Destined Mates
Books 1-3

By
Robbie Cox

Destined Mates Books 1-3
By Robbie Cox

First Edition
copyright @ 2021

Book Cover Graphics & Art: **Beautiful Mess Graphics**
Book Cover Layout: **Beautiful Mess Graphics**
Editing by CTS Editing &
Weis Editing/Proofreading Services
Formatting by CJC Formatting

www.robbiecox.com

ISBN: 978-1-955049-04-7
Library of Congress Control Number: 2021911133

For up-to-date news on Robbie's latest releases, book signing events in your area, and giveaways, follow Robbie's newsletter -
https://landing.mailerlite.com/webforms/landing/z2c3u2

You can also join Robbie's reading group, Robbie's Rascals, for more updates, extra giveaways, and even more fan involvement -
https://www.facebook.com/groups/RobbiesRascals/

PUBLISHING

To the amazing crew at the Sun Shoppe

Magic's Mate

One

dira Brenna shoved, stretching her arm out, palm up, as magic blazed from her hand to strike Jensen Harper full force in the chest. He flew across the room, tumbling over her ottoman to land on the floor. "You knew all this time you were destined to mate another, and you still played hide the sausage with me?" Adira stood, arms crossed over her chest, not because she was scared or nervous, but to keep her from reaching out with her power again and turning Jensen and his wolf into something hideous. "How the hell could you do that? How could you allow me to believe we had a future?"

Jensen hauled himself back to his feet, shaking off her attack as he paced back and forth in her living room, although she wasn't sure if it was him or his wolf who sensed the danger they were both in right then, making him

1

act erratically. Jensen ran a hand through his dark chocolate hair, his gold eyes looking everywhere except at her. "I know, Adira, I know. It was stupid to allow you to think this could be anything other than a little fun. I'm sorry."

"A little fun!" Bursts of power sparkled from her fingertips as she uncrossed her arms and took a step toward him. She knew she allowed her anger to rule her right then, not a good move considering the powers of magic at her disposal. Magic was to be used for good, not evil, and this little temper tantrum of hers could cross a line she didn't need to cross. However, there was no reining her anger in right then. Not with how foolish she felt. "A little fun is playing pool down at Shades. A little fun is a family picnic. A little fun is at least knowing you're only a stand-in for the real, true mate, so you don't allow your heart to get involved. Hell, Jensen, I would have had fun in the sack with you until you decided who your real mate was. I just would have preferred knowing ahead of time this wasn't going to be anything long term, you know. A little head's up. Then I could have looked for what I assumed I had found in you."

He sighed, his shoulders rising and falling with the action, and she instinctively knew she wouldn't like what came out of his mouth next. "I've always known who my mate was," he said, his voice tired, scared. "I've known since before she went away to college. My wolf scented her the first time he saw her in high school, but she left before I could mark her."

She just stared at him. Adira had been around shifters long enough to know how most of their rituals and habits worked. Their animals controlled who they were destined to spend the rest of their lives with, rather than their own hearts. She accepted that as part of the deal when she started dating Jensen, knowing that shifters mated with humans often. That didn't mean she comprehended everything or even had a clue as to what it all really meant. She only knew the basics. "You knew who she was? You have a name? A person to attach to this whole mating thing? And yet you still...You still let me believe I could...that we could...?" Her heart felt as if it shattered, splintering into a million shards, and the sparks of blue light at her fingertips started to sputter. "Get out."

He took a step toward her instead. Not a smart man. "Adira, look, Cynthia will be here tomorrow. She graduated and is moving back home. I just..."

"You just want to make sure I stay out of your way," she practically growled. "That I don't make trouble for you and your...your mate!" She felt every muscle in her body constrict, ready to explode with magic. "Get out, Jensen."

"Adira, I just..."

"Get out!" She lifted her right arm again, her palm out, as a ball of blue power shot from her hand and into his chest, picking him up, and knocking him back into the wall behind him. She heard the crack of a bone as he hit, heard his head crack against the wall, but she didn't care. Tears rained down her cheeks, her vision blurry, as she readied to strike him again if he stepped toward her instead of leaving.

Jensen held up a shaking hand, holding her off. He pushed back against the wall, sliding himself into a standing position, as he wrapped his good arm around his broken one. He nodded, his lips curled down in a frown. "I'm sorry," he whispered, as he moved to her front door and out of her life.

As soon as the door shut, and not a second before, she collapsed onto the floor, sobs ripping from her chest as she huddled into herself. How could he do that to her? Shards of power sparked at her fingertips, sputtering in her misery, wanting to lash out and strike something, anything. How would she face everyone, knowing that they all probably knew what she had just discovered? How did she not know that something was wrong since he hadn't asked to mark her already, marking her as his? Isn't that how it all worked? Their animals scented their mates and leaped? Tears fell down her cheeks, streaking her face as she sat there, crumpled on the floor. *How could I be so stupid?*

She wallowed on the floor until her tears were all dried out, then took a deep breath, and decided she needed to get out of her house. There were just too many memories around the place as Jensen spent most of his nights off with her. *Pull yourself together, Adira. It's not the end of the world. He's just a damn man after all.*

Outside, night began to fall, bringing its darkness into her house. She reached out with her fingers to light some candles on the wall, but nothing happened. Shards of sparks burst from her fingers, then fizzled and whiffed out. She tried it again, but nothing. Again. Nothing. Oh, god. She started crying again, her body shaking under her sobs. She knew she risked her magic when she used it in anger, bringing harm instead of building up. She snapped her fingers again. Still nothing. She cried harder.

She wasn't sure how long she sat there on the floor, lost in the agony of her broken magic. She wasn't even sure how long someone knocked on her door, calling her name, but eventually the female voice filtered through Adira's tears, bringing her out of her sorrow for a moment. She forced herself to move, shoving her body into a standing position as her muscles screamed at her for being stuck in the same spot for so long. She had to have been down there longer than she thought. On her way to the door, she swiped her cheeks and eyes with her arm, trying to remove the tears, but knowing she probably only made the streaks on her face worse. Peeking through the front window, she saw Agatha Rochester standing there and gave an inward groan. Somehow, someone must have found out about her use of magic to hurt Jensen, and Agatha was there to reprimand her. With a deep breath, Adira opened the door, braced for the scolding she expected.

However, it never came.

"Oh, my dear," Agatha said as she stood there, her head tilted to the side as she took in Adira's appearance. "I was afraid of this." She nodded and then moved to enter the house. "Well, let's get some tea in you so we can talk. Tea always helps soothe our aching minds and souls."

Adira turned, her gaze following the older witch as Agatha entered the house, moving as if she owned the place. "Agatha, why are you here? How did you..?" She shook her head and then took another deep breath. "How did you know I was hurting?"

Agatha, her dark hair pulled tight against her head, her thin body moving with deliberate intent, hiding a power underneath her frail frame, just kept walking toward Adira's kitchen. "Farren Covington called." Agatha walked into the kitchen, moving to the kettle on the stove. As she carried it over to the sink to fill it, she glanced at Adira. "Seems one of the wolves in his pack returned a little scorched around the edges." She filled the kettle with water, her back now to Adira. "I also heard that Cynthia Rogers returned to town." She turned and faced Adira again, a soft smile on her face. "It doesn't take a spell to conjure up what happened and why." Then she shrugged as she returned the kettle to the stove. "So, I thought you might be needing some tea and a shoulder."

Adira felt the tears threaten to fall again and did her best to hold them inside. How could she tell the matriarch of witches that she had used her own magic to bring harm? Agatha Rochester had stood by the witches of Draven Falls for decades, training those who couldn't get a handle on their magic and guiding them in the path of the White Goddess. While she didn't participate in coven business, for what reason Adira couldn't tell, the older woman always seemed to have her hand in things behind the scenes. Her family was one of the founding families in Draven Falls, and Agatha seemed to know everything that happened to just about everybody. "Oh, Agatha, I screwed up." Adira wrapped her arms around her waist, doing her best to hold the turmoil inside. "I didn't mean to do it. I just… I just lost control. I was so damn angry. I felt like an idiot. If I never see another shifter again, it'll be too soon."

Agatha leaned back on the counter, her hands in her jean pockets, her face a mask of sympathy. "I'm sorry, Adira. I know how much that must have hurt, and Jensen was wrong not to be upfront with you from the beginning. Farren told me about everything. I told him he's lucky Jensen is still able to mate anyone." She smiled even bigger when she said the latter. Then Adira saw the woman's shoulders rise with her deep breath. "I also have another reason for stopping by. I was wondering if you were up to taking a trip."

"A trip? To where? Why?" Although, Adira thought, a trip may just be what I need to get the hell away from Draven Falls and Jensen Harper.

The tea kettle whistled, and Agatha moved to pull it off the burner. Adira finally forced herself to move as she walked over to a cabinet and pulled out two teacups. "Well, how does Florida sound to you?"

Adira felt an eyebrow arch. "Sounds hot and sweaty. Why? What's in Florida?"

"Not so much what as who." Agatha poured the hot water into the teacups while Adira reached for the tea bags she kept in a box on the counter. Agatha looked at the tea bag and sighed. "We really need to teach you how to make tea without the store-bought bags." She took a deep breath. "Well, hopefully, you have honey."

"Agatha, who is in Florida?" Adira walked over to a cupboard and pulled out a bottle of honey.

"Dimitri Everest, and he runs a small camp there called Bull Creek. The place is a haven of sorts for those who need a

7

place to escape the prejudices and hatred of the world. When he left Draven Falls a year ago, he became alpha of sorts of the place, helping people regroup and get their lives back. I think the two of you can help each other."

"Agatha, my magic is on the blink. It hasn't worked right since I attacked Jensen. I'm not sure what help I could be to whoever this Dimitri is."

"Well, let me explain," Agatha said as she gestured to the kitchen table. "You see, there's a pack of coyotes trying to stir up trouble and drive the humans out of Bull Creek." They both slid into seats around the table, their hands wrapped around their teacups. "Apparently, a shifter named Bane Kastner thinks humans are about as evil as some of the humans in Draven Falls think shifters are. This might be just what you need to help your magic repair itself. You go down there, help Dimitri drive the coyotes away, and that balances out what happened here tonight."

"But Agatha, I don't want to live in Florida. I love the mountains here. North Carolina has been my home since I was born; I've finally found people who accept me for who I am. Why would I give that up?"

"My dear, I never said move there." Agatha shrugged. "Just go and help out. Bull Creek doesn't have any witches, and your powers might be the difference between Bane succeeding or not."

Adira glanced down at her tea, the dark liquid steaming in the ceramic cup. *If I can get my powers back, that is. I doubt I'd make much difference anywhere right now.*

Two

Dimitri Everest just stared at the man, fighting the urge to reach out and break his nose. "Why the hell are you here, Bane? I thought I told you to leave this area." Dimitri could feel every muscle strain as his panther fought to rip out of him and attack the coyote in front of him "This is a peaceful place, and you aren't exactly the peaceful type."

Bane pushed past Dimitri and his friend, Josh Rayburn, and walked further into Everglades. "This is a shifter bar, is it not?" Bane asked as he looked around, his gray eyes taking in every detail with mock amazement. "I thought I would come in here and enjoy a drink with my kind."

"This is a bar where shifters hang out," Dimitri said. "Big difference from being a shifter bar. Everyone is welcome here. Wes makes sure of that."

Bane turned again, his grin annoying as he widened his eyes as if just realizing something. "Then I should be welcome here, right? I mean, I am part of everybody."

"There will be none of your hatred in here, Bane," Wes Stapleton said from behind the bar, both hands pressed down on the wooden top as if he was ready to leap over and take the coyote leader out himself. Dimitri could see the rage in the bear shifter's eyes and knew Wes had no choice, even though he didn't like it. People cannot fight prejudice with prejudice. "If you stay here, you leave the rest of my customers alone. Understood?"

"But of course," Bane said, his expression one of shock that anyone would suggest he would behave in any other way "We merely wish to enjoy your best scotch." He then looked at Wes, his brows furrowed in doubt. "You do serve scotch, right?"

Wes just growled at Bane, who only laughed as he walked toward the back of the bar, his mangy minions trailing behind him.

Dimitri stared at their retreating backs, wondering how someone could be such an ass and think they were justified in their behavior. Bane Kastner arrived back in Bull Creek a couple of weeks ago, making the human population of the area as uncomfortable as possible, threatening them with harm if they didn't pack up and get out of town, move to the big city where humans belonged. He didn't believe that humans deserved the forests and wooded areas of Florida, or anywhere for that matter. They didn't know how to balance their habit of wasting natural resources with taking care of the wilds around them. There were enough cities of concrete and steel for the humans to inhabit; they didn't need to be in what Bane considered his forests.

Dimitri slid into a barstool, Josh beside him, and waved for Wes to bring them two whiskeys. He needed to wash the taste of Bane Kastner's hatred away.

Wes slid two glasses in front of them. "Don't let that ass get to you," he said. "His kind are always around. The best thing to do is walk away."

Dimitri pulled his glass closer. "I can't walk away. He's threatening the humans in Bull Creek. These people look to me to protect them. They're all hiding from something with nowhere else to go. I left Draven Falls to help protect these people and ignoring thugs like Bane is not how that gets done. Somehow, we have to figure out how to get those coyotes out of our area again. When he left almost a year ago, I thought we had seen the last of him."

Josh lifted his glass, holding it in front of him. "Any idea how we do that?"

"Keep patrolling and hope Bane or his coyotes screw up so we can take them out. I've talked to Sheriff Einstein, warning him of the trouble that's brewing. He said he noticed an influx of new people and wondered what it was about."

Josh nodded. "This world needs more humans like Chet. Your sister's lucky to be working there."

Dimitri laughed as he shook his head. "Chet's the lucky one. Having a panther shifter on your force is almost as beneficial as having a wolf. Makes tracking a whole lot easier."

"Don't let Alanna hear you say that. She'll make sure they're trying to track your body next."

Dimitri laughed harder. "True story. True story." He took a small swallow of his whiskey, the amber liquid burning his throat as it went down. "I thought I left all this nonsense behind me in Draven Falls, all this hatred and prejudice. It's just wasted energy when so many other things need to be accomplished in this world."

"Have you talked to anyone from back home?" Josh turned his glass in slow circles on the bar, his gaze fixed on the whiskey. "They helped form this little haven after all. You'd think they'd want to help protect it."

Dimitri downed the rest of his whiskey and gestured to Wes for another drink, hating to have to pull the man away from flirting with Noel, his server. "I called Farren Covington of the wolves and Jed Hawkins, alpha of the panthers. Both said they'd see what they could do, but I don't expect much, to be honest. Draven Falls has its own issues with the Order of Wardens trying to stir up hatred against the paranormal citizens of the town. We're pretty much on our own."

Wes set another drink in front of Dimitri and returned to Noel. Dimitri watched as the two leaned into each other, laughing and giggling, the look in each other's eyes saying everything Dimitri couldn't hear from where he sat. He wished he had time for flirting like that. Or someone to flirt with, but there just wasn't time.

"You think Bane has a secret society name like Order of

Wardens?" Josh grinned as he said it. "Something like Society of Assholes or the Order of Pricks?"

Dimitri just shook his head. "I think Bane is his own secret society." Dimitri couldn't believe such organizations still existed, groups that thrived on hatred and chaos.

Laughter from the back of the bar jerked their attention in that direction as Bane and his goons demanded another round of drinks.

"Wes, you're letting the clientele in this place go to the gutters," a female voice came from the entrance.

Turning, Dimitri saw Alanna Bradbury and Eve Hartlow walking into Everglades, Alanna moving to sit beside Josh while Eve sat on her other side. Eve, the short blonde who rarely left Bull Creek, was one of the humans Bane tried to drive out of their community. "What brings you two here?" Josh asked as he motioned for Wes.

Alanna brushed the loose strands of her light, red hair out of her eyes as she shrugged. Her emerald eyes shone with mischief as she asked Wes for a beer. "It's ladies night. Besides, it's dusty out there. Bull Creek doesn't have a paved road in the whole damn township."

Eve snorted in laughter. "It's barely a township." She motioned to Wes to give her a beer like Alanna's. "And for the record, this is the quietest ladies night I've seen here."

"Perhaps it's the quality of the ladies who are here that's keeping the others from showing up."

Everyone turned and saw Bane standing there, empty whiskey glass in his hand as he glared at Eve. Dimitri stiffened as he swung his legs around and stood to put himself between Bane and Eve. Wes could be heard coming down the bar as the others all rose, and Bane's coyote pack stepped up behind him. "Watch it, Bane," Dimitri practically growled.

Bane never took his eyes off Eve. "This is the problem with Bull Creek. It was meant to be a haven for paranormals to escape human society, and you've opened the roads to the riffraff, allowing humans to walk among their betters. The forests belong to shifters. Only we can truly appreciate this environment. Man has chased us out of every city we've ever tried to live in, deeming us beneath them, a threat to their existence." He turned to Dimitri and snarled. "I'm the prejudiced one? Please. Mankind has been attacking us since they learned of us. Now, they can keep to their cities of concrete and steel. Get the humans out of Bull Creek. The coyotes are taking over." He glanced over Dimitri's shoulders at Wes, then ran his gaze over the other shifters surrounding Eve before shaking his head. Setting his glass on the table behind him, he turned to walk away, his pack following behind him.

Dimitri stared after Bane as he left, his body trembling with the rage that coursed through him. "We're going to need to keep tighter patrols around Bull Creek for a while. I don't trust Bane to play fair."

"Agreed," Josh said.

Dimitri turned to Eve, noticing how she stood there, shorter than all of them, weaker, gripping the handle of the knife she always wore at her waist. "I'm sorry," he told Eve. "You know that's not how all paranormals feel."

Eve nodded. "I know." She turned her gaze to the door. "Just the assholes."

Three

A dira could not believe she agreed to this move into hell. What in the world was she thinking? No seasons, one-hundred-degree weather, and palm trees. Who in their right mind liked palm trees? They didn't even have real branches. They were basically long sticks with floppy leaves at the tip. They provided no actual shade, and no child ever built a tree fort in one. Squirrels didn't even like them. Palm trees didn't even deserve the classification of a tree. Why was she doing this?

She took the exit off the Turnpike and onto Highway 192, heading east, eager to reach the end of her journey and the beginning of her escape from a nightmare that still sent anger pulsing through her and from the humiliation of being a man's toy while he waited for another. She drove through Kissimmee and St. Cloud, hating every minute of it, as tourist traffic brought everything practically to a standstill. People either made their way to the house of the mouse or left it, clogging up the lanes. She just wanted to get through the damn city. This place was nothing like home.

Her cell phone rang, providing her with the distraction she needed to survive the bumper-to-bumper traffic of a tourist town. She didn't check to see who called, not wanting to take her eyes off the road and the drivers who insisted on riding their damn brakes. Swiping the green button to answer the call, and then hitting the speaker button, she said, "Hello. This is Adira."

"Well, of course, it is, sweetie," Agatha Rochester chuckled into the phone. "That's who I called, after all."

Adira shook her head. She should have expected the woman to call and check on her. After all, Agatha was the main reason Adira was out here. "Sorry, Agatha, I didn't look to see who was calling. How are things in Draven Falls?"

"A veritable morass of paranormal politics, but what else is new? I hear the wind around you, so I take it you haven't reached Bull Creek yet. How much longer until you get there?"

"Depending on this asinine traffic, probably about forty-five minutes. These people down here are crazy behind the wheel. Did you send me out here to get me killed? I thought it was just to get me away from Jensen."

"Now, Adira, don't be bitter," Agatha said with that tone that told Adira the matriarch witch of Draven Falls thought Adira was being childish. "We both know you weren't

Jensen's mate, and you being near him would only stir up trouble neither of us wanted. Besides, Bull Creek could use a witch of your talents. I told you what Dimitri was up against. We've dealt with prejudice and hatred enough in Draven Falls. That's why our town was founded after all. Coyotes are as vile as hyenas and jackals. No sense of honor or respect. Rude buggers, who would rather see Dimitri's land turned into something foul, as opposed to the safe haven he envisions. I think you could just be the help he needs."

Adira shook her head, knowing Agatha always knew more than anyone else ever did. She always tried to move people toward specific goals as if she had her fingers on the pulse of the world around her. She also seemed to think she knew what people needed, even if they didn't. "Agatha, I hope you're not pushing me toward another relationship. I don't even want a fling at the moment. Things are still too raw after that row with Jensen."

"Dear, who said anything about a relationship?" Agatha's tone, however, failed to be convincing. "Dimitri needs help, that's all. Who you permit in your bed while you're down there is totally up to you. I would never try to impose someone on you."

"Uh huh, right." Adira took a deep breath. "I'll see what I can do to help out, Agatha, but that's it. Don't get your hopes up."

"Whatever you say, dear. Have a safe trip." As she hung up the phone, Adira knew the matriarch already had her hopes up. However, the woman would be sorely disappointed.

As soon as she hit the outskirts of St. Cloud, Adira rolled her window down, turning off the car's air-conditioning to allow the Florida air to clean out her cluttered mind. That was a mistake. She kept the window down but turned the air-conditioning back on to battle the stifling heat that flooded through the window. As much as she hated this move, Adira knew she needed the new adventure, a break from the past and her old life, a new place away from Draven Falls and what she left behind. Or rather, who she left behind. Bull Creek would be that break. She laughed, as she stuck her hand out the window, allowing it to ride on the wind, like a surfer on a wave. *Okay, I'm still dealing with shifters and their drama, but it's still a new start.*

She drove through Celebration and Holopaw on her way to Bull Creek and the new cabin that waited for her. Deer lined the road, some squirrels darted across the asphalt, and a giant hawk flew overhead, almost as if it paced her car. She wondered if any of them were part of the local packs or tribes that inhabited the area. She continued to scan the woods as she passed them. She wasn't sure if she wanted to meet the local shifters. Not after losing her heart to that wolf, Jensen. She sighed. If only her magic allowed her to take away her memories of him and his taut muscles as he pinned her to the bed. She needed the distance. At least, until she came across the spell that would take her pain away. She understood the mating urges of shifters, how it made the pack determine who were the right matches for mates or not, compatible in both human and animal form. She was a witch. She didn't fit in that world. She glanced around at the passing oaks and pines. She would create a world where she did fit, and it would happen right here in Bull Creek.

Two panthers darted across the road, forcing her to slam on her brakes, the car skidding to a stop, as she watched the tawny brown beasts dodge her vehicle, their pale gray underbellies stretched out as they leaped off the asphalt and back onto the soft grass and into the woods. She sat there, her breathing ragged, her hands trembling, as she followed them with her gaze until they vanished among the trees. What the hell? Unbelievable! She took a deep breath, doing her best to calm her nerves, as she released the brake and pushed gingerly on the gas, fighting the urge to send a bolt of power after the insensitive creatures. Instead, she continued toward her goal.

And peace and quiet.

None of the roads in Bull Creek were paved, making each one bumpy as hell, the rain having washed out parts of the road. She slowed to a snail's pace, her car jerking, rocking with each hole and divot in the streets. She rolled her window back up, the air-conditioning cranked high, to keep the road dust as well as the Florida heat outside. Her cabin was in the middle of what would be classified as her yard, with just enough clear space for her to park her car and shove the door open against the high grass and squeeze her way out. She could use her powers to clear the area, pull back the foliage that grew up around her new home, but she looked forward to working with her hands, sweating the nagging thoughts of what she left behind out of her head.

She shut her car door and turned to the porch on the front

of her cabin... And stopped. He was tall, his thick arms crossed over his stocky chest, as he stared at her with eyes that penetrated her. As she allowed her gaze to travel down the rest of him, soaking in his powerful legs, she found a bulge in his pants that she suddenly wished was penetrating her as hard as his gaze was. If this was Bull Creek's idea of a welcome reception, she was glad she chose to move here. Maybe she had found a spell that would help her forget Jensen after all. She put a smile on her face, swung her purse over her shoulder, and started toward the porch. "Well, hello there," she said. "Shouldn't there be a fruit basket or pound cake or something as a welcome basket in your hands? I didn't even know anyone knew I was arriving today."

His smile dazzled her, as it pushed his cheeks up and made his eyes sparkle. "I actually saw you pull into the neighborhood," he said, his baritone voice making her sex quiver. She glanced around the area, grass overgrown everywhere, trees with moss hanging from their limbs, shrubs growing up between the trees around her cabin, around every cabin. If this were his idea of a neighborhood, she'd hate to see what he thought of as a slum. "So, I thought I'd stop by and say hello. See if there was anything you needed."

She took a deep breath. There was something she needed all right, but she didn't think now was the right time. Besides, she just told Agatha she didn't want a fling, no matter how enticing the fling appeared at the moment. "Thanks, but unless you're willing to mow the lawn and pull weeds, I think I'm doing all right."

He chuckled as he looked around her yard. "Yeah, people don't really take great care of empty cabins around here. Perhaps your law firm should have sent someone out ahead of you to clean it up." He continued smiling, even though his words seemed cold, filled with a meaning she didn't even understand.

"I wish I had a law firm then, if that's the type of things they do," she said. "I work alone, so I guess that means I'll be cleaning all this up by myself." She stopped before she reached the porch, crossing her arms over her chest, her purse dangling from the middle of her arms. "Just why do you think I came from a law firm?"

He didn't answer her. "You work alone? An investigator?"

She cocked her head to the side. "You really are curious about my line of work for someone I just met. Do you interrogate everyone who moves into the area like this?"

He shrugged. "Just until I get to know them. I'm kind of protective of Bull Creek, you could say."

"Founding family? Mayor?" She glanced around at the woods surrounding her cabin. "Smokey, the Bear?" She assumed the gorgeous specimen in front of her was Dimitri Everest, the man Agatha and the Paranormal Council sent her to help, but since he seemed standoffish, she wasn't volunteering any information.

He grinned. "Protector of these lands," he said. He looked off into the distance. "Several of us are having a bonfire later tonight to celebrate the weekend. It's kind of a ritual around here." He turned back to her, his eyes still sparkling. "You're welcome to join us, meet some of your other neighbors. Let them meet you."

"Inspection time, huh?" She nodded. "Thanks. I'll think about it." *Like hell, I will. Being put out for inspection is not my idea of a first night in town.* "For now, I need to open up the house. You know, air it out and all. Unpack."

He nodded, uncrossing his arms, as he stepped off her porch. "Just be careful at night," he said. "Coyotes are prowling around that we normally don't see in these parts. Until we get them under control, you might want to carry a bat or stay indoors."

"I don't even own a bat and staying indoors would kind of make it hard to attend the bonfire, don't you think?" She smirked, as she moved to her own front porch, keeping her eyes on him as he walked around her car and to the edge of her drive. "Did you really want me to go or not?"

He turned, his hands in his back pockets, as he continued walking. "Well then, maybe I should pop back by and escort you. You know, sort of protect you and all. Would be the neighborly thing to do."

She grinned. "Oh, it would, especially me without my baseball bat and all."

"See you later then..." He waited to see if she would give him her name or not.

She just smiled, giving a soft wave with her fingers. "Bye," she said. "For now." She turned, knowing he still watched her and entered her dusty cabin. The moldy air assaulted her as soon as she crossed the threshold. *It's definitely time to use magic.* She lifted her hand as power

23

pulsed from her fingers, sputtering at first before sending the damp air out the door. Glancing around the dust-covered furnishings in the cabin, she took a deep breath. *Looks like it's going to be a very magical day. I just hope my magic holds up.*

Four

S he wasn't the lawyer we expected?" Josh Rayburn asked as he piled fresh logs into the pit, preparing for Bull Creek's weekly bonfire. "Then who is she?" The area was a small clearing circled by thick oaks and cypress that shaded the center and provided some covering for the attendees. The grass was kept low, the ground mostly dirt to keep sparks from snapping and setting the whole place ablaze.

Dimitri stood, his hands in his back pockets as he stared back in the direction of the cabin he had just left, as if he could see the structure through the woods. "The scent of Draven Falls still clung to her, so my guess is she's been sent by the Paranormal Council to help us somehow. Of course, it would be nice if someone had told me they sent the woman and how she's exactly supposed to help us." He smiled, as he recalled how confident the newcomer seemed when she faced him from her car, feisty and confident. She was a small woman in height, but her mouth more than made up for her size. Her long, dark hair framed her oval face, bringing out the deep blue of her eyes. Her curves had made him want to shift his cock in his pants, as he swallowed her with his gaze, knowing he already showed signs of arousal. His animal practically growled at the sight of her, as she shoved her way out of her car and toward him, undaunted and determined. He may not know her name, but he knew her: strong, focused, and cheeky. She was definitely going to be a fun addition to their little community. "And, to be honest, I'm not even sure a lawyer's coming. Doing things the legal way just isn't Bane's style."

Josh stood, staring at Dimitri. "Draven Falls, huh? Good to know we still have friends there."

Dimitri turned and smiled. "The Paranormal Council helped establish Bull Creek. Of course, we still have friends there. The coyotes, however, are not friends. Mangy pack of…" He took a deep breath. "They're as bad as hyenas and jackals, but they won't worm their way into our territory, bringing their prejudice against humans with them. Bull Creek is a safe haven, and I'm determined it'll remain that way, a sanctuary for any who needs one. We've worked too hard to protect this area, opening it up to people who need a home. I'm not giving it over to some scavengers to come in and muck it all up."

Josh nodded. "I agree, but Bane Kastner is a sneaky son of a bitch. If he's set his sights on this land, he's not going to let go easily."

Dimitri nodded. He couldn't argue with what Josh said. "Still, easy or not, he's not taking over this land without a major fight. People need Bull Creek. What they don't need is the hatred of old school shifters." More than that, however, Dimitri needed this safe haven. It gave him a purpose. These people gave him a purpose.

"Are you going to help me build this fire or are you just going to stand there staring at the new woman's cabin while making speeches I've already heard?" Josh laughed, as he reached for more firewood. He paused before tossing it onto the pile. "So, what's she like?"

Dimitri turned at the waist, his feet still facing the cabin, his brows bunched in confusion. "What's who like?"

"What's who like?" Josh repeated as he rolled his eyes. "The new lady. The one who wouldn't give you her name? You know, the one who almost ran our asses over on the main road, while we patrolled the area?"

"Almost ran your slow ass over, you mean," Dimitri said with a chuckle as he turned and picked up a log. "And she's cute, with curves in all the right places, and a mouth that can cut you with its snark." He glanced back at the cabin. "Of course, she also had a scent of sadness about her as well. Like she was recently hurt or something." He turned, as he heard wood banging against wood.

Josh just shook his head. "Here it goes. Dimitri the heart doctor."

"Aren't we all heart doctors here? That's kind of the purpose behind Bull Creek." Dimitri tossed a log onto the pile, which was beginning to be as tall as Josh. "If the Paranormal Council sent her, there must be a reason, something our new resident can offer as well as something she needs."

"They sent a woman to aid the alpha of Bull Creek," Josh said with a laugh. "I think someone might be doing a little matchmaking." Then Josh cocked his head to the side as he asked, "Shifter?"

"Not a shifter. I didn't smell it on her. Not a vampire, either."

"Witch? Elf? Retired schoolteacher?"

Dimitri laughed, reaching for another log. "I guess we'll find out soon enough. I told her I'd pick her up and escort her to the bonfire."

"Such a noble beast, you are," Josh chuckled. After throwing one more log on the pile, he turned and grabbed a towel to wipe his sweaty brow. Florida heat was horrendous. "Remind me why we're having a bonfire again? I mean, it's ninety-eight frickin' degrees out here."

Dimitri shrugged. "Brings the community together. We need to keep close until Bane and his coyotes are dealt with."

"And a party in an air-conditioned house wouldn't have done the same thing?"

"Nah. Bonfires have a certain feel to them. I want that."

"Just make sure you have the beer and smores. Otherwise, I'm going back to my place where it's cool. And I have cable."

Dimitri shot his friend a grin. "But all the available women will be here."

Josh made a dramatic sigh. "Damn it. You can be so cruel at times, you know that?"

"Just didn't want you making a poor decision, that's all. You know, looking out for you. Besides, Alanna will be here, and I know you wouldn't want to miss her, not with the way you two have been sniffing around each other over the past few months." Alanna Bradbury was Bull Creek's resident wolf, and she and Josh had been panting after each other likes mates denied since they met.

"What would I do without you?"

Dimitri shrugged. "Stay home with a beer in one hand and your cock in the other, more than likely."

"My savior," Josh said with a laugh.

"Just be here on time."

They finished piling the wood in a giant tee-pee shape before calling it an afternoon and returning to their homes to get ready for the evening. Dimitri walked the dusty road, taking in the homes and cabins he passed along the way, each filled with a hurting soul, a drifter looking for an escape from the outside world. Each person had their reasons for being there. Some they shared; some they kept to themselves, tucked down into the hidden recesses of their minds. Dimitri never pushed for reasons as to why people arrived in Bull Creek. He just offered them a place to stay and helped them integrate into the community. Everyone belonged who wanted a place, a home, as long as they abided by the rules, his rules. There weren't many, and they only existed to protect the community, his community.

Dimitri knew he felt possessive about Bull Creek more so

than normal lately, but that was why the Paranormal Council back in Draven Falls sent him down here a year ago. They knew he would make it personal when he stood against his parents and their purity of pack mentality. His older brother got trapped by their parents' beliefs, and Fitz had been miserable ever since. Dimitri was sick of the prejudice coming from paranormals and humans alike. Bull Creek was founded as a safe haven against such hate-filled viewpoints, and he would be damned if someone like Bane would come in and wreak havoc on what Dimitri had built.

His thoughts shifted from all the residents in Bull Creek to just one in particular. One of the facts Dimitri had kept from Josh was that Dimitri had also scented magic when he was near the new arrival. A witch. Perhaps that was the real reason the Paranormal Council sent her, knowing what Dimitri was up against. He welcomed any help that ran Bane off.

However, that wasn't the only thing he didn't share with Josh. Dimitri also kept quiet about the fact that his panther went crazy at the sight of the witch, making it hard for him to keep his cock hidden as he interrogated her. Some interrogation it turned out to be, too. Whoever she was, she was spunky, and he liked spunky. She would be fun getting to know if he could calm his panther down long enough to wait. His animal wanted to take her right then, bend her over the hood of her car, and plow his cock into her. Now, he wondered if he should have offered that to her as a welcome basket.

"Dimitri!" Turning, he saw Sheriff Einstein driving

toward him, his arm outside his window, waving Dimitri down.

Dimitri stopped walking, glancing around to see if anyone else was near. Sheriff Einstein eased his car up next to him until they were side by side. "Chet, what's up? My sister driving you crazy, yet?" As soon as Dimitri set up shop in Bull Creek, his younger sister, Lainie, followed, taking a job with the sheriff's department, giving Chet Einstein a shifter perspective on crime.

"Nah, she's pretty good at keeping me on my toes," the sheriff chuckled. "I just thought you should know, Bane's over at Everglades in Holopaw, and he's gathering more of his coyotes around him. Of course, they're all drinking and shooting off their mouths about their plans for Bull Creek and the kitty cats they plan on skinning. Their words, not mine."

Dimitri glanced up into the sky, as he took a deep breath. Great. He glanced back at the sheriff. "Thanks for telling me, Chet. I appreciate it." He'd have some of the other shifters patrol the area, keeping their noses to the ground for coyotes.

"No worries. I hate people like Bane." Chet shook his head. "I know you have that bonfire tonight, and I thought you might need to be on your toes. A pack of drunken coyotes could very well lead to trouble. I'll make a few passes, try and keep an eye on things. I'll even have my deputies do some extra sweeps."

Dimitri nodded. "Thanks. Hopefully, Bane and his thugs will stay in Holopaw."

"Hopefully." The sheriff said his goodbyes and drove off.

Dimitri watched as the sheriff disappeared, his tires kicking up more road dust as he drove away. Dimitri doubted Bane and his pack would stay in Holopaw and leave Bull Creek alone. The man itched to take over the small community, driving the humans out. Surely, however, he wouldn't do it the old-fashioned way, with brute force. Would he? Dimitri's hope when he came to Bull Creek was that it would get him away from shifter prejudice on all sides. That wasn't the case, however. He took a deep breath. Hatred existed everywhere. There was plenty of land in Florida, so why was Bane trying to move his pack into Bull Creek again? What was here that he wanted, besides his disgust of humans? Dimitri wished he knew.

Five

She knew he was outside long before she heard the knock on her door. Right after Mr. Welcome Party left, Adira decided against using magic to clean the small cabin, choosing rather to do it the ordinary, mundane way. She needed the monotony to keep her mind off Jensen and Draven Falls. Besides, with the way her magic had been acting since she slammed Jensen into the wall, she wasn't sure her magic would do what she wanted or blow her cabin to pieces instead. The first thing she did, however, before cleaning up the place was set wards all around her property, protection spells, which would warn her the moment someone stepped onto her property. Fortunately, her magic lasted long enough for that, and it was a safe spell to work. The man who greeted her earlier on her porch seemed to be expecting trouble, which seemed faster than she was led to believe. Of course, Agatha Rochester sent her here—okay, suggested she come here—so that she would get involved in the drama of the small community and out of the drama that would happen in Draven Falls if she stayed. Agatha expected Adira to assist this Dimitri guy in his quest to protect humans from shifters. Adira only agreed to do it, because Agatha threw in the cabin, and Adira needed to escape Draven Falls. She didn't really want to fight coyotes, but it was a better option than fighting Jensen's Cynthia.

Adira took a deep breath, as her senses felt the man in front of her cabin moving closer. She worried that her power would fail her. Again. She hadn't exactly been at full strength since the sting of being rejected by the wolf who toyed with her heart for the past few months. The crushing blow of his rejection broke more than just her heart. She understood the mating rituals of the wolf packs, but thought, as long as Jensen kept her around, she was his, and he was hers. When it all ended, when she was told she wasn't his mate and then told about the female wolf who was, Adira felt her power shatter into shards of magic with no cohesiveness. Agatha suggested getting away to regain her strength, and what a coincidence that she even had a place in mind that needed a witch's skills. Adira shook her head as she sighed. Nothing with Agatha Rochester was ever a coincidence.

It didn't really matter, Adira knew. She needed to escape if she was to regain any semblance of her magic back. She needed to heal. As it turned out, the further away she drove from Draven Falls, the more she felt her power returning, as if putting the past behind her forged her a new future. She felt the man step onto the first porch step. *Not that I'm ready for that future to contain a man yet. Agatha's matchmaking plans are wasted.*

"One, two, three…" She pointed to the front door of her cabin just as he knocked. She smiled. Yes, she was definitely getting stronger. "Come in."

He opened the door, his brows furrowed over the bridge of his nose. "You know, it's not safe to tell someone to enter if you don't know who it is."

She arched an eyebrow at him. "Who says I didn't know it was you?"

He turned, scanning the area around the door, stepping back outside, looking for cameras, more than likely. Adira just stood there, arms across her chest, as she watched him investigate the front of her cabin. He wouldn't find anything, of course, but it was fun watching him search, especially when he turned around and bent over, his jeans pulling taut over his ass. It was definitely a sight that made her smile, even though she needed to strengthen her resolve about no men in her future.

"Are you looking for something?" she asked, a smirk in her tone.

He shook his head, turning back around to face her. "You're a witch?"

She felt her right eyebrow pop up. "How did you know I'm a witch?" There was more to this guy than a firm ass, it seemed. All right, so maybe a romp in the tall grass would be worth changing her mind. After all, sex wasn't mating.

He shrugged, slipping his hands into his back pockets, which, to her delight, made the fabric tighter over his cock. Even flaccid, his manhood left an impression. "Magic around the perimeter," he said. "I could smell it. Faint traces, but it's there." He gestured around the door. "With no cameras or peephole in the door, I decided to take a sniff."

Damn shifters and their noses. "I guess you know then that I don't really need a baseball bat."

He laughed, as he nodded. "Yeah, I guess that makes sense." He took a couple of steps toward her. "Still, it's my job to protect the residents of Bull Creek, so you might as well get used to me being around."

She smiled, not saying anything. However, in her mind, she thought, I can definitely get used to that. "You're more than welcome to stay around all you want, but just remember, I can take care of myself. Always have, always will."

He just grinned. "Of that, I have no doubt." He leaned back on the doorframe. "Ready to go to the bonfire?"

She glanced around the cabin. While she still had unpacking to do, she could use a break. She turned back to the man at her door. "And would the protector of Bull Creek have a name? Or is this one of those secret identity things? Like a superhero or something?" She kept her smile on her face as she spoke, making sure he knew she was teasing him. "I mean, you wouldn't want me wandering off with a stranger, right?"

He nodded, that sparkling grin spreading across his face. "No, definitely not. You must be protected by someone you know well." He pushed himself off the doorframe, taking a couple of steps toward her as he held out his hand. "Dimitri Everest. Pleased to make your acquaintance. Welcome to Bull Creek."

So this is the man Agatha sent me to help. Yet, it didn't seem as if Agatha, or anyone else from the Paranormal Council for that matter, had told Dimitri that a witch was coming.

Taking his hand, she gave it a shake, sending a shard of power into the grip, assuring him that she meant what she said about being able to protect herself. She returned his smile. "Pleased to meet you. I'm Adira Brennan. Now that the introductions are over, I think that bonfire sounds great." She waited for him to open the door.

Without reacting to her little power display, he smiled, dipping his head as he opened the door. "After you," he said, his cocky grin back on his face. *Okay, this could definitely be a fun distraction. I'm going to have to rethink my anti-male stance.*

She stepped past him and out into the sweltering Florida humidity. "And just what made you decide a bonfire was the best way to celebrate in this heat?" she asked. "I mean, in the mountains, or even during winter, I can see it, but what is it outside? In the high nineties? How many people will actually show up in order to just melt?"

He grinned, as he followed her off the porch, and then joined her, as they walked down her dirt drive. "Oh, I'm sure there will be a few. It's a Bull Creek tradition. We do this every Friday night unless it's raining, which in Florida means we only do it twenty-six weeks out of the year."

Few was an understatement. When the two of them reached the clearing, Adira was surprised at how many people gathered around a giant bonfire in the middle of a ring of giant trees, the night air, warm and sticky. Men and women stood around, talking and drinking, while small children ran around playing tag, chasing each other without a care in the world. The bonfire's flames licked up into the darkening sky, the crackling of the fire as it ate the thick logs snapping in the background. Tables were set up around the fire, loaded down with finger foods and other snacks, while coolers full of sodas and beer sat on the ground. The gray of dusk left enough light for Adira to get a glimpse of the surrounding area. Giant trees—pine, oaks, and cypress—surrounded them with palm frond bushes and shrubs overrunning the underdeveloped area. The small clearing where they held the bonfire, which she was told resided in the middle of Bull Creek, sort of like a town center, had been mowed, but that was about all that was done to the area. Most of the small space was damp earth anyway. Everywhere else, the grass grew wild and free. Off in the distance, she could hear the mooing of cattle, realizing a dairy farm or something like it resided nearby.

Dimitri introduced her to people as they passed, like Eve Hartlow, one of the humans Dimitri was protecting and the coyotes were trying to drive out, and Doc Henderson, who specialized in shifter medicine. Each one welcomed her as the newest member of their small community with hugs and smiles. Dimitri then led her over to a man with light brown hair and the brightest yellow eyes she ever saw, who was talking to a tall, robust woman with light red hair and full lips curved up into a smile. "Adira, this scoundrel is my longtime friend and partner in this little venture, Josh Rayburn. He left Draven Falls with me to begin this adventure. The lovely lady next to him is Alanna Bradbury, a wolf without a pack."

Now, that's unusual. Most female wolves stayed close to their pack, never venturing away too far or for too long. Agatha had said Bull Creek was a safe haven of sorts, a sanctuary for those who were tired of dealing with things beyond their control. Perhaps Alanna was one of those escapees, but if so, why was she running and from what? Or perhaps who? While Adira was curious about the other woman's story, she thought it should be a conversation for another time. "Pleased to meet you both," Adira said, shaking each one's hand. She glanced up at the clear, dark sky. "Great night for a fire, although I would not have believed it."

Josh chuckled. "I tried to tell Dimitri it was too damn hot, but he never listens to me. Of course, that just means we'll have to consume a lot of beer to stay cool."

Alanna shook her head. "Like you ever need an excuse to drink."

Josh shrugged. "Well, no, but the excuse helps make the drinking sound better." He gave Adira a wink, which brightened his smile.

She felt the blush heat her cheeks as she turned to Dimitri, who gave Josh a dirty look. She hid the grin that wanted to crease her cheeks. Well, he became possessive pretty quick.

That thought made her honey drip, causing her sex to quiver. She couldn't deny that she enjoyed this side of Dimitri. She smiled at him, about to say something to tease him, when suddenly the air filled with the baying of coyotes. She jerked her head to the perimeter of the clearing, trying to fixate on where the cry originated, when another howl filled the air on the opposite side of them. She turned her gaze in that direction, taking a cautious step toward it, when in even another area, another coyote called out. They were surrounded, but why?

Then she felt Dimitri's hand on her arm, holding her in place, keeping her close to him. His gaze, however, was not on her, but searching the darkness around the fire, his eyes narrow slits.

Josh stood next to Alanna, both looking in different directions. Parents called their children to them, their arms surrounding them protectively as they hid their children behind them. Eve Hartlow, the small blonde Dimitri introduced Adira to when they first arrived, stood straight, one hand on a knife hilt at her waist Adira missed seeing before, causing Adira to arch an eyebrow. Seems there's a story there, as well. Adira turned back to the darkness, waiting to see what the coyotes planned. "I take it they weren't invited to the party?"

"They're not even welcome in the area," Dimitri said, his voice almost a growl.

Six

The howling continued as bushes rustled at the edge of the clearing among the trees. Dimitri knew the coyotes were prowling, searching for a weak spot, an opportune moment to strike and attack. He grinned, hoping they would do just that. He knew something like this might happen, knew Bane would be foolish, refusing to wait too long to press his advantage in an attempt to take over Bull Creek and drive the humans and their sympathizers out. The woods were filled with panthers, cougars, and bears, patrolling the area for just such an attack. They waited, watching for Dimitri's signal.

He glanced over at Adira. If he expected her to be scared, he was pleasantly disappointed. She stood beside him, her back straight, and he could sense the power at her fingertips, ready to be unleashed. She wasn't afraid; she was ready. He even moved to step in front of her, a shield against whatever might happen next, but she moved to stand beside him instead. She wouldn't hide. There was too much fight in her.

He felt his animal growl, approval, protection, and hunger for the witch filling him. *Down boy, now's not the time.*

Turning back to the perimeter, he waited to see what Bane had planned. He didn't have to wait long.

Several coyotes, their silver-gray fur glistening in the moonlight, saliva dripping from their snarling jaws, as they snapped their threats at the residents of Bull Creek, entered the clearing, circling those within. The coyotes didn't attack, but Dimitri knew it wouldn't take much to provoke them. Everyone stood, braced for whatever was about to happen. Several men reached under the tables loaded down with food, pulling out shotguns, holding the weapons in front of them, the barrels aimed at the coyotes as if daring them to charge. The residents of Bull Creek wouldn't permit themselves to be provoked into making the first attack, but they were more than ready to defend themselves.

Bane Kastner stepped out of the woods and into the clearing, two mangy looking men a step behind him, their backs straight, arms barely moving as they walked. Dimitri could smell the stink of the coyotes the closer they came, the night wind ruffling their gray hair, their dark eyes staring right at him. The men walked with purpose, determination. Whatever their reason for being there, they seemed unconcerned about anyone stopping them or barring their way, not even those with shotguns. Dimitri's panther fought to get out, to shift and attack, and it took all Dimitri's strength to keep his animal at bay. Might as well see how this plays out first before he unleashed his panther. Human cunning was more important, right then, than animal instinct.

Bane continued his approach, his hands clasped behind his back as he walked, giving the appearance of nonchalance, even though Dimitri knew there was nothing casual about what the man intended. The snarling coyotes were proof of that.

"Well, he looks charming," Adira said, never taking her eyes off Bane.

"He's an ass," Dimitri said. "And one I wish I didn't have to encounter."

Bane stretched his arms out once he reached a few feet from where Dimitri stood. "A nice night for a farewell party," the man said, a fake grin on his face. "It's always nice to send people off with a celebration." He cocked an eyebrow at the men wielding guns. "Such a human approach to things."

Dimitri tilted his head to the side, placing his hands on his hips, as he stared at Bane. "Are you going somewhere that we should be celebrating? If I had known, I would have been more than happy to throw a few extra hot dogs near the fire for you. Perhaps even in it."

Bane chuckled as he gave a shake of his head. "Ah, Dimitri, always assuming you possess wit." He returned his arms to behind his back, his hands clasped together. "No, no. I'm not leaving. You are. You're not wanted here." He stretched an arm out, waving at all those gathered. "None of you are wanted here. This is coyote land. There's no place for…humans."

"I think you're the one telling jokes now," Dimitri said. "There's room for everyone here, but you. This land doesn't belong to you. It never did. You just wish to slither your way in and take over. For what purpose, I have no idea."

Josh stepped up next to Dimitri. "Why exactly do you want this land anyway? There's plenty of woodland south of here, good enough for you and your friends."

Bane gestured toward Highway 192. "A major interstate to the north." He gestured to the west. "A couple of productive towns to the west." He then gestured to the east. "And the beaches and even more towns to the east, with plenty of woods for prowling and hunting in between. Bull Creek is perfect for what I want. It's just infested with vermin, that's all."

Dimitri arched an eyebrow at that last statement. "Vermin?" He took a deep breath. "I think it's time for you to go. Now."

The howl of coyotes filled the night air, angry snarls following in its wake as if Bane's men tried to press their leader's point. Dimitri didn't care. He would not be bullied, and he was not going to allow these families to be kicked out of their homes. With a deep breath, he crossed his arms and just stared at the man before him, refusing to budge. "Do you need to be escorted out of here, Bane?"

Bane grinned, his yellowish teeth adding a sinister air to his face. "What? This isn't a party for everyone?" He nodded, chuckling under his breath. "You have until tonight to clear out, Dimitri. I suggest you make good use of your time. We will give no mercy to those who ignore this warning, humans or shifters."

"I just got here," Adira said, dropping her arms to her sides, palms out. "I like my cabin. It's homey, cute little roosters on the curtains, a shag rug in the living room, even a fireplace, although I have no idea when I would ever use it." She shrugged. "I don't plan on leaving. I mean, I just unpacked and everything."

Dimitri worried his feisty witch bit off more than her power could handle with Bane. The man had a horrendous mean streak when it came to hurting people.

Bane took a couple of steps closer, his grin shifting to a leer. "Well, you're cute," he said. "Spunky, even. Perhaps I'll permit you to stay."

"No one permits me to do anything," she said, as shards of magic sparked from her fingertips. "I don't need your permission, trust me."

Dimitri's panther growled, and he felt the shift begin as fur oozed from his skin. He clamped down hard before he lost control. "Leave," Dimitri growled, his voice deep, gravelly, as he took a step toward the thicker man.

Bane laughed, deep and menacing. "Down, kitty cat. I'm just conversing with the pretty lady. I didn't realize she was your girl. I'd be sure to take her with you when you leave if I were you." He winked at Adira, and Dimitri took another step, ready to lash out. Bane ignored him, however, and instead glared at Adira. "I'd be careful, witch. You're known by the company you keep, and right now, you're slumming."

And then he just laughed harder as he turned and walked away, his two men turning and following him as the coyotes slithered back into the woods. None of them even bothered to check behind them, obviously not worried that Dimitri and his friends would attack. It grated on Dimitri's nerves.

"Like I said, charming," Adira said, her magic snapping from her fingers, dissipating a second later.

Dimitri glanced at her, shaking his head as he gave a soft laugh. "Yeah, charming." He took a deep breath, giving his head another shake, this time to shed the irritation he felt due to Bane's visit. He then turned, offering his arm for Adira to take. "Come, I could use another beer."

He felt her turn and join him, her arm slipping into the crook of his as he walked back over to the coolers under the tables. "What does he want with Bull Creek?" she asked as they walked. Josh and Alanna joined them as Eve walked back to the bonfire, her back still straight, her posture tense. Dimitri wished he knew what the small blond woman's story was.

Dimitri opened the cooler, pulling out beers and passing them around. He twisted Adira's open first before handing it to her.

Josh glanced at him and shrugged. "I think I'd prefer something stronger, right about now," he said before twisting the cap and taking a long pull.

Dimitri gave a short nod. "You and me both." He then turned to Adira. "It's not that he wants it, really. It's more that he just doesn't want humans to have it. From what Sheriff Einstein told me a few days ago, they wander from area to area, looking for places such as ours where they can move in, chase the residents out, believing humans should keep to the cities while the woods and forests belong to shifters. They bully and threaten, sometimes using violence to get their way." He glanced at her with a serious expression. "They've even been known to kill. When I first arrived a year ago, he was here pulling the same shit. He left for a while, and I had hoped that was the last of him. Looks like I was wrong."

"Yeah, it probably wasn't a good idea for you to provoke him," Josh said to Adira. He then glanced up at Dimitri. "His threat seemed pretty real to me."

Dimitri nodded, catching the meaning behind his friend's words. He turned to Adira, his brows knitted with concern. "You should stay with me until this is settled with Bane."

He thought she appeared ready to pounce on the idea, but then her face grew pinched in anger. "I have my own cabin, thanks," she said, her tone clipped. "I'll be fine. I don't need a babysitter."

He couldn't believe how stubborn she was being. Had she not just witnessed the man who threatened her? Noticed his size? The men who accompanied him? Saw the coyotes? Did she not hear the coyotes waiting in the woods for a fight still? Her wards wouldn't protect her from all that threatened her. "Adira, now is not the time to be pigheaded about this," he said. "Bane means what he says. He'll use you to get to me and Bull Creek. You don't want to be in the middle of that. Of this."

"Pigheaded?" She spun on him, her voice dripping with

venom. "Did you just call me pigheaded?"

Josh raised his eyebrows and quickly averted his gaze from what he believed was about to happen. Dimitri didn't blame his friend. It wasn't the best choice of words. "That's not what I meant. I just…"

"You just thought I was some weak female who needs a man's big, strong arms to protect me," she snarled. "Well, Catnip, I don't." She put the beer bottle to her lips and tilted it back, draining the bottle. When she finished, she shoved the empty bottle at him, pinning it to his chest until he took it. "Nor do I need your help getting home." She turned and stormed off, her anger causing shards of bright light to sputter from her fingertips as she left.

He watched as she thundered her way back up the dirt road to her cabin, unsure what just happened. She probably didn't even know she leaked magic in her anger. He didn't understand. One moment, she seemed happy, standing at his side, ready to face Bane and his coyotes, and the next, she became pissed and stormed off. He felt his animal stir, aroused at both sides of the woman he watched walk away. He didn't doubt that she could protect herself, but he wouldn't risk finding out he was wrong.

Josh laughed beside him, his beer dangling from his fingertips. "Now that's a spunky one," he said. "You have your hands full with that one, Catnip."

Dimitri nodded, knowing it was more than that. Adira Brennan was his mate. Of that, he was positive. He only hoped he hadn't screwed up what was fated.

Seven

Well, that was pretty damn stupid," Alanna said, as she watched Adira stalk off toward her cabin.

Dimitri held his hands out to his sides, his face a mask of exasperation. "I know, right? She should know I would do anything to protect her."

Josh turned to him, his right eyebrow arched. "You mean…"

Dimitri ran a hand through his walnut-colored hair, letting out a breath as he did. "I felt it when she arrived, my panther going berserk the moment he scented her. Adira's my mate."

Alanna turned to him, her brows furrowed over her nose line. He dropped his arms to his sides again and took a step back. "Are you serious?" she asked, her hands on her hips. "She should know? Why the hell would she know that?

She's not a shifter, you dolt; she's a witch."

Josh lifted his beer to his lips and took a sip, ignoring the imploring look Dimitri gave him as if to say, leave me out of it.

Dimitri turned back to Alanna, still unsure he understood. "But she's been around shifters. She lived in Draven Falls for the last ten years. I called Jed Hawkins earlier and verified that the Paranormal Council sent her to help us. Agatha Rochester convinced Adira to come give us a hand against Bane, thinking we might need the aid of a witch. He even told me Adira even hung around a wolf named Jensen for the past few months. Surely she knows about mates? She has to know I would never allow anything to hurt her."

Alanna laughed, as she shook her head. "Just because that critter inside of you told you Adira is your mate, doesn't mean Adira knows it. Have you even talked to her? Asked her about it at all?" When he just stared at her dumbfounded, she sighed. "Yeah, I didn't think so. Men. You're all a bunch of idiots."

Dimitri turned his gaze back to the path Adira just stormed down. He should have talked to her, he knew, but when was there time really? Hell, she hadn't even been in Bull Creek twenty-four hours. The mating call hit him so hard and fast, followed by the appearance of Bane, that Dimitri hadn't even had time to process what it all meant. He just knew he needed her, needed her in his arms, his bed, his life, needed her safe, away from Bane and his coyotes. Did Agatha Rochester know this would happen when she sent Adira to him? Probably. The matriarch of the witches in

Draven Falls possessed a habit of matchmaking. "Great," Dimitri said with a sigh.

Alanna walked over and placed a hand on his shoulder. "I'll go talk to her," she said. "You stay here with Josh and see if you can keep this party from going sour."

He gave one short nod. "Thank you."

"No problem." She squeezed his shoulder before walking off after Adira. "Catnip," she teased, as she wiggled her fingers over her shoulder at him.

He watched her leave, yearning to rush ahead and fix his own mess. His animal agreed, urging him to do just that, but Dimitri tamped the desire down until his panther relaxed. Josh stepped up beside Dimitri, a beer held out for him. "Thanks," he said as he took the proffered beer. "I really screwed that up, huh?"

"Well, you helped me look good in Alanna's eyes, so, yeah, you screwed up."

Dimitri rolled his eyes. "Gee, thanks."

"Hey, I needed help. I appreciate it." Josh winked at him, and then both men chuckled before sipping their beers.

Pulling the sweating bottle from his mouth, licking his lips as he did, Dimitri took a deep breath. "I never knew how hard this was, finding your mate, dealing with the intensity. I just assumed she'd feel the same thing."

Josh shrugged. "She's not a shifter. She's a witch, yes, but a human witch. She'll think and feel like a human."

Dimitri shot his friend a dark look, taking Josh's words as an insult to his woman.

Josh held up his hand. "No offense intended," he said. "I

just mean, she doesn't, and probably won't, feel things as intensely as you do. You're going to have to be patient with her. As is your panther."

Dimitri didn't think he could be that patient. At least Bane would prove to be a distraction for a while. "What are we going to do about the coyotes?" he asked, trying to change the subject and get his mind off Adira. "He was pretty brazen coming here tonight." He glanced around as families started stabbing marshmallows with sticks and putting them near the fire. Others shoved hot dogs on their sticks, ready to get on with the festive night. Eve turned the music back on, and even cranked up the volume as drinks were made and laughter filled the small area. "These people came here to hide from the world, to escape some dark past they don't even want to talk about yet. I promised to protect them."

Shuffling was heard among the branches on the other side of the fire. Both men turned and watched as another man, with dark hair and thick arms, walked around the blaze, seeking them out. Once he spotted them, he picked up his pace until he stood in front of Dimitri. "Ezra, what's wrong?" Dimitri asked.

The tall man shook his head. "Nothing," he answered. "The area was full of coyotes a short while ago, watching as Bane entered and faced off with you, but as soon as their leader left, so did they. They knew we were there but didn't try to pick a fight with any of us, which surprised me. They seemed ready, though." He shrugged. "If you ask me, I think Bane was here trying to instigate something. To be honest, it's probably a good thing for everyone gathered here that the new lady distracted the man. Otherwise, I'm not sure what would have happened."

Dimitri nodded as he turned his gaze to the woods around them. "She's a spunky witch for sure." He then turned his attention back to Ezra. "Go ahead and call in the others. I doubt Bane will make another appearance tonight. No sense in anyone missing the fun."

Ezra nodded, but before he could turn away to call the others, they heard the rumbling of a vehicle coming down the dirt road. *Was I wrong?* Dimitri felt his panther tense within him, ready to pounce, as they waited for whoever approached.

Sheriff Einstein's car finally came into view, and everyone relaxed. Dimitri sent Ezra to bring the others in as Josh and he turned to greet the sheriff. The older man parked and then slid out of his car, walking over to where the party was most active. He waved at several people as they called out greetings, knowing most who lived in Bull Creek. Chet Einstein resided in Holopaw, the next township over, but kept a rapport with most of the people in the surrounding towns and communities. He had even watched many grow into adulthood, and helped with a couple of births. But more than being well known, he was also well liked by most who knew him.

"Hey, Sheriff, what brings you by tonight?" Dimitri asked as he approached the heavyset man.

"The bar in Holopaw was empty, so I grew concerned Bane and his crew were stirring up trouble," the sheriff answered, as he hooked his thumbs into his belt. "To be honest, I'm surprised he's not here."

"He was," Josh said. "But Adira scared him off. Or amused him so much that he changed his mind about causing trouble. He just gave us a warning, instead."

"Apparently, he's giving us one night to get out of here," Dimitri added.

The sheriff laughed. "Well, wasn't that right neighborly of him."

The rustling of leaves and snapping of branches under heavy feet was heard around the perimeter, bushes being shoved out of the way, causing the men to turn as those who stood guard came into the clearing to join the festivities. Bane made his threat and left, so everyone assumed the danger was over for the evening.

"Can I offer you a hot dog or soda?" Dimitri asked the sheriff. "You're here. Might as well enjoy some of the fun."

"I won't even tell on you if you have a beer with us," Josh said, that mischievous glint in his eyes.

The sheriff chuckled as he shook his head. "Thanks for the offer. I'll take a rain check on the beer, but a hot dog sounds like a great nighttime snack."

Josh laughed as he patted the man on the back. "I'll find someone to get you hooked up." He walked away, leaving the sheriff and Dimitri alone to talk.

"So, what happened?" the sheriff asked as soon as Josh left.

Dimitri gave the man a rundown on Bane's visit, telling him how Bull Creek's new resident, Adira, amused the leader of the coyote pack enough to get him to leave the festivities without stirring up more trouble than his arrival did. "He just left us with threats, but I highly doubt that's the end of it."

Chet cocked an eyebrow at him. "Bane took notice of your lady friend? Dimitri, that may be a bad thing. Have you thought about the chance that Bane will go after her for standing up to him? He's the type to do it, you know, just to make a point and send a message to anyone else who might want to follow her lead. He's a bully. That's how they operate. Intimidation. Instilling fear in people."

Dimitri didn't bother telling the sheriff that Adira was more than his friend; she was his mate, but Chet didn't understand all the nuances of shifter life yet, even working with Lainie. No sense in giving him a crash course now. "To be honest, I did think of that, and you're right. He seemed taken with her. Found it amusing she would mouth off at him. What is it with spirited women?"

Chet chuckled. "Men take it as an exciting challenge. We like to think there's a lady out there that doesn't need us, even though she does. We like strength, not some timid doormat of a female. Spirited means strength." He shrugged. "Who wants to babysit all the time?"

Dimitri nodded. It was true. He liked the fire in Adira, the way she stood up to Bane, even how she stood up to him, but it could also bring unwanted attention. He'd have to stand guard at her place, just in case Bane sent someone to take care of the mouthy witch. She wouldn't like it, but then again, who said she needed to know. "The coyotes need to go," Dimitri said as he stared at the mixture of humans and shifters having fun around the bonfire. "There's too much at stake here."

The sheriff nodded. "Agreed, but how? So far, they haven't done anything to break the law, so I can't force them out of town, or even stuff them into a jail cell."

"I'm afraid this isn't a problem you can handle," Dimitri said. "This is a shifter issue." He turned to the sheriff as Josh stepped up with a soda in one hand and a hot dog in the other, handing them both to Chet. "Shifters believe strongly in family and will do anything to protect that family. It's a bond that surpasses any other." He gestured to the people gathered around the bonfire. "These people are my family. I'll do whatever I must in order to protect them."

Josh nodded. "As will I."

The sheriff stared at each man in front of him, gauging them and the seriousness of their statements. "I'll help all I can, even if it's cleaning up the mess left behind."

Dimitri said he appreciated it and would call when he needed the sheriff's services. Then the men ended the conversation and moved over to the fire to join the others. The party continued for three more hours, the residents of Bull Creek laughing, roasting marshmallows, and enjoying the calmness of the night. Alanna never returned, and Dimitri didn't know what to make of that. Was Adira really that mad at him for wanting to protect her? It didn't really matter, though. With what the sheriff said still echoing in his mind, Dimitri already decided he would stand watch over her cabin tonight. He left Josh and Ezra to supervise the cleanup of the clearing, as he made his way to Adira's new home. Before crossing her wards, Dimitri stripped, stuffing his clothes in a bag he brought from the party and then shifted. He hoped her wards were set for humans and not animals. Otherwise, his secret guard duty wouldn't be secret for long. He clamped the bag in his teeth and then padded up her drive to the porch. Once there, he dropped the bag against the exterior of the cabin. He also believed he would be more comfortable sleeping like his animal than as a man stretched out on her porch. It also might not appear as odd to passersby.

The interior of her place was quiet, so he assumed Alanna left, and Adira was now in bed. He knew she had wards to warn her of danger approaching, but he wasn't taking any chances. Tonight, he would sleep as close to his mate as he could without pissing her off anymore. He turned a few times, getting himself settled, before laying down, his massive head propped on his crossed paws. With a deep breath, he closed his eyes, his ears perked for any unusual noise, and waited until sleep took him. It was a long time before slumber claimed him.

Eight

She fumed all the way back to her cabin, the dust from the road kicking up with her passage. *How dare he? I am not some weakling, some poor female needing a man to protect me. I'm a witch damn it!* The words continued stewing a morass of anger in her mind until she reached her cabin. With a flick of her wrist, the door burst open, slamming back against the wall. She continued her rampaging pace into her home, using her hand, as well as her anger, to slam the door shut behind her, sealing out her frustration with Dimitri.

Entering the small kitchen area of the cabin, she pulled out a wineglass from the cabinet and then reached for the wine on the counter to pour herself a full glass. She downed half of the dark, red liquid with one swallow, and then refilled the goblet as she took a deep breath. She couldn't believe how fast Dimitri went from sweet and understanding to an overprotective moron. It must be a record or something. She had already proved to him that she could take care of herself. Hell, she stood beside him and faced that behemoth of a man, Bane, ready to unleash her power in order to defend a land she just entered. What did Dimitri think? She was bluffing? She can handle her own, damn it.

Adira sighed as she turned and leaned back on the counter, one arm over her stomach, while the other held her wineglass in front of her. She couldn't deny how her sex stirred at the thought of being alone with Dimitri at his home; however, both of them snuggled tight together, his arms wrapped around her. There was definitely something about him that pulled at her, even though she arrived determined not to get involved with anyone again. Then the sexual heat, which flared up between her legs, was doused when his words struck a different chord within her. The embers of passion burst into flames of anger as she realized that he saw her as some weak female who needed to be protected. She couldn't stomach the notion. She didn't need a babysitter, and in no uncertain terms, told him just that.

She saw the confusion on his face, the disbelief that she didn't pounce at his words, his masculine superiority and strength. He was probably used to women falling for his macho bullshit. Oh, but Dimitri was a stubborn, stubborn man, refusing to give up. His persistence might even have won her over if he hadn't called her pigheaded. Even his friend, Josh, knew that was a mistake, as she saw his eyes widen as he turned away from his friend, distancing himself from Dimitri's stupidity. Now that was a smart man.

Dimitri's expression shifted to one of panic, knowing he screwed up. Good. He needed to panic. He was lucky she only pinned the beer bottle to his chest, instead of shoving it through him. She knew when she turned and stormed off that her anger caused shards of bright light to burst from her fingertips. She didn't care. She allowed them to spark, a warning to the shifter she left behind not to follow.

A knock came at the door, soft and feminine. Adira closed her eyes and checked her wards. Alanna. Adira blew out the breath she held, relieved it wasn't Mr. Macho come to berate her for her feminine hysterics.

Walking over to the door, she opened it and stared at the robust redhead on her doorstep. "If he sent you to try and calm the overreacting witch down, please, just go tell him to mount himself."

Alanna giggled at Adira's choice of words. "He didn't send me," she said. Then she pointed to the glass. "Got any more of that?"

Stop being rude and agitating your new neighbors, Adira scolded herself. She nodded and then moved out of the way so Alanna could enter. "Sorry. Come in. I just don't like the whole she's a woman and weak shtick."

"I don't blame you. It's how shifters get with someone they see as their mate, though. My guess is, Dimitri sees that in you."

Adira moved back into the kitchen and pulled out another wineglass, before filling it to a normal level for the other woman. "Mate? I just got here. He does know that's a little fast, right?" She handed the wine to Alanna.

The redhead cocked her head to the side. "Aren't you from Draven Falls? You have to be familiar with shifters."

Adira took a sip of her wine, her free arm wrapped around her waist as she leaned back on the counter, visions of Jensen popping unwillingly into her mind. The truth was, she was all too familiar with shifters. More than she wanted to be if she was honest. She knew about their mating rituals, the mark they leave on their mates, and even how fast the animals are attracted to their mate. It was what should have warned her that Jensen was just a passing fling and never intended to be in a longterm relationship with her. He never even thought of marking her. Not even a little nibble. While the sex was great, it was never she's-my-mate great. Otherwise, she'd have his bite mark in her upper shoulder and be with him now, him being the one acting like Dimitri, all macho and overprotective. She hated macho and overprotective. "Yeah, I know all about shifters. Too much at times."

"Then you know that as soon as the animal scents the one they plan to be with forever, the human has little control over it. Dimitri is driven by his animal instincts to protect his mate, to protect you."

"I'm not his mate. I'm not marked. Hell, we've only had a beer and a hot dog together. That's it. Besides," she said with a sigh, "I'm just not ready."

Alanna shrugged. "The mark will come in time. The mating process doesn't happen in order all the time. His animal has already scented that you're his mate. It'll drive Dimitri crazy until the two of you are together. In the mind of his panther, you already are. You're his, and he's going to make sure everyone knows it, whether you're ready or not."

Adira poured them each another glass of wine, and then, they settled on the couches, legs folded as feet were tucked under their rumps. After another sip, Adira told Alanna how she threw Jensen into a wall back in Draven Falls. Adira knew everything Alanna said about shifters and their mating urges was accurate, which is why Adira felt even more foolish that she had allowed Jensen to string her along. She wouldn't make that mistake again.

"And that's when Agatha offered me her cabin here in the guise of Dimitri needing help protecting the human populace from a rogue coyote pack that was trying to drive them from their land." Adira turned to Alanna, a weak smile on her face. "I'm going to be honest, Alanna, Jensen hurt me bad. Even my magic was affected by his betrayal. Instead of streams of magic now, my power comes out in shards. I really don't think Dimitri deserves a broken witch."

"Broken witch? Sweetie, you faced off against Bane, and he's a total bastard. You stood beside Dimitri, even when he tried to block you. Broken witch?" She laughed, shaking her head. "Sweetie, in my eyes, you're anything but a broken witch. You're a sassy woman, and deep down, I think you've already felt what Dimitri's felt."

"I was only doing what Agatha asked me to come here and do; I was protecting this community. I'm just lucky I didn't have to use my magic, not knowing if it would actually work or not."

Alanna lifted her wine to her lips, but before she sipped,

she said, "Sweetie, you keep telling yourself that. If you were a shifter, your animal would already be telling you how wrong you are." She took a sip of her wine, as Adira thought on the woman's words, wondering if there was even a chance that Alanna was right.

Adira shifted on the couch, taking another sip of her wine. When she was done, she asked, "So, what is the deal with Bull Creek anyway? There seem to be quite a few residents for a town that doesn't even seem like a town. Does everyone live in cabins?"

Alanna laughed. "For the most part. Some actually live in tents. Bull Creek, itself, was formed in the early 1900s as a small logging area for its cypress, which fit in well with the loggers back in Draven Falls. When the area went through some issues, the Paranormal Council of Draven Falls turned it into a sanctuary of sorts. When people come here, they just want to escape some prejudice or injustice. They just want a simple life, to be able to be who they are without recrimination. As the place grew, they decided Bull Creek needed an alpha to help protect the residents and offer guidance, so about a year ago, the Paranormal Council selected Dimitri. So far, he's done a kick-ass job."

"And then Bane showed up." Adira took another sip of her wine, trying to recall how she knew the Everest name. If Dimitri was from Draven Falls, Adira just assumed she would have heard of his family but, if she did, the knowledge refused to make itself known. "How do people hear of Bull Creek? It's not like it even has a dot on any map."

"Same way you did, word of mouth. It gets talked about among the paranormal community and the darker underworld of the humans, those who aren't afraid of supernatural beings. Some come to see what we're about, while others come here to live, needing a new start on life.

"Is that why you're here? A new start in life?"

Alanna shuffled in her seat a little, looking a tad uncomfortable. "Let's just say family can be complicated at times."

Adira just nodded, deciding not to push the subject further. Everyone deserved their privacy, and she was the new girl in town after all.

They stayed up for three more hours, the conversation shifting to their hometowns, family, friends new and old. When Alanna finally left, the moon was high in the sky, and Adira was more than ready for bed. She washed the dishes, stripped down to her bare skin, and crawled between the cool sheets. Her sleep was restless, tossing and turning, as thoughts of the night replayed in her head. Her power came out in short blasts, mixed with visions of Jensen being thrown across her living room back in Draven Falls. She tried to shove the images out of her head, but nothing worked. Finally, she surrendered, jerking the covers from her body, and deciding to sit outside and let the cool night bathe her mind with fresh images.

She wrapped her robe around her and padded across the wood floor in her bare feet. As she opened the door and stepped out onto her front porch, a movement off to her right snapped her attention. Sleeping, snuggled against the front of her cabin, nestled up close to her front door, was the tawny panther she knew she almost hit with her car when she first arrived in Bull Creek.

Nine

"Why the hell are you sleeping on my porch?" Adira stood there, her hands planted on her hips, legs slightly apart, which allowed her robe to fall open slightly, exposing her creamy thighs. "I told you I did NOT need protecting, damn it."

The panther jerked awake at her words, or rather at the seething tone in her voice. He jumped to all fours, his ears perked back as he stood, braced for whatever was wrong. He jerked his gaze to the left and the right, searching for the attack until he realized that it came from right in front of him. His gold eyes told her he knew just how pissed she was. Then he shifted, his fur slipping back into his skin, his bones popping as his four legs turned to two legs and a pair of arms, his paws shifting to feet and hands, and his body completely naked. As soon as the shift was over, he stood, his thick muscles stretching back into shape from being cramped in his animal form for so long and asleep.

Adira couldn't take her eyes off his body, his powerful legs, strong arms, broad shoulders, and… And his cock, which was already twitching to life as he stood in front of her. There was no way he could hide it this time. She felt her pussy stir as she wondered what it would feel like to have him pounding into her from behind, his hands on her hips, as he thrust deep inside…

She gave herself a mental shake, reminding herself she was pissed at him. *Now is not the time to fantasize about his cock. But wow, what a cock. No! Stay pissed, or he won't learn I'm not some weakling.* "Not like the Incredible Hulk, huh? You don't shift with pants that seem to stretch with the transformation?" She had been around shifters enough, especially Jensen, to know they were nude when they shifted back, but she still attempted to irritate the man in front of her. Nudity was never an issue in Draven Falls, and Adira assumed it wasn't here, either, with shifters transforming from human to animal all the time.

He didn't say anything, just stood there, his hands on his hips, not caring that he was naked as he stared at her in her robe. His expression revealed his wariness at her mood, which she thought was a good thing. Apparently, her tantrum last night hadn't taught him anything. "Why are you here?" she repeated.

He took a deep breath, then moved to where he dumped his bag, probably holding his clothes, on her porch. *No, don't get dressed just yet.* She was having too much fun watching his nude form move around. He stopped at the stack of clothes, and then turned to her, choosing to remain naked for now, it seemed. Lucky her. "The sheriff came by last night after you left and made some valid points," he said. "Points I tried to make to you. Bane seemed to take special notice of how you stood up to him. He won't like that for long and will probably try something. I wanted to make sure you were where I could protect you, so I chose to come here and sleep, keeping an eye on you."

She arched an eyebrow at him. "And yet, I caught you sleeping and scared the hell out of you," she pointed out.

He shrugged. "What can I say? I didn't expect the attack to come from inside the house."

"The attack wouldn't have come from outside, either, you dolt. Before I turned in, I set the wards to warn of coyotes. I told you; I know how to protect myself."

"Well, how was I supposed to know that?" He stepped toward her, his hands going to her arms. The suddenness of the move caught her off-guard, and her robe fell open a little more, exposing her soft belly. "Adira, I won't risk anything hurting you. Bane is a dangerous man. He's also smart. Who's to say he'll even use coyotes to attack you? There are plenty of other rogue shifters eager to do his dirty work."

She felt the heat between her legs fan to a roaring fire at his touch. God, it was hard to stay pissed at him when he was naked and concerned, his cock a growing rod between them. It took all her resolve not to pin him to the wall and take him right there on her porch. Her eyes widened as she glanced around the area. Had anyone seen him shift on her porch, privy to his nakedness? "Perhaps you should get some clothes on," she said, words she really didn't want to hear, not to mention even say. She wanted him to stay naked, wanted to feel his body against hers.

He moved closer, one of his hands leaving her arm to slide inside of her robe. "This area is full of shifters. Everyone is used to seeing naked people after a shift. They're also used to the sexual habits of shifters."

She swallowed the lump that filled her throat. Oh god, where was her anger now? "Dimitri, I..." She felt his thumb rub across her nipple, the tiny nub shriveling into a hard pearl of sensitivity. She moaned as she pushed her breast into his hand, her fury gone with his touch.

"Adira, I can wait, but only so long," he said. "You're mine. I knew it from the moment I saw you first pull up in your car. My animal has already claimed you as his and is demanding to make his mark." He tweaked her nipple, pinching it, as he stared into her eyes, knowing full well what he did to her.

"Dimitri, I... I'm not sure I'm ready for another fling with a shifter."

"Fling?" he repeated, and it came out as a growl. She could see his animal in his eyes, the green-gold circles of passion penetrating her. "I don't know what happened to you before, but I'm not talking about a fling, Adira. My animal wouldn't be so eager and passionate for a casual encounter with you. This is how it feels when they've discovered their mate, my mate. This isn't a fling; this is a lifetime. I cannot live without you in my life."

She stared at him, her eyes wide at such a passionate, deep declaration of love and commitment. She didn't know what to say. Jensen played with her heart, allowed her to believe that what they had was real and forever, even though he never technically said those words. Yet, Dimitri not only said them, but it was also obvious he deeply felt them. He believed every word he uttered. These weren't just statements; they were vows. "Oh, Dimitri…"

He leaned down and kissed her, his warm lips pressed firmly to hers, his tongue forcing its way inside of her, tasting her, claiming her. She fell into his arms, her robe coming completely open with the sudden embrace. She didn't care, her passion overcoming her fear of being caught naked outside.

When he broke the kiss, he stared into her eyes. "I don't know who hurt you before, but I won't allow anything to hurt you ever again. Adira, it would drive me crazy if Bane were to attempt to harm you because of me."

She held him close. "It wouldn't be because of you. It would be because of my mouth at the bonfire. But, Dimitri, that's why I'm here, remember? To help you fight him and protect this sanctuary. There are hurting people here who can't protect themselves. Agatha sent me here to stand beside you in this fight, and I'm not going to hide behind you. Or anyone, for that matter."

"But that was before I knew you were my mate. That changes things. Changes everything."

She shook her head, her hair swishing across her back. "No, no it doesn't. It only makes the stakes that much more important. I told you yesterday; I'm not some weakling human. I'm a witch, very capable of defending myself. I'm in this fight now and refuse to hide from it."

He smiled at her, and it warmed her heart, stirring the feelings she hoped to escape when she left Draven Falls. "You're such a feisty thing, Adira. Agatha knew what she was doing when she sent you my way."

Adira snorted in laughter. "When does Agatha Rochester not know what she's doing? The thing is figuring out the real purpose behind her actions."

He laughed as he nodded. "True story." He then slid a hand up into her hair, strengthening his grip on her as he pulled her tighter against him, his face growing serious. "I make no apologies for wanting to protect you. I'll do my best to remember how strong of a woman you are, but Adira, I will never allow harm to come to you if I can prevent it. I'm sorry, but you're just too important to me."

"Dimitri, you've known me less than twenty-four hours. How is that even possible?"

"It's the call of a mate. That bond is stronger and runs deeper than any other."

She shook her head, still having a hard time comprehending it all. "It's going to take me some time to come to grips with everything." She slid her hand down his stomach until she gripped his hardness. "However, in the meantime, I bet I can think of something to keep my mind off the uncertainties I'm feeling right now."

He groaned as she slid her hand back and forth on his throbbing cock. "Um, yeah, we can definitely do with some distraction right now."

She held a finger up. "But no biting. I've heard about the mate mark, and I don't want to feel that just yet. Understood?"

He nodded. "I'll do my best. Promise."

She eyed him as if she didn't believe him, but then she gripped his hand and led him into her cabin, slamming the door behind them. She turned once they were out of sight of any peeping toms, and dragged him over to the couch, twirling him until he faced her. With a smirk, she shoved him down on it. He was already naked, so there was nothing between her and his hard cock. She slid her robe down her body, allowing him his first glimpse of her completely nude form. At first, she worried he would balk at her curves, but he just stared, mesmerized, his eyes filled with passion.

He reached out to her, and she stepped forward, straddling him, her arms around his neck. She slid her slit back and forth on his cock, feeling her pussy lips wrap around him, her wetness coating his thick shaft. Then she raised her body just enough to allow the head of his cock to find her entrance, and as she stared straight into his green-gold eyes, she dropped down onto him, allowing him to fill her. She cried out as he groaned, his hands going to her waist, guiding her as she rode him, his cock slipping in and out of her pussy, stretching her, filling her. She gripped his neck, her arms pressing down on his shoulders, as her hips rocked back and forth on his. She felt his mouth on her flesh, his lips planting wet kisses all over her chest and neck as she leaned down, giving herself to him.

He held her, and she used his grip to let herself go, her body tensing into a tight ball of sensations as she continued to ride him. Nothing else mattered. It was all gone from her mind. Jensen. Draven Falls. Bane. All she could think about was Dimitri and the way his cock felt inside of her. Her body twisted itself into a tight wad of building tension, her orgasm ready to rip from her as her clit rubbed against his pelvic bone, grinding against him, building, climbing, until she felt him grip her waist and yank her down onto his manhood. She opened her eyes and stared at him, his eyes wide, as she felt his cock twitch inside of her, filling her with his cum. The first explosion hitting her walls sent her over the edge. Her body exploded with her orgasm, shuddering, as it tightened into electric jolts that ripped down her nerves, up her spine, and into her mind. Her eyes widened, and her mouth made a perfect O as she cried out.

It was the most amazing orgasm she could remember ever having, her mind lost in the typhoon of emotions and sensations that rippled through her. She couldn't stop and felt tears well up in her eyes as she surrendered to the ride she relished. It was like a giant wave pool, and she kept going up to the crest of the wave and then slammed back down only to rise again. An eternity must have passed before she caught her breath again, her vision an explosion of white dots that popped in and out. She fell onto his chest, and he held her tight against him, keeping her from falling over.

"That...that was amazing," she said, her voice a raspy whisper. "I just...wow...I need some time to rest. And some water."

She felt his lips on her neck, and he kept kissing her. "You rest," he whispered in her ear. "And I'll get you some water. And then breakfast. I built up an appetite, and all I did was sit there." He grinned at her as he nuzzled into her neck. "Maybe I should get you mad at me more often."

She nibbled into his neck. "I wouldn't if I were you." She sent a surge of power into him through her teeth as she bit down.

He yelped a little and then moaned. "I don't know. That could be fun, as well."

She could only laugh. "Go get me some water."

"Yes, ma'am," he said with a chuckle. He slid her off his lap and onto the couch, kissing her shoulder as he did, before pushing himself off the couch to carry out her wishes.

"And then breakfast," she called after him.

"Yes, ma'am," he said, still laughing.

Wow. What was I missing before? Screw breakfast. I could make a few meals out of him. She made a mental note to call Agatha and thank the woman for sending her to Bull Creek.

Ten

"Shots! We need shots," Alanna called out once they found a table. Adira slid into the empty chair, as did Deputy Lainie Everest and Eve Hartlow. It was ladies night at Everglades, a shifter bar in Holopaw, and Alanna was determined that Adira would have a good time and be able to unwind and forget men and shifters, especially coyotes. It was a dive bar, really, nothing like Shades back in Draven Falls, but it held its own rustic charm. It was a wooden structure, appearing to be constructed of discarded planks, rather than finished wood, with scratched up wooden chairs and tables, weak mirrors and flashing beer logos on the walls. Serving girls wandered from table to table, taking orders and flirting with the men patrons, whether the men had dates or not. Country music blared from a broken-down jukebox, bouncing off the walls, as couples line danced and chugged their beers. It was the perfect place to get drunk and forget.

While they were there to put coyotes out of their minds, there was one shifter Adira didn't want to forget. She couldn't, even if she tried. Dimitri consumed her thoughts and, if she was honest with herself, her fantasies. She could still feel him between her legs from that morning. If they had only tumbled in her bed once, the sensations probably would have faded by now, but after three rounds on the mattress, she almost couldn't walk.

"Of tequila," Lainie Everest shouted, echoing the call for shots as she tapped the table several times. Her long, dark hair swished around her shoulders with the movement. "I'm not on duty tonight, so I definitely need tequila." Lainie was the only shifter on Sheriff Einstein's unit, a panther he hired to help him navigate the shifter realm. As such, her hours varied depending on what was happening in Bull Creek at the time. One of the reasons she attended girl's night out was because Chet didn't trust Bane to leave Adira alone. Nor did Dimitri, for that matter. Adira knew the women were babysitting her, even if Lainie denied it. However, as long as alcohol was involved and no men, Adira allowed it.

"Yeah, how did you manage the night off?" Eve asked, her brows wrinkled with confusion. She was one of the humans who took up residence in Bull Creek a little over a year ago, running from a past she still refused to discuss. When Alanna told Adira about the other woman, all she said was that when Eve arrived in their community, her body was covered with more bruises than healthy flesh. "Saturday night should be all hands on deck, shouldn't it?"

Lainie just laughed, shaking her head. "First, shifters can't get drunk. At least, not with this stuff. We're lucky that way. And seriously? All hands? In this area? The most action we ever see around here are hunters shooting off their sticks out of season." She rolled her eyes as if Eve's question was ridiculous. Adira knew the real reason Lainie had the night off, however. "They see way more action in St. Cloud and Kissimmee. If it weren't for old man Tucker losing his keys once in a while, I would never get a call."

"You should have been out at Bull Creek last night, then," Eve said, ignoring the look Alanna shot her way. Instead, Eve tucked a strand of her sandy hair behind her ear and pressed on with her tale. "Bane Kastner stopped by and brought some of his coyote buddies. I thought they would trash the place until Adira got all sparky on them." She grinned as she glanced over at Adira, wiggling her fingers in the air. "It was… shocking to watch."

Adira rolled her eyes, ignoring Eve's poor attempts at wordplay. According to Alanna, Eve was fascinated with all things paranormal, and it seemed after last night, Adira was young Eve's new fixation.

"Yeah, we definitely need shots," Alanna said as she waved down one of the serving girls making the rounds. "Beers and tequila shots," she ordered, once the woman came close enough to hear her. Alanna then turned back to the others. "Now, enough about last night. Let's talk about Adira and how she woke up this morning." She grinned as she leaned over, waggling her eyebrows at the witch on the other side of the table.

Adira felt her face flush with heat at the thought that they all knew she slept with Dimitri that morning. *Slept with. It sounds so lame compared to what we did, which was... Incredible.* "How on earth do you know what went on between Dimitri and me this morning?" she asked. "Were you sleeping on my porch, as well?"

Alanna shook her head. "Not hardly. The ground is too hard. My wolf isn't even happy sleeping on the ground. No, my cabin is close to yours. Too close from the sounds that woke me up this morning." She grinned at her friend. "Shifters have great hearing, remember?"

Adira's blush deepened, as she closed her eyes. She forgot about how open the shifters were about all things sexual. She'd rather talk about coyotes. She had no idea what was really happening with Dimitri, and she didn't want to figure it all out in front of her new friends. "Definitely need tequila."

"Wait a minute," Lainie said, straightening in her chair. "You got it on with my brother?" Then she pointed at Alanna. "And you want to talk about it with me here? I don't want the low down on how my brother goes down."

Eve grinned, her eyes going wide as her brows popped up. "I wouldn't mind talking about it," she said. "How was he? He looks like he could be wild in bed."

"Don't!" Lainie shouted as she held her hands out. "Not one word."

"I thought shifters were pretty open when it came to being naked and sex," Eve said.

"Not when it comes to my brother," Lainie said. "Now, let's pick a new topic."

"Agreed," Adira said.

Alanna just grinned, and Adira knew the topic was bound to come back up sooner or later.

Eve shrugged, surrendering her curiosity for which Adira was grateful. Of course, that only left one other topic. "What is Chet going to do with the influx of coyotes in Bull Creek?" Eve asked the deputy. "Bane means harm. You can see it in his eyes."

Lainie shrugged. "There's nothing Chet can do right now. Technically, Bane hasn't done anything but overflow at the mouth and trespass at your party, a community party at that, so it wasn't really private or trespassing. Nothing's happened that's worth the paperwork to hold him even for a few hours."

Noel brought their drinks over, setting the beers and shot glasses in front of the women. They ceased talking until she disappeared again. There were no men at the table, so no real reason for Noel to linger, flirting her way into a bigger tip. Once she was out of earshot, Alanna asked Lainie what the sheriff told her about the bonfire.

Lainie shrugged. "Just that Bane appeared, and Dimitri said he'd handle it. We're not supposed to interfere in any official capacity until called. To me, that means it's going to be a shifter thing, which means I may be in it after all."

"What do you mean, a shifter thing?" Adira sat up straighter, reaching out and wrapping her hands around her beer bottle. The whole it's a shifter thing sounded ominous at best.

Alanna shook her head, probably to warn Lainie from saying anything else, but the deputy didn't notice the motion the way Adira did. "It means that Dimitri and his boys are going to handle it, more than likely," Lainie replied. "It's not going to be pretty. Bane has some strong men in his pack. I'm not saying Dimitri's enforcers aren't capable. I just worry that they'll be outnumbered."

Adira turned to Alanna, her brows dipped in confusion. "Dimitri is going to fight Bane? Why?"

Eve was staring at her beer. "To protect us humans," she said, her voice low.

"To protect us all," Alanna said. She ran her hand through her hair as she reached out and lifted her shot glass. The other women followed suit.

Adira stared at the amber liquid. Dimitri couldn't go up against Bane. Bane was not the type to fight fair. She just found Dimitri. She couldn't lose him. Not now. Not ever. There was still too much sex to be had, too many emotions and sensations to experience. She would stand beside him; of that, there was no doubt. That's why Agatha sent her to Bull Creek after all. To help Dimitri in his quest to protect the community and its residents. Adira would not allow him to face Bane alone. She would be by his side when it happened. Nothing would stop her.

"To Bull Creek," Alanna said as she lifted her shot glass into the air.

The others followed suit, echoing the toast. Then they all downed the liquid, allowing it to burn its way down their throats to start a fire in their bellies. Adira knew a war was on the horizon. *I need to get my full powers back. Dimitri is going to need me at my best.* She stared across the table at Alanna, who stared right back, her expression revealing that the other woman thought the same thing as Adira. They both needed to stand by their men, even though those men would do everything they could to keep the women away from the battle. *Male chauvinist...* She sighed as she reached for her beer. Now she had to figure out how to make Dimitri see her point of view.

The conversation turned from Bane and his obsession with Bull Creek to more important matters, like the way Brad Pitt's ass looked in jeans. The drinks kept flowing, shots kept coming, and the laughter grew louder. Adira didn't know what tomorrow would bring, but tonight, she was all about the other three ladies around her table. She really hadn't taken any time to relax since the breakup with Jensen and Agatha sent her to Bull Creek. From one chaos to another seemed to be her journey.

She became so lost in the merriment that she almost missed the shift in Alanna's posture. The other woman stiffened, her back going straight as her head turned toward the door, her eyes narrowing into thin slits of agitation. Adira turned her attention, following Alanna's gaze, until she noticed the two men walking into Everglades. She recognized them as the men at Bane's side last night. Four others accompanied them, each with thick muscles and dark hair, their black eyes menacing, even as they smiled at the ladies they passed. She strained to see if Bane was with them, but they seemed to be alone. Blue sparks tingled at her fingertips, and she took a deep breath, reining in the power that wanted to shoot from her hands, her agitation sparking her magic.

Tamping down her power, she watched as the men walked around the bar, stopping here and there to flirt with a lady, whether she had a date or not. They thought they were the catch of the evening, and acted like it, their arrogance overbearing and nauseating. She took a deep breath. "I think it's time to go," she said.

The others nodded, downing their beers, and grabbing their purses. As they slid out of their chairs, the coyote pack noticed them, and their smiles turned to leers. They ignored the women they harassed, moving through the crowd toward the four from Bull Creek. Adira ignored them, keeping her gaze on the target—the exit. They almost made it, too.

The men howled as they reached out and grabbed the women by the arms, stopping them, and turning them back around. "Where are you ladies going? The party is just getting started now that we're here." He was tall, his dark eyes spotted with gray flecks. He leaned in toward Adira, sniffing her as he did. "I thought I recognized your scent from last night. You're that witch. You should definitely stick around. Let's get in a few slow dances."

She jerked her arm out of his grasp. "Thanks, but, um, ew. I'm sure someone in here is slumming. You're sure to find a last call booty mate."

The men with Mister Leer laughed at her remarks, razzing

their friend. "The girl has your number, Augur," one said.

Augur glared at the one who spoke, as he shooed the rest to silence with a glance. He reached back out and jerked Adira against him. "Not very friendly, are you? I can fix that."

Adira gripped his arm, raking her nails across his flesh. He cried out, jerking his arm away from her, lines of blood popping up on his arm. "You bitch," he snarled as he raised his arm to backhand her. He never got the chance.

"Back off," Deputy Everest shouted as she reached between the two other men to shove the man off Adira. "Now, before I haul your ass to jail."

One of the other men sniffed into the air. "I thought I smelled pig." He turned to his fellow coyotes, gesturing to Lainie with his thumb. "This dame works for that old sheriff." He turned back to Lainie and sneered. "A shifter mingling with humans. Doesn't seem right, does it?"

Lainie stepped closer to the man, her narrowed eyes threatening him to say anything more. "It's time for you to leave. Now."

The man snatched out, ready to grip the deputy's throat, but never connected. His arm froze in midair. He strained, sweat popping up on his brow, his coyote growling as his upper lip curled upward. Adira stood, her arm outstretched as shards of blue light wrapped around the man's arm, holding him in place. He jerked his gaze to her, his lips curling even more. She just smiled. "I think the deputy said it was time for you to leave." She shoved with her arm, sending the man flying out the doors behind him and into the parking lot.

The other men stared at their partner and then turned growling eyes to Adira. Alanna stepped in front of her friend. "I wouldn't," she said.

Eve puffed out her chest as she drew the knife she kept at her waist. "Yeah, I'd leave if I were you."

"Now," Deputy Everest repeated.

Augur, the one who sniffed at Adira, just sneered. "This isn't over," he threatened. "Bane has plans for you." He then sneered at the rest of the women. "For all of you."

"No doubt plans he drew up with crayons," Alanna said.

"It's over for tonight," Adira said, and then she led the way out of Everglades. It was time to go home and prepare. The first shots in the upcoming battle were just fired.

Eleven

Y ou did what?" Dimitri couldn't believe what he heard. "Adira, Everglades is not a normal bar." He turned to Alanna and Eve. "You two know about that place. Why the hell did you take her there?"

Eve looked at him like he was crazy. "Because it was ladies night. You know? Two for one? Duh."

It took everything he had not to throttle the woman. "Damn it, Eve, this isn't a game." He could feel the panther pushing at him, wanting free to wreak havoc on whomever he could. Fur pushed through his skin a little, claws pushing out of his fingertips, the pain of the shift just beginning. He tamped it down quickly. He didn't need to lose control now, not with so much at risk. He spun to Alanna. "Everglades is a paranormal bar. You should have known they would be there. Hell, Sheriff Einstein even told me they were there the other day, shooting off their mouth." The three women returned to Alanna's cabin when they left Everglades, and Lainie went to the sheriff's department to file a report on the drunken men. The only reason Dimitri knew what happened tonight was because Wes Stapleton, who ran Everglades, called and gave Dimitri a heads up.

"I handled it," Adira said as she moved into Alanna's kitchen to get a glass of water. "No big deal."

Dimitri looked at her, unable to hide the disbelief he knew masked his face. "No big deal? Six of Bane's men accosted you in a bar, a bar overrun with coyotes more than likely. You're lucky you got out of there alive."

Adira slammed the glass of water on the counter, luckily not breaking it. "Lucky? I wasn't lucky, Catnip. I'm a witch. I'm prepared for asinine people like them. There is a reason Agatha Rochester sent me here, remember?"

"I don't care why Agatha sent you here," he said, his tone seething. "That was before I found out you were my destined mate. I'm not going to let anything happen to you. You're too important."

"I'm not more important than anyone else in Bull Creek." She lifted the glass to her lips and drained half of it. She then licked her lips as she pulled the glass away from her mouth, and the sight of her tongue gliding across her lips sent him into an instant erection.

His panther growled within him, straining to be released. He wanted his mate, and Dimitri couldn't blame him. He wanted her, too "You're the most important person to me," he said, taking a step toward her, taking her arms in his hands. "I don't know what I'd do if anything happened to you. You can't take chances like that anymore, Adira. I couldn't take it." He tried to give her his most pathetic look, so she'd believe him.

Alanna just rolled her eyes as Eve said, "Gee, thanks. So, we're not important. Did you hear that, Alanna? It's okay if we get hurt."

Alanna shook her head at the other woman, warning her to be quiet. Now was not the time. Alanna was smart enough to recognize that. As a shifter, she knew the importance of mates, those destined to spend the rest of their lives together, and the bond that drives them crazy with passion. Dimitri couldn't help the way he felt. It was beyond his control. It was beyond all their control.

Eve just shrugged. "I'm going home," she said. "This night's a bust."

Alanna and Adira said goodbye, but Dimitri would not let go of his mate's arms. Nor did he say goodbye to Eve. She knew better than to go to Everglades. Thirty more minutes west and the ladies could have been in St. Cloud at a decent, safe bar where shifters didn't venture. Adira wouldn't have been put in harm's way. He took a deep breath. He needed to get rid of Bane and his goons. Soon. Sooner than soon. He needed to end Bane now.

"Come on, I'm taking you home," he said, pulling Adira toward the front door.

Alanna arched an eyebrow at him but kept quiet.

Adira, however, did not remain quiet. "Excuse me? Take me home?" She jerked her arm out of his grasp. "Did you really just say that? Take me home? You are not my babysitter or my guard dog or guard cat or bodyguard or whatever the hell you think you are. I'm not yours to protect. I protect myself." She gestured with her hand waving back and forth between them. "That's the only way this—us—works."

He just stared at her, wanting desperately to argue with her, but knowing she was right. Her fire burned hot, and it drove him crazy, making him want to rip her clothes off and take her right then. If Alanna weren't there, he would have done just that. He needed to get Adira home, and not just for her safety.

He gave her a cocky grin as he reached out and pulled her against him, squeezing her body to him so that she could feel how hard she made him. "You are so sexy when you're plucky," he said before leaning down and biting her softly on the neck. He wanted to do more, wanted to mark her now, take her and drive his cock into her, but he would wait until he got her alone. He only hoped it would be soon. Very soon.

"Then perhaps, you'll at least allow me the honor of escorting you home?" he asked, his grin pushing up his cheeks. She started to say something, probably to argue with him again, but he released her long enough to hold up a hand and halt her objections. "Not to protect you, just to keep you company."

Alanna laughed. "Adira, he just wants to get you home so he can satisfy that bulge in his pants. You might as well let him. I have earplugs."

Adira spun her head, her eyes wide, as she stared at her friend. Dimitri didn't know what the earplug comment meant, but he didn't care. He needed to get Adira alone so he could ravish her body. He needed to feel her against him, flesh on flesh, his mouth on her nipples, his cock buried deep in her sweet honey.

Adira turned back, so she faced him, her temper somewhat abated as she smiled at him. "Fine. But only as a companion and not as a bodyguard."

He crooked his arm, waiting for her to take it, and then they both said goodnight to Alanna. He couldn't get Adira alone fast enough. She must have felt the same way as well, because she didn't drag her feet on the way back to her cabin.

As soon as they were through the door and she locked it behind them, he grabbed her, spinning her until he could press her back against the door, his body against hers. His mouth found hers, their lips pressed tight to each other, as he slipped his tongue inside her mouth to dance with hers. He groped her sides, searching for the hem of her shirt, and yanking it over her head as soon as he could. She pushed herself away from the doorway long enough to unhook her bra, and then stripped it off her shoulders and dropped it to the floor. He pulled his shirt off at the same time, and then they both yanked themselves out of their pants. He could hear his panther growling in his ears, the lust of the mate bond pulling at him.

Naked, their hands were back on each other, and he pressed her against the wood door again, their lips mashed together, their hands roaming all over each other's body. His breathing grew ragged, his heart thudding in his ears as he felt her hand go to his hard cock, stroking it, flicking the head with her thumb. He growled, as he took a deep breath, doing his best to slow down just a little.

Adira wouldn't have it, though. She shoved him back, pushing him toward the couch in the middle of the living room until he fell backward on it, bouncing slightly. She straddled him as he gripped her waist, trying to hold her back from going too fast. She didn't seem to care, as she reached between her legs, clutching his swollen cock, and guiding it to her pussy. "I need you," she said, her voice throaty, breathy. "I want you now."

He groaned at her words, lifting her slightly so she could guide him into her sex. With one hard drop, she swallowed his cock, allowing it to stretch her, as she cried out. He opened his mouth, the growl erupting from deep within his gut. She wrapped her hands around his neck as she started rocking back and forth on his cock, her clit pressed against his pelvic bone. Her breathing filled his ears, mixed with her moans. He felt her nails digging into his neck as she tightened her grip.

It wasn't long before he felt her body tense on top of him, her legs tightening around his hips and thighs as she rocked faster, her head falling forward slightly. He dug his fingers into her, his claws coming out slightly, pinning her to him. She yelped but didn't stop. Instead, she sent little shards of power into him, allowing it to course throughout his body. He felt his eyes go wide as the magic mingled with his passion, sending tendrils of sensations through his body until he felt his cock twitch inside of her, his orgasm ripping out of him and exploding into her tight pussy.

He knew she felt his release, her eyes popping open, as she squeezed tighter onto his neck, her elbows pressing against his chest. Then her body tightened into a tense ball as her orgasm exploded, her cries filling the cabin. She kept rocking on his cock, but it was obvious she no longer controlled the situation. Her body did everything, the motions sporadic and sensation driven. She kept rocking until her orgasm subsided, leaning down to kiss him, this time her tongue delving into his mouth, her heart beating so hard he could feel it against his chest.

When she finally broke the kiss, she leaned back, taking a deep breath. "Wow. I needed that," she said.

He grinned. "Yeah, I agree." He pulled her back down to him, her head on his chest, as he stroked her back. "Which is why I need you to be careful, Adira. I can't lose you. Not when I just found you. Promise me."

She nuzzled down into his chest, rubbing her head against him. He relished the feel of her on him. "I promise," she said. "But I need you to trust me, as well. We're partners in this. In everything."

He squeezed her to him, his hands leaving her hips and roaming to her ass. "Partners, huh? I think I like the sound of that." His panther purred his agreement. This was one partnership that held extra benefits.

Twelve

H ere are the stones you asked for," Josh said as Ezra and he entered Adira's cabin, both carrying an armload of small ordinary stones. "Planning on hurling them at Bane to drive him away?"

A new day dawned and, so far, Bane's threat was unfulfilled. That didn't mean it wasn't imminent, however.

Ezra chuckled as he walked over to her kitchen table, piling the stones on top. "Might not be real effective, but I'm sure it would be fun."

A cloth covered the table with various oils and gemstones lined along the edges and circled by a trio of tall white candles flickering shadows onto the cabin walls. A mortar sat in the center of the cloth, the pestle ready for action. At the far edge of the table, sage burned in an incense holder. Soft Native American music played in the background, not because she needed it for the spell, but because it helped soothe her nerves, calming her for what she needed to do. If I can focus long enough to pull the shards of my magic back into a steady pulse of power, that is.

She smiled at the men helping her. "I admit, after meeting Bane, that would be the fun idea, but no, these are not for throwing. I'm going to convert them into wards that we can set around the community to warn us if evil crosses over, Bane in particular."

Josh nodded, adding his stones to the pile. "How do you attune it to the coyotes?"

She grinned as she walked over to her kitchen counter and grabbed the tissue she used to wipe the coyote's blood from her fingertips after she gouged his arms at Everglades last night. It was the first thing she did when she reached Alanna's place. "Luckily, that brute last night helped us out with that. His shifter blood will provide me with what I need to set the spell to warn against his pack."

Ezra stood, his thick body a sure sign of the bear who lived within him, shaking his head, as he placed his hands on his hips. "I wish I were there when they tried their shit," he said. "I would have been able to give you more blood to use."

"Agreed," Josh said. He then looked around the cabin, searching for something. "By the way, where's Dimitri? I assumed he'd be here."

"He went to see his sister and Sheriff Einstein about last night," Adira replied. She shrugged. "Lainie already told us there wasn't anything that could be done, but he's determined to at least file a complaint on them. Something about making a paper trail for when there's something to throw at them."

"Probably a smart idea," Josh said. "Anything else you need us to get you?"

She shook her head. "No, this should just about do it. I'll get these done, and then Dimitri said he'd go with me to place them around Bull Creek."

"Okay, then." Josh slapped Ezra on the back. "Come on, Baloo, let's go prowl the woods and sniff around some. I don't like how daring these coyotes are getting."

"Baloo. Hmpf," Ezra shook his head as he turned toward the front door. "Don't even think I'm going to call you Bagheera. Now, that was a noble panther. Not some flea-bitten pussycat like you."

"You wound me," Josh said with mock seriousness. "To the core, Ezra, you wound me. Not one flea has ever dared bite me."

"Probably afraid of catching something." Ezra opened the door, and the two men stepped out into the Florida heat, their bantering shifting into song as they started to sing The Bare Necessities.

Adira chuckled as she shook her head. Never before had she thought it possible that so many different shifters could get along so well without the snobbery and prejudice that sometimes fills self-righteous minds. It was refreshing to her view of things.

Turning back to the table, she stared at the stones the men brought her. It was time to do her part in helping Dimitri protect his family. With a deep breath, she set about the task of creating wards for Bull Creek. *Magic, don't fail me now.*

If she were honest with herself, she would admit how nervous she was that she wouldn't be able to pull off the power needed to create the wards. Ever since Jensen sent her packing, her magic splintered into shards, just like her heart, sparking here and there, sometimes holding it together, other times, she wasn't even able to draw forth a firecracker burst. It disheartened her to say the least, and when Agatha asked her to come to Bull Creek, Adira almost said no, afraid she would only fail the matriarch of the witches and let everyone in Bull Creek down. Now she feared letting Dimitri down, something that would surely crush her beyond repair. Yet, she had to try, of that she had no doubt. Dimitri needed her, and she would do everything within her power, even if it were slim, to assist him in his endeavor to protect this community. If Agatha held faith in her, then Adira needed to maintain that same faith.

She took a deep breath and began. This would take a couple of hours and drain her of most of her energy, but it would be worth it, as long as the wards functioned as they should. They had to work. Too many depended on the wards. On her. Dimitri depended on her. She closed her eyes and called on the power within, using it to reach out to the natural energy of the forest, the nearby streams, the very earth around her, drawing it into herself, adding it to her power, and pushing it into the stones, each and every one of them.

~ ~ ~ ~ ~

Three hours passed before Adira could sit in her rocking chair on her front porch, a cup of hot orange spice tea between her hands as she stared out into the afternoon sun. Exhaustion pulled at her, her energy depleted from the spell she cast over the stones. She would recover, but it took time. She'd need her power back when she set the stones, tuning them to the area where she placed them. Later tonight. Not now. Now, she just needed to sit.

"Now that looks cozy," Alanna said as she turned off the main road and started walking down Adira's drive. "I wish I had time to just laze around."

Adira was too tired to laugh at her friend. Instead, she just shook her head. "I wish I was just being lazy." She gestured back inside the cabin. "There's about a hundred stones we can place around Bull Creek to help warn us if Bane or his men come sniffing around."

"Oh, so a busy lady, huh?" Alanna stepped up the first two steps to the porch and then slid herself onto the railing, gripping it with her hands. "Not a fun way to spend the morning. I thought for sure you'd be doing a certain resident panther."

Adira grinned, not embarrassed at all. "That was last night."

"Nice," Alanna giggled. "I'm sure you were already tired then, before the spell. I'm sure Dimitri appreciates your hard work, though."

Adira cocked her head to the side a bit, looking at her friend, curious, but worried she might be crossing a line. Still, she was curious enough to ask. "So far, I've met panther shifters, a bear, and I know you're a wolf. Are there other shifters here? Other wolves?"

Alanna shook her head. "I'm the only wolf in Bull Creek. There's an assortment of others here, even a couple of vampires at the edges of the community. It's a hodgepodge little family."

"Don't wolves stay in packs, though? Hell, I thought most shifters stayed in packs."

Alanna nodded, her lips pressed into a thin line. "They do for the most part, but what do you do when your pack no longer seems like a family to you?" She gestured to the area around her, indicating all of Bull Creek. "Everyone here is here because they feel like they have nowhere else to go for one reason or another. They've wound up here, and this is their home, their pack if you will. Dimitri is Alpha. He takes care of everyone, protecting us all. We're his family, and he's our leader. The great thing about Bull Creek is that it's truly a community of diversity. That's also what scares some people, like Bane and his coyotes. They don't like change or shifters coming together, crossing packs and intermingling. They want pure bloodlines. Separation. Segregation, even." She shrugged. "It's a constant battle, but one we're not walking away from."

"What drew Dimitri here?" He didn't act like a man who was missing family or an outcast. He seemed quite content in his role as Alpha of Bull Creek.

"For that story, you would need to ask him. Bull Creek is full of tales, but not full of gossip. I won't be the first. What I told you about Eve was more than I normally share." Then she grinned at her friend. "You're here. Something drove you to our little community. You wouldn't want me to share that story with everyone, right?"

Adira sipped her tea. Alanna was right. She didn't want her story to get out. She took a deep breath, reconsidering. Yet, did it really matter? "While it's true I needed to get away from Jensen and that Dimitri needs my skill to help protect Bull Creek, it wouldn't surprise me if matchmaking wasn't Agatha's real goal in sending me here."

"Well, every Alpha needs a strong woman at his side. I think Agatha's choice was pretty on target. And it seemed to work."

Adira felt the flush of heat warm her cheeks at her friend's words. "It definitely has its perks, that's for sure." She felt the passion between her legs stir, as she thought of Dimitri's naked body pressed against hers, his cock buried deep between her legs. Perk wasn't a strong enough word.

She found herself looking toward the road, wishing Dimitri would return from the sheriff's office already. She could use his body to help regain her strength. Of course, he'd probably deplete her energy a little more first... She couldn't hide the grin that sent shivers down to her pussy, clenching her legs together. *Damn, Dimitri, where are you?*

Thirteen

The evening sun dipped in the west, barely visible through the trees surrounding the small community of Bull Creek. A cool breeze whispered through the branches, rustling the leaves as Adira eased her way along the trail following the panther as he led her to where he knew the wards needed to be placed. It was hard not to be mesmerized by the feline's lithe body as he meandered through the woods, keeping his gaze bouncing around their surroundings. A smile spread across her face, knowing he protected her, keeping an eye out for Bane and his coyotes. After her run-in with Bane's thugs last night, Dimitri would not take any chances. She couldn't say that his over-protectiveness upset her. Not this time, anyway. In fact, if she were to say anything at all, it would be that his protective nature made her sex throb. If they didn't have to get the wards up so quickly, she would have loved for him to take her right there in the woods, driving his cock into her, spreading her open before him.

Adira took a deep breath, shaking the distracting thoughts out of her mind. It didn't work.

She watched as the tawny panther sniffed the ground in front of him, the sound of his padded feet soft as they made their way through the woods, stepping over fallen logs and through bushes. She placed a couple of wards as Dimitri led her around the perimeter, setting the spell into motion as she did, her eyes closed, her power radiating from her hand, pulsing into the stone she positioned on the ground. They appeared natural, the stones she used. No one who saw them would think them anything other than that they were common rocks found in the woods. The stones would also go unnoticed, another aspect she added to her spell. They didn't need children picking up her wards and using them as skipping stones in the nearby Crabgrass Creek. No, the wards would go unnoticed until she needed to recharge them. At that time, a simple location spell would show her where they had placed them, and she could reapply the spell.

She placed another one on the soil around a giant oak, squatting as she did, one hand on her knee as the other placed her ward in place. She took a deep breath, closing her eyes and setting the spell. When she opened her eyes, Dimitri's panther sat beside her, his head cocked to the side as he stared at her with his deep green-gold eyes. Adira reached out and stroked behind his ears, loving the way he pushed into her hand as if begging for her to scratch harder, the panther's purrs melting her heart. "I see you're greedy in both of your forms," she said with a giggle, giving him the scratching he wanted. She looked down at the bag at her feet. "Five more stones and then we're all set. Shall we get this over with?"

Dimitri pushed at her palm, then leaned his head back and licked the back of her hand, bringing images of the places where his human tongue had been. Forcing herself back into a standing position, she took a deep breath. She didn't need to get distracted by what his tongue could be doing to her pussy right then, or his cock pounding into her, his hands digging into her flesh. No, she needed to get the rest of the stones set. Then she could think about his hardness claiming her.

However, as she took a few steps, she heard rustling coming from up ahead. The panther's ears flipped back as he hunched down, ready to spring. Adira stopped walking, dropping the bag near her feet as she allowed her arms to go straight down, her fingers flared outward, ready to summon her power if needed. She only hoped the shards of her power would be enough. The way Dimitri acted, she assumed it would be necessary.

From out of the woods in front of them stepped Bane with two of his thugs. Augur, from last night at Everglades, was one of them. Adira spread her legs slightly, bracing herself for what was sure to be a scuffle of some sort. She glanced down at the panther, but Dimitri showed no sign of shifting back to his human form. Probably better for fighting. Fangs.

Claws. Definitely better than fisticuffs.

Bane grinned at them as his thugs stepped to either side of him, yet still slightly behind their leader. They were ready to spring to his defense, but Adira doubted the gray-haired man needed anyone standing up for him. "My, my, look what we have here, boys," Bane said, his head cocked to the side. "Our neighborhood witch is out walking her kitty cat."

"Do you have to pick up after a cat like you do a dog when you take them for a walk?" Augur asked.

"I don't think so," the unknown guy answered. "Don't cats usually cover their shit with dirt when they're done? I think I heard that somewhere."

Adira didn't smile. "Your bitches seem to have an odd obsession with animal feces. Don't take them out much, do you?"

Bane's smile disappeared. "Be careful how you talk about coyotes, witch."

"I wasn't talking about coyotes," she said. "I was talking about your little bitches there. You know, the ones who like to get rough with women in bars. Pretty sad, really. I guess their normal pickup lines just weren't successful, so they resorted to bullying. Over-compensating? Pitiful."

Bane narrowed his eyes at her, his voice low, threatening. She could hear the growl of his coyote underneath. "Just because you have powers, doesn't make you any better than any other human. You all need to go. Will go. This is shifter land, no matter how hard your little pet there tries to make it more..."

"Diverse?" Adira filled in for him before he could finish

his sentence.

"Polluted," Bane said with a sneer. "You need to get the rest of your vagabonds and move to the city. I'm sure your kind will appreciate the comforts of tourist town more than Bull Creek. These woods are off limits to your ilk."

"Haven't you made that threat already?" she asked. "And yet, we're still here."

"Not for long, I assure you."

The panther let out a hiss as he stepped toward Bane. Augur stepped toward the panther, his gray eyes narrowing as he let out a growl of his own. "Panthers can't even growl or roar like a real animal," Bane sneered. "They only hiss like pussies."

The other man with them started to shift, his bones popping, twisting, shrinking as gray fur oozed from his body, his fingers stretching into paws, his fingernails into claws. Adira lived around shifters for most of her adult life, but she would never get used to seeing them transform from human to animal and back again.

As soon as the coyote finished shifting, he pounced, his claws aiming for the panther's neck. Dimitri lunged at him, his scream filling the woods around them. Augur reached for Adira, his massive hands going for her arms. Obviously, he learned nothing from Everglades. She was sure he believed all women to be inferior and, therefore, an easy target. She relished disappointing him. He gripped her arm, expecting to jerk her to him, she was sure. With her other hand, she reached out, her fingers flared. Power lashed out as shards of blue sparks ripped from her fingers and into the thug's body, sending him backward, his arms flailing in the air.

She turned to see Dimitri, but before she could focus, Bane gripped her arms, pinning them to her side. She stared into his face, his gray eyes burning into her with his intense hatred. "I told you to leave," he snarled. "You really should have listened." She saw his teeth shift, fangs forming. He planned to bite her! She tried to twist out of his grip, attempted to use her power, but it only sputtered. Fear gripped her, blocking her magic. She didn't need to be bitten by a coyote.

Then Bane screamed, his grip on her arms loosening enough for her to jerk free. Dimitri pinned Bane's leg in his jaws, clamping down, sinking his teeth into the man's flesh. Adira stretched her arm out, her fingers wide as she shoved her power at Bane. No shards this time. A steady stream of blue flame shot from her fingers, hitting the larger man in the chest and hurling him up into the air and backward. He flew back five feet before his body slammed into the ground, driving his breath from his lungs.

Adira took a deep breath, readying her power again. A quick glance to the side revealed the coyote who sprang at Dimitri was dead, blood oozing from his throat. Augur started to climb back to his feet, but a quick burst from Adira sent him sprawling back on the ground, unconscious. Bane started to move, but Adira sent a blast of power to the ground beside him. "I wouldn't, if I were you," Adira threatened. "Someone of my ilk might just take it the wrong way. I mean, it's not like you didn't just attack us or anything."

The panther stepped to her side, his head low as he hissed at the man on the ground. Blood dripped from his muzzle.

"Now, just in case you forgot what I said the other night, let me repeat it. I'm staying," Adira said, her eyes narrow slits as she glared at the bully. "As are the humans who live here. As are any others who wish to remain in Bull Creek. And there isn't a damn thing you or anyone else can do about it. If you can't handle our kind being here, then I suggest you pack your shit and get out yourselves. You're the ones not wanted here. I don't care for bullies. Come at me, or anyone else here again, and I'll shoot a blue spark right up your ass."

Bane stared at her, his menace glowering on his face. "You haven't seen bullying yet," he spat. "If you won't leave voluntarily, I'll drive you out."

The panther hissed, taking a step forward, but Adira placed her hand on his back, halting him. "You'll try, you mean," she said. "And I dare you to try. However, I promise you, you'll lose. And I don't mean just this battle." She made sure her voice said everything her words didn't.

She stroked Dimitri's head as he nuzzled into her leg. Every stroke of his muzzle sent shivers throughout her body. She wasn't sure if it was just his touch, the fact that her power didn't fail her for once, or that together they just whipped Bane's ass, but she needed to get back to her cabin and feel Dimitri's cock spearing into her. Or perhaps it was everything combined. She pulled on the panther's fur, tugging him back and away from the three on the ground. There were still five more wards to place, but they would have to wait. She needed Dimitri to fuck her. Now.

Fourteen

Dimitri craved her. As soon as they were back to the cabin, he shifted again, taking her in his arms as soon as he possessed arms again. The entire time he stood by her as they took on Bane and his henchmen, it drove him crazy. Her strength, the passion in her voice as she stood up for herself, the way she defended the others in Bull Creek, it came as no surprise to him that his cock was rock hard when he shifted back.

He didn't wait for her to strip. He didn't even wait for her to be in the cabin. He ripped her clothes from her body, tossing the shreds to the ground as he devoured her mouth with his, using his hands to explore her body. He cupped her breasts in his hands, his fingers grazing across her swollen nipples, teasing them. A hum of satisfaction slipped from her lips, her gasps at his touch spurring him to a hotter fire. He felt her hand grip his cock, stroking him, as she begged him to take her, pleaded with him to fuck her.

Adira gripped his shoulders, yanking him toward the front door and through it, their lips never parting. With his foot, he kicked the door shut, the air switching from the hot Florida afternoon to the air-conditioned coolness of her cabin, chills racing up their bodies at the temperature change. Dimitri swept her into his arms and carried her to the couch, where he dropped her, and then spun her, pulling her ass into the air. "God, you were so hot out there," he said, his voice a growl, as he ran a hand over her ass. "My woman taking on the coyotes." He dragged his hand up her back, his nails leaving white lines along her flesh. "Mine!" he roared as he thrust into her, riding her with the hunger of his beast.

Adira's cry of pleasure tore from her lips, and it was music to his ears, to the panther within him, driving him to thrust harder, pound into her with an animalistic hunger. He clawed her ass, his nails leaving bloodlines on her flesh as his panther's claws darted out, puncturing her as he fucked her. She screamed but begged for more. He kept driving into her, leaning down until he could place a hand on each side of her, his mouth so close to her shoulder it drove him crazy. The scent of her filled his nostrils, urging his panther to bite her, mark her, and claim her as his, as theirs. He felt his teeth shift into fangs as he took a deep breath, her pussy clamped around his cock.

"Do it," she hissed, her voice a throaty whisper. "Mark me. Make me yours."

He couldn't hold back any longer, his panther craving to fulfill her cries. He sank his teeth into her shoulder, puncturing her flesh, tasting her. She screamed, pushing back onto him, her ass pressing into him, as he lost himself in her wet warmth.

With his teeth embedded into her flesh, he felt his body shudder, his cock twitch and throb as his storm of lust exploded inside of her. Her body tensed at the same time, as her muscles spasmed around his cock, her body shivering as her own orgasm ripped through her, bringing a scream of ecstasy from her lips. He reached around, tweaking her nipples as he pulled the pearled tips downward. She moaned, shoving herself back onto his cock, her back arching as she finished her orgasm. He lifted his head, the taste of her on his lips, his tongue. He would never be able to get enough of her. Never.

Spent, he slipped from her with his climax complete, spinning so that he sat on her couch, pulling her down and over onto his lap. She laid her head on his shoulder, her arm across his waist, as he wrapped an arm around her, holding her close. "I think you have powers no one else knows about," he said, kissing the top of her head. "You've definitely put a spell on me."

She nuzzled into his chest, squeezing him tightly against her. "You're not the only one bewitched."

Those words made him smile. Too bad they needed to deal with a gang of coyotes. He could stay right here on the couch, naked, with her in his arms forever. "You need to be careful," he said, pulling her tighter against him. "Bane will be more determined than ever to get at you now that you've stood up to him twice. He doesn't like to be put down in front of his followers."

"He needs to be put down, like a rabid dog."

"Trust me, it may come to that. No one messes with my community. The residents of Bull Creek need this place, this sanctuary. I'll not allow the likes of Bane Kastner to take it away from them. Prejudice and hatred will not win. Not now. Not ever."

"Is that why you're here?" she asked, shifting as she did. "Something made you become a guardian of this place."

He ran his thumb over her bare shoulder as his thoughts drifted back to a year ago when he first moved to Bull Creek. "I didn't necessarily plan it," he said, his voice distant. "I left Draven Falls because of a family squabble. My parents wanted me to be someone I wasn't and did their best to apply pressure, to force me into what they desired for their family legacy. Lainie already disappointed them by entering law enforcement, and I watched my brother succumb to our parents' pressures, leaving him depressed and miserable. My parents behaved a lot like Bane, believing humans and shifters should remain apart. However, they took it even further, believing shifter bloodlines should remain pure; no interspecies mating should exist." He took a deep breath. "My brother dated a human at the time, and my parents did everything in their power to ruin it. They succeeded, of course, but my brother was never the same. It destroyed him. They arranged a mating for him with another in the panther tribe back in Draven Falls, and he succumbed to their wishes.

I didn't hang around to see how it worked out, but I feel sorry for both him and his wife. They both have to be miserable, knowing it's not what their animals wanted."

"Was she his mate?"

"I never found out for sure, but I believe so. It's the only reason I can think of for how devastated Fitz became, and how he just gave up on life." He leaned over and kissed the side of her head. "Losing a mate is like death."

She squeezed him tightly. "I'm so sorry."

He brushed the side of her head with another kiss. "It's why I left, why Lainie left. It's why I won't allow Bane to win. There's too much hatred in this world, and too much of it wins already. It won't win here. I won't allow it."

He felt her nod against his chest, her hair brushing his flesh, sending thrills throughout his body. His cock twitched at the sensation, and it took all his power to keep his panther in check. As much as Dimitri wanted to take her again right then, they needed to figure out how to deal with Bane. "So, how do we stop him?" she asked, finally allowing herself to shift, sitting up straight.

He moved as well, stretching his muscles as he did. "That's the big question, isn't it?" As much as he dreaded leaving her side, he pushed himself off the couch. "To be honest, outside of just killing him, I'm not sure what we can do. He's going to keep coming at us, attacking humans and the shifters who befriend them." He kissed the top of her head. "And witches who stand up to him. You're marked now, love, in more ways than just as my mate. You've made yourself a target and, while I'm proud of the guts it took, I can't say I like that you're in Bane's crosshairs. I need you to be more careful. I couldn't handle it if anything happened to you."

She pushed herself off his chest so she could stare into his green-gold eyes. "I won't allow a bully to cause me to cower. Bane needs to be stopped, and we're the only ones who can do it. He's skirted the law so far. We can't allow him to keep up his reign of terror."

He couldn't feel prouder of her than he did right then. Yet, he also feared for her safety. Bane was not someone to trifle with, even if that someone was a witch. Dimitri needed to make sure Adira was safe, but he knew he needed to do it in a way she didn't expect. If she realized for even an inkling that he coddled her, she'd never forgive him, of that he had no doubt. Of course, he had no idea how he would go about that little task, either.

An incessant pounding shook Adira's door as Josh screamed Dimitri's name. One pounding wasn't enough, apparently, as the man kept beating on the door until Dimitri opened it—after slipping his pants back on, that is. "What the hell?" Dimitri stared at the man. Josh appeared as if he had just run miles, his hair plastered to his sweaty head, his shirt soaked, and his chest heaving with his struggle to catch his breath.

Josh leaned on the doorframe, his shoulders rising and falling with his panting. "Lainie….accident…." He shook his head, still struggling with his breathing.

Dimitri felt his eyes widen. "Where is she?"

Josh waved off to the west. "Sheriff," was all he could say.

Adira came out of the bedroom, having left the living room before Dimitri opened the door to put on some clothes. She stared at him, the pain she saw on his face reflected in her own expression. She could feel his anguish. "Go," she said. "Make sure she's all right. I'll be here when you get back."

His panther urged him not to leave, or to take her with him. But this was his sister. He needed to be with her. Adira would be fine for just a little while. Bane couldn't retaliate that quickly. He nodded once before turning to Josh. "Get patrols started. Contain any coyotes you find in the vicinity of Bull Creek. I want answers."

Josh nodded. "You'll have them."

As Josh left, Dimitri turned to Adira, walking across the floor to take her in his arms. "You need to stay inside with the doors locked and be safe. If Bane's taken to attacking people now, especially my sister, a deputy, then who knows what he'll try next. I need you safe."

She placed a hand on his cheek, and his panther struggled to pounce her right then and there. He pressed down the desire, the urgency to get to his sister a priority. He leaned in and brushed a kiss on Adira's cheek. "Remind me to send Agatha Rochester a thank you note."

She smiled as she pushed him toward the door. "After this is over. Now go and give Lainie a hug for me. I know she's got to be all right. I'm not thinking any other way."

He squeezed her. "I'll be back as soon as I can, and we'll go for round two." His grin made her blush, which in turn made his panther purr. He needed to get back to her. And

113

quick.

She shoved him toward the door again. He nodded once, and then turned, rushing toward his truck, and then to his sister. If Bane did something to Lainie… If he hurt her in any way…

Fifteen

Adira watched as Dimitri closed the door behind him. She felt terrible, blaming herself for the attack on Lainie. Dimitri's sister must have been attacked because of the way Adira mouthed off to Augur at the bar. This was the coyotes' way of retaliating. They couldn't get to her, so they went after her friend. Adira came to Bull Creek to help, but so far, all she did was make things worse. *Not such a big help, huh?* She only hoped Lainie was all right. Adira wasn't sure if Dimitri would forgive her if his sister was seriously hurt because of her. Hell, she wasn't sure if she could forgive herself.

Turning to fix herself some tea, she placed her hand on Dimitri's teeth marks, and almost yelped at the touch, the sharp, electric sensations sending tendrils of pain throughout her body. Even without looking, she could imagine the bruise that formed on her lower shoulder. With a deep breath, bracing for the tender stings of pain, she caressed the deep impressions left by Dimitri's teeth, especially where his fangs sank into her. A smile broke across her face as she thought of what the mark meant and the bond that now connected the two of them. Mates. While she had heard stories, knew the premise behind the mate mark, now she truly understood it. It was more than just the sensations of the bite. It was the feeling of unity she now felt washing through her for Dimitri, a bond that could not be broken.

As she reached for a teacup, the wards around her cabin sent a tingling through her senses, warning her of someone crossing her property line. She turned to the front of her house, but then heard glass breaking in the back. She spun, her arms flying up to shoot whatever power she could muster at the intruder. She focused so much on the back of her cabin that she didn't hear the front door open until it was too late. The board creaked behind her; she spun, lashing out her witch's power only to have someone hit her arm and throw her shot wide, the power shattering a shelf and everything on it. As she turned to face her attacker, she felt the hard, sudden blow to the side of her head, and then nothing as her body slumped to the floor, darkness enveloping her.

~ ~ ~ ~ ~

Dimitri darted into the sheriff's department, his pulse racing as his panther fought to get free. As protective as they were about their mates, shifters were equally protective of their family. Lainie moved here to help him keep others from being hurt, and instead, she was the one who wound up injured, attacked because of him. He wasn't sure what he would do if anything happened to her because of his mission in life. Bull Creek was his purpose, given to him by the Paranormal Council back in Draven Falls, and Lainie only followed out of a sense of loyalty to him.

"Dimitri, over here," Sheriff Chet Einstein waved to Dimitri from his office door.

Dimitri picked up his pace as he rushed to the sheriff's office and his sister. When he entered, Lainie sat on a chair next to the sheriff's desk, a cold compress pressed against the side of her head. Doc Henderson hovered over her, doing his best to clean up Lainie's wounds. Her face was covered with bruises and small gashes, and a cut still oozed blood on her left cheek. Her clothes were ripped, the collar of her shirt dangling over her chest. Dimitri growled, his panther eager to lash out at whoever did this to her.

He knelt down beside her, his hands going to the arms of the chair. "Are you okay? When did this happen? Who did this?" He shot the questions at her rapid-fire, as he stared up into her face. He craved answers. He demanded retribution.

Lainie gave him a weak smile. "Cool it, oh brother of mine," she said. "I'm fine. They just roughed me up, and then left before I could get in my own licks. They kept hitting me, keeping me from shifting."

"So they knew you, knew you were a shifter," he said. He glanced up at the sheriff. "Do we know who did this to her?"

The sheriff shook his head. "They got her from behind, just kept pummeling her, keeping her off-balance."

Dimitri turned back to his sister. "They could have killed you."

Lainie nodded. "You're right. They could have." She narrowed her eyes, her mind chewing on something. "But they didn't." She turned to face him, her eyes still narrowed. "Why? Why didn't they kill me?" She shoved Doc's hand away from her as she sat straight in her chair, glancing back and forth between Dimitri and Chet. "What better message to send you that they meant business than to kill your sister? Yet, they didn't. So what was the purpose other than to beat the hell out of me? What did it accomplish?"

Dimitri was confused. Why did there need to be a message? Bane and his pack were vicious brutes, bent on destruction, wanting to hurt the humans of Bull Creek and any shifters who sympathized with them. Wasn't that reason enough? Wasn't beating up Dimitri's sister enough of a message as to how far they would go?

Chet scratched his head, pondering her question. "The only thing it accomplished that I can see so far is that it brought your brother here." He shook his head. "Other than that, I can't come up with anything else."

Dimitri's eyes went wide as Lainie slapped his shoulder, both shouting at the same time, "Adira!"

Dimitri shoved himself away from his sister, standing as he did. "They lured me away from Adira. I have to get back out there." He could feel his panther shoving at him, wanting to break free and run. He could feel claws punch from his fingers, as fur oozed from his skin. He gritted his teeth, clamping down on the anger his panther felt, the

118

urgency to get to his mate.

"Go. The doc has your sister," the sheriff urged. "I'll send Johnson out to Adira's cabin to check on her."

"Thanks," Dimitri said, gripping Lainie's shoulder and squeezing. "Take care of you. I'll be back."

She nodded. "Go protect our girl."

Our girl. The words rang in Dimitri's mind. Lainie accepted Adira as Dimitri's mate. He squeezed Lainie's shoulder one more time, then turned and bolted from the office, his only focus on getting to Adira before Bane and his goons did. He shoved his way through the sheriff's department, out the door, and to his truck. He crammed the key in the ignition and turned it, shoving his truck into gear as soon as the engine revved. He floored it as he gripped the steering wheel with white-knuckled fingers. How could he be so stupid? He should have brought her with him. He was foolish for leaving her behind, knowing that the coyote pack was after her. He only hoped her wards would keep her safe until he got there. Then a panic seized him as he realized they never finished setting those last few stones. Bull Creek wasn't entirely safe. Bane could still sneak into the community.

As he hit the accelerator again, turning onto the highway, he slipped his phone from his pocket and punched Josh's name. A horn blared as Dimitri almost ran into another vehicle. He swerved, cussing at Josh for not answering the phone. While he appreciated Chet sending his deputy out to Bull Creek, Dimitri knew Johnson wouldn't get there soon enough. Dimitri needed to get his own people out there, his own pack. This wasn't something for regular law enforcement. This was beyond an ordinary court of law issue. This was something only shifters could handle. This demanded shifter justice.

"Dimitri?" Josh's voice sounded in his ear. "What's up? How's Lainie?"

"Get everyone over to Adira's cabin," Dimitri snapped into the phone. "Bane's men attacked Lainie as a distraction to lure me away from Bull Creek. We're pretty sure they're on their way over to Adira's cabin now."

"Damn. I should have stayed with her. On our way, man. We'll be there." Then the phone went dead.

Dimitri dropped the cell phone into the passenger seat, as he took the next turn. He needed to get to the cabin. He couldn't allow anything to hurt Adira, not his mate, not after he just found her.

When he pulled up to Adira's cabin, Deputy Johnson was already there, walking up to the front porch from his squad car. Josh, Ezra, and Eve stood on the porch, hands on his hips or over their chests. When Josh glanced at Dimitri, his expression held no good news. Dimitri's panther hissed within him.

Dimitri shoved his way out of his truck and ran to where Josh and the others waited, almost beating the deputy there. "Adira?" he questioned as he hit the first step.

Josh shook his head. "She's not here, and from the looks inside, she didn't leave willingly." He gestured inside the cabin with a tilt of his head. "Place looks to have been ransacked just for the fun of it."

Dimitri felt the panther pushing out of his skin, and he clamped down tighter on his control. He had to wait just a little longer.

Ezra stood off to the side on the porch. "One plus is that we didn't find blood," he said in his deep voice. "I don't think they hurt her. I think they just wanted her, so there's still time to find her and get her back."

Dimitri nodded. "And make whoever took her pay for their insolence."

"That goes without saying," Josh said.

"And without hearing," Deputy Johnson said. "What I don't know, I can't prevent." He glanced at Dimitri, who nodded his understanding. Chet told the deputy to give them plenty of leeway in this. "I'm going to search around the highway and leave the inner part of Bull Creek to you folks. I'm sure you know it better than I do."

"Thanks," Dimitri said. "For everything."

Deputy Johnson nodded and then moved back toward his car. However, before he was able to get too far, a dark gray wolf darted out of the woods surrounding the cabin, tongue lolling in its haste. Dimitri recognized the shiny fur of Alanna's wolf as she raced toward the porch. Stopping just shy of the others, she lifted her head and howled, prancing backward a couple of steps as she snarled. *I have Adira's scent*, she sent to everyone with the power of the shifter mindspeech. *It's mixed with coyote, but I can follow it. She turned and made for the forest's edge again.*

"Let's go," Dimitri said, and everyone shifted. Animals moved a lot faster than humans. Two panthers and a bear raced after the wolf, leaving Eve and the deputy behind, watching, and hoping everything turned out all right.

Sixteen

dira's head throbbed where Augur cracked it with…well, with whatever it was he used to hit her. Adira had no idea what that was, only that it hurt like hell. Then and now. Her eyes fluttered as she tried to open them, the light in the room stinging. She could hear voices off to the side—Bane and Augur—discussing what to do with Dimitri when he arrived to rescue her. She struggled against her bonds, pressing against the ropes that held her in place. She couldn't allow Bane to use her to hurt Dimitri. She wouldn't allow it.

She tried to twist her hands, so she could use her power to get out of her bindings, but the coyote pack was smarter than she gave them credit for and bound her wrists so that she couldn't move her fingers. She grinned as she glanced off to the side where they stood, Bane conversing with Augur, while two others sat at a table in the corner playing cards or something. Not one of them seemed concerned with the woman bound to the chair. They were so naïve. So stupid. It would cost them in the end.

She took a deep breath as she closed her eyes. With her inner core, she reached out to her surroundings, called to the earth around the building in which they held her captive, reached for the wind as it brushed through the trees, pulled in the power of the nearby Crabgrass Creek that ran to the south of Bull Creek. She called to the energy from every life source around her, filling her own reservoir of power. When she opened her eyes, she could feel the power thrumming within her, filling her, ready to explode. She bit her inner cheek, tamping down the power, holding it at bay until she needed to unleash it. With another deep breath, she opened her eyes and stared at the men who set off to the side, knowing she didn't need her fingers to cast her magic.

Bane looked up and noticed her watching them, his leer turning up the corners of his mouth. "Nice of you to join us," he said, as he crossed the floor to where she was held. "I hope Augur here hasn't hurt you too badly. He's always been a little overzealous in his pursuit of our cause."

She arched an eyebrow at him. "Your cause? This isn't some charity you're trying to raise money for or some political issue to which you're trying to raise awareness. This is a bunch of shifters being a prejudiced gang of bullies. You don't have a cause. You have a fucked-up view of life."

His mouth turned into a sneer as he leaned down, his face inches from hers. "Ah, but it is an issue of which we're trying to raise awareness. You see, humans are such inferior creatures, and it's about time they were put in their proper link on the evolution chain. Shifters need to rise and take control."

"Shifters and humans coexist, and they do it peacefully until bullies like yourself try to think themselves better than they are," she said. "Your chest thumping only means you have a tiny dick and a narrow heart. What's the matter? Did mommy not love you enough when you were little?"

He backhanded her, and her cheek stung from the blow as her head snapped to the side. "I'd be careful, my little witch. I've noticed your sporadic magic the last few times we've been close. I kind of think you're in no shape to be so mouthy to me. The other shifter races may like that. Coyotes prefer a female who knows her place."

She slowly turned her gaze to Bane, her eyes narrow slits of hatred. "This woman's place is to see you're banished from Bull Creek." She was about to show him just how wrong he was about her magic when Augur called out to him. She held off, waiting for another opportunity.

"What?" Bane yelled as he left her and walked back over to his first-in-command who peered out the window. The other two at the table paused their game and stared at Augur.

Augur didn't turn to face the bigger man. "Looks like we have company."

She wished she could see what they saw. She didn't want to be the reason Dimitri walked into a trap. She needed to get out of her bonds, and now!

Bane grabbed at the curtain, pulling it to the side to give him a better view of what was happening outside of the cabin. "Do you see anyone else or just him?"

"No one else that I can see," Augur answered. "I've got coyotes hiding around the perimeter. If he did bring others, they'll find them and put them down."

Bane nodded his approval without turning to look at the other man. "Show no mercy," he said. He then turned his focus to Adira. "Anyone who sympathizes with the riff-raff will join them in their fate."

She strained against her ropes, wanting desperately to get her hands around the man's thick neck and snap it. She'd show him no mercy once she was free from her bonds.

Bane just smiled at her before turning toward Augur. "I'm going out to meet our neighborhood panther. You keep an eye on Witchy Poo there." He then gestured to the others. "You two keep an eye on the back door. We don't need any surprises."

They jumped to obey as Bane crossed the distance to the front door. As he gripped the doorknob, he turned once more back to Adira, a smirk on his face. "I do hope you had a decent farewell kiss," he said. "You won't get another one. At least, not from Dimitri." He winked at her as he turned the doorknob, opened the door, and stepped out into the Florida heat to face his adversary.

Adira growled as she felt the sparks sizzle from her fingertips behind her. She couldn't wait to wipe that smug smirk from his pathetic face. He would regret ever sending his goon squad to fetch her.

Augur smirked at her before he turned his focus back to the window and the scene that unfolded. Good, she thought. Keep your attention outside for just a little while longer.

~ ~ ~ ~ ~

Dimitri watched, as Bane stepped out of the cabin, the smug, over-confident grin on his face taunting Dimitri's panther. He could scent Adira inside, could smell her blood in the air from where they hurt her, and it took all Dimitri's will-power not to give in to his panther's urgent desire to rush in and rip everyone inside the cabin to shreds.

"Dimitri," Bane said, "I warned you. I told you to send everyone packing, but oh, no, you just had to show how pathetic you are by sticking up for people who can't stick up for themselves."

"Isn't that the opposite of being pathetic?" Dimitri said as he took a few steps toward the cabin. "I kind of think you're the weak one, Bane. You're afraid of anyone who's not like you, afraid of diversity. You're a coward, and you only want to run everyone off, so you don't have to deal with what you're afraid to face."

Bane growled. "Your words mean nothing. Humans are a scourge on the forests, and they need to go. They destroy what we cherish, wasting resources that we need. You keeping them here only prolongs the inevitable. My patience has run out. It's too late for you to save them. My pack will kill them, just as soon as we finish with you and your little girlfriend."

Snarls and howls erupted from the woods around the

cabin, and a loud roar from a bear burst from the woods behind it. From off to the side, a panther and a coyote tumbled out, their claws ripping into each other as they bit down on the other's neck, doing their best to get a grip on their opponent. They sprawled out on the earth, snapping and clawing at each other. Dimitri ignored the fight Josh was in and stayed focused on Bane. The leader of the coyote pack did the same, his gaze riveted on Dimitri. More fights broke out in the woods around the cabin as coyotes found the shifters Dimitri brought with him. He heard the howl of Alanna's wolf fill the air, followed by a yelp of pain. He needed to end this and now.

His panther hissed as he began to shift, claws stretching from his fingers as his panther's tawny fur slid out from his skin, his bones popping and snapping as he surrendered to the transformation from man to panther. This ended tonight.

As soon as he was on all fours, he hissed again and sprang toward Bane who was also transforming into his coyote. Dimitri hit the other man in mid-transformation, knocking him down on the cabin's porch, Bane's bones still popping as he shifted. The door behind them opened, and Augur lunged out, reaching out for Dimitri's neck. Dimitri leaped backward out of Augur's reach, just as he heard Adira scream from inside the cabin along with the sounds of breaking furniture.

Seventeen

The sounds of fighting could be heard outside the cabin—panthers, a wolf, coyotes, even a bear. Their cries mixed with pain and agony. Augur jerked away from the window and darted toward the front door. Whatever happened outside, apparently scared him. Adira watched as he jerked the door open and reached outside. One of the men who went to the back emerged and darted to the front door to take Augur's place. A quick glance over her shoulder showed that the other guy remained in the back. Now was her chance. Taking a deep breath, she sent power through her arms, sending blue light from her forearms to sizzle and help her break the ropes that held her. They shredded, charred, and fell to the ground as she sprang from the chair, knocking it backward.

The noise startled the goon who headed to the front door,

causing him to spin toward Adira. She jerked her arm out, palms up, as blue fire erupted from her hand and sent a ball of energy into the man's chest. The power picked him up, sending him flailing through the air and into the wall, which he crashed into with a shattering crack, causing shelves and knickknacks to fall around his body.

She focused so much on the man in front of her, she forgot about the one in the back of the cabin until it was too late. He grabbed her from behind, spinning her to the ground and into the tipped-over chair, smashing it as she fell. The shattered pieces of wood sliced into her, causing her to scream as it drew blood. Rolling over onto her back, she called the power she stored and sent it into the man's chest as he leaned down to grip her neck. The blue fire hit him like a wrecking ball, lifting him into the air and sending him flying to land on the table where he had sat earlier, playing cards spewing into the air. Adira glanced in his direction to see if he would attack her again. He wouldn't. The table leg protruded from his chest, blood oozing out, soaking into his shirt.

The other man picked himself up off the ground, tossing the remnants of the shelf he broke in his fall to the side. His eyes flashed yellow, his coyote struggling to get out. There was no hesitation. No time for fear. She lashed out, gripping him with her power, and lifting him into the air once more. With a shove of her hand, she sent him flailing through the air until he hit the wall once again, his head snapping back and cracking against the wooden structure. His body slid to the floor, motionless.

As she took a deep breath in a feeble attempt to steady her nerves, she heard the hiss of a panther outside the cabin along with the snarl of a coyote. Dimitri! She didn't think; she just reacted, moving quickly through the shattered mess of the cabin to the front door. She needed to get to her panther.

Reaching the door, she gripped the knob and flung it open, stepping out into the pandemonium that enveloped the grounds around the cabin. Bane lifted his body off the porch as he continued to shift into his coyote, while out in the yard Dimitri wrestled with another coyote, who she assumed was Augur. Since Dimitri had Augur, Adira turned her attention to Bane. Claws poked out of his fingers as his hands shrunk to paws, his arms and legs popping, twisting into his coyote's legs, his torso shrinking as fur oozed from his flesh, covering his body. She needed to halt his transformation.

She heard the rustling of the animals behind her, jerking her attention back around. Augur's coyote was on top of Dimitri's panther, whose jaws were clamped down on the coyote's shoulder. She forced her attention away from the fighting animals and back to Bane. Dimitri would have to handle himself for the time being. She needed to put an end to Bane.

With a flick of her wrist, she sent her power outward, wrapping Bane in a web of blue energy, bringing a halt to his transformation. As she lifted her arm, Bane's body rose into the air, the transformation stopped. It was weird to see him that way, half human, half coyote, his face covered in fur, his ears pointed and flipped back, while the rest of his face remained that of the bastard who kidnapped her. She held him there, his legs—part man, part animal—dangling, as she stepped closer, her lips curled in a snarl. "As you can see," she said as she drew closer to him, "my power is no longer in shards. It's pretty much back to normal." She squeezed her fingers together, and Bane screamed out as if she squeezed him. "We warned you to leave. A pity you didn't heed it."

He jerked his twisted face to her, his gold eyes filled with rage and hatred. Through clenched teeth, he sneered, "I'm going to kill you and everyone else in this god damn pl..."

A tawny blur darted across her vision as she heard the angry hiss of a panther. Dimitri struck Bane in the chest, his claws digging into the other man, knocking them both to the porch as Dimitri's fangs bit into Bane's throat. With a snap of his head, his jaw broke Bane's neck. He dropped the man to the ground, almost as if he spat Bane out as something disgusting.

Adira heard rustling behind her. Turning she saw the others—Josh, Alanna, and Ezra—coming out of the forest, blood covering their naked bodies, some of it theirs, but most appearing to be that of their enemies. She let out a sigh of relief as she turned back to Dimitri. He had already transformed, his naked body still on the ground held up by his hands and knees. Blood dripped from his mouth and covered his chest and arms. She didn't care. She raced to where he knelt on the ground, wrapping her arms around him, pulling him against her. He was alive, and that was all that mattered.

Sirens cried out in the distance. Dimitri waved at the others to get out of there. While Chet knew about shifters in his jurisdiction, he didn't need it thrown in his face so that he couldn't use deniable plausibility and have to start making arrests. The attacks looked like they were done by animals, and that didn't need to be contradicted by a bunch of naked, bloody shifters in human form.

Josh nodded once and then led the others back into the woods and out of sight.

"Help me stand," Dimitri said, his voice harsh, his breathing heavy.

"All right, Catnip, take it easy," she said, slipping a hand around his arm as she helped him to his feet. "You know, I did have him under control. Although, you looked sexy as hell when you knocked him out of my spell, all snarly and furry."

He chuckled, as he stood. "I couldn't let you have all the fun, now, could I?" He straightened, stretching his sore muscles. "Let's find me some clothes in the cabin. I don't think Chet or Deputy Johnson want to see me in the buff."

She gave him a salacious grin as she raked her gaze up and down his taut body. "I don't know. You look pretty damn hot to me. I may want to keep you this way."

"Later," he promised as he led her to the cabin. "So, what happened in there?" he asked, gesturing toward the cabin.

Adira shrugged. "Seems your mate mark did more than permanently leave an impression of your teeth in my flesh. My power is healed, no more shards I can't trust. Bane assumed I was still broken, but I guess I surprised him." She winked at Dimitri.

He laughed again as he stepped onto the porch. "I guess you did."

They entered the cabin and rummaged through the back bedroom until they found something that came close to fitting Dimitri. Adira had to admit, she dreaded watching him cover up his body. She would much rather he stay naked, that they both were naked, and he was pressing his body against hers, her hands running over his chest, down his legs, and grabbing his cock. She couldn't understand it. She should be exhausted after the battle they just fought, but she wasn't. It turned her on, needing him to take her, satisfy her. She grabbed him, pulling him to her, her lips searching out his as she ran her hands up and down his back. He glided a hand up her spine and into her hair, pulling her head back as he bit down on her neck, hissing as he did.

She cried out, clawing him, as she felt her body tense. Only the sound of sirens and the flashing of lights through the windows kept her from throwing him on the bed and having her way with him. She growled her frustration, to which he only laughed as he finished slipping a shirt on to cover up the blood on his arms. No time to wash up.

"Shall we go fabricate a story for Chet?" he asked, as he gestured to the door.

"Not what I really want to do, but I guess if we must," she said with an over-dramatic sigh, which she didn't really fake. She didn't want to talk to Chet about Bane and the misguided coyotes; she wanted to fuck Dimitri. Needed to fuck him if she was honest. Never before had lust filled her so much, but the desire she felt for Dimitri right then almost overwhelmed her.

He kissed her nose. "Soon, my witch. I promise. I want it as much as you do, trust me."

"Then let's get this over with quick. I need your cock."

He grinned at her. "Good." He passed through the doorway, and she wanted to spell him back to the bedroom. This needed to go quick, or she would go crazy with want. She stared at his ass as he walked away. *Scratch that. I'm already crazy with want. Chet better not be chatty.*

Eighteen

It took longer with Chet than they wanted, but by the time they fabricated explanations that could be put down in a report for what transpired at Bane's cabin, everyone was content, and Adira and Dimitri rushed back to her place. Yet, the craving they felt for each other couldn't wait, and as soon as they were out of sight of the sheriff and his men, as well as the crime scene unit roping off Bane's cabin, they groped at each other's clothing, ripping them from their bodies as they dropped to the ground, their clothes a pile of shredded fabric around them. Twigs and branches poked into their exposed flesh, but neither one of them cared. They each wanted the other, their passion a hunger that wouldn't be abated until they possessed what their bodies craved.

Adira ran her hands up his back, her nails clawing into him as he plastered her neck and shoulders with kisses, his lips warm on her flesh. She arched her back, shoving her chest into his, pressing into him until there wasn't even room for the air around them. She wanted him, needed him. His hardness pressed into her thigh, the wetness of his pre-cum on her flesh. Her pussy throbbed as he bit into her neck, causing her to scream out, gripping his sides as she sent bursts of power into him. This time, his back arched as his eyes popped wide and he grunted.

Glancing down, his smile reached his eyes. "Now, that was unexpected," he said. "Nice, but unexpected." He kissed her nose. "An accident?"

She couldn't keep the proud smile from stretching across her face as she stared up into his eyes. "Nope. No accident. Like I said, my power's returned ever since you marked me. Seems that mouth of yours has talents I never even thought about." She waggled her eyebrows at him.

His smile reached her heart. "Nice to know. Of course, right now, I just want to use my mouth on that pussy of yours." He kissed her again, leaving a trail from her neck over her chest and down her curvy stomach to the valley that thrummed between her legs.

She moaned as she felt his tongue glide between her pussy lips, tasting the nectar that waited there for him. She spread her legs wider, urging him onward as she reached down and gripped his head, holding him in place. He gripped her ass, lifting her into the air as he sucked on her clit, flicking it with his tongue. She pressed her pussy to his mouth, craving more, as the cool air whispered across her flesh, a contrast to the heat that flushed her body. Her free hand gripped the soil at her side, her fingers digging into the ground as they would his flesh, her power shooting into the earth. She couldn't control it, so lost was she in the passion that wrapped around him. Blue fire shot from her fingers, lifting them into the air as he slid up her body to drive his cock into her. Her power formed a bed under them, the wind whipping around their naked bodies.

Dimitri gripped her shoulders as he thrust his cock in and out of her pussy, the wetness of her passion coating them both. She felt his body tense, felt his cock throb within her, sending tendrils of electric sensations to her nerve endings. She heard him hiss in her ear, felt him drive into her once more, his orgasm erupting from his cock to fill her with his passion. She cried out, her own body reacting to his, shuddering, as her orgasm swept through her, sending more bursts of power from her hands to explode into the ground.

As her orgasm subsided, she eased them back to the earth, until she once again felt the twigs and branches under her. Their breathing sounded heavy and ragged in her ears as Dimitri eased off her to lay at her side. "Well, that will hold me until we get back home," she said, laying her head on his chest with a contented sigh.

He chuckled beside her, as he kissed the top of her head. "Home?" he asked. "You're staying then? The problem of Bane is finished. Isn't that why Agatha and the Paranormal Council sent you here?"

She pressed her head down on his chest, snuggling in tighter. "That was the excuse, but I think we both know the real reason she sent me to Bull Creek." Agatha Rochester always worked more than one angle. "Besides, I kind of like it here."

She could hear the grin in his voice when he spoke. "It does tend to grow on you, doesn't it?"

"Besides, where else would I go?" She leaned up so that she could gaze into his eyes. "My mate is here."

He smiled as he wrapped his arms around her tighter, pulling her into an embrace that would forever heal her heart as well as her power.

Mate's Appeal

One

Eve Hartlow stared at the top of her beer bottle, frustration filling her at how she felt. She was tired of being helpless, of feeling like everyone in the world could take care of themselves except her. Even worse, she felt like she couldn't help defend her friends, which was obvious when everyone went after Bane Kastner when he abducted Adira a few days ago. Everyone, that is, except her. The others could shift, transforming into their animals, and race off to kick the coyote's ass, while Eve was stuck at Adira's cabin watching them all run off to Adira's rescue. Eve took a giant swallow from her beer, trying to drown out her helplessness.

"Not used to seeing you in here without your all-female posse," Noel Hastings said as she set a fresh beer in front of Eve. "Of course, I haven't seen you in here this early, either.

You doing all right?" Noel leaned on the bistro table, her hands clasped together as she stared at Eve, ready to be a shoulder if needed. Eve wasn't sure when Noel arrived in Bull Creek, but the woman fit right into their little community and gave Eve another human to share the paranormal world with her. While Bull Creek was made up of a diversity of people, from human to shifter to vampire and now a witch, thanks to the arrival of Adira Brennan, the human population was far outnumbered. The day Eve finally met Noel was a blessing, even though both ladies fit in well with everyone else.

Eve nodded, brushing a strand of her sandy-blond hair out of her eyes as she thanked Noel for the fresh beer. "Was just thinking how useless I was when everyone went to rescue Adira a couple of days back. There wasn't much I could do against the coyote pack." She glanced down at the brown bottle in her hand. "All I could do was stand on the front porch and watch as everyone else shifted and raced off to rescue Adira." She sighed. "I've always been that helpless, and I hate it."

Noel leaned to the side of the table, making a point of staring at the knife Eve always kept strapped to her waist. "You seem pretty prepared to me."

Eve glanced to where the curvaceous blond looked, noticing the wooden handle of the knife she wore. The blade was a symbol more than a weapon, although Eve practiced throwing it every day. Shrugging, she turned back to Noel. "I got tired of being the only one in Bull Creek without fangs, even more so after Bane and his thugs tried to run us all out of town."

Noel nodded, giving Eve a weak smile. "I can understand, trust me." Eve watched Noel glance at the bar toward Wes, the owner of Everglades. "It's exciting being around shifters and other paranormals, but it also holds its own dangers as well." She turned back to Eve, her grin growing. "I think it's worth it, though." She winked before tapping the top of the table and walking back to the bar.

Eve watched as the other woman walked away, saw Wes turn to Noel and smile as she approached where he stood, wrapping an arm around her when she reached him and giving her a kiss on the forehead. Eve smiled around the top of the beer bottle as she took a sip, thinking how wonderful it was that Noel had found someone who made her happy. However, Wes and Noel never went further in their relationship, just like Josh and Alanna. Why they held off from taking the next step Eve had no idea, but she knew holding back had to be driving both of them crazy. The animal of a shifter drove them to mate once they scented their fated partner. To refuse usually sent the human portion half-mad with distractions. Eve took a long swallow of her beer. She was quite content not having any distraction at the moment. The last one had been...

A movement off to the side caught her attention, and she jerked her gaze to the front door just as someone with short, dark hair slipped outside. A shiver ran through her as a horrible memory flashed through her mind, but she shook it off. Nightmares were real, she knew, but she had shaken hers before. She doubted that particular nightmare would return. There was no way anyone could find her in Bull Creek.

Eve took another sip of her beer, the uneasy feeling that filled her still churning her stomach as she forced herself to look away from the front door. However, the feeling still nagged at her. Tossing some bills down on the table, she shoved her beer to the side and stood. She glanced back to the bar to wave at Noel, but the woman was still wrapped up in Wes and not paying any attention to anything else. *Good thing I didn't need another drink.* Eve shook her head and started for the front door. Perhaps some fresh air would help calm her nerves.

Dusk was just beginning to blanket the area when Eve stepped out of Everglades and into the evening. Standing outside the rustic wooden door, she took a deep breath of air, filling her lungs in the hopes that it would clear her head. Life had been going well for her ever since she moved to Bull Creek, even though occasionally the nightmares of her past returned to give her the creeps. She was safe here, among these people, her new friends. Safer than she had ever been back home. She knew this, even though on occasion she had bouts of the jitters, which made her fearful. Those feelings came with running away, even if running away meant saving your life.

Stepping out into the dirt parking lot—everything was dirt and not pavement in Bull Creek—she took another deep breath and shook the agitation that had crept up on her inside the bar. The night was balmy with the Florida heat, and crickets could be heard off in the distance chirping their song. At least, Eve hoped it was crickets making that noise. Living in a paranormal community, one just never knew. Eve then giggled to herself as she shoved her hands in her pockets and continued walking, wondering if there were such a thing as bug shifters. So far, she had seen bears, panthers, coyotes, and wolves, had even heard of a vampire living at the edge of Bull Creek, and now a witch resided there as well. Still, that was about it as far as the supernatural. That didn't mean, however, that there weren't others out there she had no clue about. The one thing Eve had learned when moving to Bull Creek was that not everything was as it appeared all the time. Monsters were real, but not all monsters were evil.

Something moved off to her right, darting in the woods, rustling the lower brush. She tried to ignore it, hoping it was a natural creature scavenging in the woods for its nightly meal. Of course, it could be a shifter in animal form as well. Just a few days ago, Dimitri and Josh did patrols in their panther forms, guarding Bull Creek against the coyotes who wanted to drive out or slaughter the human population. However, things had quieted down since Bane and his goons were driven out or killed, so she doubted the rustling in the shrubs was anything with wicked intentions.

Even with Florida's humidity, the night wasn't as bad as usual. A slight breeze whispered through the trees, brushing against Eve's sandy-blond hair as she walked the dirt road. She probably should have driven, but she didn't live far, and walking always gave her a chance to clear her head and enjoy the quietness of the woods. Bull Creek was a safe haven, but even more, the small town, made up of cabins and supernatural creatures, was a quiet sanctuary far enough from the city that darkness could actually cover the area. Streetlights and the neon signs of businesses didn't keep the night air lit up, making sure everyone knew the city was still open for business. Eve needed the quiet peacefulness of the small community and the residents who dwelt there. She looked forward to the weekly bonfires that Dimitri held to bring everyone together, the ladies night out at Everglades, and the camaraderie that she felt with those who made up the small town. This was her home, and furthermore, it *felt* like her home, more so than where she had lived before. She couldn't imagine living anywhere else now that she had found this place.

More rustling off to the side forced her to stop and this time pay attention to the bushes that were being rustled, the hair on the back of her neck standing up. She stared, peering with squinted eyes into the palm fronds and shrubs, but nothing appeared. *You're just imaging things, Eve ol' girl.* Yet, the feeling refused to leave her. The rustling stopped almost as soon as she did, and Eve worried that whatever she was staring at in the bushes stared right back at her. *Okay, so I still get the creeps, even in this quiet town.* Sometimes, quietness was just too…quiet.

A car rumbled down the street toward her, and Eve stepped off the road, but made sure to move in the direction opposite the rustling bushes. She waited for the car to pass, not wanting to risk walking on the edge of the woods and tripping over a fallen branch or into a hole and injuring herself. However, the car slowed as it neared her.

"Eve?" Alanna Bradbury said from the open window. "What in the world are you doing in the middle of the road?"

Eve glanced at the bushes one more time and then turned her gaze to Alanna. "I just left Everglades and thought it a nice night for a walk."

"Well, I'm heading home now. Want me to give you a lift the rest of the way?"

Eve would have said no under normal circumstances, but unable to shake the feeling that crept up her spine, she eagerly accepted Alanna's offer. As she moved around the car, however, she kept her gaze on the section of the bushes where the noise had come from, not taking her eyes off the overgrown area until she was in the car and her door was locked.

"You okay?" Alanna asked, her brows pinched in concern.

"Yeah. I'm fine." Eve fastened her seatbelt, her attention still out the window. "Just a night for weird noises is all."

Alanna laughed. "Honey, this is Bull Creek. It's full of weird noises as well as loud moans and groans and cries of ecstasy." She laughed harder as she continued down the road. "I thought you'd be used to all that by now."

Eve nodded. "I am, for the most part." Then she shrugged as she turned back around and settled in her seat. "Some nights, though, it's hard to keep the nightmares from creeping in." Eve didn't want to deal with the nightmares anymore. She took a deep breath. Living it had been bad enough.

Two

Shades bustled with customers as people sought to get rid of the workweek and embrace the weekend. Arlin Landry stood by the front door, making sure the younger residents of Draven Falls didn't try to slip past through the front doors and trick a busy bartender for drinks. The North Carolina night was cool, in drastic contrast with the sweaty atmosphere of the inside of the bar, with just enough breeze to keep it comfortable without making it too cold. Overhead, the leaves rustled in the wind as the moon continued to climb into the night sky. Outside was peaceful while inside was anything but, especially in the back of Shades where a small group was making enough of a ruckus to drown out the DJ stationed in the middle of the bar. The noise was enough to make Arlin grateful he was positioned at the front door with the door wide open.

Closing his eyes, he took a deep breath as another scream came from the back of the bar. Arlin understood the need to blow off steam, of having fun and getting a little out of control. However, the group that came in earlier seemed to be taking it all to the next level. The noise was enough to give Arlin a headache.

"Here, Dad said you could probably use a drink."

Arlin turned and saw Drey Hawkins standing there, a bottle of water in his hand that he held out to Arlin. "Thanks," Arlin said as he took the bottle. He gestured back inside Shades with his chin. "A little crazy in there tonight, isn't it? That group in the back seems a little out of control."

Drey ran a strong hand through his dark red hair as he turned his attention back inside the bar, nodding. "Parker Evans and his group. They rarely come to town, which makes the residents of Draven Falls quite content as well as the Paranormal Council. Hyenas," Drey said with a sneer. "Nothing ever good comes from hyenas."

Arlin nodded. "Almost as bad as coyotes." He glanced back into Shades where the group of hyena shifters hollered, playing grab ass with any female who walked by and making a general nuisance of themselves. He could feel his tiger wrestling inside to deal with the annoying group. "I wish your father would let me toss them out on their ass. I'm not sure why they're even here. They usually stick to the woods closer to the mountains."

Drey gave a snort of derision. "Someone must have gotten paid." He slapped Arlin on the back and then turned to walk back inside. Arlin watched the other man leave, knowing the panther shifter drew the eyes of most of the females in the bar, and probably even a few of the guys. Arlin couldn't say he blamed them. The other man may work the bar at night, but his day job dealing with lumber kept him in strong physical form.

Arlin turned to look at his reflection in the glass of the front door, noticing his own muscular build and dark hair. He smirked as he shook his head. The two of them were built the same, and both received the same amount of attention from the ladies who came into Shades, but Drey wasn't interested in any of them. He was quite content with the triad relationship he was in with Gavin Covington and Caitlin Carver. That left all the female attention in Arlin's capable hands. He considered it one of the perks of being a bouncer in a bar.

Another burst of cheers went up in the back of the bar, and Arlin watched as one of the bulkier of the hyenas grabbed a girl and twirled her around, pulling her into his lap, causing her to shriek. Arlin growled as he started to make his way toward the commotion. Now, he had a reason to toss the group out on their asses.

Drey left the bar, crossing the floor to join him, as Arlin passed the DJ and drew closer to the group of hyenas who apparently saw nothing wrong with their behavior. Scavengers, the pack of hyenas disgusted Arlin. They possessed no dignity, no respect for others. They were vermin on society's ladder.

Arlin stepped closer to the table where the overbearing drunk held the woman, squeezing her to him and grinding her on his lap. She screamed, fighting to get off Parker's lap, but all he did was rub his dark beard against her cheek in an attempt to steal a kiss from her. She beat at him, and Arlin worried he wouldn't reach the man quick enough to stop anything bad from happening.

The man, thick of body as well as skull, gripped the woman's chin and attempted to turn her mouth toward his. Arlin saw the woman open her mouth, only she didn't scream. Instead, she bit down on the man's hand, driving her teeth deep into his flesh. He cried out, shoving her away from him and onto the floor. The woman hit the floor, screaming, and then the goon reached down and gripped her by her shirt and jerked her to her feet, backhanding her as soon as she was within reach. "You, bitch!" he roared as he raised his hand to hit her again.

However, Arlin reached the man first, grabbing his arm and spinning him around. The tiger within Arlin struggled to break free, the orange and black striped fur oozing from his flesh as he tossed the man away from the woman.

Drey reached the woman as Arlin reached out and gripped Parker, shoving him toward the entrance. "Time for you to go," Arlin growled. He struggled to control his anger. Men didn't attack women. Period. He had watched his father beat his mother too many times when he was a kid to ever allow it to happen in his presence again.

Parker spun, thrusting his thick chest out at Arlin. "Keep your grubby hands off me, you circus act. Don't think I don't know what you are." The man spat on the floor. "You think you're so superior, but all you are is a doorkeeper." Then he laughed. "And a doorkeeper for panthers at that, smaller animals."

Arlin felt his animal growl, but he kept the tiger tamped down. *They're just words of a drunk. Calm down.* He gestured to the door again. "As I said, it's time for you to go."

Parker looked past Arlin to the woman, a leer twisting his lips. "Don't worry, sweetheart. I'll be around to finish what we started." He gave her a wink.

Arlin's tiger refused to hold back any longer, and as Arlin swung to punch the man, his hand transformed into a tiger's paw, fingers shifting to claws as he sliced into the man's face, a growl ripping from him. Parker's head snapped to the left, his body turning with the force of the blow as Arlin reached out and gripped him by the shirt, lifting him into the air and tossing him toward the back wall. Parker was hurled through the air, arms flailing as he landed hard on a table covered in bottles. Glass shattered, splintering in all directions as the man slid across the table and rolled onto the floor. Arlin didn't slow down, ignoring the cries of those around him telling him to stop. He heard Drey's voice, and Jed's, but nothing would temper his anger at that point. No one—NO ONE—made comments like this hyena just did to a woman. Not in Arlin's presence. There were lines, and the man on the floor crossed them.

As Arlin reached down to yank the drunk to his feet for another toss across the room, Drey reached him, yanking his arms away from Parker, who was on his hands and knees, panting for breath, cuts across his arms. "Stop! Arlin, enough," Drey said as he pulled Arlin around and away from the man on the floor. "I think you made your point." Drey shoved Arlin toward the bar as another of the bouncers approached to haul the hyena out of Shades. A couple of the serving girls surrounded the woman who had been the object of the brute's unwanted attention.

Arlin allowed himself to be steered away from the scene he had caused, his shoulders rising and falling with his heavy breaths, his muscles still taut with his anger. He knew he shouldn't have done what he did, should have just kept shoving the man toward the door. Parker was just running off at the mouth and probably would have forgotten what he said once he sobered up. However, Arlin had lived with a man like him before and refused to allow any other woman have to deal with the chauvinistic jackasses of the world if he could help it. Tonight, he could help it.

"What the hell were you thinking?" Drey snapped once they were in the backroom and away from the customers. "You don't attack people in Shades. You just toss them out on their asses." Drey shook his head, his red hair swishing across his forehead.

Arlin blew out a breath of frustration, hoping to calm his nerves. "Sorry. I can't handle men like him who think women are their property." He shook his head. "Watching him just brought back memories I thought I had dealt with already. I guess I was wrong."

"You think?" Drey shook his head. Then with a deep breath, he said, "Take the rest of the night off. I'm sure Dad will call you tomorrow, but I doubt anything will come of this. Everyone knows Parker's an ass. I doubt he'll get much sympathy from anyone around Draven Falls. Just lay low tonight, and let it blow over."

Arlin nodded, taking deep breaths, his nerves still raw from the encounter. "Tell your dad I'm sorry."

"Will do. Now, go get some rest. Tomorrow's a new day, and I'm sure he's not going to give you two days off in a row." Drey chuckled, doing his best to make light of the situation, Arlin knew. However, with tensions between the paranormal factions of Draven Falls and the humans who dwelt there, Arlin knew Jed wouldn't be able to ignore what happened entirely. Arlin didn't know what the consequences would be, but he was sure there would be some sort of fallout. Parker was ass enough to try and press his point somehow and stir up more shit just to make Arlin's life miserable.

"Call me tomorrow," Arlin said as he turned to the door. "And make sure to apologize to Jed for me."

"I will. Promise."

Arlin stepped out of Shades and into the night air of Draven Falls. The atmosphere that seemed so peaceful just a short while ago now seemed heavy with his screw up. He knew people would be talking about it if they haven't texted all their friends already. News like this spread faster than a wildfire in dry woods. He ran a hand through his dark hair as he stood on the sidewalk staring at the gazebo across the way in Circle Park. Draven Falls had been a home to him when nowhere else felt safe, and he suddenly feared that he had screwed it up. Where else could he feel this safe? There was no other sanctuary for people like him. He was stuck now and may have just cost himself the only place he ever felt like he could be himself.

He took a deep breath. *Well, nothing for it but to sit tight and see where the chips fall.* He started toward his car, his fate now in Jed's hands for better or worse.

Three

When are you going to stop dancing around Josh and just give in to him?" Eve Hartlow asked her friend as they wandered the dirt roads of Bull Creek. The Florida sun was high overhead, bringing the stifling heat to the wooded community and a sweat to her brow. Still, Eve would take it over the frozen winters up north any day of the week. "I'm not a shifter, and even I can smell how the air changes when you two are around each other. Why keep the poor guy at arm's length?"

A couple of days had passed since Eve's self-pity party at Everglades, and she had managed to give herself a couple of pep talks that rustling bushes didn't scare her anymore. Alanna had been right. There are too many noises in Bull Creek to start jumping at each one now.

"Arm's length? Trust me, he's been a lot closer than that,"

Alanna Bradbury said with a wink and a laugh. Then she shrugged. "I'm just not ready for that type of commitment yet. I'm a wolf without a pack, still feeling my way around."

Eve chuckled. "From the sounds coming from your cabin the other night, seems like you're doing a lot more than just feeling around. Besides, that poor boy has been panting to get you into his cabin since before I moved here. You really should cut him some slack."

Alanna giggled as they walked. "I know but making him pant is half the fun. He's so cute when he's being teased."

Eve Hartlow rested her hand on the hilt of the knife sheathed at her waist as they walked, the oak handle giving her a sense of calm when nothing else did lately. "Is that another shifter thing? Some rite of passage? I'm have a hard time keeping it all straight."

"Nah." Alanna gave a shake of her head. "It's an Alanna thing." Both ladies laughed, Alanna shoving her hands into her back pockets as they continued walking. The breeze, which did nothing to cool them off, tugged gently at their hair. When the laughter died down, Alanna gazed at the knife at Eve's side. "Sort of like wearing that blade is an Eve thing. What's the deal anyway? You trying to pick up a hunter? You've worn that thing ever since you arrived in Bull Creek, and I've barely seen you pull it out of that fancy holster you wear. You do grip it a lot, though, like right now. I know we ladies like to accessorize our outfits, but I think you went the wrong direction for wooing a man."

Eve took a deep breath through her nose in a vain attempt to calm the jitters that churned in her stomach. As the breath escaped past her lips, she shook her head. "I'm not trying to woo anyone. God, what a weird word." She laughed, the tension leaving her shoulders. "I'm pretty much over men. I prefer the quiet, unattached life."

Alanna nodded as if she understood, but Eve knew there was no way her friend could comprehend what she was talking about. She probably thought Eve was jilted by some lover and pined away over a man back home. Eve Hartlow didn't pine away for anyone. She preferred her simple life.

Overhead, mallards flew to the east, heading to Crabgrass Creek. "Is it because of the bruises that painted your body when you first arrived in Bull Creek?" Alanna asked, her tone cautious as if she knew how sensitive the subject was for Eve. Alanna was also skirting very close to the unspoken rule of Bull Creek — Don't ask personal questions.

Yet, Eve didn't call her on it. She appreciated Alanna's kid gloves with the topic she didn't understand. While she knew something lurked behind Eve's self-imposed spinsterhood, that something would remain a secret as far as Eve was concerned. Needed to stay a secret as a matter of fact. Eve didn't want someone else knowing how weak she once was, regardless that it was a weakness she was determined never to experience again. "I just think it looks good," she lied with a feeble shrug, sidestepping the whole issue. "Besides, it's practical. When you're in the woods, a knife comes in handy. Bane and his coyotes may be gone, but who knows what else is around the corner?"

"Really? We live in Bull Creek. Bane Kastner was the most excitement this place has seen in decades. That's why this area was chosen for a sanctuary."

Eve had to admit, it was definitely quiet around here. A week ago, Bane, a coyote shifter, brought his pack in and attempted to drive the humans out of Bull Creek. Bane was the leader of a mangy coyote pack, a group of bullies who thought humans didn't belong in the forests. They believed the wooded areas of the world belonged to shifters who knew how to appreciate and take care of all that dwelt within the woods. Bane was a prejudiced bully who was afraid of anyone who wasn't like him. However, Adira Brennan, a witch who just moved to Bull Creek, and Dimitri Everest, the alpha of the community, killed Bane and his second-in-command, driving out the rest of the coyotes. Bull Creek returned to its peaceful existence, the residents going about their routine of minding their own business. Eve glanced out of the corner of her eye at Alanna. *Well, not everyone minds their own business.* She shrugged "I may need to whittle or something."

A car could be heard rumbling up behind them, almost pacing them. Eve fought the urge to look back, forced herself to ignore the vehicle behind them, to squelch the feeling of panic she had the other night at Everglades. *Why am I so jumpy?*

Alanna laughed. "You whittle? Really?"

"I can learn," Eve said, a smile curling her lips upward. As Alanna laughed, Eve couldn't help but join her, the ridiculousness of her excuse apparent even to her. As they rounded the bend leading to Eve's cabin, she said, "Let's just say it's a security blanket for now." She took a deep breath.

"Let's head to my place. I could use some tea."

Alanna nodded. "Sounds good." Yet, it was obvious she wasn't ready to drop the subject of the knife. "So, have you even used that knife on anything besides poor defenseless trees? What did those trees ever do to you anyway, you big meanie?"

Eve swiped her sandy-blond bangs out of her eyes. "The noble trees around my cabin have sacrificed daily in order to help me with my proficiency with this knife. I'm sure they know the worthy cause for which they suffer."

Alanna shook her head, her dark hair swishing across her back slightly as she did. "Trees are noble like that," she said with a chuckle. "Of course, the fact that they have no choice..."

Eve shrugged. "What can I say? I'm not ready for a moving target yet."

"So you have been practicing." Alanna crossed her arms as they walked. "And just why are you practicing? Bane and his men are gone, the whole pack of mangy coyotes either dead or in hiding."

Eve nodded, remembering quite well the battle her shifter friends fought just a week ago in order to protect the humans in Bull Creek. She knew she should feel safe again, but the coyotes weren't what worried Eve. Her past, however, scared the hell out of her. Eve shrugged, "I like to stay ready. Who knows when something might pop up again?" Her reply was weak, she knew, but she wasn't exactly ready to spill her guts. Not yet. Maybe not ever.

Alanna nodded, her expression showing that, while she

didn't really believe Eve, she wasn't going to press the subject any further. Alanna was one of the few who was around when Eve first arrived in Bull Creek and saw her battered condition. Yet, no one knew the reasons for her appearance, and Eve never offered an explanation. That was the great thing about their small community. It was a safe haven for anyone who needed to escape their reality. Bull Creek was full of misfits and vagabonds, each oppressed in one way or another. All kinds of shifters resided here as well as humans, and even a vampire or two stayed hidden on the outskirts of their community. While everyone knew that everyone else was there, hiding from something, no one asked what that something was. If people wanted to speak about it, there were shoulders to lean on, ears to listen. If they didn't, then it remained their secret as long as that secret didn't spill over onto anyone else in Bull Creek. Eve didn't think her secret would ever harm anyone else, but she wouldn't take that chance. Ever.

She also wouldn't take the chance that her secret would return and hurt her again. Once was enough. More than enough. Only one other person knew she was even in Bull Creek, her mother. As far as the rest of the world was concerned, Eve Hartlow vanished from the face of the earth.

"So, you're telling me no one is sniffing around your skirts worth talking about?" Alanna asked, apparently ready to change subjects.

Eve shook her head, not really liking the rehash of the dating topic. "I haven't really made myself accessible. As I said, like you, I'm just not ready. Not yet." She shrugged.

Alanna glanced over at her, her expression sympathetic. "You know, if you ever need to talk about whatever it is you're keeping inside, I'm all ears. Sometimes, it pays to talk it out. Get it off your chest. Helps you move on."

"Thanks," Eve said with a slow shake of her head. "But I'm not ready for that, either." She wasn't sure she'd ever be ready. While it was over six months ago, it was still extremely raw. Nightmares woke her up, screaming, leaving her shaking. She took a deep breath. She was tired of waking up shaking.

They turned down one of the streets leading to Eve's cabin and the promise of sweet tea to cool them off. "We need another ladies night out. Take the edge off the monotony. The last one kind of ended poorly."

Eve chuckled. That was an understatement. One of Bane's goons tried to make a move on Adira, and she used her powers to shove him out the door and into the parking lot. "I was surprised I was even allowed back into Everglades. I figured we'd be non grata there after last time."

"No way. Wes knows it wasn't our fault." Some rustling in the trees to their left startled Eve for a second, and she chided herself for her nerves still being so on edge. "Besides, we haven't been out in a while. I think we could all use it. I'm sure Lainie will want to get out. I'll check with Adira and have her join us if I can get her off Dimitri's pecker long enough."

Both women laughed at the truth of that statement. Even with Eve being human and not a shifter, she was around them long enough to know the basics of how the mating of shifters worked. It was a heat that kept them panting after each other, unable to keep their hands and mouths from devouring one another. Adira and Dimitri were going at it nonstop ever since the fight at Bane's cabin.

"Sounds like fun. What time?"

"Nine sound good? Of course, you might need to leave the knife at home. I'm sure you'll be safe with a witch and two shifters." She glanced over and winked at Eve as she said it.

Eve just nodded, choosing not to comment. She'd keep her knife on her. It wasn't that she didn't trust her friends to have her back. She just didn't like being unprotected or dependent on others. Not anymore. She learned a long time ago that others could disappoint you and that she needed to take care of herself. "Nine works for me. Gives me time to shower and fix dinner. Want to join me?"

"For the shower or the dinner?" Alanna nudged Eve as she waggled her eyebrows at her friend. Eve just rolled her eyes. "Thanks, but I'm meeting Josh for dinner. He's cooking lasagna or something like that."

They turned the corner and started to walk into Eve's front yard when Alanna grabbed her and brought them both to a stop. "You may need that knife yet."

The front door of Eve's cabin was kicked in and, on the front wall, the words, "There's no escape," were painted on the wood in bright red. Two of the front windows were broken, glass everywhere, the drapes pulled out and blowing in the breeze. The plants that usually lined Eve's porch had their pots smashed, the pottery strewn throughout the yard, the plants destroyed and dirt scattered over the porch.

Alanna was already pulling her phone from her back pocket, hitting nine-one-one. Eve just stood there and stared. Not again. Not here. She rested her hand on the hilt of her knife, knowing without needing proof that her past had somehow found her.

Four

rlin Landry shook his head at the two women who seemed clueless as they walked down the dirt road, blindly going about their business, lost in whatever conversation had them so absorbed that they couldn't even pay attention to the vehicle coming down the road right at them. He sighed as they turned the corner down the dirt road just before his brother's cabin and finally out of his way. He wasn't sure if it was because they were female or the fact that they lived in this backwoods community that had them so negligent about their surroundings, but it would frustrate him to no end if everyone in Bull Creek were the same way. Draven Falls may not be a metropolitan, but people paid attention to what they did and where they walked. He blew out a breath, trying to calm his nerves. *Relax, Arlin old boy. This is precisely why Jed Hawkins sent you out here, to chill your over-stressed emotions.*

He pulled into the dirt drive of his brother's cabin with a shake of his head. He knew he needed solitude, but when Nathan said Bull Creek was a quiet, out-of-the-way community, he had definitely kept to himself the full extent of just how quiet and out-of-the-way it was. Arlin sighed as he shifted his car into park and stared at the front of the cabin, taking in the overgrown weeds that lined the front porch and the sides of the structure. Nathan hadn't been to the cabin in months, and it showed. Well, Arlin wanted solitude after all, and by the looks of it, he would get it. Besides, the manual labor of pulling weeds and cleaning up the place may be just what the doctor ordered, if he had seen a doctor, that is.

Turning the ignition off, he opened the driver's door and stepped out into the Florida humidity, taking a deep breath as the wave of heat hit him. *Arlin, you're not in Kansas anymore.* Or Draven Falls for that matter. As much as he needed a vacation from working at Shades, when Jed suggested Arlin use his younger brother's cabin in Bull Creek, Arlin knew he should have asked for more details. If Nathan Landry hadn't made the place his homestead, there had to be a reason, and Arlin wished he knew what it was. A little forewarning might keep what happened in Draven Falls from happening here as well. Arlin did not need a repeat of his loss of control, the bloodlust of his tiger consuming him once again. No one needed that.

He closed his eyes as he recalled the last night he worked the door at Shades, the drunks who ventured in desperate to stir up trouble. *Damn hyenas.* They managed to get more than they bargained for that night, and it almost cost one of them his life. Arlin took a deep breath, turning his gaze to the sky full of clouds in an attempt to calm his nerves. There was a special place in Hell for men who preyed on women, trying to bully the females into the backseats of their cars, and Arlin did his best to send one of those men there that night. Only Drey Hawkins' interference kept Arlin from crossing a line from which he would never recover. Of course, now he was on vacation until the heat died down. It was worth it.

He locked his car after popping the trunk lever, walked around to the back, and pulled his duffel bag out of the trunk. *Might as well get settled.* He was here now and would make the best of it, whatever that turned out to be, as long as wandering pedestrians paid better attention to moving cars, that is.

The interior of the cabin was musty from where it had been closed up for several months, a fine layer of dust coating everything. Before he could use anything in the cabin, he would need to spend some time cleaning up the place. As it was, he couldn't even sit on the furniture. He needed to teach his brother how to cover things with old sheets before leaving the cabin. Some proactive measures would have made the clean up a little easier. At least, Arlin would have been able to sit down as soon as he walked into the place after such a long drive. Of course, his younger brother was never one for much forethought in things, preferring to rush out and deal with everything later. Arlin should be happy Nathan at least closed the door and locked the place up.

He chuckled to himself as he dropped his duffel bag on the floor just inside the front door. With a deep breath, hands on his hips, he shook his head. Hopefully, Nathan kept some cleaning supplies here.

Luckily, Arlin discovered bottles of cleaning fluids and old rags under the kitchen sink. He had just pulled everything out and filled an old mop bucket he found in the back room with water when he heard sirens breaking the natural peacefulness of Bull Creek. He turned his attention to the front windows as he finished filling up the bucket. *Now, I bet that's unusual for around here.* Turning off the water and dropping the rag in the sudsy bucket, he decided to check it out and see what constituted a nine-one-one call around such an isolated community.

Blue and red lights bounced off the giant oaks and pines that filled the wooded area around the cabins, guiding him to where a sheriff's car was parked in a dirt driveway down the street that he witnessed those ladies turning down earlier. *One of them probably walked right out in front of a passing car.* He gave another shake of his head as he turned down the road to see how bad it was.

He was pleased—surprised, but pleased—to see that neither of the women he passed earlier had wound up being struck by a passing motorist. However, he was shocked at what he did find in what he assumed was such a peaceful community. The flashing lights of a sheriff's car ricocheted off a cabin that had been vandalized severely. Windows were smashed, plants destroyed and scattered everywhere, and in dark red paint over the front of the cabin were the words, *There is no escape*. With a cock of his head, he stared at the words, wondering, *Escape from what?* Nathan had obviously left out the dramatic aspects of his home away from home at Bull Creek.

Arlin glanced around at those gathered in front of the cabin, and his nose twitched at the mixture of shifter scents he sensed mixed in with humans, and…he took another deep breath….witches and vampires. He gave an appreciative nod. Jed did tell him the place was a diversity of paranormal personalities. Arlin just didn't expect it to be a melting pot.

Next to the sheriff's car stood a portly elderly man in uniform along with a female deputy and a muscular man with shaggy, tawny hair, his arms crossed over his chest as he listened to the sheriff speaking. Near the front of the porch, stood three women, two of them were the ladies he saw on the road earlier, and the third was a smaller woman with dark hair and a powerful stance. The shortest of the three, with sandy hair and a knife hanging at her waist, attempted to get past the other two ladies and into the cabin, but was blocked every time. *Must be her cabin. I'd want inside as well to see what else the asshole who did this destroyed. Probably some teens thinking they found an easy score out here in no man's land.*

Walking over to where the sheriffs stood with the other man, Arlin slid his hands in his back pockets to make himself appear less of a threat. With the damage to the cabin and him being a stranger, he didn't want any misunderstandings that would cause his tiger to bust loose and get him in trouble again. He'd filled out enough police reports over the past couple of days to know he didn't want to go through that again.

The man not in uniform turned his attention to Arlin as he approached, an eyebrow arched over narrowed eyes as he watched the newcomer. Arlin just nodded once, doing his best to appear charming and not threatening. He cleared his throat, gaining the sheriff's attention, and all conversation stopped. "Pardon the intrusion," Arlin said. "I heard the sirens and noticed the lights down the street. I passed the ladies walking just a bit ago, and they weren't really paying attention to where they were walking, so I wanted to make sure nothing happened to them. I'm glad to see they're all right." He pulled a hand from his back pocket and gestured to the cabin. "Although, this is far from all right, I know."

Arlin thought for sure the sheriff would be the one to speak first, but instead, the civilian took the lead. "And you are?" He crossed his arms over his chest, definitely doing his best to appear intimidating.

Arlin slid his hand back into his pocket, leaving himself open, remaining as calm as possible. He was the stranger after all, suddenly here during a crisis. "Arlin Landry. My brother, Nathan, owns the cabin up the road. I'm staying here for a bit of a vacation."

The tawny-headed man nodded, uncrossing his arms and letting his hands discover his own pockets. "Jed Hawkins told me you were coming." He pulled a hand out of his pocket, reaching out to shake Arlin's. "I'm Dimitri Everest, kind of the overseer of Bull Creek." He then gestured to the other two. "This is Sheriff Chet Einstein, and my sister, Deputy Lainie Everest."

"You didn't happen to see anyone else on the road as you were driving, did you?" the sheriff asked.

Arlin shook his head. "No, just the two ladies. As I said, they were so lost in whatever they were talking about that they didn't even notice me behind them. I could tell by the way they meandered over the road as they walked."

"I don't meander."

Arlin turned and noticed the other three women approaching. The shorter one with the sandy hair practically snarling at him.

"And for the record, I did notice you. I just didn't care. I would assume if you had a license, then you knew how to avoid people walking on the side of the road."

Arlin arched an eyebrow at the small woman, small but apparently formidable. His tiger growled within, as well, wanting to pounce the little spitfire in front of him, and Arlin felt his cock twitch inside his pants, stirring to life. His heart beat faster as his breath caught in his throat. *Why the hell did Jed send me to Bull Creek?* "Since I was the one behind you, I'm pretty sure I know how you were walking," Arlin said. "You were meandering." Then he shrugged. "I didn't say it was a bad thing. Why would you be worried about cars running you over in this area, after all? I mean, you were only walking in the middle of the road."

"The middle...." The woman took a step forward, her hand dropping to the hilt of the knife at her waist. Arlin's tiger purred inside, instead of growled, and Arlin knew he was in even more trouble than he first thought. "I was walking on the side of the road, thank you, and that heap you were driving wasn't exactly quiet, you know. I'm sure they heard you in St. Cloud with that clunker."

"Clunker?" Arlin slid his hands out of his back pockets and crossed his arms, ignoring the looks the others gave him. While the sheriff had a confused expression, the others just stood there grinning. *Probably all shifters,* Arlin assumed. Then he detected the scent of the witch next to the robust redhead. Yet, she grinned as well. All of them knew what his tiger had just detected, all of them except the short, sandy-haired piece of sass in front of him, that is. He did not come to Bull Creek to find his mate, but it appeared his mate had just found him. So much for a vacation of peace and quiet. "My car is not a clunker, thank you. It's a classic."

The short woman laughed. "Classic? That's what they call something that's old and worn out, right? Something that has a musty odor? I bet the music you listened to as a child is a classic, as well, being played on one of those oldie stations with a DJ born while 8-tracks were popular. Who the hell are you again and why are you even here?"

Arlin sighed. *It looks like I'm here to find out who trashed your cabin, my vivacious vixen.* Yet, he knew now was not the time to bring that up, not with the first impression he had just made. His tiger growled, wanting to claim the lady in front of him right there and didn't care if he did it in front of everyone else, and the awkward part was that at least four of the others knew it as well. *Me and my big mouth.*

Five

Everglades was a shifter bar in Holopaw, a dive bar, really, and nothing like Shades back in Draven Falls, but it held its own rustic charm. Unless you knew what type of bar it was, anyone looking at it in passing would probably just drive on by, thinking the place needed to be condemned, even with cars parked outside. The ancient wooden structure appeared to be created of discarded planks found in abandoned buildings, rather than the finished wood of a newer structure. The interior consisted of scratched up wooden chairs and tables, appearing as if the place was thrown together in much the same way as the exterior of the building. Weak mirrors and flashing beer logos covered the walls, while serving girls wandered from table to table, taking orders and flirting with the male patrons, whether the men had dates or not. Country music blared from a broken-down jukebox, bouncing off the walls, as couples line danced and chugged their beers. It was nothing like a nightclub in the city. Instead, Everglades held the feel of a homier, comfier environment. That was exactly what Eve needed right then, considering her own home was ripped away from her today.

Noel, one of Wes's serving girls, brought over a tray full of beers and tequila shots, setting them on the table in front of Eve and the others. While quite a bit of alcohol was required to get shifters drunk, since their metabolism is a lot sturdier than humans, it didn't stop them from enjoying the tastes as well as the social aspects. Right then, Eve needed her Bull Creek sisters to help her get drunk and forget about the ransacking of her place. Noel must have heard about the break-in because the curvaceous blond set an extra tequila shot in front of Eve. "This one is on me," she said with a wink before walking back to the bar.

Eve thanked the woman as she walked off and then reached for the small glass and downed the fiery liquid, allowing it to burn her throat and warm her belly, before slamming the glass back on the table and picking up the second shot.

"Hey, hey." Lainie Everest stopped Eve before she tipped the shot glass back. "Let us have a chance to join the festivities."

"Agreed," Adira Brennan, Bull Creek's resident witch, chimed in. "I hate being left out, especially when it comes to drinking shots."

Alanna picked up her shot glass, the wolf shifter lifting it high in the air. "To finding the ass who tore our girl's cabin up and kicking his ass."

All four ladies lifted their glasses, cheered, and downed the tequila, slamming the glasses back on the table when finished. Eve grabbed her beer and took a long pull from the bottle, allowing the cold liquid to contrast in her throat with the burning tequila. Wiping her mouth with the back of her hand, she set the beer bottle back on the table, but didn't release it. She knew if she didn't hold onto something, she would be gripping her knife for security, probably not the best thing to do in a bar. Out of the corner of her eye, she noticed Lainie watching her. Eve continued to stare at the bottle in her hand. "What?"

"I know the code of Bull Creek," Lainie said. "No one asks nosy questions about why someone else is here. It's a safe place for those who are escaping something they would rather not discuss." She shrugged. "Hell, I'm here to get away from my parents and their idea of a perfect mate for me. Still, it seems whatever you're hiding from has found you. I think it's time you fill us in so we can help protect you."

Eve pressed her lips into a thin line as she shook her head. "I don't need help."

"Really?" Alanna said, her tone shocked. "We all saw your house, Eve. What would have happened if you were there when whoever did it decided to come calling? I know you love playing with that knife you wear, but even you said you weren't ready for a moving target. We're your friends. More than that, though, we're also shifters and a witch. We can do more than fight like girls if you know what I mean. We can kick ass like women."

"I can make you some wards for your cabin, like I put around the area for Bane's coyotes," Adira said. "Of course, they would be more effective if I knew what they were warding against."

Eve stared at a drop of condensation on her bottle as it trailed a path down the dark brown glass and onto her knuckle. She knew these ladies were her friends, but she never wanted anyone to know how weak she once was. She hated thinking of herself as a victim, but that was what she allowed herself to be back then. She swore then that she would never be that helpless again. Never. Not today. Not ever.

The music shifted from Willie Nelson to Tim McGraw as Eve blew out a frustrated breath. She glanced up as couples hit the dance floor, two-stepping to the beat. Why couldn't she be normal like everyone else? She stared at the front door, wanting desperately to run and avoid the questioning looks from her friends. Then she saw him again, that stranger who suddenly appeared at her cabin earlier, accusing her of not paying attention to her surroundings. She growled as she watched him head to the bar after giving her a cursory glance. A giggle to her left made her turn a questioning gaze to Alanna. "And what's so funny?"

"You." Then she pointed at the newcomer with her chin. "Him. That poor man had no idea what hit him today. You were frustrated and angry, scared if you were smart, and you took it all out on him." She shrugged. "It was fun to watch, I admit. Almost as much fun as it was watching Adira dig into Dimitri a couple of weeks ago, clueless to the fact that Dimitri had scented her as his mate."

Eve tightened her grip on her bottle. "Well, that was them. This is me, and I don't need someone I don't even know passing judgment on how I do things."

"Oh, trust me, I'm sure he gets it," Adira said with a chuckle.

Lainie took a swig of her beer, setting the bottle back on the table and running her tongue over her lips when she finished. "It doesn't matter, though. I don't think he's going anywhere anytime soon. I'm not sure he could now if he wanted."

Eve cocked her head at the deputy, a nagging suspicion of what the others were trying to insinuate making the hair on the back of her neck stand up. "And just why couldn't he leave? No one invited him here. I sure as hell don't need him sticking his nose into my business."

Alanna giggled. "I think it's already stuck, and you're stuck with him."

Eve was about to make a smartass comment about shifters and their noses when she spotted another person entering the bar, only this one did more than just aggravate her; he scared the hell out of her, a feeling she swore she would never experience again. She couldn't help it. It was the first time she had seen him since she snuck out one night months ago while he went out for a drink. Her heart pounded in her ears, her breath caught in her throat, and all she could do was stare. When she saw the damage to her cabin, the note in red paint across her wall, she prayed he had not found her, that it was merely a threat by teenagers with wild imaginations. Yet, his appearance at Everglades told her that the warning was very much real. Her escape was only in her mind.

Eve swallowed the lump in her throat that threatened to choke her.

"Eve, sweetie, you okay?" Alanna placed a hand on Eve's upper arm, hoping to shake her from the trance, Eve assumed, but it didn't work. Eve couldn't move. She could do nothing but stare as Kyle Wagner turned to her, his dark eyes narrow slits as he glared at her, his coal black hair disheveled from the breeze outside. He sneered at her as he started her way, menace in every step he took. Panic seized her, her eyes going wide in fear. No! No, no, no. Whatever she swore never to feel again didn't matter. The icy grip of fear clawed at her nerves, rooting her in place.

"Eve, what's wrong?" This time it was Adira who asked, one arm across the table wanting to touch Eve and shake her out of her frozen behavior.

Kyle stepped up to the table, his sneer plastered across his face, as he ignored the others with Eve. He leaned on the table, his hands clasped in front of him, his lips curled up in a snarl. "Hello, Eve. What a pleasant surprise to see you here. Or rather, I bet you're surprised to see *me* here. Or ever again, for that matter."

Eve forced herself to swallow the lump in her throat, her hand gripping the knife hilt tightly. "What are you doing here, Kyle?"

He just smiled bigger. "You mean, how did I find you?" He reached across the table and took her beer, watching her with intense eyes as he tilted it back and drained it of what was left. Then he shrugged as he set the bottle back on the table. "What can I say, your mom has a soft spot for me. When she saw how distraught I was with your little vanishing act, she quickly told me where to find you." He glanced around Everglades, his sneer a judgment of his distaste. "I have to say, I thought you had better class than this rat hole." He turned his gaze back to her. "Still, I guess you thought if you found a nice little hole to bury yourself in, I would never find you." He leered at her, waggling his eyebrows as he leaned closer to her. "But I found you, didn't I? There is no escape, Eve."

Lainie reacted then, grabbing Kyle by the arm and forcing him down on the table with a thud that sent the beer bottles toppling over, bending his arm behind his back. "What the hell did you say?"

He kept his gaze fixated on Eve, his smile never wavering. "Just an inside joke between Eve and myself. Right, Eve?"

Lainie leaned over, snarling in Kyle's ear. All Eve could do was watch. "And yet, those exact words were painted on Eve's cabin earlier. Wouldn't happen to know anything about that, would you?"

"A cabin? Really?" Kyle chuckled. "You actually live in a cabin out here? Oh, how quaint. Then I guess it's a good thing I arrived to save you, isn't it?"

"What did you do to my mother?" Eve asked, lifting the knife slightly from its sheath as she started to step around the table. She didn't get far, however, before she smacked into that man from earlier, who now stood there in front of her, his smile gentle as he slid his hand to her fingers on the knife, lifting her hand as he gently pulled her after him. *What the hell is he doing?* She needed to find out about her mother. This idiot didn't know what he was doing.

He ignored the pained expression on her face as he turned to Lainie. "Deputy Everest, right?" Lainie nodded, confusion on her face mixed with the anger she felt over Kyle at the moment. "Pardon me, while I whisk this one out to the dance floor while you tend to..." He glanced at Kyle, his eyes narrowing into angry slits. "...whatever this is."

Lainie nodded. "Good idea."

The others just stood watching. Eve didn't understand how they could just stand there, letting this man take her away from the answers she needed. Yet, a part of her was glad he did. She needed to get away from Kyle, because she almost did something she would have regretted in front of a bar full of witnesses. When she took Kyle Wagner down, there would be no witnesses; she'd make sure of it. And there was no doubt in her mind that she would take him down, like the rabid dog he was.

Turning, she realized she was already on the dance floor without even realizing she had crossed the bar. The tall, dark man in front of her spun her, his hand sliding to her waist as he pressed her against him, lifting her hand in the air as he began to sway. His smile sparkled, matching his eyes, and she could feel the hardness in his jeans press into her as he held her tight against him. "By the way," he said, "my name's Arlin Landry."

She smiled, feeling the blush warm her neck. "Pleased to meet you," she said. "I'm Eve Hartlow."

Six

Sorry for the intrusion there," Arlin said, enjoying the way she felt in his arms and especially against his growing cock. "However, the situation appeared to be getting a little tense for this place. Besides, you really looked like you needed a dance."

Her arms stiffened a little as she pushed back on him in a feeble attempt to put some distance between them, but he didn't allow it, keeping a firm grip on her waist as he pressed her against him. Her frustration was quite evident on her face, but Arlin just smiled at her. "Do you always insert yourself into people's lives like this?" she asked, giving up the struggle with a frustrated sigh. "First at my cabin and now here."

"Insert? I didn't insert myself anywhere. At your cabin, I wanted to make sure someone didn't run you over due to the way you carelessly walked in the middle of the road." She started to make a smartass comment, but he talked right over her. "And as for this dance, I'll be more than happy to let you return to your table and whoever that is making a nuisance of himself if you'd like, just say the word." He twirled her as she opened her mouth, and then jerked her back against him, his hand sliding lower down her back. He knew he wouldn't let her go back to that table even if she wanted. His tiger would rip out of him and tear the place apart if he did, and that didn't work out so well in Draven Falls. As it was, his tiger was hard to contain just witnessing the scene that took place at Eve's table. It would only have made things worse for him and probably for her as well if he lost control. "Some people would think I was chivalrous," he said, smiling.

She rolled her eyes, the gesture triggering his tiger's urge to take her outside and have his way with her. Did she really not know how he felt about her? The mating call was instant and powerful, but she was clueless, even after living with shifters for however long. "Do I look like I need someone to be chivalrous for me?" Her body stiffened again in his arms, her frustration shifting to irritation. "Do all men insist on portraying the white knight of sappy romances? Women aren't fragile creatures, you know. We can take care of ourselves." Just then two guys helped a drunk female across the floor and toward the front door, the sagging woman blubbering about wanting just one more drink and how she could drive herself home. Eve blew out a disgusted breath. "Well, most of us can, at least."

"A man being chivalrous has nothing to do with a woman being weak, and everything to do with him being a gentleman. It's about respect and giving the lady honor." He shrugged as they danced. "If anything, I think it elevates the woman in everyone's eyes, especially his, not diminish her."

A scuffle jerked their attention to the side, and Arlin watched as the man at the ladies' table snatched his arm out of the deputy's grip. The man turned and glared, first at Eve, and then at Arlin, who only smiled back, giving the man a wink as he did. "When a man doesn't treat a woman with chivalry, then that's what you get."

"That's what you get when the man is a class-A asshole." She shook her head. "I need to get back there. They shouldn't have to put up with him."

"Looks like they can handle things pretty well," he said, wanting to keep her in his arms. Of course, he would much rather have her in his bed, but he was willing to take what he could get for now. "Care to tell me what his problem is?"

"Outside of being a douche," she said with a sigh, and he knew then he'd do whatever it took to keep that man away from her. He wasn't sure what the deal with the guy was, but Arlin was damned sure going to protect her from him. She turned away from the scene at the table. "Kyle's just someone from my past who doesn't want to go away. He thinks me leaving somehow is a personal affront and can't handle it. He lost, and he despises losing."

They heard a crash and watched as Wes's bouncer, a burly man with arms the size of Arlin's thighs, grabbed Kyle by the arms and shoved him toward the front door. Kyle tried to turn back around, but the other man was taller, thicker, and quite a bit stronger. Even Arlin wouldn't have wanted to go up against him. The man's size didn't seem to be deterrent enough for Kyle, however. He snarled some nasty comment Arlin couldn't make out and then took a swing at the man. The bouncer ducked to the side, Kyle's swing going wide and missing its target, causing Kyle to spin and fall into the man's arms. People watching cheered as the bouncer grabbed Kyle by the nape of his neck and strong-armed him out the front door, shoving him into the parking lot. While it was fun to watch, Arlin knew it would just bring more trouble to Eve's front doorstep eventually. Arlin needed to know more about this Kyle guy so he could keep catastrophe from chasing her.

Turning her, Arlin smiled down at her, relishing how lost he could get in her pretty golden eyes. "Let's go join your friends and get another drink, shall we?"

She only nodded as she let him guide her off the dance floor and back to her table. He flagged down the waitress as they walked and ordered another round for the table. While he knew the alcohol did nothing for the others unless they were really determined to get plastered, Eve could use it to help calm her nerves.

"That man is an ass," Lainie said as they approached.

Arlin noticed Alanna stared at Eve with sympathy and care. "Are you ready to tell us the story now?" Alanna asked. "I don't think this is something you can keep quiet anymore. First, your cabin is ransacked—and I'd guess we're pretty sure we now know who did it—and now that ass shows up at Everglades to stir up trouble. I'll say that shows he's following you."

Adira reached out and placed a hand on Eve's, patting it sympathetically. "It's okay, sweetie. We all have reasons for being here. We just want to help."

Arlin decided to allow the women to talk Eve into sharing her story, while he just stood there and waited, hoping they would forget he was there until he had the information he needed. Luck was not on his side, however. All three women turned to him with questioning, suspicious eyes. He just stood there, smiling innocently.

"And who are you again?" Lainie asked, her eyes narrowed as she leaned on the table, staring at him with a deputy's intense glare.

Alanna cocked her head to the side as she stared at him. "That's twice now you've shown up right after something has happened to Eve. You wouldn't know about Kyle and what he's planning, would you? Perhaps his scout of sorts?"

Adira placed her palms on the table, blue sparks bursting from her fingers. She didn't need to say anything else.

Arlin held his hands up in surrender, just as the waitress brought over the round of drinks he ordered and set them on the table. "I'm the guy buying this round?" *Smile, Arlin boy, or they're going to have that bouncer toss you out on your ass as well.* "I'm Arlin Landry. I worked for Jed Hawkins at Shades back in Draven Falls, and I'm on vacation, staying at my brother's cabin."

"Nathan Landry's your brother?" Alanna asked, her gaze still saying she was suspicious.

"You came to Bull Creek for a vacation?" Lanie snorted a burst of laughter. "You didn't have high hopes, did you?"

He glanced at Eve, his smile genuine as he felt the stirrings of his tiger wanting to take her in his arms again right there. "I don't know. The place seems to have everything going for it so far—adventure, intrigue, pretty ladies. What else could you really ask for?"

"Some peace and quiet," Alanna said. "Thanks for the drinks and all, and trust me when I say I understand the urges your animal is feeling, but this is ladies night." She made a shooing motion with her hands. "Time for the male to leave."

He kept his gaze on Eve. "Do you want me to leave?" God, he hoped she said no.

However, she disappointed him, and he knew he would have a hard time getting his tiger to just walk away. "Thanks," she said, "but the four of us need to talk. I appreciate the distraction and the dance."

"And the beer," Adira said, holding up the bottle with a smirk.

Eve gave a soft laugh that was music to Arlin's ears. Still, she didn't change her mind. "Perhaps we can have drinks another time," she offered.

He nodded, not letting his smile slip, even though he felt more like growling. He lifted Eve's hand to his lips, kissing the back of her knuckles softly. "As you wish," he said, gazing up into her eyes. "You know where I'm staying if you need anything, or if that idiot comes back." He then said goodbye to the others and left, leaving money on the table for the drinks.

He fought the urge to look back as he reached the door, his tiger growling inside at the thought of leaving her unprotected. Yet, Arlin knew she was far from unprotected. She was surrounded by shifters and a witch. She had more protection than anyone else in the bar. No, he felt all right leaving her, and to be honest, he had something else on his mind that he needed to do before Eve returned home. He needed to make sure her cabin was secure enough for her return. She didn't need a reminder of the destruction that shattered her life earlier. While he might not be able to stand guard over her right then, he sure as hell could make sure her place was presentable for when she came home and not a reminder of what had happened.

Seven

Eve couldn't help but keep her gaze fixated on Arlin's ass as he walked away, his back straight, shoulders thick and square. If she was honest with herself, she really didn't want him to leave, but her friends deserved to hear the story first, just for putting up with her. Besides, she didn't know Arlin, where he was from, what he did, what he was really doing in Bull Creek. For all she knew, he could be in cahoots with Kyle to drive her crazy, keep her distracted, make her drop her guard enough so that Kyle could slip in and finish what he started months ago.

The memory sent a shiver down her spine.

Eve hit the floor, her back smacking against the coffee table before she landed on the carpet. Her face stung from where Kyle backhanded her. The only plus to it was seeing him shaking his hand from where it hurt him as well. Her joy was short-lived, however, as he reached down, yanking her partway off the ground only to slap her again, her head snapping back, only to spring forward again for him to repeat it, over and over. She tried to fight him, but he just laughed at her, daring her to hit him again. For every one of her blows that struck him on the shoulders or arms, he'd land two on her face. He squeezed her so hard at one point, she had bruises on her arms for weeks. Bruises covered the rest of her, as well, from where he knocked her around the house, slamming her into the furniture and walls.

"I told you," he snarled, "I don't like other people sniffing around my woman. Yet, you just had to flirt with that waiter tonight, didn't you? Didn't you?"

She tried backing away, doing a backward crabwalk until her back hit the couch, halting her escape. He reached down, gripping her shirt front and yanking her to her feet. "I wasn't flirting," she cried out. "I just smiled at him. That's all. I never flirt with anyone, Kyle. I swear."

"I was there," he shouted, his spittle spraying her face. "Are you calling me a liar? Are you telling me I didn't see what I saw?"

"No, Kyle, I would never say that. I promise. I'm only saying what I did. Or rather didn't do. I wasn't flirting. Stop hitting me. Please." Tears streamed down her face, her pleas echoing off the walls. At one time, she hoped her neighbors would call the cops, but after the third time of no one hearing anything, she gave up. This was her life from now on, and everyone around her must have thought she deserved it, because no one ever came to her rescue.

"You lie! You always lie. You're always flirting with men we meet. If you do that in front of me, what the hell do you do behind my back? I always treat you so well, give you everything you want, and this is how you treat me?" He hit her again. And again. And again.

And all she could do was take it, crying, begging for it to end, but she knew it wouldn't until he spent all of his anger on her. When it finally ended, him throwing her down on the ground and kicking her for good measure, he spit on her and walked toward the front door. "I don't know why I keep putting up with you," he snarled. "You're just lucky I do."

She straightened against the couch, doing her best to appear brave, strong. "I don't need you. I can escape this life. I will escape it." It was her mistake, mouthing off to him, trying to put up a front, posturing. She should have just kept her mouth shut and snuck out once he left. Then there would be no more beatings, no bruises and cuts, no more pain.

He spun on his heels, stomping his way back to her. She sat there, her chin held up, her back straight. He backhanded her, her head snapping to the side, and she took it. He did it again, grabbing her hair and holding her head still. He leaned down, snarling, his lips twisted in a nasty pinch. "There is no escape. Never. You and I will always be together." He shoved her back on the couch. "I'm going for a beer. Clean this mess up. Consider it your punishment for embarrassing me in public."

Eve watched as he walked away, barely closing the front door behind him. She didn't know how long she sat there, huddled on the floor, crying her eyes out. It seemed like hours, but in reality, only a few moments passed.

When the sobs finally subsided, she wiped her eyes as well as her nose, with the back of her hands, her sniffles loud in the quiet that swallowed the tiny home after the storm that was Kyle Wagner.

She stared at the mess, the broken coffee table, the knocked over lamps and knickknacks. She needed to clean the disaster of his anger up before he came back, or she knew there would be more beatings. It was her life. She deserved it, she knew, for whatever she did wrong in her life. This was her punishment. Kyle was her penance.

She wiped her face again. That is, he was as long as she allowed his abuse to continue, and she was tired of allowing it. Pushing herself off the floor, she decided Kyle was wrong. She could escape. She would *escape.*

She went to her room and stuffed her clothes and anything else she could grab into a green garbage bag and tossed it into the trunk of her car. She didn't even turn around to take a final look at what was her home for the past three years. All she wanted was to escape.

And she did.

"Oh, baby," Alanna reached out and squeezed Eve's hand when the story was finished. Pity and sympathy was the last thing Eve wanted from her friends.

"How in the hell did he find you?" Adira asked, her arms folded, one on top of the other on the table as she stared at her friend. "It's not like Bull Creek has a massive spot on a map. I wouldn't have known it even existed except for Agatha Rochester sending me to help Dimitri with the coyotes."

"Oh my god, my mother!" Eve snatched her cell phone out of her purse and punched her mother's name. *If Kyle's hurt her...*

Eve let out the breath she held until her mom finally

answered the phone, cheerful and perfectly fine. And talkative. Eve almost regretted calling to check on her. The others stood there, sipping their drinks as they waited for Eve to get off the phone with her mother.

Once she was finally able to hang up, she grabbed her beer and took a long swig. Setting the bottle back on the table, she blew out a deep breath, letting the stress roll off her shoulders. "Well, needless to say, Mom's fine."

The others just laughed as some of the tension relaxed from around the table.

"Let's get one more round and then head home," Adira suggested.

Eve stared at her beer bottle. *Home. How can I go back to that place?*

"Why don't you crash at my place tonight?" Alanna suggested. "Then tomorrow, we can get your windows repaired and clean up the rest."

Eve nodded. While she didn't want to sleep anywhere else besides her cabin, she knew it would be miserable in the condition it was in right then. A night to gather her strength would be best, even if not ideal.

"Now that we're pretty sure Mr. Scumbag did it, I can steer my investigation his way and see what I can dig up," Lainie said. "We're not going to allow him to get away with it."

Adira nodded her agreement. "I can also make wards specific to him to keep him from getting onto your property. He won't reach you so easily next time."

Eve sighed, her lips pressed into a thin line. She didn't

want there to be a next time, but she knew if he traveled this far to get her, Kyle would not give up. She appreciated her friends' help, but she wanted to take care of herself. She *needed* to take care of herself. They may not understand it, but being self-reliant was important to her. She would not allow herself to be the helpless victim ever again. She had allowed it too long as it was.

Eight

Arlin drove to his brother's cabin first. If he knew Nathan at all, and he did, there would be a pile of unfinished projects in the shed behind the cabin. Once he had scrounged around enough, gathering plywood, nails, and a hammer, Arlin set about gathering up whatever cleaning supplies he could find. In a box tucked into the back of the shed, he also found some old drapes he thought would work for now to replace the shredded ones he saw earlier at Eve's cabin. They probably weren't what she would pick — not his mate — but they would do for now in order to get rid of the reminder of what that creep did to her cabin. While he wished she would have told him the story with Kyle and the threat the man posed, he refused to allow Eve to return home and find her cabin still a mess. She deserved better than that, and he would damn well make sure she got it. He would get the story later. For now, he just wanted to take care of his mate-to-be.

He loaded everything into his car and headed back to Eve's place, backing into her drive so that the supplies in the trunk of his vehicle were more accessible and quicker to reach. The first thing he did once he was out of the car, was turn on her porch light, luckily one thing Kyle didn't destroy. With the light on, he set about hooking up power cords and measuring the windows. Plywood wasn't the best answer, but it would keep the weather and small creatures out until she could replace the glass.

Once he had the windows boarded up, he hung the drapes he found at his brother's, making sure he picked the glass out of the windowsill before he did. At least from the inside, there would be some semblance of normalcy. Arlin then set about the task outside of picking up the shattered pots, taking care to save all the plants he could. He'd plant them for now, making sure the roots were well-tended until she decided what she wanted to do with them again. He swept the dirt from the porch, again making sure to sweep up the glass from the broken windows. The red paint on the front of the cabin would be the worst thing to clean up, and Arlin had to admit, he wasn't sure he could do it completely. Still, he was determined to give it his best shot. Eve didn't need that flashing reminder when she pulled into the driveway.

As he tied a knot in one of the garbage bags he filled, he heard tires on gravel announcing someone turning into the driveway. He panicked at first, worried she had returned before he could finish. With the way she dismissed him at the bar, as well as the way she snapped at him when he saw her here earlier, he wasn't sure of the reception she would give him if she caught him at her place now, regardless of his motives. He blew out a breath of relief, however, when he noticed the truck pulling in behind his car, and Dimitri sitting behind the wheel. Arlin walked out to his car, the bag of trash in his hand, as he watched the other man turn his truck off and slide out of the driver's seat.

"I thought I saw lights on when I passed by," Dimitri said as he walked to the front of his truck, while Arlin tossed the trash bag into his trunk to haul away. "I wanted to make sure Eve hadn't returned and attempted to stay, or that whoever did it hadn't returned to do more damage."

Arlin nodded. "Neighborly of you. It's just me. I didn't want her to come home and see the chaos again. She's still with the ladies at Everglades, so I thought I'd try and see what I could do before she came home."

"I should have considered that, but I wasn't sure when Chet's team would be finished." Dimitri glanced around the place, giving an appreciative nod. "Seems like you did a pretty good job, though. Anything left I can help with?"

Arlin chuckled. "Just make sure she doesn't kill me when she finds out I did it."

Dimitri laughed as he leaned on the side of Arlin's car. "Eve's a pistol, I'll give you that. I'm not sure what her story is, but my guess is that something tragic happened for her to be here. She's never opened up to anyone, even those she classifies as friends."

Arlin closed the trunk, before walking to the front of his car, placing his hands on the hood, and sliding his ass up onto it. "Does everyone here have some tragic past?"

Dimitri shrugged his thick shoulders as he turned his gaze out to the dark woods around the cabin. "Not perhaps what you and I would call tragic, but most have something they want to escape, even if it's life outside of here and crowds." Then he turned his focus back to Arlin, and Arlin felt the scrutiny under those brows. "Even you, as I hear it. As I said earlier today, Jed gave me a heads up that you were coming to Bull Creek. He told me about the incident at Shades."

Arlin took a deep breath, wishing Jed would have at least warned him that he said something to Dimitri, but understanding why the alpha of Bull Creek needed to know. "Well, I'm not sure exactly what he told you, but I can assure you that's not a habit of mine. Some drunk decided he wanted the attention of a lady who didn't want to give it to him. It would have been fine if he had just left when he was told to get out, but before he did, he insinuated that he was going to wait outside for her to finish what he had started. I can usually keep my tiger in check, but it seems we both lost control that night, and I shifted before I could tamp down the rage that flooded my senses. By the time it was over, the asshole was pretty beaten up with tiger marks across his face, the girl crying, and Jed was shooing me out of town." He shrugged, glancing off into the distance. "I decided to take my brother up on his offer to use his cabin." The irony of Arlin's situation was not lost on him. The fact that he was very close to being in the same predicament that made him leave Draven Falls in the first place troubled him a little, but only a little.

"Everyone comes to Bull Creek for a different reason," Dimitri said. "As long as those reasons don't interfere with the other people here, it's all good." Then he cocked his head, and Arlin had a sick feeling he knew the next topic of conversation. "So, earlier when you arrived after Eve discovered her cabin vandalized, was I imagining the tension between the two of you as well as the...scent that tends to attach itself to a mating call?"

With a sigh, Arlin shook his head. "No, which is another reason I can't allow her to come home to a disaster." He turned his gaze to Dimitri, and he knew the fire of his tiger's over-protectiveness blazed in his eyes. "And we know who did it. The deputy is looking into it, but it seems there's an ex that doesn't like being an ex. He discovered she was here and made his presence known at Everglades."

"And your tiger..?"

"Growled, but I kept him in check. Instead, Eve and I danced while your sister took care of Kyle."

"Kyle?"

Arlin nodded. "The name of the ex-boyfriend. Or ex-husband. I'm not really sure which. She told me to leave before the story came out."

Dimitri chuckled, and Arlin found himself smiling as well. "Told, huh? That sounds like the spirited nature of a Bull Creek woman," Dimitri said. "Just because someone is escaping something, doesn't mean they're weak or timid. I don't know of one person here who wouldn't step up to the plate if needed. It was a mess a couple of weeks ago when some coyote shifters tried to run most everyone off, but the people of Bull Creek stood their ground and had each other's backs. We're a family here, tighter than any other shifter family I've ever known."

"Sounds like a great place to be," Arlin said. And he meant it. He needed a family around him like the Hawkins surrounded each other. If he was honest, he was kind of hoping his brother, Nathan, would have been here when he arrived. It had been too long since Arlin had seen his family. "Family is important, whether it's blood or commitment."

"It's about love and a common ground. I don't envy your road with Eve. She's a spunky gal, but also very shielded. You're going to have your work cut out for you there."

Arlin just smiled. "I like a challenge."

"Be careful what you wish for around here."

Both men laughed a little, knowing full well that any lady worth having had some spunk to her and could keep her man on his toes while making him feel like a king at the same time.

"Well, I'll let you get to it," Dimitri said, pushing himself away from Arlin's car with a bump of his ass, "if you're sure there's nothing I can do to help. If you need anything, just give me a yell. I'm two roads over, cabin in the middle."

"Thanks, I appreciate it."

Arlin watched him go, thinking Dimitri an affable enough fellow. The man seemed to have the right balance of nonchalance and authority, while remaining friendly. He was probably an outstanding leader for Bull Creek where a diversity of personalities existed and everyone hid something. *I'll fit right in,* Arlin thought as he walked around the cabin to gather up the rest of his belongings.

Once everything was loaded up, he turned back to eye his handiwork one more time. He hoped she'd be pleased with what he did, at least happy that he finished the major cleanup. He wished he could be there to see her reaction, but seeing him again would more than likely not go over so well. Then he grinned as an idea struck him. *Seeing me may not go ever so well, even if I stay hidden in the woods. However, my tiger can be a little stealthier than me.*

With his mind made up, he hopped into the driver's seat, started the car, and drove back to his brother's cabin. He only hoped he had enough time before Eve returned.

He didn't bother to put away his tools or supplies yet. There would be time later for his own cleanup. He wanted to get back to Eve's cabin. He stripped, tossing his clothes recklessly onto the top of his car, and as soon as he was naked, shifted, his tiger fur oozing from his skin as his bones popped and twisted, arms and legs becoming the legs of his tiger, feet and hands becoming paws. Once the transformation was complete, he bounded into the woods to avoid possible drivers and made his way back to Eve's cabin. Too bad she didn't know she was his mate yet, a situation he needed to remedy quickly, for the night could have gone down a more erotic path. The snap of dry leaves and twigs sounded under his massive paws as he weaved through the woods, memories of her body pressed to his bringing a frustrated snarl from the beast that consumed him.

Nine

The ladies finished that last round and then called it a night. Emotions were strung tight as Eve's tale still reverberated in everyone's minds. Alanna followed Eve back to her cabin to gather what she needed for the night and the next day, insistent that Eve not be alone. Eve didn't argue. The attack on her cabin had been a violation that left her feeling dirty.

It wasn't a long drive, the night quiet and the traffic light, but it was long enough to allow Eve's nerves to once more be set on edge. She didn't look forward to seeing her cabin trashed again, the damage Kyle inflicted, a reminder that her past had returned. Sheriff Einstein had not permitted her to clean anything up until his crime scene unit processed the place, which would probably make more of a mess left for her to clean and fix. Now it was too dark to see the disaster

Kyle made of her home enough to clean it up, even if she had the stomach for it. Alanna was right. Eve needed to sleep somewhere else because her place wasn't secure. Not just from prowlers tempted by broken locks, but also from nocturnal critters that weren't the shifter variety as well as bugs, mosquitoes being the worst. She dreaded the cleanup job ahead of her and was more than willing to put it off one more night.

She was about to make herself sick just thinking about it when she pulled into her driveway, prepared to witness the nightmare all over again. Yet, what confronted her was not what she expected. Her jaw dropped as she stared at her cabin, confusion furrowing her brow. *What the..?* The windows had been boarded up, plywood covering the broken glass. The front porch had been swept, all the fractured pots picked up and thrown away, while the dirt and ripped up plants were swept from sight. Some of the plants were even planted in the ground around the front of her cabin in a quick effort to save them. Someone had also tried to wash away the words that Kyle spray painted on the front of her cabin, the spot now a dull smear of red. *Who would do this?*

Stunned, she turned her car off as she opened her driver's door, her face still a mask of bewilderment. Stepping out into the night air, she turned as Alanna pulled in behind her, her face also a mask of confusion. As soon as her friend stepped out of her own car, Eve asked, "Did you know someone was doing this?"

Alanna shook her head. "Nope. I didn't expect Chet and

his team to be done with it in time to do anything to it tonight."

Together, they entered the cabin through the front door, which had also been repaired, the lock replaced and secure, or as secure as it could be in its condition. Eve could only stand in the doorway, barely making room for Alanna to enter as well. Everything had been picked up and a feeble attempt of order made. Anything broken was cleaned up and thrown away, while the place had been swept, the glass inside the house picked up and tossed into the trash, which itself had been carried off. Even new curtains replaced the old, shredded ones. Except for the boarded windows, it almost looked as if the break-in never happened. "I don't understand," Eve whispered.

"Don't look to me for answers," Alanna said. "I'm just as surprised as you are. You're still not staying here, however. The door may be locked, but those windows are not so secure. Put a bag together for tonight, and we'll head to my place."

Eve nodded, still dumbfounded, as she trudged her way through her cabin to her bedroom, trying to make sense of the scene around her. Who would have done this? Not the Crime Scene Unit. They destroy in their quest to investigate, not clean up. Who else would have known they were finished? She froze, Kyle would have known if he watched the place. She shook the thought from her mind. Kyle wouldn't waste his time fixing his mess. He'd want her to deal with the aftermath of his chaos like he always did, a reminder of his power, his rage, as well as her place in life, his life. So, who then? She didn't have a clue.

It didn't take long for her to put an overnight bag together. She only grabbed the bare necessities, eager to be out of the cabin, and the memory of Kyle and his vandalism put behind her. Alanna followed her out as they made sure the place was as secure as possible considering its condition before heading to their cars. As Eve opened the driver's door, she paused a moment, looking around the place one more time. Movement in the woods to the east of her place snagged her attention, and she squinted, trying to make out what—or who—lurked there, at first worried that Kyle watched her. However, what she saw surprised her even more than if it had been her ex. Standing at the edge of the tree line stood the biggest tiger she could imagine, bigger even than the ones she had seen in the Orlando Zoo. He didn't move, just stood there watching her, his golden eyes blinking once as he dipped his head in her direction as if bowing.

She stared for a moment, a small smile turning up the corners of her mouth, not sure what to do, and then she collapsed into the driver's seat and started her car. She'd have to ask Alanna if there was a tiger shifter in Bull Creek. She hadn't heard of one before, but that didn't mean anything. People came to Bull Creek to hide who they were from the outside world, not draw attention to themselves.

She sighed, wishing she had been able to stay hidden, as well.

Glancing one more time at the woods, the only possible answer struck her. The tiger could only be one person. But why? Why him? Why her?

She sighed. Why now?

~ ~ ~ ~ ~

Arlin heard the voices from the front of the cabin as he neared a massive oak right at the edge of Eve's property line and instinctively slowed his pace, not wanting to be heard. He arrived just as both ladies left their vehicles. Through golden eyes, he stared as Eve stood there, staring at his hard work on her behalf, her face a mask of shock and surprise. *But not fear.* He worried she might misconstrue the intentions behind the good deed, thinking it more of an intrusion than a helping hand. He watched as they went inside, each of Eve's steps tentative, cautious. He shifted slightly, hoping to get a better angle for when she exited the cabin, hoping Alanna tagged along to whisk her away from the chaos.

He didn't have to wait long before he heard footsteps on the front porch again. Turning his attention back to the cabin, he watched both ladies exit, Eve with a bag in her hand. He let out a sigh of relief. *She's staying at her friend's place. Good.*

Keeping his gaze riveted on her, he watched as Eve neared her car, opened the door, and threw her bag in the front seat. Then she froze, her back straightening, and very slowly turned her gaze to where he stood. He braced himself, ready to run if she should scream out. Their eyes locked, it seemed, even though he couldn't tell if she could see him in the dark. He stood to his full height, his legs planted, back straight, just in case she could see him, and then he gave her a small bow of his head. She stared for a moment, her face unreadable, before smiling and getting into her car.

Arlin remained still until her taillights vanished, and only then did he make his way back to his place, pride at the knowledge that he pleased her with his work puffing out his chest. Perhaps there was hope for this mating yet.

Ten

What the hell were you thinking? I know that was you in the woods last night, so don't even deny it. Were you standing guard or something? Protecting the poor weak female?" Eve stood on Arlin's front porch, doing her best to ignore how sexy he looked standing there in his doorway clad only in his gray pajama pants. Lust was not something she needed to feel right now, wanting to hang on to her anger just a while longer. She'd think about how much she wanted to jump his chivalric bones later. "What? You just randomly go around cleaning up people's cabins? Sticking your nose in where it doesn't belong? Why are you always around anyway?"

He stood there, mouth parted slightly in his shock at her outburst. It took him a moment to get his voice, and she relished every second he struggled. She ignored how cute the masculine specimen appeared caught off-guard right then, not needing the distraction. "I...I just...you know...wanted to help," he said with a shrug. He glanced down at the coffee mug in his hand, holding it up to her. "Want some coffee? Fresh pot."

"What I want is to not be cosseted like some weak, pathetic female." She stared at his coffee mug. "And a cup of coffee." He grinned, and she felt her anger slipping away at the twinkle in his golden eyes.

Pushing the door to his cabin open wide, he motioned with a tilt of his head for her to enter. Keeping the scowl on her face, she walked past him, determined not to give him the satisfaction of knowing how wet he made her or how her pussy throbbed right then. As much as she hated the idea that he took care of her last night, fixing her cabin and keeping an eye on her, protecting her in a way, from another sneak attack from Kyle, she couldn't get past the feeling that overwhelmed her of someone actually putting her needs first, instead of their own. Kyle had been a user, sucking her dry in his attempt to bully her into submission. His words made her feel weak as if she had no better option than to suffer at his hands. Arlin was different. Much different.

"Look," she said as she walked over to his kitchen counter, "it's not that I don't appreciate what you did at my cabin. Or that you even gave me a distraction at Everglades last night when Kyle showed up." She turned to face him, surprised when he was almost on top of her. She hopped back a couple of steps, giving a little yelp of surprise to which he just chuckled as he walked around her to the cabinets. "Sorry, I'm a little jumpy, I guess." She took a deep breath, crossing her arms over her chest. "Anyway, thank you for all of that, but I need to take care of myself. I'm not used to relying on others. I did that once, and it didn't turn out so well."

Arlin pulled a mug from the cabinet, his back muscles rippling as he stretched, and then filled the cup with coffee. When he turned to face her, offering her the cup, she noticed how golden his eyes were, a definite sign that he was a shifter, and how strong his jawline appeared, the dimple in his left cheek when he smiled only adding to his charm. She took the cup from him, holding it with both hands against her chest.

"Kyle?" he asked, his voice soft, not pushing her.

She appreciated the care he took in his curiosity. Nodding, she said, "He wasn't always such a brutish dick. At first, he was romantic in the whole bad boy kind of way, only the bad boy became a worse man, and he expected me to be his punching bag, taking out all his frustrations on me, blaming me for his failures in life." She shrugged. "Somehow, he made me believe I deserved it, that I couldn't do any better than him."

Arlin sipped his coffee while she talked, licking his lips when he pulled the cup away from his mouth. She watched his tongue as it glided across the redness of his lips, imagining it on her sex, her hands on his head... She shook the images out of her mind. *Now is not the time, Eve girl.*

"Until you didn't believe it anymore, obviously. Otherwise, you wouldn't be here."

She nodded, agreeing with him. "One night, he hit me one

too many times, and I escaped. That was actually what I told him before I left, that I was escaping."

"Which is why he wrote those words on the front of the cabin." Arlin nodded his understanding. Yet, she doubted anyone could understand her world unless they lived through the hell she endured.

"He thinks he's going to make me go back with him, I'm sure, but I won't. Not now, not ever. I'll kill him first."

He stared at her, his gaze measuring her, the sincerity of her words. Yet, she meant it. She wouldn't allow Kyle to hurt her ever again. The time of being his victim was over.

Then Arlin nodded as he set his coffee cup on the counter behind him. Stepping up to her, he cupped her cheek with the palm of his hand as he gazed into her eyes. "I know you don't want to be cosseted, and I promise, I never intended that, but Eve, I can't just let you handle this on your own. That's not how it works."

"How what works? Arlin, you don't even know me."

"You're right; I don't. However, that pesky tiger inside of me already scented everything about you that he needs and has claimed you as his. We're mated in his eyes." He gave her that dazzling smile of his. "And to be honest, I'm quite happy with his choice. We'll deal with Kyle, one way or another, but we'll do it together."

She felt the pounding of her heart in her chest, felt the warmth of his hand on her cheek, the promise in his eyes. She had lived around shifters for a while but thought all their habits and traditions were strictly for them. "But I'm not a shifter…"

"You don't have to be. Then again, you may be once I mark you." He shrugged. "It'll be fun to find out." He winked at her. "I'm not going anywhere, Eve, and you won't be facing Kyle alone. I'm sorry he did that to you, for everything he's ever done to you. You deserve so much more, and I swear, I'm going to spend the rest of my life proving it to you." And then his lips were on hers, pressing against her, warm, his tongue slipping between them, into her mouth, tasting her, claiming her, as he squeezed her tight against him.

She surrendered to his kiss, his hardness pressing into her, stirring the honey between her legs, her passion, a passion she thought squelched long ago, into a roaring fire. She needed him. Now.

She raked her nails up his back, bringing a moan from his lips, his arms flexing, holding her tighter. Her pussy quivered at his strength. It had been too long since arms held her that weren't attached to hands hitting her. With Arlin, she just melted into him, unable to get close enough, needing to feel all of him.

And then he stopped, holding her back at arm's length as he looked into her eyes. She knew he wanted her, could see the hunger in his eyes, so the fact that he waited to claim his prize confused her. And irritated her, as well. "What?" she asked, a little harsher than she intended. "Please don't tell me you're going to pull that gentleman card. Trust me, now is not the time."

"I don't want to stop, believe me, but this is stronger than just a chance encounter. My tiger already scented you as his mate, Eve. I may not be able to stop myself from marking you." He gave her a sheepish smile and a shrug. "I haven't exactly been able to control him lately. That's why I'm here as a matter of fact. If you're not ready to be marked, then I think it safer that we just stop."

Stop? He really thinks I can stop? "Can't you shifters ever just fuck? What is it with the mate thing all the time? I mean, Alanna and Josh can fool around without marking each other, so why can't you?"

"I could if my tiger hadn't already marked you in his mind. Now the pull is too strong for me to risk it without you knowing what the consequences could be. I can't treat you like any other woman at the bar last night, because the truth is, you're not like any other woman."

You have got to be kidding me. Eve rolled her eyes. This is not how she saw this going. She was finally willing to give herself to someone, and he turned all righteous and caring on her. Of course, she hadn't seen herself throwing herself at him when she first arrived, either. When she pounded on his door earlier, she was pissed. Now, she was still pissed, but for a whole other reason.

Like the shifters she lived around, Eve growled. *The first time I'm ready to give myself to someone and this happens.* She reached for the knife at her waist, pulling it out and stabbing his counter with it so hard the thunk of the blade sinking into his countertop echoed in the cabin. "Are you going to fuck me or not?"

He smirked at the knife, still vibrating where she thrust it into the counter. "As long as you know the risks, my little warrior." He reached out, grabbing her by the waist and pulling her tight against him, his cock pressing into her. "I'll try to be as careful as possible not to mark you, even though I so badly want to do so." He reached for her shirt, claws poking out of his fingertips, and she could see the glint in his golden eyes, the hunger there for her. Her breath caught in her throat as fear clutched her chest. Perhaps, she shouldn't have been so aggressive.

With a growl of his own, he ripped her top, tearing it from her body to fall in shreds to the floor. He lifted her in the air, Eve wrapping her legs around his waist as he turned and carried her to his bedroom, where he dropped her unceremoniously onto his bed. She bounced, her arms bracing herself on the mattress as she stared at him with wide eyes.

He didn't give her time to react as he reached for the buttons on her jeans, ripping the zipper downward. Gripping the waistband on her pants, he yanked them off her body, lifting her in the air as he did, stripping them down her legs, and tossing them carelessly to the floor. His lips turned up into a passionate grin as he reached for his own waistband, making quick work getting his pajama pants off, his boxers going with them. Once he was naked, he crawled up her body, his grin mischievous, hungry. "I believe you wanted something," he teased as he slid the head of his cock up and down her wet slit.

She tried to say something—anything—but nothing came out. She reached up, grabbing his shoulders, her nails digging into his flesh as she took a deep breath. His presence over her overwhelmed her. She wanted it. God, she wanted it.

He leaned down, kissing her, his lips warm on hers. Then he thrust deep into her, his cock spreading her before him until his hips slapped hers, her moans slipping out past their lips, her back arching. He held himself there, buried deep inside of her, as he broke the kiss and gazed into her eyes with a smirk. "Is that what you wanted, Little Warrior?"

"Yes," she moaned, her voice a throaty whisper. "Oh god, yes." She thrust her hips up at him, grinding against him to prove the desperation of her need.

He just grinned as he slid out and then thrust back inside of her, and then he kept thrusting, pounding into her. She clutched his shoulders, wrapping her legs around his waist again, pulling him into her as deep as he could go. She heard him growl in her ears, keeping his mouth away from her shoulders, his arms cradling her head. Harder he thrust, faster, the sounds of flesh on flesh filling her ears, mixing with her moans.

She slid a hand down his shoulder, slipping it down his chest, her hand on his nipple, toying with it between her fingers. As he thrust into her, his body shifted upward, his chest hovering over her face. Without even thinking, she licked his flesh, her mouth opening as he drove into her again. Then she bit him, her teeth sinking into his pectoral. He cried out, thrusting into her harder, his body tensing, his cock twitching.

She ran her tongue over the flesh between her teeth, biting just a little harder before letting go. His cock throbbed once, and then she felt his orgasm rip through him, filling her. It was enough to send her over the edge, her body tightening into a tense ball as her climax rippled through her, her breathing ragged gasps as she cried out.

She felt his cock slip out of her as he rolled to her side, his arm draped over her stomach, his breathing heavy in her ears. She giggled as she placed a hand over his. "Is that what you meant by a bite mark?"

He just chuckled as he shook his head. "Oh, Little Warrior, this is going to be so much fun, I can tell."

You have no idea.

Eleven

Arlin kept her in bed for most of the morning before she forced him to get up and fix her some breakfast. As he stood in front of the stove, he ran his hand over her teeth marks embedded in his chest, shaking his head at how sensitive the marks felt. *Now, this is definitely a twist on things,* he thought with a chuckle. *I wonder if I'll turn into a human.* He flipped the stove on and then rummaged around his cabinet for a pan in which to fry some bacon. He glanced behind him at her knife still sticking straight up on his counter. She definitely deserved some bacon.

He heard her coming from the back bedroom and turned his head as she shuffled into the front room wearing nothing but an old T-shirt of his. His tiger growled, and he had to agree with his animal's assessment, although he would have much preferred she came out of the back room naked. The image of her under him, the freckles across her pale breasts, the sexy vulnerability she displayed, made his cock twitch even now. He'd never get tired of looking at her body.

Or touching it, caressing her flesh with his hands, tasting her skin with his lips. *Down boy, or she'll never get her breakfast.* He shook his head, but not the image from his mind, as he walked over to the fridge for the bacon and eggs.

When he turned around, he gestured to the counter. "I made some coffee if you're interested."

She ran a hand through her sandy hair, the T-shirt climbing up her bare legs as she did. Both he and his tiger purred, and he had to tamp down the urge to press her against the wall and bury his cock between her legs, saying the hell with breakfast. He took a deep breath and turned back to the stove, setting the food on the counter next to the knife. "So, am I forgiven for cleaning up your cabin?" he asked, needing to change the subject before he acted on his impulses.

She walked over to the counter, leaning back on it, propping herself up with her hands, which made her shirt ride high on her thighs again, one leg swinging back and forth. "I think the jury's still out on that." She reached over, pulling the hilt of the knife back and letting it twang as she released it. "I mean, after all, I did have to threaten you in order to get you to take me to your bed. Not really a good impression, you know?"

He slipped some bacon into the pan and then leaned over, kissing her on the lips. "I promise, you'll never have to threaten me again."

"Good," she said, with a curt nod, as he pulled away. Out of the corner of his eye, he saw her reach out and yank the knife from where it was stuck. "I'd hate to have to leave more holes in your counter."

"Yeah, I'm going to have fun explaining that to my brother."

She shrugged as she ran a finger over the edge of her knife. "Just tell him I did it. Nathan won't be surprised."

Arlin felt a twinge of jealousy stiffen his spine. "There isn't anything between you and my brother, is there?" He needed to have a talk with Nathan. And soon.

She giggled as she set the knife on the counter behind her. "And if there is?" Her eyes sparkled as she said it, and at first, he didn't know how to take it.

He turned to face her, an eyebrow cocked. "Then I think I'm going to be kicking my brother's ass." She laughed as if he was joking, but Arlin was far from joking. He grinned, however, as he reached for the eggs. After he cracked a couple into a skillet, he tilted his head as he looked at her from the corner of his eye. "Care to tell me about last night? Who that guy was?"

She sighed, turning her gaze to the floor, her lips pressed into a thin line. "He was a very bad decision that I thought was finished." She shook her head and then gave him the full story.

As she leaned back on the counter, her leg no longer swaying back and forth, telling the tale of Kyle's abuse, he continued to cook them breakfast, frying the eggs while the bacon sizzled. If her story hadn't been so dreadful, making his anger growl for a different reason than it did earlier, Arlin would be distracted with the way her legs kept drawing his gaze away from the stove. He took several deep breaths, focusing on the story she shared.

His anger boiled just below the surface with every instance she recounted of where Kyle beat her for his own failings. At the same time, his heart went out to her for everything she endured. He didn't feel sorry for her, not by a long shot. She may have suffered at Kyle's hands for a brief period, but she refused to be a victim for long. He glanced over at the knife on the counter, wondering how far she was willing to take it if Kyle came at her again. His tiger growled within him. *Don't worry, boy. That scumbag won't get the chance.*

As they sat down at the table to eat, she finished with her story. Her voice was soft, neutral in tone, as she spoke, her breathing even, almost as if she distanced herself from the story she told. He refused to reach out and hug her, even though that's exactly what he wanted to do. However, he knew she wouldn't appreciate it. Not in the least.

"And the knife?" he asked. "Is that something you carry now because of what happened with Kyle?"

She glanced back to the counter where the knife lay, her eyes distant as if looking backward in time. "It's more than just something I carry for protection. It's become a symbol of sorts." She shrugged, turning her attention back to him. "It reminds me that I don't need anyone else to protect me, that I'm a capable woman who doesn't need to rely on anyone else."

He scooped up a forkful of eggs as he nodded. "You know it's okay for other people to help you once in a while, right?" He shoved the eggs into his mouth, watching her.

She reached for her juice glass as she nodded. "However, there's a difference between getting help and being dependent upon someone. I was dependent on Kyle, which is why I suffered the abuse. I believed him when he said I couldn't do any better, and only he would take care of me, only he would love me."

"So, what finally broke?"

She grinned as she lifted the glass. "Not me." She waggled her eyebrows at him as she took a sip of her juice. Shrugging, she said, "He finally hit me one too many times, and I guess it knocked some sense into me. I realized Kyle would never change or stop or put me first, and if he wasn't going to do it, then it had to be me. So, as soon as he was out the door, I packed my bags with everything I could carry and ran." She sighed, setting the glass back on the table. "Sounds cowardly, doesn't it? I ran."

Arlin reached out, seeing the self-doubt in her eyes, and placed a hand on her wrist. "Not at all. What else could you have done?" He shook his head as he moved his hand, setting his wrist on the table next to his plate. "You only had one real option; get the hell out of there. Never doubt that."

She gave him a weak smile, and he knew she didn't believe what he said. He felt his tiger whine within him. *We'll prove it to her, boy. Don't you worry.*

When breakfast was over, Eve said she needed to get back to her cabin. Someone was due out to replace the glass in her windows, and a local of Bull Creek named Josh planned on replacing her locks with stronger ones. Arlin watched her get dressed, dreading every second of it. He wanted to go with her, stay by her side until Lainie put Kyle behind bars, but after everything Eve said, he really didn't think she'd take it as anything other than him believing her weak and coddling her. Eve Hartlow was anything but weak.

He stood on his porch after hugging her goodbye and watched as she walked down his dirt driveway, keeping his eyes on her until she turned and headed out of sight. He wasn't thrilled with her walking home alone, not with Kyle still out there. Keeping his eyes on his driveway, he slipped out of his pajama pants, dropping them carelessly in a heap on the porch. Once he figured enough time had passed, he shifted, legs and arms popping and stretching, feet and hands transforming into paws, the striped fur of a tiger oozing out of his skin as whiskers slid from his nose. It only took a few seconds, agonizing seconds to be sure, but ones he would endure to ensure Eve's safety. He hunched down on his back paws and then leaped off his porch, slipping into the woods between his cabin and Eve's. She may not want him beside her, babysitting, but that didn't mean he wouldn't keep an eye on her as best as he could. She just wouldn't know he did it. After all, what Eve didn't know, couldn't hurt him.

At least, that was his hope.

Twelve

S he left Arlin's cabin and, to be honest, the fact that he allowed her out of his sight amazed her. Considering she just met him yesterday, his over-protectiveness seemed quite obvious. And annoying. She would not permit anyone to cosset her ever again.

Then she grinned as she left his street and turned onto the dirt road leading to her own cabin. Of course, with the way he drove his cock into her, she just might permit him to try. She could still feel him between her legs, knowing her pussy lips were swollen and aching. Months had passed since a man made love to her, not that she would call having sex with Kyle making love, and she would savor the soreness for the rest of the day. She could have remained in bed all day enjoying his body. She chuckled. *The look in his eyes when I bit him was priceless. Shifters and their whole mate mark thing crack me up. Turning the tables on him was nice.* She sighed contentedly, slipping her hands into her pockets. She had heard all about shifters and how fast the attraction to their mates erupted. How could someone live in Bull Creek and not know the mating habits of shifters? However, she never understood it until that morning and seeing Arlin standing there in his pajama pants, shock covering his face at her outburst. God, it was so worth it. His assumption that she'd know why he did it and accept his actions baffled her. Men. Shifter men, especially.

Of course, she had to admit, as much as it annoyed her that he did it, she truly appreciated his cleaning up her place after the crime scene people left. The thought of returning home to a disaster, knowing Kyle had ransacked her place, was almost too much to stomach. Her mother really wasn't to blame for giving her location away. It wasn't like Eve told anyone why she left Kyle, feeling the shame usually associated with domestic abuse, even if it wasn't her shame to bear but Kyle's. She was embarrassed at the time. The truth was, she was still embarrassed, even though she tried to overcome it. Talking to her friends helped quite a bit. And to Arlin. Revealing her secret lifted the burden of keeping it from her shoulders, and she actually felt herself walking taller. None of what she endured had been her fault. Kyle was a sick bastard, who needed help. Serious help. He wouldn't get it from her, though. The only thing he would ever get from her was the point of her knife, and she would have no regrets about doing it.

Her eyes popped wide, as she jerked a hand to the sheath

at her waist. The empty sheath. She closed her eyes and groaned as she pictured her knife sitting on Arlin's kitchen counter. How on earth could she forget her knife? This is what happens when she allowed herself to become distracted.

Pausing in her tracks, she debated within as to whether or not she should go back and get it. With a shake of her head, she decided against it, realizing that she wasn't sure when the glass repair guy would arrive. For all she knew, the man already waited at her cabin, pacing, or giving up on waiting and leaving. She needed those windows fixed so she could stay at her own place tonight, instead of Alanna's. She liked her friend, but not as a roommate, and especially not with Josh trying to sneak into Alanna's bedroom late in the night. She giggled as she shook her head, beginning her trek again. For two shifters who knew all about mating, Alanna and Josh did everything except the marking. They were hornier than any other...

"So, I see without me, you've turned into a bed-hopper."

Eve jerked around to see Kyle standing there, staring at her with disgust on his face. Her heart raced, drumming in her ears, her breathing caught in her throat as fear shook her, making her knees, her arms, tremble. She slid a hand down her waist to the sheath, swallowing more fear as she remembered it was empty. She took a deep breath. *I will not be afraid. I will not be afraid.* "For the record," she snarled at him, "I'm not a bed-hopper as you say. Even if I was, however, it's no longer your concern or business. You gave up that right when you hit me that very first time. It just took me a while to realize it."

"I hit you?" he sneered. "You're blaming me for all of that? You were a sad individual when I met you. I made you into something, gave you everything, took care of you." His voice rose as he spoke, and she watched as he took a couple of steps closer. However, even though she trembled, she refused to back down. Oh, she was very much afraid, but she would face that fear. "Yet, you just couldn't stop pissing me off. You never appreciated everything I did for you. Selfish. You've always been selfish. Never satisfied." He was so close to her, she could feel the spittle from his outburst strike her face. She flinched but refused to move.

"Then you should be happy I left." She straightened her back, doing her best to appear taller, stronger. "Why are you following me?"

He shook his head. "You never appreciate what I do for you." He shrugged. "I was worried about you. I know how much trouble you have getting along with people and staying organized. I came here to make sure you were all right, and all I get for my trouble is a smart mouth and a snotty attitude." He reached out, gripping her arm and jerking her toward him, sneering into her face. "Is that any way to treat the man who's always taken care of you? Huh?"

"Let go of me, you ass!" Eve jerked her arm out of his grasp, trying to shove herself away from him. She spun a little, stumbling from the force of her reaction. "You don't own me." She turned back around, regaining her balance, only to feel him backhand her, sending her spinning around, stumbling to the ground.

Catching herself with her hands, the tiny pebbles digging into her flesh, she jerked her gaze back around to stare at him, tears stinging her eyes. He loomed over her, his eyes narrow slits as he growled at her. "I will always own you, Eve. Always." He straightened, his arms dangling at his sides as he gazed up the road. "I'm giving you until tonight to get your belongings and head back home." He gazed back down at her, an artificial smile turning the corners of his mouth up. "Don't make me come back for you." He winked, and then turned and walked off.

She watched as he walked away, his hands in his front pockets, his lips pursed as he whistled. If she had her knife, she'd run after him and sink the blade into his back.

Rustling could be heard off to the side of the road. She turned just as a giant tiger hopped over a fallen log and padded his way toward her. His lithe body moved with grace as he padded over to where she lay sprawled on the ground. When he reached her, he butted his head against her shoulder, pushing her slightly as he purred.

She sighed as she reached up and scratched his head, leaning into him. "It's okay, Stripes. I've suffered worse."

Arlin growled as he turned his face in the direction that Kyle vanished, sniffing the air.

Eve nodded. "Yeah, you just missed him." She moved her hand to scratch behind the tiger's ear as he growled louder. "Yeah, I wish I had just missed him, too." She fell back into him as Arlin sat on his haunches, his tongue lolling out the side of his mouth. *So much for escaping.*

Thirteen

Someone needed to die. Correction. Kyle Wagner needed to die, and he needed to die at Arlin's hands. What kind of a man hit a woman? Arlin twisted his hands on the steering wheel, his knuckles turning white from the pressure. If he had just arrived a couple of minutes sooner, he would have been able to sink his fangs into Kyle's weaselly body and put an end to the threat over Eve's head. It was time to make sure that her ex-lover knew that no meant no.

Once they arrived at Eve's cabin, Arlin had her call Alanna to come over with her boyfriend, Josh Rayburn, to sit with her. Boyfriend was a very loose term, Eve told Arlin. "The two of them are more like friends with extra, extra benefits who happen to have no one else with the same benefits," Eve said. "Apparently, Alanna has an issue with titles and roles, preferring everything to remain casual."

Arlin just laughed at that. When Eve asked him what was so funny, he only replied, "Little Warrior, those two sniff around each other like mates denied. I don't care what she's saying out loud; inside, her wolf wants to mate with Josh's panther."

"Can they do that?" she asked. "Have sex and deny the actual mating part?"

"They can do it, but it's not always easy or fun. They'll have to give in sooner or later or go crazy with the calling. It's a powerful pull on shifters."

Once the others arrived, Arlin left Eve in their capable care and headed for the sheriff's office. He wanted to get some type of restraining order on Kyle. It wouldn't work, of course, but it would at least show there was cause when Arlin just happened to over-react in defending Eve.

The sheriff's department was a small building, typical of what he would expect in a small town—single-story, brick exterior, with a brown shingle roof. The parking lot was small, and the inside had nothing in the way of security measures to keep the bad guys from going after the sheriffs. There wasn't even bulletproof glass in front of the receptionist, who happened to be a small, gray-haired lady with the thickest reading glasses Arlin ever saw. How she kept them on her nose was a miracle at best.

Stepping up to the desk, he asked if Lainie Everest was available and then was promptly told to take a seat as the woman stared at him over the top of her glasses as opposed to through them. He just smiled, withholding the chuckle that bubbled up, and took his seat. The hall behind the woman seemed to hold tiny offices off to each side, along with another hall breaking to the right. The noise was nonexistent as if everyone was out, and Arlin worried that he should have called first.

However, his wait wasn't long, and soon, Lainie walked out of one of the offices near the back of the hall and motioned for him to join her. Arlin smiled at the woman behind the desk, who only watched him through cynical eyes as he passed her. She was probably deciding whether or not he was culprit or victim.

"Arlin, right?" Lainie extended her arm, shaking his hand as he returned her grip, nodding at her remembrance of his name. "What brings you by?"

Arlin stepped in behind her, following her to her office. "Eve was attacked a little while ago," he said. "I want to file..."

"What?" Lainie came up short, spinning as she did, causing him to bump into her before he could stop his steps. "Why weren't we called? How bad is she?"

Arlin took a step back. "Not bad. He only hit her once before threatening her and walking away. I just missed him."

She arched an eyebrow at him. "Missed him?"

He nodded. "Yeah. I knew she didn't want me to follow her home, so I shifted into my tiger and worked my way through the woods between her cabin and mine. By the time I realized she hadn't made it home and backtracked, Kyle had already caught up with her and knocked her to the ground." He shrugged, giving a proud smile remembering Eve's determination when she told him what happened and how she wouldn't back down. "She wouldn't back down from him, and he made her pay for that insult. He also said he would come back for her in a few hours, and she had better be ready to leave. I want a restraining order to keep him away from her."

She looked at him sideways. "You really think a piece of paper is going to stop him?"

"Not at all," he said with a shake of his head. "But it starts a trail."

She glanced around them, making sure no one was listening. "Starting a defense?"

It was his turn to pop an eyebrow at her. "Let's just say, he won't hit her again. Ever."

Lainie turned and continued walking back toward her office, Arlin trailing behind her. "Well, a restraining order doesn't happen that fast. It'll take a couple of weeks after filling out the paperwork to get a hearing, but I can at least file a report and get it started. That'll be something."

"It'll take that long? Really? We can't do it faster?"

She entered the office, walking around the oak desk along the back wall. Arlin walked in behind her and stood in front of her desk as she sat down. Her words weren't what he wanted to hear, especially knowing Kyle would return later that night to carry out his threat.

He wasn't about to give up, however. "Seems odd that it would take so long if someone's life is being threatened."

Lainie sat in her desk chair, pulling herself up to her desk. "I agree with you but there isn't anything I can do about it. As sad as it sounds, no one's actually seen him do anything except make an ass out of himself at Everglades. We don't know what happened back where they came from, or even what he did before you arrived today."

"You think she made it up?" He couldn't believe what he heard. This woman was supposed to be Eve's friend. How could she not want to protect Eve? "I saw her on the ground right after he backhanded her." His tiger growled, and Arlin fought to keep the animal from losing his control. *Save it for Kyle, boy.*

Lainie shook her head as she folded her hands. "It doesn't matter whether I believe her or not, which for the record, I do. However, in the law's eyes, it's her word against his. No witnesses." She leaned forward as he took a seat. "And it's not a rare thing, either. Hell, twenty people are physically abused by intimate partners every minute here in the United States. And it's not just women. Men are victims as well. On a typical day, over twenty-thousand calls are made to domestic violence hotlines nationwide, and there's no stereotype for the victim; they come in all ages, races, religions, economic standings, and even sexual orientations. The problem is that most will keep it to themselves until it's too late, because they feel embarrassed or ashamed. Eve's a survivor. Not everyone is so strong. Quite a few victims suffer from a high rate of depression, which can even lead to suicide."

"And even with all of that, there's nothing we can do?"

She tilted her head to the side. "You said he told her he would come back to get her tonight?"

"No. Just that he expected her to pack and head back

home to him. If she didn't, he'd come back for her and make sure she regretted not obeying him."

"Obviously, she's not leaving, so my advice is to stay close to her and wait for him to screw up. I'll try to keep an eye out as well, and when we see him attack her, she presses charges, and I can lock his ass away for good."

"We have to allow her to remain in danger in order to catch the guy? Isn't that kind of the opposite of protecting her?" Arlin was not the sit and wait type of guy. He wouldn't risk anything happening to his mate while the police sat around on their asses. While the law might not be Lainie's fault, her enforcing it was. "I'm not going to allow anything to happen to Eve." He stared at Lainie through narrowed eyes. "You know I can't."

"Trust me, I know. Still, as far as the law is concerned, that's the best advice I can give you." Then she leaned forward even more, lowering her voice as she did. "However, you and I both know that some things can only be handled with a shifter type of justice. Protect your girl would be my personal advice."

Arlin nodded but didn't say anything. Protecting Eve had been his plan all along, regardless of what the law said. He wouldn't sit on his ass while Kyle made some move to hurt Eve. Arlin's tiger growled his agreement with a slip of fur oozing out of Arlin's arms to prove the point. The animal would take matters into his own hands—or rather paws—if he had to in order to protect his mate.

Don't worry, boy. I'm right here with you. Nothing is going to harm our girl. Arlin thanked Lainie for her time and then turned and walked out of her office. He had been away from Eve too long as it was and needed to get back to her. He wouldn't feel calm again until he knew he was there at her side to protect her; it didn't matter how many others were there already. Eve was his, and he would be the one to make sure Kyle did nothing else to hurt her. Not and be able to walk away from it anyway.

Fourteen

Eve tested the sharpness of her blade with her thumb before sliding it back into the sheath at her waist. The first thing she did when she arrived back at her cabin was select a new knife to replace the one she left at Arlin's. She would not be caught unawares again if Kyle reappeared, and there was no doubt that he would. If he followed her all the way to Bull Creek, then he wouldn't give up that easy, which meant his threats were more than threats; they were promises.

She walked back over to the kitchen counter, needing more coffee. Alanna had left a few moments ago, along with Josh and Ezra, after making sure the repairs were finished and Eve's cabin was safe and secure. She could tell by the look on Alanna's face that she didn't really want to leave, but Eve needed to be alone to figure out what she needed to do next. She didn't doubt that Kyle would be watching. Glancing at the front door—the locked front door—she wondered if she'd be able to spot him in the woods around her cabin. It only made sense that he'd be out there after threatening her to pack up and head back to where they had lived together. He'd want to know his threat worked.

He had to know there was no way in hell that she'd listen to him. There was no going back. He'd have to kill her first, and if it came down to one of them having to die, it would be Kyle Wagner. She'd be sure of that.

The sound of tires on gravel broke the silence. Panic gripped her for a moment as she stared at the front door. *No! I will not allow myself to fear him. Not anymore.* With her hand on the hilt of her knife, Eve walked to the window at the front of the cabin, blowing out a breath as she did. It was one thing to tell yourself to calm down and quite another for your body to listen to the pep talk.

Pulling the curtain back, she saw Arlin stepping out of his car, his gaze scanning the surrounding area. *He probably has the same thoughts I do, that Kyle is out there somewhere.* Then she couldn't help but giggle as she pictured Kyle crossing paths with Arlin's tiger. Kyle had no clue shifters even existed, so she could only imagine the look on his face when he actually saw one, and she highly doubted his first encounter would be a good one.

By the time Eve opened her front door, Arlin was taking the first step up to the porch. "Well?" she asked. "Were you able to accomplish what you wanted?"

He shrugged as he crossed his arms and leaned against

the porch pole. "Yes and no. I filed a report, but to be honest, according to Lainie, there just isn't much they can do until something further happens, and there are witnesses. Filing a restraining order takes over two weeks, and we don't have that kind of time."

She nodded her head, her sandy hair falling into her eyes. "I'm sure he'll be back around once he realizes I'm not packing up and hightailing it out of here."

Arlin glanced at her, a smile creasing his face as his gold eyes sparkled. "I'm glad to hear you're not planning on going anywhere."

"Hell no, this is my home. He can kiss my ass if he thinks he can scare me away from it."

Arlin took two steps, crossing the porch, and gripping her arms in his rough, massive hands. "No one kisses your ass, but me." He leaned down and kissed her, his lips warm, hungry.

Eve fell into his embrace, sliding her hands up his back to wrap around his shoulders as he held her. She felt his tongue part her lips, tasting her as she tasted him, his breath warm on her cheeks. She really hoped Kyle was watching right then, just to see how a real man treated a woman. Then she felt herself grinning, her kiss deepening. *Might as well give the ass a real show.* She slid her hand from Arlin's shoulder and across the ever-growing bulge in his pants. Gripping his cock through his jeans, she stroked his fire into a full blaze, feeling his body stiffen against her as his breathing grew huskier. She squeezed his shaft harder, urging it to life.

When Arlin broke the kiss, keeping her tight against him,

he grinned as he looked down at her. "I think we should take this inside," he said, taking a step toward the front door, urging her backward.

"Why? You don't like right here? Right now?" She pushed herself away from him as her hands went to the hem of her shirt, pulling it over her head and dropping it to the porch. Reaching behind her, she unclasped her bra and slid it off her shoulders to land on top of her shirt. "I thought shifters were past the whole shyness thing when it came to sex and nudity." She felt the cool afternoon air brush against her breasts, stirring her nipples to life. She didn't hesitate, but instead, reached for her pants button and stripped her jeans from her legs, taking her thong with them. She stared at him, grinning a shit-eating grin as she wiggled back and forth in front of him. "Are you saying you don't want me?" She walked around him until she could lean across the porch railing, her ass wiggling back and forth in front of him. "Is that what you're saying?"

She heard him growl as he reached for the bottom of his shirt to yank it off. "Little Warrior, I've warned you before about tempting me. Soon, I will not be able to hold my tiger back from marking you." His shirt slid over his head and joined hers on the ground. He took a step toward her as he undid his pants button. Before he slid them down his powerful legs, he reached out and ran a hand over her bare ass, bringing goose bumps to her flesh. She pushed back against him, pressing her ass into the palm of his hand. "And, I think, it'll be sooner than later."

She glanced at him from over her shoulder. "I don't want

you to hold back. I want you to take me. Claim me. Make me yours. Right here on this porch. Right now. Do it, Arlin. Do it now." She knew she taunted him, and even though she lived with shifters, she wasn't truly sure what the mark of a mate really meant outside of bonding two people together, but she was through worrying about it. She wanted Arlin and wanted Kyle to know she now belonged to another. *Let the bastard try to get me now.*

Arlin slid his pants down his legs, his boxers sliding down with them, and kicked them both to the side. She felt his hands return to her waist, and as she glanced back over her shoulder, could see the lust growling in his eyes. Her pussy dripped at what she witnessed. It was almost as if his animal was in full control, and when she felt the tiger's claws slip out of his fingertips and into her waist, she feared she may have made a mistake.

He positioned himself behind her, the tip of his cock teasing her passion's entrance. Yet, he didn't shove himself inside of her. Instead, he leaned down and whispered in her ear. "Don't think I'm not aware of the show we're making, Little Warrior." His breath felt heavy in her ears, warm against the side of her face. "For all of your bravado, this will make you mine forever, and I enjoy ravishing what's mine and don't care who sees it." His claws dug into her flesh just a little sharper as he thrust deep inside of her, the ache from where he took her this morning fresh as his cock speared into her, spreading her pussy open. Claiming her.

She cried out, her back arching, his chest pushing into her as he pounded her. Gripping the porch railing, it was all she could do to hang on during the ride. She felt her own nails dig into the wood, felt her body shuddering under the sexual assault he gave her, her pussy hungering for everything he gave. Faster, he drove into her, his grunts and growls stirring her own orgasm to the front. Her whole body felt like tendrils of electricity as she shoved herself back on his manhood, felt her pussy lips sucking his cock, her walls tightening around him, holding him inside of her. Gone were the thoughts of threats and Kyle, gone even was the idea that she and Arlin were fucking on the front porch of her cabin where anyone driving or walking by could see them. She didn't care. All she wanted right then was Arlin. His cock. His orgasm. His mark.

Her body shuddered, tightening as she felt her orgasm sweep through her. Arlin leaned over her, his deep voice a growl in her ear. "Mine." And then she felt his grip tighten as he sank his teeth—fangs?—into her, his cock twitching as he filled her with his cum. She cried out again, her whole body a tightrope of sensations as she stiffened in place, his presence over her, dominating her as the pain from his bite shot through her, mingling with her orgasm.

When his body softened, his grip loosening, she could feel him stand again, his cock slipping from her. She almost cried out again as the void filled her where his shaft was just a second ago. He placed a hand under her waist and helped her to stand, turning her as he did. She maintained her grip on the railing, her knees weak and shaky as she felt their lovemaking drip from her. Gingerly, she placed a hand over the bite mark, the pain sharp, intense. *Now, that bruise, I'm going to enjoy having.* She could feel the impressions of his teeth as she gently ran her fingers across the mark, wondering if it did all the things she had heard.

He gripped her waist, pulling her against him, the curls of his chest hair ticklish against her flesh. His smile captivated her as he gazed into her eyes, his expression still hungry, ready for more. "Now that you've made your point out here, why don't we go inside and continue where it's a little more comfortable?"

"What's the matter, Stripes? I thought animals liked the outdoors."

"Not when there's a perfectly good bed inside." He bent down and scooped her into his arms, carrying her inside the cabin and to the back bedroom. As he dropped her on the bed, causing her body to bounce slightly, he said, "There's much more room to maneuver right here, and I want to explore every inch of this body." He crawled on top of her, nibbling her as he did. "Biting. Licking. Tasting. It's going to be a busy morning. You'll want to be comfortable."

She laid back on the bed, her grin reaching her eyes. "I've got nothing but time." And before she knew it, they had explored their way out of the afternoon and into the evening, no longer caring that outside the cabin her attacker more than likely watched from the edge of the woods.

Fifteen

Arlin knew why she did it. He just wasn't sure having sex on the porch was the smartest decision right then. It was one thing to turn her nose up at Kyle and tell him to kiss off, and quite another to fuck another man on her porch as a way of informing Kyle that they were definitely over. The first would probably just piss the man off, while the second would surely send him into a rage, making him even more dangerous than he seemed already.

Of course, Arlin was quite happy to perform with her, even marking her in front of the peeping tom they assumed hid in the bushes. There should be no doubts as to who Eve preferred now. Besides, Arlin rationalized, it just might be what they needed to spur the man to make an asinine move, which permitted Arlin to put an end to him once and for all. All of that rage Arlin felt at Shades would surely have a place to be vented once he got Kyle in his grasp.

"You seem pensive," Eve said from her spot on the bed beside him. "What's wrong?" Then she shot up on her elbows so she could stare him in the face. "You're not regretting marking me, are you?"

"What?" He turned to her, reaching a hand out to cup her face. "Not at all, Little Warrior. The tiger within me can now relax, knowing we're together." He snaked his hand behind her neck and pulled her down for a kiss. He would never regret marking her; he knew that for sure, as he licked her bottom lip, pulling away from the kiss. "I just wondered what our little show did to infuriate your ex, that's all. If he watched as you suspect, and I would agree that he was, then he's definitely going to be gunning for you now. You need to be extra careful. Watch your back."

She grinned at him as she swung a leg over his waist to straddle him. "Does that mean you're going to be watching my front?"

He groaned as he felt her wetness sliding up and down his cock. Reaching up, he caressed her perky tits, flicking his thumb back and forth over her nipple. "I'm going to be watching every inch of you. You can count on that."

He felt her slide back and forth along his quickly growing cock as she leaned down, her hands pressing on his chest. "Good. I'm counting on it." She leaned down and licked where she bit him the first time they made love, the impressions of her teeth faint, but still there. He winced as she nipped at him again. And still tender, it seemed. With a push, she shoved herself straight again as she grinned down at him. "So, what's the plan?"

He chuckled. "You're on top. I thought you knew what you were doing." He winked as he waggled his eyebrows.

"Snarky, Stripes. I like it," she said with a laugh. "However, I'm talking about getting Kyle out of our lives and out of Bull Creek."

"Do we really need to talk about your ex while we're naked, and you're straddling me like this? I'm sure we can come up with something else to...um, discuss."

She rocked back and forth on him, her grin growing. "Discuss? You want to talk? Really?"

His tiger growled within, urging him to take his mate right then. "Well, perhaps discuss is too weak a word." He could feel his cock stirring to life, twitching between her pussy lips as she ground on top of him. "I can come up with something stronger, I'm sure."

She leaned back down, her grin full of want, passion. "Good. I like stronger." She gripped his arms, squeezing them, her nails digging into them, and then—he yelped again—her claws digging into him. Eve screamed, matching his yelp as she jerked back up, her back straight, her hands in front of her as she stared at her fingertips, the tips of claws sticking out. "What the hell?"

Arlin reached out, taking her hands in his and pulling them to his lips, kissing each claw tenderly. When he pulled her hands from his mouth, he said, "It happens, Little Warrior, with humans. The mate bitten takes on the animal of the mate who bites her." He looked up into her eyes, doing his best to make his expression reassuring. By her wide eyes, he assumed he hadn't pulled it off.

She glanced down at him, her body trembling slightly. "A little warning would have been nice," she said, her voice holding a tinge of a growl, which made the tiger within Arlin growl as well. She glanced back at her fingertips, unable to look away, it seemed. "You mean...I'm going to shift now? Into a tiger? Like you?"

He gave her a slow nod, worried now that perhaps he should have been more upfront with her about the specifics and risks of mating. He just assumed she knew all about shifters since she lived in Bull Creek surrounded by the paranormal. As best as he could tell, her best friend was a wolf shifter, so he just assumed... He took a deep breath. By the look on her face, he assumed wrong. "I'm sorry, Eve, I just...I assumed you knew." He squeezed her thigh, hoping to reassure her of his sincerity.

Yet, the worry that creased her brow just a moment ago shifted into wide-eyed excitement. "This is so cool." She turned her hands over and over, just staring. Finally, she shoved herself off him and slid to her feet on the floor. "C'mon, I want to go try it out."

"Now?" He felt his heart—and his cock—deflate a little. "I thought you wanted to, you know, discuss a little more."

She grinned as she patted the shaft of his cock slightly, and at first, he worried she would use her newfound claws on him. "Later. Right now, I want to see how this works."

He sighed again for dramatic effect. "Fine. But, I'm warning you, the first time is going to hurt like hell. They all hurt, but the very first time is the worse. Your entire body is snapping and popping into a new shape, a new animal, fur sliding from your skin, claws from your fingertips and toes, arms and legs turning into tiger legs. I can tell you all about it, but even then, it's not enough to prepare you for what will happen."

"It'll make me stronger, though, right? I won't have to carry that knife everywhere. My claws will be my blades."

He swung his legs off the bed, his hands on his thighs, as he stared up at her. "You don't need to be stronger, but yes, it will." Then he grinned up at her. "Of course, ladies night may not be as fun or as cheap. It takes a lot of alcohol to get a shifter drunk."

"Aw, damn. That's right. Shifters are almost impossible to get drunk." Her shoulders slumped a little at the realization. Then she took a deep breath and straightened her shoulders. "That's all right. It's worth the trade. Tiger claws are much better than a knife I'm still learning to throw. Truthfully, I suck at it anyway."

"Eve, you don't..."

She stopped him by placing her fingers on his lips. "I know what you're going to say, so don't. I know what I am and how strong. I also know Kyle seems to always have the upper hand, and I'm tired of that happening. The next time he raises his hand to me, I swear I'm going to bite it off." Her grin grew. "Now, won't he be surprised that I can actually do it."

Arlin couldn't really blame her for how she felt. And, if he was honest with himself, he knew Kyle had it coming. Still, Arlin didn't want Eve to lose who she was in her quest to put an end to her ex-boyfriend. He couldn't allow her to do something that she might later regret, and which might turn her into someone besides the sweet girl he was growing to love. His tiger already knew what Arlin was just now realizing, that he would do anything to protect and keep Eve safe, to prove to her that she was, indeed, a precious lady worthy of love and adoration.

Reaching out, he took her hand in his and gave it a tender squeeze. "I can't wait to run with you. Let's do it."

Eve reached to the floor to grab her shirt, but he stopped her. "It would just be a waste of time. Clothes get ripped off, remember? Might as well save yourself from buying something new each time you shift and just stay naked."

She shrugged as she turned toward the door. "No wonder you shifters are so comfortable at nudist camps. You have to go around naked all the time anyway."

He chuckled. "True. And we'll wait to shift until we're outside. Tigers can bust through doors, but not open them real well. It's easier on the wood this way."

She glanced back over her shoulder and down at his cock. "I wouldn't want to do anything to hurt the wood." She winked before turning back around and heading to the front door.

He followed, his gaze riveted to the way her small, heart-shaped ass swayed as she walked. His cock twitched at the sight, and he groaned inwardly at the distraction to more "discussing."

"By the way," she started, reaching for the doorknob, "have you ever, you know, had sex while in your tiger form?"

He followed her outside, his head tilted to the side as he thought about her question. Finally, he gave a shake of his head. "You know what? I haven't. Ever. I mean, it's possible, I'm sure. I just haven't done it."

She grinned, running her tongue across her lips. "Great. Another thing we can try together. Now, how does this work?"

Arlin shook his head at her enthusiasm, smiling. "Just focus on the tiger inside of you and relax. She'll take it from there. It'll hurt, but don't fight it. Trying to resist will make it worse."

She nodded, her expression a mixture of determination and excitement. Then she took a deep breath and shifted, her bones popping and snapping. She released a loud wail as her body twisted, the transformation jerking bones and muscles into new shapes and positions. The orange and black striped fur oozed from her flesh, shoving its way out of her skin as she screamed again. And then, she hunched down onto her paws, growling, as her sharp teeth dripped saliva. She ran her tongue over her dark lips, her growls turning to a soft purr of satisfaction.

He couldn't shift until she was finished, his gaze frozen at the process he had witnessed a million times, yet, never before with someone for which he genuinely cared. There was a grace to the transformation, he now realized, watching her, that he never before noticed, a fluidity from human to animal that was both frightening and amazing.

As soon as she finished, her tiger's mouth open, panting,

he allowed himself to shift.

If you catch me, Eve sent to Arlin through the mental speech of the animals, *maybe we can have real animalistic sex.* She nipped at his neck and then turned and leaped off the porch.

Oh, I'll catch you. Arlin growled and followed her.

Together, they bounded into the woods. If Kyle Wagner watched them now, Arlin was sure the man was scared as hell. Good. He needed to be scared, but not of Eve. Kyle needed to be scared of Arlin, because he had already decided what he would do with Eve's attacker. He wouldn't wait for Eve to get hurt again. Arlin planned to take Kyle down; it was just a matter of time now.

Sixteen

The afternoon sun caressed the orange and black stripes of her fur, massaging her with its warm rays as the wind whispered along her lithe form. She ran through the forest surrounding Bull Creek, leaping over fallen logs, dodging trees, turning up the earth with her massive paws. All the while, Arlin, in his tiger form, followed close behind her, allowing her the freedom to explore her newfound ability while also remaining close enough to protect her and keep her from harm. While Bull Creek was a sanctuary for shifters, she knew Arlin wasn't familiar enough with the area to let his guard down just yet, especially with Kyle still stalking her. She'd have to do something about her ex soon, though, if she were to move on with her life.

Out of the corner of her eye, she saw Arlin's tiger prowling around a giant oak tree, matching her pace. She knew he was now a significant part of that forward momentum of her life, of putting her past behind her so she could enjoy this sparkling new present. And god, did she want to enjoy it. She darted close to him, nipping at his shoulder flank, and then bounded away to the right, Arlin giving chase. She knew he allowed her to outdistance him, for she was nowhere near able to match him in speed or stamina or even strength, being too new to her animal. Still, it felt good to run and taunt him a little, her powerful legs propelling her ever faster, ever forward. This was one journey she looked forward to making.

They ran for over an hour, giving their animals room to roam and explore before they shifted back once they were near her cabin. Eve figured it would be less distance to walk naked, still not as comfortable as Arlin with the whole nudity thing. While shifters may be comfortable being nude around each other, she wasn't ready to join the Wild Kingdom Nudist Colony just yet. No one needed to see her in the buff. No one except Arlin that is. Glancing over her shoulder as he finished shifting back to his human form, she soaked in his broad shoulders and sculpted abs, allowing her eyes to scan down the rest of him, his powerful thighs, his hardening cock. She licked her lips remembering how good his hardness felt between her legs, spreading her open for his pleasure.

And for hers. She couldn't stop thinking about how he made her feel when he marked her, claiming her as his. Kyle tried to claim her, but in a much more brutish, abusive way. With him, she was more like a possession to be owned and used, while with Arlin, she was a treasure to be plundered and ravished. The differences made her head spin, and her heart swoon.

"I can fix us some lunch if you want," she suggested as she headed for her porch. "Of course, if you have a different appetite…"

He chuckled, and it stirred the honey between her legs. "I will always have that appetite." She felt his hands on her waist as he yanked her back against him, his mouth going to her neck, his teeth nibbling on her sun-warmed flesh, bringing a different kind of warmth to her body.

She giggled as she pinched her shoulders to her neck, trying to ward him off. "Can't you even wait until we're inside, like normal people?"

"Normal is so…well, normal." He licked her earlobe and then growled. "I prefer the abnormal with you."

"You really have changed since you sneaked out of the house." The menacing voice behind them caused Eve to stiffen in Arlin's arms. They both turned to face Kyle, but she noticed Arlin did not take his hands away from her, but rather hid her naked form behind his. "Is that what you've turned into? Some tramp who walks around outside naked, participating in sexual behavior where anyone can see? How far you've fallen, Eve. It really is despicable."

She felt Arlin's body stiffen in front of her, his shoulders rising as his back straightened even more than it was. "Eve, go inside the cabin," he said.

Eve felt herself take a step back from Arlin. She was not some mouse to go scurrying away when trouble appeared.

He should know that by now. "I'm fine where I am, thanks."

He gave one curt nod, his gaze still focused on Kyle. It wasn't the response she expected from him. There was no arguing or demanding she do as she was told and be the good little woman. He merely nodded, accepting her decision to remain at his side.

Or his back as the case may be. While she didn't want to run away, she didn't really have any desire for Kyle to see her naked body. Not ever again if she could help it.

"I'm only giving you one warning," Arlin said, his voice calm, yet threatening, deep, yet stern. "Leave Bull Creek and stay away from Eve. This is the only chance you'll have to get away and make the right decision. If you come around again, if you threaten her again, even sneer at her, I'll make sure it's the last thing you ever do."

Kyle laughed, head tilted back, mouth wide open. He laughed. She couldn't believe it; although, she should have expected it. When he finished, he stared at Arlin, the left corner of his mouth turned up in a sneer. "I'll do whatever the hell I want, you over-compensating freak. I don't know who the hell you think you are, but this is between Eve and myself. Not some fish camp lowlife." He took a step toward Arlin as if he was ready to get into it right then, and Eve felt her eyebrows pop up in genuine surprise. Arlin was definitely the bigger of the two, and while Kyle was great at beating up women and smaller punks, she thought him stupid for even trying to intimidate Arlin. He pointed a finger at Arlin's chest, his eyes narrowing into a menacing scowl. "I'm taking Eve back home with me where she belongs, and if you try to stop me or try to convince her to do anything other than what she's told, I swear they'll be using you for alligator bait in that river over there. Now, be a good boy and..."

Arlin snatched out and grabbed Kyle's wrist, spinning the man around as he wrapped his arm around Kyle's neck, pinning him to his chest—to his naked body. Eve watched as Arlin leaned into the side of Kyle's face, snarling as he spoke. "I'm not threatening you, dipshit. I'm making a promise. Come near her again, and you'll be the one being used for bait." He shoved Kyle away from him, bracing his feet in the dirt for what they both knew would happen next. It would have almost been comical, the scene before her if it wasn't so deathly serious. Yet, she still felt her sex throb at the image of Arlin standing there, naked, ready to defend her.

Kyle, if he was smart, should have just quit and walked away, but bullies rarely give up, and Kyle was never smart. Even before he had his feet planted firmly on the ground for balance, he spun, his fist aiming for whatever connection he could make. Arlin, however, knew it was coming—as did Eve—and before Kyle finished his swing, Arlin jabbed out with all his might and caught the other man in the nose, then swung a right, clocking Kyle on the left side of his jaw. Kyle tumbled backward, arms swinging to recapture a balance that never came. Arlin shook his hands, the pain from his hits stinging his knuckles, Eve knew. Kyle hit the ground with a thud and a whoosh of air leaving his chest. Arlin— naked and threatening—stood over him, his hands up and ready for more if Kyle chose to continue fighting.

Blood oozed from Kyle's nose as tears poured from his eyes. His breathing was ragged as he struggled to get back to his feet, his hand on his nose, blood dripping from between his fingers.

Eve could only stand there, watching. Part of her prayed Kyle would just get up and walk away, while another part of her wanted him to fight so he would get his ass kicked even more. She could feel her tiger wanting to shift, wanting to put an end to the man who had beat her so often and caused her so much pain and humiliation. Clinching her teeth, she struggled to keep the transformation from happening, fighting to maintain control over herself. Now was not the time for Kyle to discover her new ability, if he hadn't witnessed it earlier. She assumed he didn't know yet, had not actually been watching from the woods like she hoped, or he would have made some nasty comment about it. No, this was a card she was determined to keep up her sleeve for now.

Groggy, Kyle made it to his feet, his body swaying slightly as he tried to regain some semblance of his pitiful intimidation. His hand still on his broken nose, he said, "That was a mistake. I'm not so easily scared away. I'll return, and when I do, I'll be taking what's mine, and doing away with any interference." He pulled his hand away from his nose, staring at the blood that dripped from his fingers. "If you're smart, you'll stay the hell out of my way."

Arlin didn't move a muscle, keeping his stance. "If *you're* smart, you'll disappear, or you'll suffer more than a busted up nose."

Kyle grinned, and Eve knew this wasn't the last that they would see of him. "I'll be back," he promised, as he turned and walked away, his hand back on his nose, his steps awkward and unstable. "Be ready to go, Eve, for your boyfriend's sake."

They stood still watching as he walked away, making sure he actually left. When they were finally sure he was gone, at least for now, Eve placed her hands on her bare hips and grinned at Arlin as he turned around. "I bet that's the first time Kyle's ever had his ass handed to him by a naked man."

Arlin laughed as he shook his head. "Not exactly the way I pictured that confrontation in my head, but I think he still got the message."

"Got it, yes, but heeding it will be another story." Then she tilted her head to the side, her brows bunching up over her nose. "You pictured that confrontation?"

Arlin walked back over to her and pulled her into his arms. "Of course. No one threatens my mate. I knew he wouldn't give up, and I wanted an idea of what I would do when he showed up again. It pretty much went like I thought, only I pictured myself wearing clothes." He winked at her, and she couldn't help but giggle.

"I don't know; I think the picture of you standing over his face with your junk dangling over him will be an image he won't forget for quite a while. I know I won't." She winked back at him.

He swatted her on the ass, and she yelped a little, still giggling. "C'mon," he said. "You mentioned lunch, and I'm hungry."

She slid a hand down between them, stroking his cock. "So am I, but not for food."

He kissed her nose. "Insatiable. I like it."

You have no idea.

Seventeen

T here were coyotes everywhere," Eve said as if Arlin hadn't heard the story already. He just smiled and stared, listening to her retell the tale of when Bane and his band of miscreants invaded their Friday night ritual of a bonfire to celebrate the coming weekend. Of course, Arlin hadn't heard anyone mention jobs as of yet, so he wasn't really sure how the weekend was any different from the weekday, but he'd take any reason to celebrate with his mate. "They backed down quickly, however, when Adira sparked some of her magic at them. You should have seen it."

"I don't think that's how it happened," Adira said, the small dark-haired witch glued to the alpha of Bull Creek's side. "I didn't use my magic until they tried to accost us at Everglades."

"And then at the final battle," Dimitri added. "You used a lot of magic then." He pulled her into himself, squeezing her tight. "For which I'm glad. They were a right nasty bunch."

"Wanted to take over the area, huh?" Arlin asked. From the scent the witch and panther put off, it was obvious they had recently mated, which meant they could probably scent his mark on Eve as well. He was glad Dimitri was there, however, when Bane tried to put an end to the human population in Bull Creek. Arlin didn't know what he'd do if he weren't able to find his mate. If he could be honest with himself, he was lost up until the time he met Eve at Everglades. If it weren't for that encounter, he'd probably spend years searching for scmeone, bouncing from one cheap, pointless encounter to the next until he finally settled down with someone he pretended to love, but really only tolerated to cure his loneliness. He glanced over at Eve who started the tale of Everglades again and couldn't keep the smile from pushing his cheeks up. No, this, this was much better.

"What's all the chatter about over here?" Turning, Arlin saw Alanna and her boyfriend, Josh Rayburn, walking over to them, a behemoth of a man he had yet to meet following in their wake, each carrying a beer bottle and wearing a smile.

"Eve is regaling us with her storytelling capabilities," Dimitri said, smiling over at Eve and winking.

"Stories I'd rather forget, to be honest," Adira added. Arlin couldn't blame her considering she was abducted and had the crap knocked out of her. He'd want to forget that story, too.

The giant man reached out a powerful hand to Arlin. "Welcome to Bull Creek. Nathan's brother, right? I'm Ezra."

Arlin took the hand, noting the more-than-human strength in the grip. Ezra wasn't trying to be intimidating; it was just a natural trait of his. If Arlin had to guess, he'd say the man was either a bear or a gorilla shifter. "Arlin. And yeah, I came to visit my brother, and he's not even here."

Ezra nodded, laughing. "That man comes and goes faster than anyone can keep track. Where is he off to this time?"

"With Nathan, who knows?" Arlin said with a laugh. He then turned to Dimitri. "So, you do these every Friday night?"

Dimitri nodded. "We do them as often as possible. It's just a way to celebrate life, bring the community together. For some people here, we're the only friends and family they have." He shrugged. "It's a way to check in without being intrusive and pounding on doors."

Arlin nodded as Dimitri spoke. "Nice. I like it. A diverse family feel."

"That's what I've come to love about it," Adira said.

"Me, too," Eve agreed. She turned to Arlin, wrapping her arms around his. "I've found everything I need right here."

Leaning down and kissing her nose, he said, "As have I. Who would have thunk it?" They both laughed at his comment. "I'll need to send Jed a thank you note for kicking me out of town for a while."

Adira laughed. "The Paranormal Council back in Draven Falls has a habit of sending people where they need to be when they need to be there. I'd swear they have an inside scoop on this mating business."

"Well, I think I need to call them," Ezra said, laughing. "Maybe they know where mine's hiding."

Arlin noticed Josh and Alanna doing everything they could not to look at each other. He just smiled. That was one battle the two of them would have to fight sooner or later.

"Hey, I notice you have no knives at your waist," Alanna said, quickly changing the subject, as she pointed to Eve's waist and the missing sheath. "That knife is always at your hip. What gives?"

Arlin watched as Eve reached for her hip and the absent knife. She laughed softly as she felt it missing. "Well, to be honest, I wore it as a means of protection, but since...well, you know...since I'm now my own form of protection, I decided it was time to store it away." Her smile grew timid with the admission as if she bragged too much. Yet, Arlin was glad to know she felt that confidence within herself. It brought a glow to her that Kyle's appearance had dimmed.

Dimitri grinned as he nodded. "Well, I thought I detected a familiar scent." He squeezed Adira to him as he said it. Then he glanced over at Josh and Alanna. "Maybe it's contagious."

Alanna rolled her eyes, but Arlin noticed Josh shuffling his feet at the idea. Perhaps, Dimitri's comment hit closer to home than the other panther shifter was ready to admit. How Josh and Alanna were able to deny the call of fated mates so far was beyond Arlin's imagination. The minute his tiger scented Eve, it took everything Arlin had to resist marking her for as long as he did. Sooner or later, he knew something between the others would snap. He just hoped they were both ready when it did. Denying the call could be torture, a torture he was glad he didn't have to endure. If Eve had decided she didn't want anything to do with him, Arlin wasn't sure what he would do.

The night went on without incident, which Arlin had to admit surprised him. He truly thought Kyle would have made some sort of appearance to try and prove himself to Eve, to show he wasn't intimidated. Yet, it seemed like he wasn't going to be so brazen. Or so stupid.

As the party started to wind down, Arlin and Eve offered to help clean up, but Dimitri told them to go ahead and get out of there. New people apparently got a pass the first bonfire night. Arlin wasn't going to look a gift horse in the mouth, so he grabbed Eve's hand and headed out of there. The moon was high, the sky clear enough to see Orion's Belt, and a cool breeze blew through the surrounding trees—a perfect night for a moonlit stroll with his mate. Grabbing her hand, he led her away from the cleanup crew and down the dark street, the wind pulling at their hair. His tiger wanted to bust loose and run, and he was sure Eve's gave her the same temptation, but not tonight. Tonight, he wanted nothing more than to be alone with his mate in a slow stroll through what would be his new home.

"I like this tradition," he said, after they walked for a few minutes, the bonfire clearing behind them. "It's a great way to bond the community together."

Their arms swung back and forth in slow motion as they

walked, Eve giving a soft nod. "It is a fun tradition. I've been going to them since I arrived here. It's where I met most of my friends." She remained silent for a moment, but Arlin could sense that wasn't the end of it. He was right. "This is actually the first place I've actually felt like I belonged. No one judges you or cares that you're not like everyone else." She giggled, and it stirred his heart. "Actually, they prefer that no one is like anyone else."

"It must have been hard, starting over." He couldn't imagine what she went through when she finally left Kyle. It seemed as if she left everything and everyone behind, truly starting over. "I'm sorry you had to go through all of that."

"Me, too, but in a way, it worked out. It brought me here and got me to you."

They turned the corner, an animal scurrying in the underbrush off to the side. Arlin stopped, twirling her until he had his arms wrapped around her, holding her against him, her breasts pressed to his chest. He was sure she could feel his growing cock against her. "I'm glad at the destination, but I hate the path you had to take to get here." He leaned down, kissing her softly, first her lips, and then her nose. "Of course, that only means I'm going to spend the rest of our lives making it up to you and proving to you how a lady should be treated." He loved the way her eyes sparkled when she gazed up at him. "Eve Hartlow, you make my heart happy."

He felt her squeeze him to her, her head on his chest. "You make me happy, too. I never thought it possible, to be honest. Or that I deserved it." She leaned back and stared up into his eyes. "But I do deserve it, and what's more, I'm ready for it. I'm ready to finally be happy. I'm ready for us."

"So am..." And that's all he got out before he felt a skull-cracking thud against his head, stars flashing across his vision before darkness swallowed him, his legs turning to jelly, no longer holding his weight. The last thing he heard was Eve's scream.

Eighteen

Kyle stood there, a broken tree limb in his hands as he glared down at Arlin's body, Arlin's motionless body, Eve noticed. She couldn't tell whether he was dead or just unconscious, but he definitely wasn't moving. Her heart lurched in her chest, the pounding echoing in her ears. They should have known Kyle would not give up that easily. They were careless and arrogant, and now Arlin paid the price for their flippant behavior.

"People should learn to mind their own business," Kyle snarled as he sneered down at Arlin. Glancing up at Eve, he shook his head. "This is your fault. If you would have just done what I told you to do, just packed your bags and headed home instead of sowing your wild oats, none of this would have happened." He pointed at Arlin with the end of the branch he wielded like a club. "You made this happen.

You did this." With each word, his voice grew louder, angrier. "Don't blame me. I didn't want this to happen, but I told you it would if you didn't come home." He stood straighter, his shoulders flat and his chest puffed out. "Now," he motioned the way she had been walking, "let's go get your stuff and go home. We can put this whole mess behind us."

"No," she snapped, doing her best to keep the fear from making her voice quiver, or the tears that threatened to fall from revealing how scared she was. "I'm not going anywhere with you. You don't own me, Kyle. I'm not some prize you won or some helpless female you can bully. This is my life, and it no longer includes you. Just go away."

Kyle raised the branch high over Arlin's head, his lips twisted into a crazed leer. "I'll bash in his head if you don't get moving. If he's the one making you act this way, then I'll get rid of him. Only you can spare his life." He motioned as if to bring the branch down on Arlin's skull, making Eve cry out for him to stop.

Hands held out as if warding off Kyle's threat, the tears finally fell. "Okay, okay. I'll go. I'll go. Just leave him alone." She took a few steps backward, hoping to lead Kyle away from Arlin's prone body. Her tiger raged within her, wanting to bust free and attack, the orange and black striped fur slipping through her flesh. Eve gritted her teeth, biting the inside of her mouth as she fought to tamp her animal down, doing her best to control her tiger. *Please, not now. We're too close.* If she shifted now, it might scare Kyle and cause him to attack Arlin. She needed to lead him away from her mate, far enough away so she would have time to shift and not risk Arlin being hurt. Then she could turn and take the bastard out with pleasure. But first, she needed to create some distance between her past and her future.

He gave her a wary look, only lowering the branch a little as he stepped over Arlin's body. She backed up a couple of more steps, turning only slightly, wanting to keep Kyle in her line of vision. To her relief, he followed her. To her dismay, however, Arlin still wasn't moving. *I just need to get him away from Arlin.* She allowed herself to face forward, determined to make Kyle believe he had won. *Then, I'm going to kill him.* She took a deep breath and kept walking.

"You could have made this simple, Eve. Could have kept all this from happening." His voice held a tinge of anger, the threats of the past coloring his tone. "But, oh no, you just had to make me come looking for you. You shouldn't have done that. Nope. Shouldn't have done that at all."

She heard him walking behind her; it sounded like he drew closer to her. Chancing a quick glance over her shoulder, she noticed the branch still in his hand, but now dangling at his side as he walked. He focused more on chastising her than protecting himself. Taking a deep breath, she clenched her fists. *He still sees me as some weak female he can bully. Won't he be surprised?*

With another deep breath, she flexed her fingers, ready to unleash the tiger inside of her. Yet, just as she was about to shift, a blur roared past her, taking Kyle with it, the two of them tumbling over and over on the dirt road. She stared, unsure what had happened or what to do. Kyle screamed as whatever took him—an animal—growled, its massive paws and sharp claws slashing the man across the chest, knocking him across the road and into the grass. Eve stared at Arlin in his tiger form as he braced, paws apart ready to pounce one more time, his mouth open, lips curled back, growling, attention focused solely on Kyle.

Glancing at Kyle, she watched as he rolled over, his hands behind his back as he did a backward crab crawl to get away from the tiger. "What the hell? Why is there a tiger here?" Arlin took a step closer, and Kyle screamed. From Eve's angle, it appeared he wet his pants as well, which made her smile.

Eve closed the distance between her and where Arlin stood, reaching out and stroking his raised fur when she reached him. Keeping her gaze on the tiger, she spoke to Kyle, however. "I warned you. I told you I wasn't going back with you, and I meant it." She scratched behind Arlin's ear as she turned her gaze back to Kyle. "I don't need knives or restraining orders or anything else to make sure you understand me. I have Arlin. He's the best thing that ever happened to me, and he gave me the greatest gift anyone could ever give."

Kyle's gaze stayed riveted on the tiger. "What did he give you that I didn't?"

She smiled, soft and warm. "He gave me his love, unconditional and open." Then she grinned. "And then he gave me this." With a smirk, she took a deep breath and shifted, her bones popping and snapping as her body transformed from the small, sandy-haired woman to a strong, powerful female tiger, the perfect counterpart to her mate. When the transformation was complete, Kyle gawked with wide eyes and an open mouth, his bottom lip quivering. She roared, taking a small leap toward him, Arlin's tiger roaring with her, and it was all Kyle could take. He jerked himself off the ground, spinning as he did, and ran into the woods, screaming. It was the most significant sight Eve had ever seen.

Her roars turned to purrs as Arlin brushed his muzzle up against her, rubbing her, his own contented purr mixing with hers. After a few moments of mingling fur, she heard his voice in her head. *As much as I want to continue this, Little Warrior, we should follow him and make sure he truly leaves.*

She growled, nipping at the ruff of Arlin's neck. As much as she didn't want to agree with him, she knew he was right, and with a burst of speed, she shoved off the earth and headed after Kyle. She'd thank her mate properly soon enough.

Kyle wasn't faking it. They followed his scent to the edge of Bull Creek and an oil-burning Chevy that left rubber track marks on the road where it had been parked, heading west. When they reached the edge of the forest where Kyle vanished, they both shifted back, the evening breeze brushing against their naked flesh. Remaining hidden from passersby who didn't need to see their nude forms, Eve stared at the open road, the empty open road. It was over. It was truly, finally over. Kyle was out of her life. Gone.

She felt Arlin's strong hand on her arm, pulling her to him. Turning, she placed a hand on his chest as she gazed up into his golden eyes, his smile brightening up her night. "It's over, Little Warrior," he said, reaching up and brushing her hair out of her eyes.

She reached up, turning his head to the side, causing him to wince. "How's your head? I was worried Kyle had succeeded in killing you."

His voice seemed strained when he answered, the pain evident in his tone. "Oh, it hurts like hell, but it'll take more than that to knock me out." He grinned, giving a soft chuckle. "It wasn't even hard enough to knock some sense into me." He winked at her as he turned his head back toward her. "I just needed him to move away first so I could shift. Besides, we're a hardy breed, quick healers."

She felt the grin pushing up her cheeks. "Thank you. For everything." She pressed her head against his chest, taking a deep breath of him into her.

He stroked her hair, and she had never felt so much love in a touch. "Little Warrior, you haven't seen *everything* yet." He pulled her back so he could gaze into her eyes. "But you will. My entire life is going to be all about showing you."

She squeezed him, the emotions washing over her like a waterfall. This is what life was supposed to be about. Not fear, but love. This was Heaven, and she had to go through Hell to find it. Now that she did, she would never let it go. She heard the growl within her. Not that her tiger would permit her to let it go. No. This was her life. Her future. And she would enjoy every minute of it. This was the journey she craved all her life, and she would savor every step.

Mate's Touch

One

Looking into another person's eyes usually revealed…well, something. There was always emotion behind the eyes, some hint as to what the person felt or thought, a motivation, a truth, or a lie. Yet, looking into the eyes of a corpse only revealed that life was too damn short, and you needed to grab everything out of it you could while you still drew breath. For one Mister—Lainie Everest glanced down at her notes—Roger O'Brien that chance was over, and whatever he had failed to grab out of life was now lost forever. *And now I'm stuck trying to figure out why.*

"What can you tell me?" The portly Sheriff Chet Einstein stood beside her, his sheriff's hat clasped in both hands in front of him, the afternoon breeze making a mess of his gray hair as he stared at the prone body on the ground. Deputy Johnson stood opposite Lainie, his hands in his pockets as he waited for her answer, letting her take the lead. She appreciated the opportunity, even though it made her nervous as hell.

Lainie squatted beside the corpse, her forearms resting on her thighs, her gaze still fixed on the lifeless man. "Roger O'Brien, age forty-two, been in Bull Creek less than two weeks, although I haven't really seen him around or talking to anyone. The only reason I know how long he's been here is because I noticed when his cabin came to life. He's never even made it to one of our weekly bonfires, and you know how big of a deal those are." She glanced up at her boss, her lips twisted into a grimace. "This is Bull Creek, though. People sometimes stick to themselves. Hell, there's a few residents at the edges of the community I've never even seen." Glancing at her notes again, she said, "According to his license, he seems to have arrived here from Pensacola, reason unknown obviously, but he never bothered to change his address, so I'm not sure if he's just visiting or planning to take up residence. Of course, like I said, it's only been two weeks. It's possible he's on an extended vacation. From all appearances, he was shot while out taking a walk, two in the chest, no defensive wounds so I can assume no struggle. He may not have even seen it coming." She pushed herself into a standing position as she took a deep breath. "I can ask my brother if he knows anything about him. Dimitri usually makes it his business to at least talk once to new folk, making sure they know the rules of our little township."

Chet nodded. "Whatever the man was running from seems to have caught up with him."

"What makes you think he was running from something and that this wasn't just a robbery or something?" Deputy Johnson asked, his brows pinched in puzzlement.

Chet shrugged. "Because this is Bull Creek." He glanced over at his deputy. "And no one here has much to steal and everything to hide."

Both, Johnson and Lainie, nodded in agreement. "I'll do a full background check on him when I get back to the office," Lainie said, tapping her notepad with her palm.

"No, Johnson can do that," Sheriff Einstein said. "You go talk to your brother. Find out what he knows about our victim." He then glanced around the area, making sure no one was within hearing range, before turning back to Lainie. "Any chance to know whether this man was anything besides human? Might help us know a little more about why he was killed."

Lainie glanced at Johnson, who just shrugged, and then gave a quick scan around them before kneeling back down, leaning forward, and inhaling deeply of Roger O'Brien. Sitting back on her heels, she shook her head. "Human. I doubt this has anything to do with our paranormal community."

"You're right; it doesn't."

They all turned as a tall man, dark hair and golden eyes, strode over to them. Lainie's panther purred at the sight of the newcomer, and at first glance, Lainie had to agree with her animal's assessment.

"And you are?" Chet asked as Lainie stood, concern about the man overhearing her comment about the community knitting her brow.

The man flashed an ID and badge at them, Lainie noticing his powerful hands and strong fingers as he did. She also saw the way his shoulders squared off and the cute little dimple on his chin. Just as her eyes started to scroll down the rest of him, she stopped herself, biting the inside of her cheek. "Rance Culpepper," the man said. "Detective for the Pensacola District Attorney's Office." He then pointed to the dead man. "I've been trying to track this man down for over a month now. He's a witness in a gang shooting back in Pensacola. Key witness, unfortunately."

"Seems the gang had better resources than your office," Chet said, as he slipped his hat back on his head, shoving his hair out of his eyes first. "I hope your case didn't hinge on his testimony."

"Not if I can find his phone." The man stuffed his ID back in his jacket before jabbing his hands onto his hips. This time, Lainie couldn't stop herself from following the motion and blushed when she noticed where her gaze landed.

"His phone?" Lainie asked, jerking her gaze upward, while inwardly scolding her panther for its urges. *Now you want to get frisky? At a crime scene?*

Rance nodded. If he noticed where Lainie's gaze went, he didn't show it. "Apparently, he has a video of the shooting. If I can find that, we can save the case. You didn't happen to find a phone on him, did you?"

Lainie nodded. "It's been bagged as evidence."

"Great. I need it." He looked around as if he could see it lying about carelessly.

"Um, no. When we get back and go through everything, if there's a video on it, I'll let you know." Lainie squared off against the agent, ignoring the purring of her panther. "This is a murder investigation. The phone belongs to us. It's our case."

"Your case is connected to mine, which happened first. I need that phone." Rance's chest puffed out—a chest Lainie found herself wanting to pounce on—and his golden eyes narrowed as he stared at her.

"And you'll get it when we determine it's not connected to our case. Roger's murder happened here, in our jurisdiction, and this is my case. You're not getting shit until I say you can have it."

"Well, I'll just go over your head to your boss." He took a step toward her, trying to be intimidating.

Chet cleared his throat, and Lainie and Rance both turned to look at him. "I'm her boss, so consider your request noted. However, as she said, she'll get the phone to you when she's done with it. This man was murdered in our backyard, and I'll be damned if some agent from a big city is going to swoosh in here and take over until we have a chance to discover who killed the man."

Lainie shot Rance a smug smile, but he had already turned toward Chet, dismissing her as someone inferior, no doubt.

"But our case goes to trial in just over a week." Rance moved closer to Chet, no longer attempting to be the big bad agent. Lainie shook her head. *Chauvinistic ass.*

"Then you better hope my deputy solves the case fast."

He then turned to Lainie. "Keep me posted. I'm heading back to the office." He stepped around the dead body and toward the sheriff's car. "C'mor. Johnson; you're driving."

Rance, his hands still on his hips, just stared as the two men walked away, his shoulders tense with his agitation even through his finely pressed jacket. He turned his gaze to the ground and shook his head.

Lainie did her best not to reveal her victory smile when he turned around. *Yup, he's definitely not happy.* "So, if you want to leave me your card, I'll make sure to reach out when you can have the phone."

"No way."

She shrugged. "You heard my boss. The phone's ours until I'm through with it."

"I heard him, but I'm not going anywhere. My case hinges on you closing your case, apparently, so I'm staying right here with you until it's closed."

"I don't need a babysitter or a ride-along."

"Doesn't matter. I'm staying by your side, so what's next?"

You have got to be kidding me. "Look, Detective Culpepper, this will go a lot faster without you interfering, so go back to your hotel, drink some cheap booze from the mini-fridge, and enjoy the hot tub. Or, better yet, go back to Pensacola, and I'll Fed-Ex the phone to you when I'm through. I can even send you the video in an email. However, what I can't do is allow you to be a pain in my ass while I try to solve this case. Now, go away." She hung her notepad in the pouch on her belt and started to walk away. She only took a couple of steps before she paused and pulled a business card from her shirt pocket. Handing it to the detective, she said, "You can leave me a message where to contact you once I'm done."

The detective took the offered card, annoyance covering his face.

Lainie then turned her back on Detective Rance Culpepper and his arrogance, as well as the purring of her panther. Both of which were more than getting on her nerves right then.

Ten minutes later, she knocked on her brother's cabin door, still struggling to put Rance out of her mind. She didn't need the distraction, not on her case, not in her day, and definitely not in her life. She also didn't need her panther getting all hot and bothered over some out-of-towner. She left Draven Falls to avoid an arranged mating. Relationships just left you heartbroken and damaged. She had done well following Agatha Rochester's advice and getting the distractions out of her life. She sighed as she heard the doorknob turning. *And Rance could very well be a distraction.*

"Hey, what's going on?" Dimitri stood in the doorway, wearing only a pair of jeans and holding a cup of coffee.

Lainie glanced behind him to see if he was alone, and then grinned as she spotted Adira, Dimitri's mate sitting on the couch, covered up with a blanket. "I won't be long. Hate to disturb the happy couple. You really should start thinking about a proper wedding, you know. That is if the two of you can keep your hands off each other long enough to endure one." She gave Adira a finger wave. "Don't you two have jobs or anything?"

"Is that jealousy I hear?" Dimitri asked as he leaned back on the doorframe. "And we both have the day off, thanks. Now, is there a reason you're here or did you just want to cock-block me?"

"Is that even possible anymore?" Lainie grinned, and then grew serious. "Actually, I wanted to know if you knew anything about a Roger O'Brien. He was shot a little while ago. Some kids found his body in the woods."

Dimitri ran a hand through his shaggy, blond hair. "Wow. Unreal. Any suspects?"

"Not yet, although some detective from Pensacola showed up claiming Roger was a witness in a murder. The jerk even tried to take over my case. Some balls he has."

"Got that close to him, did you?" Dimitri smirked, laughing at his own joke.

She knew he teased her, but she also recalled how her panther wanted to get closer to Rance Culpepper's cock and balls. The urge grew even when the man was out of sight, but Lainie didn't leave Draven Falls, avoiding a mating her parents wanted, just to get stuck in a mating here. She needed to get this case solved and Rance out of her hair. "Roger O'Brien?" she repeated. "What can you tell me?"

Dimitri shrugged. "Pretty much a loner. I'm not even sure how he heard about our town. He said he needed a quiet, secluded place to lay low because some pretty bad people hunted him back home. He promised he didn't do anything wrong, that he witnessed something terrible, and now those people wanted him dead. We went over the rules of living here, and I invited him to the Friday night bonfires. He never showed, of course. Hell, I'm not even sure he ventured out of his cabin."

"Taking the hiding thing really far, huh?" She took a deep breath, as she glanced out at the woods around her brother's cabin. "Seems that detective told the truth about Roger witnessing something." She turned her gaze back to Dimitri as she nodded her head. "I think I'll check out his cabin before heading back to the department. Thanks for your help." She leaned into the door, waving at Adira again. "Bye, Adira. Make sure my brother treats you right." She grinned. "Of course, if he doesn't, you can always zap him or something. Maybe turn him into a frog?" She grinned as she patted her brother's arm. "You'd make a good frog, I think."

"Get out of here," he said with a shake of his head. "And good luck with your case."

Lainie waved as she turned and headed back to her car. She didn't need luck with her case. She just needed that moronic detective to stay out of her way.

Two

Rance knelt behind the giant oak, watching as Deputy Lainie Everest slid out of her patrol car. He would not allow some small-town deputy to steal his case, regardless of how his wolf panted after her back at the crime scene. Now was not the time for animal lust to distract him. Roger O'Brien was his; Roger's phone was his. Rance needed the video on that phone to put that punk, Snake, and four of his friends behind bars for shooting up a family's house and killing the father. Gang violence in Pensacola was out of control, contributing to almost eighty percent of the criminal activity in the county. Rance's office was determined to do everything within its power to put as many of them behind bars as possible. Roger was to be a step in that direction. Was to be, that is, until the man turned chicken and ran. Now the only witness to the fatal shooting had been fatally shot, and some one-horse deputy was doing her best to impede Rance's investigation. *Well, she's going to try anyway.*

Rance finished tying his shoes as he kept one eye on the cabin. When the deputy left without him — correction, when she refused to allow him to accompany her — he decided to do his own investigating by following her. One of the things that made him good at his job was the wolf who dwelt inside of him, and Rance had no problem shifting and following the deputy as she did all the legwork, which is exactly what he did. As soon as she was out of sight, he stripped, tossing his clothes into a small duffel he kept in the trunk of his car, shifted, and then took off after her through the woods, the duffel bag clenched in his teeth. He followed her to her brother's house but was unable to get close enough to hear what the two of them discussed on the front porch. Still, Rance waited until she returned to her car and then followed her here to what he assumed was Roger's cabin, hiding in the woods while she went inside to investigate. Realizing that this was where he needed to be, he shifted back and started to get dressed.

Now he stood there, hands on his hips, staring at the front door of the cabin, wondering what the deputy discovered inside without him. Rance hated waiting, especially since it was his case to begin with. He needed to know what was happening inside Roger's cabin and being stuck on the outside was driving him crazy. Perhaps if he hadn't been such an ass back at the crime scene, he'd be in there right now, assisting the deputy instead of blocked from the investigation.

He blew out a breath between his lips, allowing the frustration to drain from his shoulders. He needed more than just to get inside that cabin, and he knew it; he needed to get beside that deputy. Ever since he came upon her at the crime scene, his wolf chomped at the bit to be near her again, and Rance had to admit, the idea of taking her long, dark hair in his hand and yanking her toward him for a passionate kiss lingered at the forefront of his mind. Her passion for her job and the sass with which she had put him in his place only added to the cause of the bulge in his jeans and the panting of his wolf. He wanted her, and there would be no calming his wolf until he possessed her, even though he knew from their brief encounter she was not a woman to be owned. Deputy Lainie Everest would give as much as she received.

Rance was just about to step out into the open to confront the deputy when he noticed some movement off to the west of the cabin. Pausing in his steps, he made sure he was tucked behind the oak where he stood and squinted his eyes in a desperate attempt to get a better look at whoever skulked around in the woods besides him.

A stocky man with short-cropped, dark hair and dark skin crouched among the trees, taking his time moving from one spot to the next. He had about four days' worth of stubble on his face, and his clothes looked as if they could use a washing, his jeans grungy and frayed at the ends, while his T-shirt seemed to have just as much dirt on it as the man's face. Rance was about to make some crack about the denizens of the small community of Bull Creek when he noticed the tattoo of a snake wrapped around a falcon's torso on the man's neck. Rance's back stiffened as he felt his heart thud faster in his chest. *Why is someone from the Serpents still here?* It didn't make sense since Roger was dead.

The phone. Damn it; they're looking for the phone. Rance kept his gaze on the man as he drew nearer the cabin and the deputy inside. Rance's wolf struggled to shift and intervene, but Rance kept the transformation from happening, needing more answers. *Did the idiots really forget to search Roger's body when they killed him? The deputy said she had the phone in evidence, so that had to be it, but wouldn't the gang member know that? So, what is that punk up to?* Unless, of course, Roger made a copy of the video. Rance stood straight, his hand reaching for the gun at his waist, realizing the gang member was there to make sure no other copies of that video existed.

The wolf inside of him growled, and Rance agreed with the animal. The time for hiding was over.

He stepped out into the east side of the property, making sure to stay as low to the ground as he could. He unholstered his gun, gripping it firmly in his right hand, the hard metal cold and rigid. He needed to get between the gang member and the deputy before the Serpent could get the jump on her. Swiveling his head, Rance made sure no one else accompanied the gang member. He didn't need anyone sneaking up behind him, either. As far as he could tell, it was just the one man.

Glancing around the place, Rance decided on a different tactic. Changing course, he eased around to the back of the cabin and the rear door. If he could sneak in without the deputy shooting him, they could set a trap for the Serpent member and then perhaps find some answers. He kept looking over his shoulder, making sure he was still ahead of the other man. By the time he reached the back of the cabin, Rance knew he only had a few moments to get in and gain the deputy's attention.

Reaching the door, he tried opening it, but as he feared, it was locked. *Damn it!* With a deep breath, he knocked as loud as he dared, hoping the deputy would hear him. His wolf urged him to break the door down, but that was more noise than they needed. He waited a few more seconds and then knocked again, his ear pressed against the wooden door, his shifter hearing on high alert.

Footsteps, slow and cautious, could be heard on the other side of the door. Leaning back, he glanced around, but nothing appeared out of the ordinary. The doorknob turned, the click loud in his ears. Turning his attention back to the cabin, he waited as the deputy eased the door open, her own gun in her hand, her brows pinched in question.

Rance gave her a weak smile, his wolf panting at the sight of her. "You have company sneaking in from the front," Rance whispered. "I recognize the tattoo on his neck. He's from the gang back home, the Serpents. I'd guess he's the one who killed Roger."

The deputy leaned out the door, glanced around making sure Rance was alone, and then gave him a curt nod as she waved him inside, her expression anything but welcoming. "We'll deal with why you just happen to be here after we deal with your friend," she whispered.

Rance just nodded, deciding silence the best course of action right then. He followed the deputy toward the front of the cabin, locking the back door before he did. With his attention facing front again, he couldn't help but notice the way her khaki pants hugged her hips, cupping her ass as she walked in a way he wouldn't mind his hands cupping it. Her dark hair barely moved along her back as she walked, her gait slow, cautious. Rance closed his eyes. *Deal with the Serpent first, then admire her ass.* Pep talk over, he opened his eyes again just as they stepped into the front room.

The deputy motioned for him to take the right side of the door as she stepped over to the left. He nodded as he carried out her wishes, once again admiring the way her uniform fit on her. *Okay, boy, you are going to have to calm down until we deal with the matter at hand.* His wolf had shown no desire for anyone in ages and just so happened to perk up at the most inopportune time. Great. Rance didn't need this right now, although he knew the call his wolf felt would not be squelched for long.

The wood on the front porch squeaked, announcing the arrival of the Serpent. There was a pause, and Rance could imagine the man standing there waiting to see if he was heard or not. The deputy kept her eyes on the door, while Rance kept his eyes on her. The woman had fortitude and guts; he'd give her that. Of course, he couldn't imagine his wolf panting over some weakling of a doormat. Too bad she lived all the way out in no man's land.

The sound of the doorknob turning snapped his attention back to the task at hand as he tightened the grip on his gun.

He steadied his breathing, his gaze riveted to the door. The man would see him first, the deputy on the backside of the opening door. Rance sucked in his gut, pressing as flat as he could against the wall, hoping the man would step in before noticing him.

The door eased open, and the nose of a small Glock entered the room first. Rance waited, his eyes on the barrel of the gun in case it suddenly started to turn in his direction. They wanted this man alive, needing answers, first of which would be if there were any other Serpents in the area.

The gang member eased into the cabin, one foot, a hand, then his head. He turned, his eyes going wide when he saw Rance standing there. Rance lowered his gun level with the man's chest. "I'd stay right where you are if I was you," he said.

The deputy stepped out from behind the door, her own gun aimed at the gang member. "I'd listen to him if I were you," she said.

The man jerked his gaze to her, the panic settling into his breathing. Rance could see the man's heartbeat thumping at his temple, see the sweat starting to pop up on his forehead. Rance could almost hear the thoughts flitting through the man's head and knew he wouldn't like the trail they followed. "There's nowhere to go, so just put the gun down and tell us why you're here," Rance said, stepping slightly away from the wall but keeping his gun level to the man's chest. "C'mon, look around you. You're in the middle of nowhere. Who knows what wild animals are out there, just waiting for a snake snack. Let's just put the guns down and talk."

The man jerked his gaze back and forth between Rance and the deputy, unsure who was who and who to listen to. The deputy tightened her grip on her gun, but otherwise stood there, letting Rance handle it. *Now that's a shocker.*

The man took a deep breath and then jerked around and bolted, jumping off the porch onto the grass as he attempted his escape.

"Damn it!" Rance shouted. "I hope he gets eaten by an alligator." Then he shouted at the fleeing man. "Did you hear that? I hope you get eaten by an alligator!"

The deputy, however, was already out the door, chasing the man, screaming at him to stop.

Rance sighed, wondering why she was doing this the hard way. With a heavy sigh, he started to strip, preparing to shift.

Three

Lainie knew just by looking at the man in the doorway that he was ready to bolt. Yet, Rance seemed determined to attempt to talk the man out of his weapon. She gripped the handle of her gun tighter, wanting to shake her head, but not wanting to give anything away to the thug enduring an intercession with Rance. *Big town cops and their stupid ways. He's had a chip on his shoulder since he showed up at my crime scene, thinking he knows how best to handle things. All big city cops are the same, no matter how much their eyes smoldered.*

Lainie watched as the intruder took a deep breath, and her panther sensed what was about to take place and growled. Then, just as she knew would happen, the punk turned and darted away, jumping off the porch onto the grass as he attempted his escape.

"Damn it!" Rance shouted, just standing there staring as the man made a quick retreat. "I hope he gets eaten by an alligator." His frustrated mumble almost made her laugh, but then he shouted at the fleeing man. "Did you hear that? I hope you get eaten by an alligator!"

What a frickin' idiot. Lainie shoved past the detective in pursuit of the other man. There was no way the kid would get far, not in her woods, not some city-slicker who thought he was all bad-ass because he belonged to a gang. Her panther begged to be let loose, but Lainie resisted the urge, mainly because she didn't need either of the men—the one she chased *or* the one she left behind—seeing her naked when she shifted back. Besides, where would she put her handcuffs?

She leaped over a fallen log, swiping at a low hanging branch as she passed it, knocking it out of her face before it left a mark. With the stamina of her panther, she raced after the man, gaining quickly. Movement off to her right tried to snag her attention, but she ignored it, choosing instead to keep her focus on the man in front of her. Of course, then she wondered if he was alone or not. There was no doubt the kid was involved in Roger's death. There really was no other explanation as to a gang member being in Bull Creek. Yet, Roger was dead, the deed done. So why the fleeing man even showed up at the cabin baffled her.

She heard a roar as something burst through the foliage in front of the man she pursued, a giant wolf leaping out to block the man's path. The gang member screamed, skidding to a halt, but his feet slid out in front of him, and he fell to his ass. She watched as he crab-walked backward trying to get away from the wolf in front of him. She slowed her pace to a walk, her chest heaving with the breaths she took as she reached down and grabbed the man by the collar, rolling him over. Pulling her handcuffs from behind her back, she started reciting the man's Miranda rights, her gaze on the wolf who stood in front of them, his tongue lolling out from his exertion. Her panther purred its admiration within her, a thirst for the wolf in front of her overwhelming. *Knock it off,* she scolded her panther.

"Get that thing away from me, man," the punk said, as he squirmed on the ground, doing his best to flip over.

Lainie picked the man up and slammed him back down on the ground. "What's the matter? A big tough shit like you is afraid of a little dog? Ah, that's so adorable."

"You're crazy, lady." The man's breathing came in rapid gasps as he kept his gaze on the wolf, still doing his best to roll over and get away from the animal.

Lainie picked his shoulders off the ground again and slammed him back down. "I said knock it off, damn it." She shook her head as she stood up straight. She left the handcuffed man on the ground for now, placing her hands on her hips as she stared at the dark gray wolf, its golden eyes staring back at her. Things just became a little more complicated.

Her panther salivated within her, wanting to shift and be with the wolf. *Okay, a lot more complicated.*

With a shake of her head, she pointed back to the cabin. "Go on, get out of here," she said with a frustrated tone. "I'll meet you back at the sheriff's office."

"What?" the man on the ground shouted. "What the hell you talkin' about, lady? You're not leaving me here with that thing."

Lainie blew out a breath as she ran her hand through her hair. "If only I could."

The wolf barked once, the sound almost like a laugh, and then it turned on its hind legs and darted back into the woods. She did not doubt that Rance Culpepper would be waiting for her at the sheriff's office by the time she arrived.

With a shake of her head, she reached down and gripped the gang member under the arm. "Come on, get up." She was sure the kid was alone or else someone would have come to his aid by now. "Wanna tell me what you were hoping to find at the cabin?"

"Go to hell." The kid tried to jerk away, and Lainie was tempted to trip him and watch him hit the dirt, but she needed to get back to the office before Rance ran his mouth to Chet. Still, it would be nice to know what the kid wanted from within Roger's place.

She spun the kid around and shoved him toward the cabin. "If I were you, I wouldn't try and get away. That detective was right; there are alligators out here, and I highly doubt they get much to eat in these woods."

The kid turned and glanced at her over his shoulder, his eyes wide, his expression unsure whether she told the truth or not. She just gave him a blank look as she continued walking. He turned back around, only this time he kept staring around them, checking for wild animals, she was sure.

When they arrived back at the cabin, she glanced around, trying to discover if Rance was still around or not. *Where did he come from anyway?* She was sure she would have heard a car pull up, and even if she hadn't, the idiot in front of her surely would have seen Rance get out and approach the cabin. So how did Rance get here?

She took the gang member to her vehicle, shoving him into the back seat, doing her best not to be gentle with him. It was his fault, after all, that she had to deal with Rance in the first place.

"You really should let me go, Missy," the kid said, his eyes narrowed as he tried to look menacing. "You don't know what you're getting in the middle of. The Serpents aren't a group to be messed with."

She just stared at him a moment, and then shut the car door, turning back to the cabin as she put the kid out of her mind. She came here to get a look around and wasn't going to leave without getting it. Making sure the car was secure, she stepped back into the cabin, her hands on her hips as she gazed around. *What were you hoping to find?*

While she already planned on searching the cabin when she first arrived, now with the appearance of the Serpent gang member outside, she knew there was something to find here, so she searched with a more thorough intent. Opening doors, peeking inside cabinets and closets, Lainie searched every drawer and cubby, nook and cranny, she came across. Nothing out of the ordinary stood out to her, however. Roger O'Brien lived a minimalist, subdued lifestyle. Of course, he had only been here two weeks, and he was on the run, so it stood to reason he didn't have much baggage in case he needed to vamoose pretty quick again. Still, the gang member must have thought Roger possessed something vital or he would have run back to Pensacola after killing the man, instead of hanging around to sightsee. So, what was he looking for?

As she wandered through the back half of the cabin, she came across a desk in the extra bedroom. She searched the drawers, the file cabinet, even did a scan for secret compartments, having watched too many spy movies. She stared down at the desktop, her hands on her hips, knowing she was missing something, but not sure what it was. Then it hit her. There was no computer, but there was a clean square spot in the middle of a dusty desktop, the perfect size for a laptop. But why was it missing? They caught the man in the back of her car before he could search the cabin, and to the best of her knowledge, she was the only…

Rance. *Damn him!* She turned and bolted back out of the cabin and to her car. The detective had plenty of time to search the place before she returned with the Serpent member. She should have known better than to trust a city boy.

She started the engine even before she had the driver's door closed, ignoring the man in the back seat and his protests as she jerked the car into gear and hit the gas. Rance Culpepper better hope she didn't get her hands on him, because as much as her panther wanted to jump his body and see how well a wolf and a panther could do together,

Lainie wanted to throttle the man. And she would if she found him.

She slammed her palm into the steering wheel. *Damn!* She should have known better than to let him out of her sight.

"What's the matter, pretty lady?" The Serpent said from the backseat. "Someone take all the Frosted Flakes out of the cabin?"

"Shut up," she snapped, both hands on the steering wheel, pretending the hard plastic was Rance's neck. She sped through the dirt roads of Bull Creek on her way to the sheriff's office, ready to put an all-points-bulletin out on Rance's car. She'd arrest him for interfering in an investigation, eager to throw the handcuffs on him and slap him behind bars.

Her pussy dripped, her panther drooling at the thought of Rance in cuffs and at her mercy. Lainie growled, doing her best to ignore the images her panther kept shoving into her mind. *Stay out of it!* Of all the times for her panther to be horny, now was not it. Lainie knew what her animal tried to tell her, but she refused to listen. She didn't need to be mated to some jackass of a detective who probably couldn't find his way out of the woods even if he did shift into his wolf. No, the man was a sneaky, mangy...

She sighed. Good looking, strong, seductive man. *God, I so do not need this right now.*

Four

Rance walked into the sheriff's office, the laptop tucked under his arm. Once he had reached the cabin again and shifted, he dressed and did a quick scan of the structure. The only thing of importance in the whole place was an ancient laptop. Rance shoved it into an evidence bag he found in the deputy's car and then stowed it in his duffel bag along with his clothes. Roger was doing more than hiding in Bull Creek; he was hiding from life. He only had a few changes of clothes, no other electronics, such as a music device or television, no books to mention, which made Rance wonder what the man did out in the middle of nowhere to keep from going off the rails. Bull Creek was a quiet getaway, but Rance wasn't sure if he could last without something to distract him besides watching the hands of a clock tick.

He grinned as he walked up to the receptionist's desk. Of course, if he had Lainie Everest in his cabin, he could let time pass without worry. Spunky, sassy even, but it suited her. He couldn't wait to get her off this case and see where the two of them could go. His wolf already made his claim, but Rance knew there was no way the deputy would give him the time of day if she still thought he intended to steal her case away from her.

"Can I help you?" the gray-haired lady behind the desk asked, looking up at him over the rim of her glasses.

"Rance Culpepper here to see Sheriff Chet Einstein. Is he here?"

"One moment." He watched as she picked up the phone and hit a button in the middle of the ancient rotary device. Rance just stared at it, wondering where in the world they dug it up, and then realized it probably came with the building. He tapped the laptop with his thumb, his impatience making him jittery. "Yes, sir," she said, then hung up the phone and peered back at Rance over her glasses again. "He'll be right out."

Rance nodded and then turned to wait, his thumb still tapping against the laptop. He had assumed Lainie wouldn't have time to search the cabin with the Serpent in her custody, so while the place was still open and not locked down, he took it upon himself to search the cabin. The laptop was all he came up with, but he hadn't opened it yet. As much as he wanted to see if the video was on the thing, he didn't need a wall to come up between him and Lainie just because he took a sneak peek. His future with her held other plans.

"Detective Culpepper, right?"

Turning, Rance saw the sheriff, his leathery hand extended for a handshake. "Yes, Sheriff Einstein, thanks for coming out." He handed the man the laptop wrapped in the plastic evidence bag. "I discovered this at Roger's cabin. Your deputy should be behind me shortly with a prisoner in her custody." He then started to relate the tale of what transpired at the cabin with the Serpent member.

The sheriff took the evidence bag with the laptop but gave Rance a skeptical look. "Lainie permitted you to go with her to the cabin? Last I heard, she didn't want you anywhere near her case."

Rance gave a slight shrug, not really wanting to admit to the sheriff how he had tracked the deputy and followed her to the cabin from the crime scene. "Let's say I turned up at the right time. The gang member who probably killed Roger was sneaking into the cabin to attack the deputy. I arrived in time to give her a heads up and assisted in the guy's capture."

The sheriff nodded slowly, his expression clearly showing he knew he was missing something. He held the laptop up. "And you didn't go through this? If I remember correctly, you were searching for a video for your case."

Rance shook his head. "As tempting as that was, I decided to go the proper route through channels." Then he gave his own weak shrug. "I'm pretty sure I've already pressed my luck with your deputy as far as is safe."

"There you are, you son of a bitch." Lainie's voice came

from behind them, her tone making it quite apparent she was not happy about his search of the cabin. "What the hell did you think you were doing?"

The sheriff chuckled, giving a shake of his head. "Yup. I'd say you pretty much pressed your luck. I'll hold onto this." The man then turned and headed back to his office, leaving Rance to deal with the irate deputy.

"Watch him," Lainie ordered as she shoved the Serpent member toward another deputy.

Rance watched as she stormed toward him, her expression dark and thunderous. "Look, I can explain," he said, holding his hands up in front of him. He didn't think she'd strike him in a room full of witnesses, but he wasn't taking that chance. "I've already given your laptop to the sheriff. I didn't even open it. Just bagged and tagged it."

"And you think that gives you the right to steal my evidence?" She jabbed him in the chest with her finger as she continued her tirade, her nail digging into him. "I told you I didn't need your help or even want it on this case. I told you to stay away from it, but oh no, you just had to go and dive right in." She kept stabbing him with her finger, making him back up a step each time until his back was against the receptionist's desk and he was forced to stand there and take it.

And take it he did, his wolf purring at her temper and the way she came at him like she did. This was no weakling in front of him, and his wolf more than approved. He wanted her and almost busted through Rance's flesh to take her, not caring that they were in the middle of the sheriff's department. Every eye in the place had turned, everyone halting whatever they worked on and gawking at the spectacle in the foyer.

While Rance was being berated in front of the entire sheriff's department by a woman an entire head shorter than him, he couldn't stop thinking how sexy she looked in her anger. Her nostrils flared a bit, her eyes narrow slits, and her mouth was pinched even as she yelled at him, and instead of wanting to argue back, all he wanted to do was take her out of there and bend her over, ramming his cock into her from behind and claiming her for all to see.

Something in his expression must have suggested his thoughts were not on her outrage because she stopped yelling, her hands thrust onto her hips, and glared at him. "What the hell are you smiling at?" she asked, her fluster now a confused annoyance.

He felt the grin spread across his face, knowing he should stop it, but unable to do so. "You look cute when you're pissed off, that's all."

"What..?" She shook her head, her dark hair swishing across her back. "Are you fucking kidding me? You think flirting with me is the best way out of this situation?"

He gave a slow shake of his head. "No, but I wasn't really flirting. I meant it. And for the record, I was just trying to help back there. I already gave the laptop—untouched by me—to your sheriff, all nice and tidy in an evidence bag, which I found in your car." He leaned back on the receptionist's desk, his hands gripping the edges. "I assumed you would be busy with the Serpent kid and didn't want to take the chance of someone else from the gang being around and searching the cabin before you had a chance to send the crime unit out." He shrugged. "I didn't even open it, just bagged it and brought it here."

She stood there, her hands going across her chest as she glared at him, and he could tell she wanted to find something else to yell at him for but couldn't think of anything. His actions surprised her, he knew, keeping her off-guard, which was to his advantage if he was going to give his wolf what the animal wanted. Her breathing was ragged, the heaviness of it causing her breasts to rise and fall under her arms, her cheeks flushed. He'd kiss her if he didn't think she'd slap the hell out of him.

With a tilt of his head, he offered what he hoped was a disarming smile. "Maybe we can go look at that laptop?" he asked. "Perhaps both of us will find what we need for our cases, and then, if you really want, I can get out of your hair. Or, perhaps, we could get a drink or something."

Her eyes widened, and he could smell the effect his offer had on her, the pheromones of her—panther?—shouting to him that her animal gave her the same urges his wolf gave him. "You're unbelievable," she said.

He nodded. "I've been told." Then he grinned. "But you didn't say no."

She blew out a frustrated breath, the rush of air flapping her bangs over her forehead. He couldn't take his eyes off her lips, wanting to kiss her with a hunger he never before felt.

She dropped her arms to her sides as she turned and

walked toward the back of the department. "Fine. Come on. The sooner we get you your damn video, the sooner I get you out of my hair."

He watched her storm away, her ass sashaying, drawing all eyes to her, and she probably didn't even know the effect she had on the men around her, especially him. He grinned as he pushed himself off the desk with a bump of his ass. *You may get me out of your hair, but you and I both know you won't get me out of your mind. Not with your panther feeling what my wolf feels.* This was definitely going to be a fun mating.

Five

nfrickin' believable! Lainie stormed through the sheriff's department, her hands clinched into tight fists. She didn't need Rance's charm or assistance. She didn't need him anywhere near her, no matter how much her panther panted in his direction. Besides, his entire story reeked of bullshit. She wasn't sure what game he played, but he definitely worked some angle, and until she knew what it was, she would keep him as far away from her as possible.

She rapped on the doorframe of Chet's office before barging inside. "Did this idiot give you a laptop?"

Chet glanced up at her from underneath his gray bangs, a grin pushing up his cheeks. "Nice to see you're playing well with others." He reached out to the top of his desk and tapped the plastic bag perched there. "I think this is what you want."

She reached out, taking the evidence bag, and stared at the laptop. "Have you looked at it yet?" Noise from behind her caught her attention, but she didn't turn around. She knew it was Rance. The man could wait.

Chet shook his head. "No. I figured you'd want the first go round. Of course," he glanced behind her to where she knew Rance stood, "looks like you might have an audience." Chet grinned again and then waved them out of his office.

As Lainie shoved past Rance, who just stood there, his hands out to the side in a gesture of surrender, Deputy Johnson yelled out. "Lainie, where do you want this guy?" He held the Serpent member by his forearm, his own posture bored, as if he wanted to hurry off to anything but what he was doing.

"Just stick him in the box and put someone on him. I'll get to him in a minute." She turned back to Rance, even though it was the last thing she wanted to do. "Well, are you coming with me or not?"

She didn't face him long enough to wait for a response, but she knew he wore a smug smirk. Her panther purred within, and Lainie just shook her head. *This is not the time.* But then, the way his jeans wrapped around his ass and the strength in his shoulders just made her…

Stop!

God, she really didn't need this now.

Turning into an empty office, she plopped into one of the chairs, ignoring Rance as he did the same, not wanting to see his thick thighs wrapping around…

Stop it, damn it!

She ripped the evidence bag open, sliding the laptop onto the desk. She took a deep breath, staring at the device a moment before opening it. She wasn't sure why she even bothered. Roger was dead, and she couldn't imagine anything on this computer telling her who did it. Looking up, she glanced over at Rance who just sat there, patiently waiting for her to do whatever she was going to do, hands clasped in front of him on the table. The angelic schoolboy. She rolled her eyes.

She flipped the lid of the laptop open, hitting enter to wake it up. As she waited for it to boot, she looked over at Rance, his golden eyes expectant, almost hopeful. "I wouldn't get your hopes up," she said. "There may be nothing on here."

"I'll take my chance."

The laptop beeped, drawing Lainie's attention back to the screen. *Great. The damn thing needs a password.* "You've followed him," she said, her tone frustrated and snappy. "Any ideas what his password would be?"

Rance stared at the screen a moment, his brow furrowed in concentration. Finally, he shook his head. "No, not a clue." He glanced over at her, his gaze hopeful. "Don't you have a team who can crack it?"

"Yeah, but not as fast as either one of us wants right now." *Not fast enough to get you out of Bull Creek.* She fell back into her chair with a sigh of aggravation. "Great." *Now what?*

"There's always the gang member we brought in," Rance said.

"*We* brought in?"

"What? I helped you catch him, and you know it. Not that I want credit or anything. It's your collar. I'm just saying, maybe now is a good time to talk to him."

As much as Lanie didn't want to agree with anything Rance said, he made sense, and it pissed her off. "Fine, let's go." She didn't wait to see if he followed her. There was no way he would be left behind. If she didn't know better, she would swear Chet set this little partnership up just for shits and grins. She'd have to find some way to get even with him, the old coot.

A deputy stood by the door to the interrogation room, the square, bare space called the box by the sheriffs, his hands clasped in front of him as he stared off into space. Lainie didn't envy him but knew his situation was the price for being low man on the totem pole in the department. She nodded to him as she passed him, opening the door, Rance right behind her.

The kid sat at a boring table, his hands handcuffed with the cuffs attached to a ring in the table in front of him. As they entered the room, he jerked his attention toward them, yanking on the cuffs. "What the hell, woman? I didn't do nothing for you to do this. You need to let me go. Now."

Lainie walked around to the other side of the table, ignoring the kid's words. They all said the same thing. It was a misunderstanding. They didn't belong there. They did nothing wrong. Then, they were all found guilty and sent to prison. She was sure this kid would suffer the same fate.

She slid into the chair across from the gang member,

Rance taking the chair beside her. She did her best to ignore the detective, but her panther paid more attention to him than the man who wanted to kill her. She didn't need this distraction right now.

"Look, I thought it was my friend's cabin, okay," the gang member said. "I was playing a practical joke, you know. When I saw you, I got scared and ran. See? A misunderstanding." He lifted his arms as high as they would go, feigning innocence. "Now, can we get these off?"

Lainie gave a slow nod as if she contemplated what the kid said. "A practical joke, huh? So, whose cabin did you think you were entering?"

"I told you, lady. My friend's. I was wrong, that's all."

"And your friend's name?" She gave a noncommittal shrug. "You know, just so we can verify your story and get you out of here." She leaned forward on the table, hands clasped in front of her as she gave the punk a smile, knowing he lied and just waiting for it all to play out. None of them would just admit their crime and make the whole thing easy. They always made her jump through hoops.

Rance stared at her a moment, but she didn't look his way. Then, out of the corner of her eye, she saw him match her posture and stare at the Serpent member, waiting as well. The kid squirmed a moment, shifting in his seat, his hands clasped in front of him. "Johnnie, I think."

"You think?" Lainie leaned forward a little. "You don't know your friend's name? You must not be all that close."

The kid shrugged. "He's more a friend of a friend. So can I go now?"

Rance leaned forward, closer to the punk kid. "Snake sent you to kill Roger. We know why you're here, so how about just cutting the bullshit and tell us what you were looking for?"

Lainie stared at Rance, her mouth open slightly. *Unbelievable. He's still trying to steal my case.*

The kid jerked in his seat. "Who said I killed anyone? I didn't kill anyone. I didn't kill that Roger dude. What the hell, man?"

Lainie shook her head. "If you didn't kill Roger O'Brien, then what were you doing at his cabin? And don't tell me you were playing a prank. We know better. Save us some time, will ya, and just tell us what we need to know."

The kid turned his dark eyes on Lainie, narrowing them as he glared at her. Leaning over the table toward her, he sneered, "All you need to know is the Serpents take care of their own, and if I were you, I'd just back out of that old man's death."

"Threatening me?" Lainie shook her head. "Not really a smart…"

"What the hell did you just say, punk?" Before Lainie could react, Rance snatched across the table, gripping the kid's shirt, pulling him halfway across the table. "You don't talk to her that way."

The kid screamed as Lainie reached out and grabbed Rance's arm, pulling him off the kid. "What the hell are you doing?" she screamed at the detective, yanking on his arm. She wasn't sure he was going to let go of the kid though, and her panther was almost as furious as Rance seemed to be at what happened. Glancing down at his hand she noticed the slight dark gray fur starting to ooze out of his flesh before he got himself under control.

Tossing the kid back into his seat, Rance dropped back into his chair, his breathing coming out in heavy gasps. Lainie could swear she heard a growl come from him as well.

She remained standing, staring at the detective. *If he screws up my case...*

Rance crossed his arms over his chest as he stared at the kid through narrowed eyes. Lainie could only shake her head as she sat back down. With a deep breath, she turned back to the kid. "So, you admit to killing Roger? Why? So he wouldn't testify in the case back in Pensacola? You don't think him running off to hide was good enough indication that he had changed his mind about testifying? You needed to make sure?"

The kid dropped back in his seat, slouching down as he glared at Rance. "You're lucky I'm in these cuffs, dude, or I'd teach you not to touch me."

Rance jerked forward in his chair but didn't cross the table. The kid shoved backward as far as he could go with the cuffs holding him in place, his eyes wide. Rance chuckled. "Yeah, I can see I have a lot to be worried about."

"Will you knock it off or get the hell out of here," Lainie snapped at him. She continued to stare at Rance until he nodded his acquiescence, although she doubted he meant it. Turning back to the kid, she said, "And you shut your mouth with that shit. No one is buying your tough guy facade. Hell, you shit your pants when you faced off with a mangy mutt."

"Mangy mutt?" Rance jerked around to face her, his mouth open as he stared at her. "Who are you calling a mangy mutt?"

"So, why did you kill Roger?" she asked the gang member again, ignoring Rance.

The kid shrugged. Then he glanced up at her, his head cocked to the side in a way that made her want to slap the back of his head and tell him to sit up straight. "I didn't say I killed nobody. But if someone did, they were probably just tying up loose ends, you know. Making sure no one changed their mind about anything."

"Oh, is that right?" Lainie shifted in her seat. "And your trip to the cabin was what? Making sure his ghost didn't come back to life?"

"Nah, man. Like I said, I didn't pull no trigger on the man. My only job was to search his house for some video." He shrugged again. "I don't know who shot your man, lady, but it wasn't me. I'm just the clean-up man."

"So you're saying the murderer has returned to Pensacola now that Roger's dead?" Rance asked, his tone a little calmer.

But the gang member just shook his head. "No one goes back to Pensacola until all the loose ends are silenced."

Lainie sat back in her chair, her brows bunched over her nose. Turning to Rance, she wondered what other loose ends the kid referred to if Roger O'Brien was dead. Rance just shook his head. *Great. I hate this case.*

Six

Rance parked in front of Everglades, the only place in the small community that passed for a bar. However, looking at the dilapidated building, he still possessed his doubts about that. The building looked more like a piecemeal shack thrown together after a hurricane than an actual structure built on purpose. With his luck, Rance would walk inside and the whole place would give up the ghost and come crashing down around him. *I really hope this place at least has decent whiskey.* After the scene at the sheriff's department, Rance desperately needed a drink.

Opening his door, he slid out of his car, shoving the keys into his pocket, and took a deep breath of the stifling evening air. As he turned toward the entrance, his mind shifted back to the interrogation of the Serpent gang member. Rance had no idea what the kid meant by loose ends. With Roger dead, what else was there to worry about except the video, which was already in evidence lockup? Unless they stormed the sheriff's department, there was no way they would get their hands on Roger's cell phone or the laptop, so what loose ends did he mean? None of it made sense, and Rance chalked it up to being the punk's last-ditch effort to sound menacing.

The interior of Everglades was just as rundown as the exterior with scratched up wooden chairs and tables, appearing as if the whole place was thrown together in much the same way as the building itself. Weak mirrors and flashing beer logos covered the walls while country music blared from a banged-up jukebox. It was nothing like a nightclub in the city. Instead, it held the feel of a homier, comfier environment, more good ol' boy than hipster. Perfect for Bull Creek, but definitely a far cry from anything in Pensacola.

Being barely past five o'clock, only a few patrons occupied the barstools around the sturdiest structure in the place, the actual bar. Behind the wooden barrier stood a thick, burly man with shaggy, dark hair and gray eyes, his attention focused on a curvaceous blond leaning across the bar, her ass swaying as she gave the man a salacious grin. *Definitely, some employee fraternization going on there.*

Nodding at the burly man when he glanced his way, Rance slid onto a barstool and ordered a bourbon on the rocks. As he waited for his drink, he spun on the stool and soaked in the atmosphere of the place. In a dark corner toward the back, a couple leaned over the table and whispered to each other, probably sultry words of what they would do to each other if they weren't sitting in the dilapidated bar. Rance chuckled to himself as he allowed his gaze to wander around the establishment. Two men sat together in the back, sipping beers, and laughing about not working, while two others sat at the bar, drinking slowly from glasses and cutting up with the bartender.

Rance heard the glass hit the wooden bar behind him and turned, reaching for his whiskey. The bartender stood there, staring at him. "Haven't seen you around before. Visiting someone or just passing through?" the thick-chested man asked.

Rance arched an eyebrow at the man. "Does anyone *just passing through* even see this place?"

The man laughed, nodding. "True. Everglades is a little off the beaten path. So, that means visiting. My name's Wes, by the way."

"Rance," Rance said as he reached for his glass, and then he shook his head. "And actually, I'm working." He leaned on the bar, both hands wrapped around his glass. "I'm a detective for the D.A.'s office in Pensacola. One of our witnesses ran down here to avoid his civic duty."

Wes nodded. "A lot of people come here to hide. That's the whole purpose of Bull Creek, to escape the outside world and all of its hatred." Rance noticed the man looked down the bar at the server he was talking to when Rance entered the place, a somber expression clouding his face. With a deep breath, he turned back to Rance. "Sheriff Einstein has a good group around him. You should be able to work with them pretty well."

Rance laughed in a short burst. "I've met one of his deputies, a Lainie Everest." He shook his head, lifting his glass back to his lips. "She doesn't play well with others." *And yet my wolf wants to play hard with her.* Rance wasn't sure how he would rectify what his animal wanted, the burning desire of the mating call, and the fact that Lainie thought he was a nuisance. "I think she feels like I interfered with her case, even though it started out as my case back in Pensacola."

Wes chuckled softly as he braced himself with his hands on the bar, leaning on it. "Yeah, Lainie is pretty protective of her friends and her job. Her brother is the alpha of Bull Creek, so she feels a certain responsibility to the place." Then he shrugged. "Everyone who lives here pretty much feels protective of each other. We've had some pretty rough spots lately. It makes trusting strangers hard."

Rance took a sip of his drink. "I noticed."

Wes told Rance to let him know if he needed anything else and then wandered off to play grab ass with his waitress, not that Rance could blame the man. The blond Wes flirted with had curves in perfect places and, it seemed, eyes only for the thick-chested man. Rance only wished he could get Lainie to look at him that way.

He sipped his whiskey, turning the situation over in his mind. While he needed to put an end to the case he was on, he also needed to somehow get Lainie to think he was something more than a moron. Not that he had done a great job of turning her opinion in the other direction, of course.

That's me, always a bull in a China shop. His mind also pondered the gang member's last words. What loose ends needed to be settled? Why hadn't he just killed the man and then left? Of course, the kid denied killing Roger, but then again, who would readily admit murder? Still...

Rance downed his whiskey, starting to leave his stool, as an idea struck him. Or rather, more of a worry. As he turned, he almost ran into Lainie, her hand pressing against his chest, keeping him from knocking her to the ground. His wolf growled within him, the hunger quickly filling him as he struggled to regain his footing.

"In a hurry?" Lainie asked. "Not rushing off on my account, are you?"

Her smile brought a twitch in his pants as he settled back on the barstool. "Sorry, no, I was actually on my way to see you."

"And eagerly, it seems," she teased, sliding onto the barstool beside him. "Why the rush?" She waved at Wes, who only nodded at her as he reached into a bin of ice under the bar and pulled out a beer.

Rance waited until the man slid the beer in front of Lainie and then turned back to his own lady friend before speaking. "If that kid means what he says about not being the one who killed Roger, then that means there's someone else in town. Perhaps even more than just one. Serpents tend to travel in groups. That makes me think of the loose ends that kid talked about back there. The only one I can think of is that video."

Lainie finished taking a sip of her beer, then nodded as

she set the bottle on the bar. "Which is locked up safely in evidence. They'd have to go through a shitload of sheriffs just to reach it. Not the best scenario."

Rance ordered another whiskey, mulling over what she said. Lainie was right about them not getting the evidence by busting through the front door of the sheriff's department. Something else had to be up then, but what could it be?

Lainie licked her lips after setting her beer bottle back on the table, and the glide of her tongue snapped his attention back around, his wolf growling his hunger. Rance felt his cock twitch again and shifted in his seat searching for some relief. If Lainie sensed his discomfort, at least, she kept quiet about it. "So, do you usually use your wolf to capture criminals in Pensacola?"

Rance shook his head, his glass held in his hand in the air over the bar. "Nah, too much steel and concrete to run freely like that. I actually have to travel toward Alabama to allow my wolf to run free and stretch. To be honest, it felt good to get the drop on that punk like that earlier."

"I don't know how you do it. I love allowing my panther the freedom to run at times. I need these woods. I wouldn't have left Draven Falls if I wasn't moving to another town just like it, with less cold, of course."

"Draven Falls? That's where you're from?"

She nodded, her dark hair falling into her eyes. He fought not to reach out and swish her hair back out of the way, wanting to see her golden eyes. "It is," she answered. "My parents had plans for me that I didn't quite agree with, and so I followed my brother here. Dimitri is the alpha of Bull

Creek, keeping an eye on the community's residents. A group back home helped him set up the township, making it a refuge of sorts for those who don't seem to fit in anywhere else." She shrugged. "It seemed natural for me to come here."

He smiled, her pride of the community infectious. Then an idea struck him, and he found himself grinning. "So, how about a little shifter investigating?"

She cocked her head to the side as she stared at him. "What did you have in mind?"

"Someone from the Serpents is still here somewhere." He shrugged, twirling his glass back and forth. "Why not go back to the main scene and allow our animals to sniff around some? If that kid's telling the truth, we should be able to pick up a trail still."

She gave a slow nod as if thinking the idea over. Finally, she said, "Actually, that sounds like a pretty damn good idea." She then turned, one eyebrow raised, and one corner of her mouth upturned in a grin. "Of course, if this is just some asinine ploy to get me out of my clothes…"

"What? What are..?" He laughed as he shook his head. The fact that they would have to strip was not something he had thought about when he made the suggestion, shifting being a natural part of their lives. Still, he had to admit it was definitely a plus in his book. "If you'd rather I went alone, I don't mind. Or you can follow me as I sniff around."

She snorted in laughter. "Now you just want me to see you naked while you steal my case. Nope. We'll do it together. Just don't get any crazy ideas. I have no problem arresting another detective, especially one who doesn't live around here."

Rance grinned at her as he motioned for Wes to settle his tab, motioning for the man to include Lainie's beer as well. "Now you just want to get me in handcuffs," he said, grinning. "I can't say I'm surprised. I knew you liked me."

Lainie rolled her eyes. "I'll meet you outside. We can take my car. I prefer being in control."

Rance handed Wes his credit card, but kept his gaze on Lainie, his wolf dancing inside. "I assumed as much when you wanted to put me in handcuffs. My safe word is pineapple, by the way, you know, just in case it comes up."

"I wouldn't hold your breath." He watched as she slid off the barstool, turned and walked toward the exit, his eyes glued to the way her pants snugged against her ass. *This case definitely has its perks.*

Seven

Lainie watched as Rance pulled his shirt over his head, his muscles rippling, his abs pulled taut. She forced herself to look away before her panther urged her to take the man where he stood. She did not need these feelings right now, not with a killer still on the loose. To be honest, she didn't need her panther's stirrings, period, having made her peace with a celibate life. However, as Rance started to unbutton his pants and she heard the zipper sliding downward, she couldn't stop herself from turning back around to watch as he slid his pants down his powerful legs, the material slipping over his ass as he faced away from her, his ass firm, full. *Bite-able.* Her breath caught in her throat as she jerked her gaze back around, away from where the detective stripped, ready to shift and track the assailant.

Oh god, it's my turn. While shifters were quite comfortable being naked in front of others—it was part of their natural world after all—Lainie struggled to be naked in front of Rance right then. *Who am I kidding? I'd be nervous being naked in front of anyone these days.* It had been a long time since Lainie was naked in front of anyone and her last experience had not been a good one.

Facing away from Rance, she began to strip out of her uniform, the afternoon air caressing her bare flesh as her skin was exposed, her mind drifting back to Draven Falls and the cruelty she left behind when her parents tried to force her into a mating against her will. While the whole thing may have been great for her father's business, the coupling was far from great for Lainie. Mark Strickland made it quite clear how things would go once the mating occurred, and to Lainie, it was a journey into servitude instead of a partnership. Mark was arrogant and insufferable, thinking Lainie owed him for bringing her family into the fold of the Strickland empire. It didn't take long for Lainie to tell him where to stick his empire and followed Dimitri to Bull Creek, following the advice of Agatha Rochester.

Once Lainie was nude, she took a deep breath, ready to face whatever crack Rance would make about her body. Mark had made plenty, berating her for her curves. He was crude in his descriptions of her, and she had remained clothed ever since, even choosing not to shift since she left Draven Falls unless she was alone. Her concerns were unnecessary, however. Rance had already shifted and was busy sniffing the ground for traces of a trail. *He's either the only gentleman in the world or everything Mark said is true.*

Lainie sighed as she began the transformation from human to panther, her bones popping as her body stretched and melted from one form to another, the tawny coat of fur slipping from her flesh as claws slid out of her fingers and toes. The pain made her shudder and whimper, her tolerance diminished since it had been a while since she last shifted. The transformation was a mixture of pain and freedom. She sneezed once it was over, her feline catching a whiff of the pollen in the air she didn't like. Once the sneeze was over, Lainie padded over to where Rance's wolf sniffed around.

Well? She sent to him using the mindspeech of the shifters. *Anything popping up?*

He gave his head a hard shake, then lowered it back down to the ground. *Might be better if you give it a go. My nose is used to city life. All these scents are too new to me to pick out what doesn't belong, especially without anything really to go on.*

Lainie couldn't argue with his logic and set about sorting out the scents on the ground. She found Chet's and Johnson's, the Crime Scene Unit people, and even hers and Rance's. Then she discovered Roger, tracking it to the edge of the clearing, but stopping before tracking it any further. They didn't need to know where he came from, at least not yet. With her nose to the ground, she sniffed around the perimeter of the crime scene until she came across a scent she didn't recognize, and it wasn't the kid back in holding. Wait. No. There were two scents. She sniffed around some more, trying to pinpoint which direction they appeared and where they went. When she finally had a trail she felt confident about, she sent, *This way. If they're city kids like the last one, they won't even suspect two animals on their trail.*

Makes sense to me, Rance sent.

Lainie led the way, Rance right behind her, their paws snapping small branches and crunching on the dry fallen leaves. Lainie's panther moved with lithe grace, weaving among the trees and bushes as she followed the trail she had picked up, while Rance's wolf was more rambunctious, like a dog, excited to be out of a building and in the woods. With the noise he made, Lainie wished she had put him on a leash. She would have thought he knew better than to make so much noise in pursuit of an adversary. *City cops.*

The trail wound through the woods, the giant oaks and pines providing covering for the trail they followed, casting it in shadows. The leaves stopped crunching and turned more to a squish under their paws as they continued to follow the scent. Birds flew overhead as crickets sounded from their hiding spots in the bushes. Squirrels chittered their warning of intruders to any who would listen, displeased at the disturbance to their peaceful surroundings. In the distance, Lainie detected a slight hint of smoke in the air and slowed her pace, suddenly aware that even if they found the murderers, they couldn't exactly do anything about it in their animals' forms. They couldn't even shift back. She was sure confronting the gang members in the buff wasn't good for the report she would need to file. So much for being proactive.

Drawing closer to the smoke, she started to hear voices, at least two people, one seemed to be grumbling while the other told him to shut the hell up. *Ease up,* she sent to Rance.

I think we're almost on them. I can hear two, but not sure how many more there may be, so we need to be cautious.

Rance stepped up beside her, his tongue lolling out the right side of his mouth as he stared ahead of him. *This is your area. I'll follow your lead.*

She gave a mental nod and eased further down the trail, the evening breeze brushing against her fur. The day was starting to be swallowed by night, the temperature dipping a little but not enough to be noticeable to a tourist. As she led the way toward the voices, they became more distinguishable. Definitely two voices, both male, young, and one was definitely not happy.

"I don't get it, man," the unhappy fellow whined. "What are we supposed to do. Knucklehead got his ass caught by a woman. The evidence is already with the cops, dude. How you think we going to get it now?"

She heard the sound of a lighter being flicked, followed quickly by the odor of propane and then cigarette smoke. *Asshole. It's too dry for that shit.* Lainie eased to the edge of the path she followed. Parked between two giant pines, hidden from the main road was a clunker Lincoln, faded puke brown paint with a hard-shell top. The color was enough to ensure they wouldn't be quickly noticed by a speeding car, which worked in the gang members' favor. For now, anyway.

"Then we just got to get someone to get in there and get it for us," the other man said. He seemed older than the first one, more or less the leader of the two. "Snake said get it, so we get it."

"Did Snake have a thought as to how?"

She watched through her golden eyes as the second man shrugged, sticking the cigarette in his mouth, and taking a long drag, holding the smoke for a three-count, before blowing the smoke out. "These small-town cops don't know shit, man. They'll scare pretty easy enough. We just find the weakest one and use them to get us what we need. Hell, we'll use their family if we have to, just to have fun making them do what we want."

"And what about Jace? The cops got him in this stupid-ass town. We can't leave him here."

"Jace should have been smarter than to get caught then. Our concern is that video. Not some idiot who can't kick a female cop's ass."

She watched as the younger of the two moved around the car, slapping at his neck at some insect he felt on his skin. "God, I hate this place. Too many damn bugs, man. Can't we get a hotel or something? This is ridiculous to be sleeping in the car."

The leader of the two sat on the trunk of the long car, his ankles crossed, one arm over his waist as he held his cigarette in his other hand. He seemed confident about not being discovered or at least unworried if he was. They always think they're bigger and tougher than they really are, and if his impression of small-town cops was as low as it sounded, then he really underestimated her. She hated arrogance, people thinking less of her because she was either a female or worked in a small sheriff's department, but it always worked in her favor. Their faulty impression of her made them overstep and slip up, making it easier for her to catch them.

"Then I suggest we hurry up and get what we came here for and then we can get back to Pensacola. Snake said we're not to leave here without it, and I don't know about you, but I'm not one to go against the boss. I've seen what happens to people who do."

"Yeah, like that snitch we had to come out here and kill."

"Shut the fuck up!" The leader shot up straight, swinging his legs off the side of the car as he glared at his partner. "Don't be confessing to anything, even if it's just us you frickin' idiot."

"What? You think the trees have ears?"

"Yeah, well Snake thought he was safe as well, remember? But that dude we came here for recorded that video on him. So, yeah, even the trees can be narcs."

"Fine. So how the hell are we going to get that video since Jace fucked it up?"

Lainie hunched down, her concentration on the exchange she witnessed. If these idiots spilled their plans, she could head them off and get them red-handed, putting an end to her case. She heard enough to know who to send Rance after once they had these morons in custody. At least, that was the plan in her head, but she should have known better. So far, her plans had gone completely awry with the appearance of Rance Culpepper in her life and the pull their animals felt for each other.

"Oh, that'll be easy enough," the older of the two gang members said, his lips twisted up into a sneer. "We're going to catch that bitch sheriff and force her to get us inside to the man's phone and anything else he had on him. Who knows," he added with a shrug. "If she obeys nicely, we might even let her experience Serpent love at its best."

That's all it took for all hell to break loose. Rance's wolf roared into the night, springing from his spot on the ground and leaping after the man who spoke, his mouth open, teeth ready to do some major damage.

Eight

Rance heard what the punk said, knew he needed to sit still and wait it out. They were just words after all, and Lainie and he needed to hear more to know their next move. However, his wolf was in control now, the shift giving the animal more power than his human portion and was not about to allow the man in front of them to threaten the one the wolf had already claimed as his mate. Rance's wolf leaped out of hiding, his claws out and teeth ready to gnash at someone's arm, a growl ripping from his chest.

The man sitting on the trunk of the car screamed, jerking himself backward further on the trunk, trying to shove himself through the rear windshield in his escape. The other kid, eyes wide, screamed as well as he darted around to the front of the car, ducking as if he could hide from the wolf. Rance knew better. There was no hiding from his wolf. Or from him.

What the hell are you doing? He heard Lainie shouting in his mind. *You're screwing everything up, damn it!*

He knew he was screwing it all up, but he also knew there was no stopping his wolf when his mate was threatened. He would pay the price of it later, he was sure, but for now, since his wolf had already jumped out, he saw no reason not to go with it. The older of the two punks crawled backward still, trying to slide up the rear window and on top of the car, probably believing the higher he went, the safer he was. Rance chuckled to himself, thinking the man was an idiot. Hunching down on his back haunches, Rance shoved himself off the ground and onto the back of the car, eliciting another yelp from the gang member. The wolf growled, saliva dripping from his fangs as he walked up toward the man who threatened his mate. It was the last threat the man would ever make.

Determined to put an end to the Serpent, Rance's wolf stepped onto the glass, inching his way closer. His attention was focused on the shaking man; nothing else was in his line of sight, which is why when he was knocked off the car, hurled to the ground, it caught him quite by surprise. The only warning he had was the growl that hit his ears just before he was slammed from the trunk of the car and down to the ground. His wolf yelped as he hit but quickly skidded around back to his feet, his legs braced, ready to take on whoever dared attack him. Yet, he came up short when he saw the tawny panther standing there, snarling at him, its own legs braced for a fight.

Get out of here. Now! Lainie sent to him through the animals' mindspeech.

Rance's wolf shook his head, shaking off the dirt from where he landed on the ground. She was right, and he knew it. Turning his head back to the punk on the car, he growled once more, and then turned and padded back into the woods, fading from sight. He could hear the panther behind him as he walked but refused to turn around. He'd wait as long as possible for his ass-chewing.

Lainie didn't speak to him the entire way back to where they left their clothes hidden in the bushes near the crime scene. As soon as he reached the spot, he shifted, ready to face whatever music was thrown at him. Still, nothing was said. He turned once the shift was over, searching out Lainie. He expected to see her reaching for her clothes, but instead, she stood there, the sun breaking through the branches overhead and kissing her flesh, her hands on her hips as she glared at him. He stood facing her, his arms at his sides. Never before had he felt so vulnerable as he did right then.

She blew out a breath. "What the hell were you thinking? If you've scared them off, I swear, I'll kill you myself."

He could watch her chest heave with her heavy breathing for hours, her breasts rising and falling, his eyes drawn to her nipples, each bud shrunk in on itself and tight. He doubted she knew how beautiful she looked at that moment, standing there, clothed only in the shadows of the sun through the tree branches overhead. "Obviously, my wolf wasn't thinking. He just reacted, and you know why he did. That punk back there threatened you. My wolf wasn't going to allow him to get away with that."

"I've been threatened before. It tends to go with the job." He watched as she took a few steps toward him. "And I don't need you or anyone else protecting me. I can handle myself."

Rance sighed, his hands on his hips, shoulders slumped a little. "I know, I know, but you also know I sometimes don't have that control. My wolf was out and after them before I even knew what was happening." He shrugged, trying not to appear too beaten. "At the time it was done, I just went with it." He glanced up into her eyes, hoping she understood everything he tried hard to say and failed at so miserably. "Lainie, you know I would have avoided that if possible. I know how important it is and what we need. Yet, when the mating call comes upon our animals, there isn't anything we can really do but follow it. I know you feel the same way. Your animal has been emitting the pheromones since we met. Any shifter around us will be able to tell."

She stared at him a moment, and he was afraid he had said way too much. However, everything he said was true, and he knew she knew it. He could smell the heat from her sex, smell the hunger of her animal, the hunger that matched the craving that flooded from his own animal. She glanced around the clearing, avoiding eye contact until he wanted to scream to get her attention. He did not leave Pensacola looking for a mate, but these things were not up to them. Their animals controlled this process, this hunger which had nothing to do with how horny their human counterparts were or how attached they were to someone else. More people had been miserable because they were denied a mating for reckless decisions they made without their animal's approval. Rance had avoided that mistake by ignoring the possibilities for attachment with anyone, choosing one casual affair after another just to feel something, anything but the real thing. Now here he was, and the real thing stared him in the face. Or rather, stared off into the surrounding forest.

"Lainie, I..."

He didn't have the chance to say anything else. She rushed him, each step a deliberate punch to the ground, and at first, he thought she would attack him again, only this time in human form. However, when she reached him, she threw her arms around him instead, her lips finding his as she kissed him roughly, fingers raking through his hair, with a hunger their bodies instantly grew to feel as well.

He stood, stunned, for a moment, before his wolf growled its own hunger. Then he slipped his arms around Lainie's waist, pulling her tight against him, his cock growing against her stomach. Her body felt warm in his arms, her flesh meshed against his, her breasts pressed firmly against his chest. He slid his hand down her curves to cup her ass, never breaking the kiss as their tongues danced. He felt her hands pull at his hair, her fingers gripping it as she kissed him. No one ever felt so perfect in his arms.

When they finally broke the kiss, he looked down into her eyes, the passion reflected there. He felt the smile turn up the corner of his mouth but before he could say anything, Lainie spoke. "No one has ever wanted to protect me like that before. Thank you. But we need to get dressed and find those guys. They may have been spooked enough to move their hiding spot."

He stared at her, his eyes narrowed in his confusion. Surely he didn't hear what he just heard. "You're joking, right? I mean, after that kiss you really want to go hunt bad guys?"

She kissed him one more time, then pushed off his chest as she turned and headed for where her clothes were hidden. He wanted to enjoy the way her ass swayed as she rushed away determined, but then he remembered—she was rushing *away*. "Get dressed. We can't show up as our animals this time. We need to be able to take them into custody," she said.

"For what? What are you going to use to hold them on? A panther and wolf overheard them talking about their plans? Surely that's not enough to concern ourselves about right now, not when…" He pointed down to his rock-hard cock.

She grinned at him, her clothes dangling from her fingertips. "Do you really think after your stunt you deserve more than a kiss right now? I mean, you still screwed up back there, even if it was for the sweetest reason."

"Well," he sighed. "Now that you mention it and put it that way, I was trying to be protective. That should give me some brownie points. Besides, we're back to where we were before; we can't really charge them yet. Our animals aren't exactly allowed to testify."

She stared at him a moment and then shook her head. "But we know what they want, and even more, we know who they plan to use in order to obtain it."

He watched her, his eyes staring straight at hers, fighting the tug to allow his gaze to wander downward, to caress her beasts with his gaze, letting it travel down her stomach to the valley between her legs, and then... Then it dawned on him. "You intend on using yourself for bait?"

Her grin only revealed he was right. "Well, it won't be like they're sneaking up on me unaware now will it. We know they're coming for me, thinking me some scared female they can force to do their bidding, but we know better. We'll be prepared for them, waiting for their move." The grin grew across her face. "And we both know I am far more than a timid little country deputy."

He ran a hand through his hair as he allowed his gaze to drop to the pine needle-covered ground. It was a gutsy move to be sure, but was it too gutsy? Something could go wrong, putting his mate in danger. Then what?

His wolf growled within him. *Yeah, then we tear them limb from limb.*

Nine

Gracie's Diner was a small hole in the wall attached to the only gas station between Melbourne and St. Cloud. Travelers could stop in for lunch, fill their car up with gas, and grab a bag of chips and a drink for the rest of their journey. The building was concrete with faded white paint and walls that needed pressure-washing just to be able to see the bottom layer of dirt. The parking lot was chipped asphalt and pot holes surrounded by weeds that had choked out the grass decades ago, and the sad part was, the exterior of the building looked better than the interior. The tables were a fake-wood Formica, and what wasn't chipped was stained with no one knew what. However, it was probably the same dark liquid that stained the cheap linoleum floor. The chairs were a hideous burnt orange that seemed leftover from the seventies and had as many tears with exposed stuffing as fabric. The building even smelled old, like one of those antique shops back in Downtown Melbourne, musty with the aroma of mildew from years of storms blowing in through a leaky roof. However, for all of its lackluster posterior, Gracie's Diner served the best food for miles around, and old lady Gracie cooked it with just as much heart as an artist uses when painting. Lainie had eaten more meals at the small diner than she did her at own home.

"Are all wolves that spastic or is it men in general?" Lainie asked Alanna Bradbury as she stabbed her sweet tea with a straw, using it to stir the dark liquid, making sure the sugar didn't settle at the bottom. She had filled her friend in on everything that was Rance Culpepper and her disastrous day. Alanna had just sat there and smiled, listening as Lainie vented. "I swear, for as much as he says he needs to end this case, he's done everything possible to sabotage the damn thing."

Alanna lifted her glass, smiling around her straw as she took a sip of her cola. When she pulled the glass away from her mouth, she said, "Uh huh, I'm sure that's why he's acting the way he's acting." She took another sip of her drink, still smiling.

"I know why he's doing it; I just don't like it. Or want it. Alanna, this is more than I'm prepared for. I like my simple life." Lainie was used to being on her own, enjoying the freedom of coming and going as she pleased, of being able to work late nights and early mornings without worrying about a partner being frustrated with her hectic schedule. "It's not like being a sheriff out here comes with a normal routine."

Alanna shrugged, obviously not really seeing the merit behind Lainie's excuse. "He's a detective, right? He's probably used to crazy schedules and last-minute call-ins as well. Maybe that's why he's still alone, too. Ever think of that? You both need someone familiar with the life of a cop. Seems like a perfect match. Besides, your animals have kind of already made the decision for you."

"Damn them," Lainie sighed, to which Alanna only grinned more. Lainie thought the other woman was enjoying her discomfort way too much. Then Lainie shook her head. "I'm not leaving Bull Creek, and Rance's life is in Pensacola. It would never work, no matter what our animals are feeling."

Alanna shrugged. "You know what'll happen if you fight this."

Gracie appeared, a tray laden down with greasy burgers and fries balanced on one arm, her gray hair tied back in a tight ponytail and her red apron already smeared with today's spills and splatters. "Here you ladies go. It's hot, so be careful." She set the plates in front of the women, who had to switch the plates around as Gracie passed them out to the wrong person. "Can I get you anything else? Refills? More napkins? No hunky men available, sorry. Haven't served that in years."

Lainie and Alanna both laughed, Lainie not sure whether Gracie was joking or if she actually sold men in her past. In this area, anything was possible. "We're all set, thanks." Lainie took the tomato off her burger, smeared the bun with mayonnaise, and then cut it in half.

Alanna reached over, snatching the tomato from Lainie's plate, and adding it to her burger after smothering the bun with ketchup. She also drowned her fries in the red condiment before returning the bottle to the rack at the back of the table. She then picked up the burger with both hands and bit into it, grease dripping out the back end of the sandwich.

Lainie just watched her friend, staring at how indelicate Alanna was in her eating. Then she laughed as she picked up her own sandwich with her fingertips and took a small bite of the corner, keeping the burger aimed upward so that the juices didn't get all over her fries. The food may be messy, but it was always delicious.

"So, what are you going to do?" Alanna asked around a mouthful of burger, showing no shame in the way she was eating.

Lainie smiled as she gave a slight shake of her head. "Well, hopefully, those idiots make a move and I can shove them behind bars for being morons. That's about the only way we can make anything stick thanks to how Rance acted in the woods." His actions still grated on her nerves. Just when she thought she was past it, his loss of control would pop back into her head, and she'd get pissed all over again. "I just hope they don't wait too long." She glanced out the giant window with the logo of Gracie's Diner on it, staring at the empty highway. She shook her head. *Some highway. 192 finally became more than just a two-lane road, and Holopaw only has a blinking yellow light to warn people that there's another road out here. Although, that's one light more than Bull Creek possesses.*

"You really think they'll try and force a sheriff to break into the department? I don't know, that just seems a little too brazen to me, even for gang members." Alanna's plate was a mess. Ketchup and the grease from her burgers drizzled her fries as well as her fingers and pieces of lettuce and onion had fallen from her burger to land in her plate adding to the mixture. How she could keep eating them was beyond Lainie's comprehension. And her stomach.

"It's all they have left," Lainie said as she picked up a heavily salted French fry. "According to the kid in lockup, they have to have that video or Snake will take it out on them. He's not going to risk going to jail just because his followers don't have the balls to take on a cop. They'll do it. The question is when. The trial starts soon, so they're on a deadline."

"Still seems ballsy to me," Alanna said as she held her burger in one hand and grabbed her drink in the other.

Lainie didn't disagree with her friend, but she also knew if the Serpents were willing to commit murder for this Snake character, there was no telling what other lengths they would go to just to fulfill the man's demands. Smart people didn't join gangs, so the commonsense factor was already tossed out the window where they were concerned. She would just have to keep watching her back.

Picking up her drink, Lainie turned her gaze back out the window as Alanna droned on about Josh and how he refused to take her to St. Cloud to a real restaurant for a date. Lainie only half-listened as she stared out the window. The tale of Alanna and Josh was pretty much repetitive. They chased each other, only allowing the other to catch them long enough to get each other off in bed, and then they played the hard-to-get game a little more. The fact that they were destined to be mates was obvious, so why they fought it, no one could guess. *Maybe they think it increases the excitement of the sex.* That thought made Lainie think about how it felt to kiss Rance in the woods when they returned after finding Tweedledum and Tweedledumber. She could have taken him right them, wanted to take him right then, but she had to admit, the anticipation that built within her almost drove her to distraction. Once they finally did cross that line, she knew she'd see fireworks.

She sipped her tea, staring out the window, when she saw the Lincoln from the woods heading west. She was out of her seat before she knew she even moved, Alanna calling after her. Lainie pressed her face to the window, following the car with her gaze, confused. *Why are they leaving? There's no way they have the cell phone.* She returned to her seat, ignoring Alanna's questions as she pulled her phone from her purse and called Johnson. While the phone rang, she said, "That car that just drove by was our gang members. It doesn't make sense that they would leave town right now without Roger's phone. They need that video."

"Unless they already have it."

Lainie didn't want to think like that.

"Hey Lainie, what's up?" Johnson asked after answering his phone.

"I need you to check on that phone we have in evidence. I

just saw those punks leaving town, and they wouldn't do that without the video they killed Roger for."

"Okay, I'll check, but nothing exciting has happened around here, so I doubt they have it," Johnson said. "I'll call you back after I take a peek."

"Thanks." Lainie canceled the call and dropped her phone on the table. "What are they up to?"

"Maybe they've been called home for some other plan of getting at it," Alanna offered. "Or, maybe they just got smart and figured out attacking a cop wasn't the smartest plan in their book, regardless of how frightening their leader is. You gotta admit, that was a pretty gutsy plan."

Lainie stared down at her plate, nodding her head in agreement. Alanna was right, she knew, but if the gang members were gone, how long would Rance stick around? There was nothing to keep him here any longer, the case almost solved, and the cell phone now free to go to him as soon as their team cleared it. Suddenly, she felt the twisting in her stomach. As much of a pain in the ass he was for her, she didn't want to see him leave. Alanna was right in that as well. Lainie's panther wouldn't make it easy to ignore the call that pulled at her. But what could she do? The reason for Rance staying behind just drove off, heading back to Pensacola.

Ten

Rance stormed toward the interrogation room where he knew Jace waited, once again in cuffs attached to the loop in the middle of the table. Deputy Johnson stood outside the door, shaking his head. "You know, Lainie isn't going to like this," the deputy said. "Isn't she all over your ass enough as it is?"

Rance nodded, outwardly showing he understood the deputies concerns, while inwardly, he wanted Lainie Everest all over him in so many stimulating ways. "Then we just won't tell her." He glanced through the window in the door at the small man stuck inside the room. "You know as well as I do that something isn't adding up." He pointed inside the room. "That kid knows something, and I intend to find out what it is." Rance knew he was just lucky to be in the sheriff's department when Lainie called Johnson about the cell phone and how the other gang members were seen heading west out of town. Johnson was the only one they had told about their little jaunt into the woods and coming upon the other thugs, mainly because how they discovered their information was hard to put into a report. However, they left out the part of the two guys planning on using Lainie to get to the phone. While it wasn't Rance's idea to keep that part a secret, Lainie thought that if people knew, then everyone would try to keep her protected at all times, and they'd never get the chance to capture the bad guys. However, the bad guys had split, so what had changed?

Johnson shrugged. "I'm just giving you fair warning, that's all." He opened the door and gestured for Rance to do whatever he was there to do.

Rance gave a curt nod before entering the room and shutting the door behind him. He didn't sit, nor did he stand. He pressed his palms down on the table and leaned into the kid, his eyes narrowed, his voice a growl as he said, "Your buddies left you. They were just spotted with their tails between their legs heading for the Turnpike." He cocked his head to the side. "They must not care about you or the phone, seeing as how they left without either." He just leaned there and stared at the kid, willing the slimy man to confess something that would help him figure out what the plan was and where he needed to focus his attention.

The kid looked everywhere but at Rance. "I don't know what to tell you. They do whatever Snake tells 'em to do."

"And Snake must have told them to leave your ass behind. No such thing as loyalty these days. How does it feel to be expendable?"

Jace just shuffled in his seat, keeping his eyes on the walls around him, choosing to remain silent.

Rance didn't blame him. It sucked to finally realize that the man you worshiped never cared for you and considered you merely a pawn to be sacrificed. "Now, you get to go from being Snake's little bitch to some musclebound lifer in prison. Hell, that might even be a step up for someone like you."

The kid turned and sneered at Rance. "Fuck you. I ain't nobody's bitch. Go fuck yourself, man, and get out of my face."

"Did I strike a chord? Oh, you poor boy, you. If you're not Snake's little bitch, prove it. Tell me where your buddies went. What's the plan? I thought you said no loose ends. You're a loose end, aren't you?"

"I ain't no loose end." Jace jerked forward, wanting to strike out at Rance, but the cuffs kept him from going too far.

"Then tell me what the plan is!" Rance snapped. "Snake's going down. Why do you want to go down with him? So far, all we have you on is trespassing. Unless we can pin Roger's murder on you, which seems to be what your buddies want, since they left your ass behind. Seems they don't care about the video any longer either. So, what's the next move?"

The kid turned his gaze back around to the wall, ignoring Rance and his barrage of questions. His loyalty would cost him in the end, but not this time. If he didn't kill Roger, and it seemed even more unlikely that he did, then all they had him on was the trespassing charge, and maybe breaking and entering, even though the cabin was unlocked. He'd get a fine and be sent on his merry way to return to Pensacola and whatever punishment Snake doled out for his failure. Rance shook his head. "Fine, have it your way. But you know Snake's not a forgiving man. You failed here by not getting what you were sent to obtain. He won't take kindly to that, and you know it. Let us help you."

"I ain't no snitch. Now arrest me or let me go." The Serpent fell back into his chair, his shoulders slumped. He knew what his fate was, but he was willing to take that rather than rat out the others. Stupid.

Rance shook his head as he shoved away from the table, turned, and headed out of the room.

Johnson waited outside the door, another deputy with him, waiting to return Jace to his holding cell. "Anything?" Johnson asked as the other deputy entered the interrogation room.

Rance walked away from the door, not wanting the gang member to overhear him. "No. Nothing. What is it with these kids that they'll sell their souls to some pathetic loser who would turn on them in a heartbeat?"

Johnson just shook his head. "So, what's the plan now?"

Rance took a deep breath, his hands on his hips. "I'm going to call my boss and let him know the other two may be heading back his way. I'm still going to wait around for that cell phone, but if the Serpents who just left are the killers, I'm not sure what else Lainie can do. I'll try and catch them when I get back." *But I don't want to go back.* The wolf within him growled at the notion, clearly expressing his disagreement.

"What do you want me to do with him?" Deputy Johnson pointed to Jace as the other deputy led him out of the small room.

"That's Lainie's call. Honestly, I'm not sure what you can hold him on."

Johnson gave a soft chuckle. "Yeah, too bad stupidity isn't a crime."

Rance laughed as well. "Are you kidding? We wouldn't have enough room in the jails to hold that many people." He shook Johnson's hand, thanked him once more, and then said goodbye. As much as he doubted the Serpent members actually left Bull Creek, he still needed to give his boss, Scott Campbell, the Assistant District Attorney, a heads up that they just might be heading his way.

As soon as Rance was behind the steering wheel and heading down Madison Street, he pulled his cell phone from his back pocket and dialed Scott's number.

"About damn time," Scott's gruff voice filled Rance's ear. "I thought maybe you decided to take a vacation while you were down there. Did you find him?" Rance could hear the man's chair squeak and pictured Scott leaning back in his chair, face aimed at the ceiling. If the man was anything, he was predictable.

Rance took a deep breath, knowing Scott was not going to like the update he was about to receive. "Yeah, I found him, but not before the Serpents found him. He's dead. The local sheriffs have the cell phone and are working on getting me the video. There's a rambunctious female sheriff who seems to think letting me have it now might screw up her case."

"What the hell?" The chair squeaked again, Scott swiveling in his anger. "Roger is *our* witness. His murder belongs to us. Why the hell didn't you call me sooner?"

"Because this is the first chance I've had. We found one of the Serpents trying to break into Roger's cabin. He's in custody now, but there were two others, the ones we think killed Roger O'Brien. We couldn't get them before they bugged out."

"Where did they go?" Scott's tone held the same exasperation Rance felt with this case. He just wanted it over with so he could get things settled with Lainie.

"West is all I know. The theory is that they're heading to the Turnpike and back to Pensacola. I don't buy it, though. The video is still here. Snake sent them to kill a man to get it, so they won't return without it. My guess is they ran into St. Cloud on a beer run, but I thought you might want a heads up. The locals have put an A.P.B. out on their car, a nasty brown Lincoln with a hard-shell top."

"I'll pass the description around here. I'll also send Burkes out to the Serpents with what we know, see if we can rattle some cages. You never know who might slip up."

"Sounds good. I'm going to hang out here until the video is ready, and then, I'll head back."

"Great." The chair squeaked again, and Rance smiled, knowing Scott was relaxing a little and leaning back on his desk. The man had habits. "Did I hear you say Roger was staying in a cabin? Where the hell are you?"

"The town's called Bull Creek. This place is so far out in

the sticks, they have to import their sticks from another small town. It makes the small towns back home look enormous. Still, it has its own charm. The locals are friendly enough, and they're what make the town."

"But cabins? Instead of a house? Really?"

Rance just laughed as he told Scott he'd keep him updated and hung up. He turned off Madison onto Highway 192 heading to his hotel. Might as well wash the dust of the day from his body. There was nothing to do now but wait for Sheriff Einstein's forensics team to finish with the phone. Still, Rance wondered whether the other two Serpents did head back to Pensacola, make a quick escape, or just went into town for beer. *What happened to their plan to trap Lainie?* He didn't like his destined mate being used as bait, but it was her call, and he was not going to stand in her way again. He needed her to like him, after all.

He sighed, propping his head up with a fist, elbow resting on the interior door panel. *And just what am I going to do once I have that video? How do I convince Lainie that we need to surrender to the call of our animals?* Then he worried about the logistics of when they did surrender. They weren't exactly neighbors. Someone would have to move, and he highly doubted Lainie would volunteer. Not that he blamed her, of course. Bull Creek kind of grew on you in a slow drawl sort of way. Would he be happy here? He found himself smiling, knowing that as long as he had Lainie in his arms, he would be happy anywhere. Destined Mates happened once in a lifetime, and he refused to let Lainie slip through his fingers. They were each other's future. Now, he just had to make her see the same thing.

Eleven

Two days passed and Lainie was afraid that Rance's stunt scared off the Serpent gang members, making them actually leave town, since there had been no attack upon her for her access to the evidence locker. She sat in a rocker on her front porch, a cup of English breakfast tea warming her hands, dressed only in a flimsy tank and some silky pajama shorts as she stared out at the woods surrounding her cabin. While she had forgiven the detective for his little stunt in the woods when he attacked the one who threatened her, she still wanted to throttle him for the way he may have screwed things up. If he had left well enough alone, they could have returned to their clothes and called for backup, lying in wait for the men to admit to the murder again.

Lainie stopped rocking, following that trail of thought.

Why can't we still do that? They don't need to know we were in our animal forms when we heard them talk about Roger's murder. She shook her head. It wouldn't work. If they had heard it then, they would have stepped out of the woods right away and arrested them. They would have also intervened when the wolf attacked the gang members, instead of allowing the attack to go further. No, Rance screwed up their chances of bringing them in when he lost control of his wolf. Now they could only wait until the Serpents made a move again, and who knew how long that would be? She blew out a frustrated breath as she settled back in her rocker.

"That breath didn't sound good."

She turned and watched as Rance walked around the side of her cabin, his jeans snug against his thighs and his... Lainie shook her head. She didn't need to forgive him that quickly. "Why are you on the side of my cabin?" she asked. He was semi-dressed for work, a dark blue button-down shirt and jeans with sneakers. At least he shed his stiff jacket. Florida was definitely too hot for a sports coat in the middle of the day outdoors. Or indoors for that matter.

He gave a weak shrug. "Just trying to keep an eye out and make sure no one else hung out on the side of your place." She watched as he walked around to the front of her cabin, his hand sliding along the wooden railing. "I take it nothing has happened so far? Scott says there's been no sign of our boys back in Pensacola, so he's pretty sure they're still here."

She shook her head. "Not even a sighting or a whisper of a stalker in the woods." She gestured around her property. "I had Adira place wards around my place to give me a warning if some malcontent crossed my property line." Then she gave him a smirk. "Obviously, it didn't work."

He shook his head, giving her a soft chuckle as a reward for her quip. Then he cocked his head to the side as he stared at her. "Adira?"

Lainie finished taking a sip of her tea before answering. "Adira is Bull Creek's resident witch, mated to my brother."

Rance nodded, glancing around the place as if he could see the wards Lainie mentioned. She just smiled at him as he did so, knowing he was clueless as to what she was even talking about. When he turned back to her, his golden eyes soft as he stared at her, she smiled back at him, the cup still held between both hands. He nodded to where she sat. "A morning ritual?"

She nodded. "It's just about the only peaceful time I get to myself."

His back straightened as he stood. "Oh, sorry, I didn't mean to interrupt your morning." He started to back away, turning to leave.

She sighed. "Stop. I didn't mean it that way." She stood, turning toward her front door. "I'm not a big coffee drinker, but I keep some hidden somewhere for when my brother visits. I could scrounge around for it if you like."

"Tea is fine. Thanks. No need to put yourself out." She heard him moving behind her, his feet on the wooden steps to her porch, and it brought a smile to her lips. She knew what she struggled with, and also knew that sooner or later she would have to do something about it. She wouldn't be able to walk away from him as she did in the woods two days ago. "So, is there a plan in case they don't make a move?"

Once she was inside, she went to her kitchen, pulled a mug from a cabinet, and filled it with hot water from the kettle, the steam rising in curls toward the ceiling. "Probably need to go out and track them again. I'm sure you spooked them, and they moved hiding spots. They may just be settling in before making their move."

"They'll have to do it soon. The trial is next week. They won't risk that evidence being brought forth in Snake's prosecution." He slipped onto a stool she had by the island that separated her kitchen from the living room area of her cabin, his arms resting on the island, hands clasped. "They're going to have to attack you soon."

She turned, a soft giggle slipping past her lips. "You don't have to sound so eager for it to happen." She shook her head, reaching for the bag of breakfast tea and dipping it in the cup of hot water. "Can't wait to get out of here, huh?" She didn't really want to hear his answer, but she knew the minute he had possession of that video, he'd be gone, heading back to Pensacola and out of her life. As much as she had dreaded the fact of him sticking his nose into her case, she was quite ready for him to stick other parts of himself in hotter places. Her panther made it almost impossible for Lainie to keep resisting the urge to make the move herself. Well, make it again, anyway.

She heard the scuff of the stool sliding across her wooden floor but refused to look behind her. She kept her gaze on the water in front of her as if she needed to count how many times she dunked the tea bag into the steaming cup. Even when she felt his hands on her arms, she refused to turn, not sure what he would say or how she would react.

However, Rance didn't give in and forcibly turned her so that she faced him. "Lainie, I know you feel what I feel. I know this bond between us, this mating call our animals are shoving us toward, is strong." He sighed, his shoulders slumping a little as he tilted his head to the side. "Why are you fighting this so hard?"

She glanced up into his eyes, his golden, sparkling, soft eyes. She didn't want to do this. She didn't think she'd ever *have* to do this. "Because, Rance, you're going to go back to Pensacola. My life is here. What good is it going to do to give in to something we know won't last?"

"How do you know it won't last? Why would you think that? You know about matings just as well as I do."

"Trust me, I know, but I also know reality. You don't live here, and I'm not moving. My life is here."

He slid a hand around her neck, sending goosebumps over her flesh, as he pulled her toward him and kissed her softly. His lips were warm, soft, as he pressed them against hers, taking her mouth, claiming her as much as he could at the moment, as much as she'd let him. She wanted more, needed more, but the truth was, she didn't need to get attached to someone who would drive off in a day or two.

When he pulled back from her, his smile curling his lips, his eyes still sparkled. "For the past two days, you're all I thought about and what the future holds. I don't know what tomorrow will bring, to be honest, and yes, I'm going to have to return to Pensacola and see this case finished, but after that, who knows? What I do know is that I love it here, and I'm not ready to walk away from it. Besides you, there's the outdoors to enjoy, something I didn't realize I missed until the other day when we were running through them tracking the Serpents. I've lived on concrete so long I almost forgot what it felt like to run free, the wind through my wolf's fur, the sun baking my coat. I don't want to give that up yet." He kissed her forehead before gazing back into her eyes again. "I don't want to give you up."

She dropped her head against his chest, struggling to keep the tears from falling. His words were not what she expected to hear. The way her heart swelled when he was with her was something she never thought she would feel. This was more than she ever thought possible. His hand stroked her dark hair, falling until she felt it caress her back, and suddenly she needed him. Now.

Grabbing his hand, she dragged him toward the back bedroom before she changed her mind. *It's just sex, that's it. I just need to get this out of my system. Get him out of my system.* She hoped that once she took him to bed, her panther would be sated, and she could move on with her life. Rance would return to Pensacola, and she could get back to being alone.

Once they were in her bedroom, she pulled him in front of the bed, turning him so that he had his back to it, and then shoved him backward. He landed on the bed, bouncing slightly on the mattress, arms splayed outward as he stared at her, eyebrows arched. Yanking her top over her head, she tossed it on the floor and then made short work of her pajama shorts.

He leaned up on his elbows, his gaze raking over her body. "It's not that I'm not eager for this to happen, especially after the sudden brakes the other day, but are you sure you want to do this now?"

Placing a knee on the bed, each hand on either side of him, she began to crawl up his body, biting her bottom lip, her gaze fixed on his. She gave a slow nod once she reached his chest. "Positive. Right now. Right here." She sat up, straddling his waist. She gripped his shirt with both hands and ripped outward, buttons flying in all directions. She could already feel his cock swelling beneath her. With her hands on his chest holding her up, she rubbed herself back and forth on his cock, the jean material scratching against her clit. With eyes closed, she continued, getting lost in the sensations between her legs, his cock growing harder with each of her movements.

Finally, she had all the stimulation she could handle and needed satisfaction. Sliding back on his legs, she yanked his button open, the zipper ripping downward. She scooted off his legs, grabbing his pants by the waist and jerking them down his legs, dragging his boxers with them, his cock popping to attention as soon as it was free. She didn't need him naked, just accessible. This wasn't about him; it was all about her and her needs right now.

She crawled back up his body, stopping at his cock once she reached it again, wrapping his hardness with her hand as she lowered her mouth down to it, tasting him. His body stiffened under her as his moan reached her ears.

Swallowing him, she bobbed her head up and down, his pre-cum coating her tongue as she swirled it around the head of his cock. Too long she had gone without being fucked, and she needed him to be as hard as he could be once she slid herself down onto him. Hungry was the only way to describe how her body felt right then.

"Lainie..."

She lifted her mouth from his cock, continuing her path upward until her pussy hovered right over his shaft. With one hand holding her up, she used her other to guide him to her entrance, never hesitating once she felt the tip of his manhood slide between her wet lips. She dropped down onto him, stuffing herself with his hardness. Her eyes widened as she cried out at the suddenness, her body tightened around him, sucking him deeper into her. She could feel his hands on her waist, holding her straight as she rocked back and forth on him, relishing the feel of being full.

"Oh god, Lainie," she heard him say, and the feeling was very much mutual.

She closed her eyes her hands pressing down on his chest as she continued to move back and forth on him, the tip almost slipping from her entrance before she rocked back, shoving him deep inside of her again. *Oh god...so long...it's been so long...* She lost herself in the sensations of her movements, her clit sliding back and forth against him, his cock filling her and then almost vanishing, the air-conditioning on her flesh. Everything sent tendrils throughout her body, and she just wanted to bask in it all.

Then her eyes popped open again as she felt the

tightening of her body, her nipples shriveled into tight pearls, her body starting to shake as her orgasm washed through her. He dug into her with his fingers, holding her as she seemed to lose control of her body, her whole being shuddering with the climax that rocked her senses. She cried out, screaming her ecstasy in one long, pleasurable release. She didn't even feel when his cock twitched, his own body tightening under her as he reached his orgasm, filling her with his passion as he pinned her down on top of him. She just stared at him, mouth open, her cry now spent as the wave of her orgasm hit her shore and spread outward, the head-rush filling every inch of her insides until she just collapsed on top of him, her body numb with satisfaction.

She didn't know when he rolled her over, his arm wrapped around her waist, pulling her snug against him. She could feel his breath against her neck, her ear, just before she drifted off to sleep, lost in the sublime pleasure of finally having what she felt she had denied herself for too long. She'd worry about him leaving when she woke. Right now, she just wanted to bask in his arms, his presence, and the act of love that bound them at the moment. There would be enough time for regrets later.

Twelve

However, Lainie had no regrets. It was true she had no idea what tomorrow would bring or if Rance would leave with the next sunrise, but she wasn't going to pass up this chance to finally feel something. It had been way too long. She wrapped an arm around his waist and snuggled in tighter.

"You okay?" she heard him ask just before he kissed the top of her head.

"Just giving myself a pep talk. I'm not one for living in the moment so much. I like to know what's coming."

She felt him caress her bare arm, his breathing even, comforting. "And are you heeding this pep talk you're giving yourself?"

"Well, I haven't kicked you out yet, so that's a positive sign, right?"

He chuckled, his chest bouncing with his laughter. "I'll take it." He kissed her again, and she felt herself relaxing even more. "How long has it been since you've been in a relationship, if I may ask?"

She hesitated for a moment, not that she didn't mind telling Rance about her past, but more that she just didn't want to revisit the nightmare again. Finally, she decided if he was returning to Pensacola, then it didn't matter what he knew, and if he was remaining in Bull Creek, obeying his wolf, then he would find out eventually. With a deep breath, she snuggled deeper into his side and let the words flow. "I'm probably being more dramatic than necessary, but with the pressure my parents put on me, I kind of grew sensitive about it." She shrugged as best as she could while lying in bed. "My parents are pretty much control freaks, thinking their offspring needed to tow the line and obey in order to see the family business succeed. My father thought it was his duty, so to speak, to make sure we married into the proper families to cement his connections. Our older brother obeyed and is now stuck in a loveless marriage, while the one he truly wants to be with is lost to him. Dimitri was next, and he just flat out refused. The Paranormal Council back in Draven Falls knew of this place and knew that Bull Creek needed someone to protect its residents. They tagged my brother for the task, and Dimitri jumped at the chance. Agatha Rochester, a witch back home, knew my parents were already setting their sights on my future, actually had even promised me to a jug-headed idiot. That was a nightmare. I had to endure him criticizing my looks, my weight, even the fact that I was a panther and not a wolf. Agatha suggested I follow Dimitri, and I did, never looking back." She ran a finger up Rance's stomach, twirling the happy trail of hair that led down from his bellybutton to his cock. "Of course, my parents think we turned our backs on the family and constantly remind us of that. I can live with their scorn as long as I'm free to follow my own path."

She felt him squeeze her again, kissing the side of her head this time. "I hope you know our paths are intertwined. Your panther and my wolf have already decided. You also know that to deny that call would make us both miserable. I hate being miserable just so you know."

She kept her gaze on her fingers as they circled his bellybutton. "Didn't you say it was miserable living in a city surrounded by concrete and steel? Your wolf would thrive outdoors."

He twisted under her, and she wondered if perhaps she touched on a sensitive spot. His chest rose and fell with the deep breath he took, and Lainie was just about to say something else to change the subject when he started talking. "Small towns come with small-town prejudices, and my father found himself in trouble with some rather unpleasant men around Niceville, of all places, which is east of Pensacola. One night they jumped him, making snide comments about shifters, and throwing beer bottles at him. People who are scared usually hide behind brutality, thinking it makes them look brave and righteous, when in fact, it only reveals their fear. Dad wound up in the hospital, and my mother had tolerated enough of small minds. I was determined to do something about the injustice of it all, so I took a job with the District Attorney's office to fight hate crimes. There's more power to achieve that in the big city than in the small towns where bullies rule out in the open, instead of behind closed doors and through sneaky deals. Mom and Dad followed, moving to the west of Pensacola where the trees outnumber the buildings, so I get a little of both."

"People are idiots," she mumbled into his chest.

He sighed, deep and heavy. "That they are, but it's on both sides. Just as many shifters are prejudiced against humans as there are humans prejudiced against shifters. Sometimes in our quest to gain acceptance for ourselves, we become that which we spout off against. It's still prejudice, but since it's not against shifters, the paranormal world thinks it's all right. We can be prejudiced against humans, because well, they started it. Or so the logic goes. It's asinine."

Lainie's cell phone started ringing from where it rested on her nightstand, and she fought the urge to ignore the intrusion. She didn't want to move or lose their connection. With a groan, however, she pulled away, reaching over and snatching up her phone. Locking at the screen, she saw Johnson's name, and she groaned deeper as she slid the answer button over. "Lainie."

"Hey, Lainie," Johnson said. "Sorry to bother you while you're at home, but we got the video off Roger O'Brien's phone. I've stored it on a flash drive for now. How do you want me to proceed with it? The laptop came up empty, by the way."

"Great," she said into the phone. "I'll be right over and give it a look, and then we can go from there. Thanks, Johnson. I appreciate it." When she ended the call, she glanced over at Rance, and as much as she dreaded it, she knew her break from life was over. "Johnson was able to get that video off the phone and onto a USB. I'm going to go check it out and process it for you, then you can have it and get it to the D.A.'s office in time for Snake's trial." She scooted to the edge of her bed, her day turning for the worse.

"Why are you frowning?" He slid out of bed, scooping up his clothes as he did. With a tilted head, he stood there, his shirt dangling from his fingers as one hand rested on his hip. "This is a good thing."

She nodded, walking over to her closet and a fresh uniform. "I know. You get to put an end to the investigation and send that gang leader to prison. It's great. Really."

She felt his hand on her arm, turning her so that she faced him. He leaned over, his face an inch from hers, his smile reaching his eyes. "And then I can come back here and be with you. Do you think there's room in your department for another detective?"

She felt her eyes widen at his words, her lips parted, not knowing what to say. "You mean it? You'd move here? Just to be with me?"

He kissed her nose, slow, lingering, before pulling back and giving a shake of his head. "And just where else do you think I'd be? My mate is here, so I need to be here as well."

"I'm not your mate, yet."

"All that's left is the marking, and you know it. Our animals have claimed each other in spirit, and I can't say I blame them. Unless, of course, you don't want me here."

She reached out, one hand going to his cheek. "I want you here. To be honest, I think I need you here."

"Good, because I'd hate to keep you handcuffed to the bed. People might wonder where you've disappeared to all of a sudden."

"I'll be the one doing the handcuffing," she said with a slight giggle. "Maybe as a special treat before you leave."

He kissed her nose again. "I like the sound of that. Now, hurry back to me. I'll give my boss a call and fill him in on what's going on." He slipped his shirt over his arms, reaching to button it, then stopped, realizing that she had popped all the buttons off. "Well, first, I need to go to my hotel and grab another shirt."

"You don't keep a spare in your car? What kind of detective are you that you aren't prepared?"

His grin made her honey drip, and she fought the urge to drag him back to the bed. "I will admit, until today, I didn't really need a spare, but I'll make sure to keep one in the car from now on. You know, just in case of your spontaneous bursts." He leaned down and kissed her again.

"Why don't you just hang out here until I get back? Then we can decide what to do with our evening. If everything goes smoothly, I'll call, and you can meet me at the station for the evidence hand-off."

"You're always so bossy."

"You'll get used to it."

He pulled her toward him once more, kissing her long and hard, his tongue probing her mouth, tasting the passion on her breath. When he pulled away, his lips were twisted into a smirk. "I love a lady with a touch of sass."

She grinned back at him, unable to help herself. "Oh, there's more than a touch, trust me."

He stared into her eyes, and she knew she'd be happy getting lost in them for the rest of her life. "With everything I have, love. I trust you with everything I have."

She felt the blush warm her cheeks as she ducked her head, her gaze going to his chest. Taking a deep breath, she glanced back up at him, patting his chest. "I'll get this over with, so we can get on with our lives." Then she grinned, her body swaying just a little as she stood there. "And I'll ask Chet about a position for you if you're serious."

"Dead serious." He winked at her, and she felt her blush deepen. She turned, pulling her uniform out of the closet. She didn't want to leave his side, but she needed to get this part of things done and over with so they could move onto the next phase of their lives. She paused, staring at her uniform a second at the thought of finally having someone in her life she truly wanted to be there. She took a deep breath, savoring the feeling.

Fifteen minutes later, she was dressed, looking all prim and proper, while Rance stood in her kitchen wearing jeans and a ripped shirt making coffee. Where he found the coffee, she had no idea. Dimitri never popped in enough for her to worry about it. She turned as she scooped up her keys, slipping her purse strap over her shoulder. "You going to be okay here while I'm gone?" she asked.

He pulled a mug out of her cabinet, as he glanced at her, smiling. "Might as well start making myself at home, right?"

She nodded, blushing again. *God, I have got to stop doing that.* "That you do. I'll be right back."

"I'll be here."

She forced herself to turn and leave, knowing that she was dangerously close to forgetting what she needed to do in lieu of what her body wanted her to do. So lost in thoughts of Rance's arms around her, his body under her, that she didn't even remember the drive to the sheriff's department. She pulled in next to Johnson's sheriff's car, her mind still on Rance and how fast things had changed for her. *Sometimes, these animals can be a pain in the ass.* She snatched her purse, throwing her keys into the open pocket, and popped her car door open. Stepping out into the humid Florida afternoon, the sun warming her face a contradiction to the air-condition from inside the car, was the last thing she remembered before something slammed against the side of her, her vision exploding in colors and dark spots. She took another crack upside her head before her body crumpled to the ground, her hand sliding down the side of her car as she went to the pavement beneath her. Just before the darkness swallowed her, she saw the face of one of the men from the woods, smiling at her. *I guess the wait is over.* She felt hands on her arms, and then she was out.

Thirteen

Rance watched as Lainie walked out the door, fighting the urge to follow her. He needed that video, true, but he also needed her to see that he was serious about everything he told her. She needed to do this her way if he was going to get her to trust him and believe in them. True, he ran the risk of the district attorney he worked for getting pissed off for the delay, but Lainie was worth it. More than worth it.

After pouring himself a cup of coffee from the brewer he found under her kitchen sink, he took a quick scan around the interior of the cabin. He missed his opportunity to really see the place earlier before she dragged him back to her bedroom. Of course, he didn't complain. Nor would he ever. Now that his wolf had made his desires known, Rance had a hard time understanding how he had ever done without

Lainie in his life before. Too many things, he suddenly, realized he had been missing without even knowing it, things like the soft contours of her curves and the way she fit perfectly in his arms. He sipped his coffee as he looked at all the pictures Lainie had scattered around the cabin, pictures of her family, even the parents who wanted to use her to increase the family's holdings in business. How archaic of a concept. There were a few pictures of others Rance assumed were friends as well as a couple of her with some fellow officers. Paintings of panthers in the wild hung from the walls along with a giant dream catcher with dark burgundy beads. Everything else in the house seemed modest and simple compared to the other homes Rance had seen. It warmed his heart that she was so easily pleased and content.

Pouring a second cup of coffee, Rance went out to the porch, sitting in Lainie's rocker as the sun beat down from high in the sky. Glancing around her property, he soaked in the small palm frond bushes, the giant oaks mingled with large palm trees and towering pines. The roads were dirt, most of them riddled with potholes that rattled your teeth when you drove over them. There was a river and a lake nearby, but he had yet to see either. Highway 192 ran east and west connecting the beach to the touristy Kissimmee and all the trappings of the house of the mouse. Yet, Bull Creek was so isolated that unless you knew what was on either side, you seemed lost in tranquility and peacefulness. Life here would be a far cry from what he knew in Pensacola, but somehow Rance knew he was ready for it. He was sure that the Serpents were the most excitement this area had seen in ages, if ever. He would be happy to get it back to what it was before Roger O'Brien moved here, and then Rance could spend his evenings enjoying Lainie's curves and lips.

He grinned as he watched a squirrel dart across the dirt driveway, still able to feel Lainie's body on top of him as she took control of the first time they made love. The more he thought about it, the more he believed that she didn't even know she was about to have sex with him. The act was spontaneous and passionate, a satisfying of her panther's urges, to quiet the hunger she felt, believing that as soon as Rance had what he wanted, he'd be gone and she'd be back to being alone. She'd never be alone again if he could help it. There was no way he would leave her now, nor ever.

Another cup of coffee and an hour later, Rance decided to head back to his hotel for another shirt. If he were lucky, Lainie would call him soon with his video all bagged up and ready to be transferred. He didn't want to waste another second. He'd get the evidence to Pensacola and rush back to Lainie's arms. If he were even luckier, he'd be able to talk her into accompanying him when he returned home.

As he slid behind his steering wheel, he thought of that word once more. Home. Pensacola would no longer be his home, he knew. Not while Lainie was in Bull Creek. No, he would move back here. Hopefully, Chet would take him on, but if not, there were enough big cities nearby that he could attach himself to one of their departments, he was sure. Either way, Rance would make it work. He had to because his girl was here. He would never again be satisfied being anywhere else except by her side.

Pulling out onto the highway, he slid his cell phone from his pocket and called his boss, Scott Campbell, to give him an update as well as a heads up about his plans for the future.

"Well, it's about damn time I heard from you again," Scott snapped into the phone. "We're two days away from court. Tell me you've got the video and haven't just been boinking the locals on my dime."

Rance shook his head at Scott's tirade. "I'm picking up a copy of the video today, probably within the hour. Still nothing from the Serpents who killed Roger, though."

"Damn!" Rance could hear papers hitting the desk and pictured Scott falling back into his chair wearing that defeated expression he always succumbed to when things didn't immediately go his way. "Well, at least we have the video. We'll cut the head off one snake at a time."

"At least it'll be the head of the top Serpent. Maybe some of the others will slither back into their holes for a while."

"We couldn't be that lucky. Someone will ooze into and take Snake's place."

"They always do, don't they?" Rance took a deep breath, bracing for the next conversation. "Scott, after this case, I'm out. I'm resigning and just want to give you a heads up."

"What the hell?" Rance could hear the squeak of Scott's chair. He really should get that fixed. "Why the hell would you do that?"

Rance felt the grin curl his lips upward. "Because I found someone."

"Rance, you've only been gone a couple of weeks. How

the hell did you find someone worth quitting your job for that fast? It's not rational."

"Rational is so boring, don't you think?" He shook his head. He knew Scott would react this way, but there was nothing to do but to get it over with. "She's amazing, Scott. That's about all I can tell you. I'll get the evidence to you, but then, after this case, I'm through. Brighter things lay ahead."

Scott argued with Rance the entire way to the hotel, but all Rance could do was laugh at the man. Scott didn't know about shifters, and therefore, wouldn't understand the pull of a mating call, and without that background knowledge, it wasn't worth even attempting to explain. Scott would just have to think Rance crazy. "Just get me the video, and we'll talk when you get here," Scott said as Rance pulled into a parking spot in front of his hotel room.

"We can talk, but I'm not changing my mind. I'm going to try and bring her to Pensacola with me so you might be able to meet her if you're good."

"You're killing me, Rance. You're the best detective I have. I don't want to lose you. I can't lose you."

"Thanks for the ego boost, but my mind is made up. Now, I'll call once I hit the road and am heading your way. Start working on your opening argument. You got this case nailed."

Hanging up, Rance turned off the engine and slid out of his car. He checked his phone on his way to his room, but no messages. *Almost two hours now. I wonder what's taking her so long to process a simple video.*

Deciding to make the best use of his time, Rance stripped

out of his clothes and headed for a shower, regretting not grabbing some lunch on his way to the hotel. As the hot water beat down on his flesh, he wondered whether Lainie would travel with him to Pensacola or not. He knew things were moving fast, but that's the way things happened with shifters. Once their animals found their mate, there was no denying the pull or what the future would hold if you ignored the calling. Things went a lot better if everyone just gave in to the pull and followed the hearts of their animals. Most times, it worked out, but there had been a rare few where the humans couldn't stand each other, and the mating ended in tragedy. Rance was lucky, he knew, with whom his animal had chosen. Lainie was not some timid wallflower, waiting to be babied and pacified. No, she was a spirited female with spunk to spare. She knew what she wanted in life, knew it enough to know that what her parents desired for her wasn't her future. She had enough guts to deny her family and leave Draven Falls. Rance wasn't sure how it would have turned out if she had obeyed what her parents wanted and then his wolf found her panther. Talk about a nightmare situation.

Once he was out of the shower, he began to truly worry about how long it was taking Lainie to reach back out to him. After the morning they spent together, as well as the things they shared, he would have thought she would have called by now. Wrapping a towel around his waist, he snatched his phone off the nightstand and scrolled his contacts until he found her number. With a deep breath, he hit the call button. Nothing. It didn't even go straight to voicemail as if she had declined the call. He tossed the phone onto his bed and reached for some clean clothes. Maybe she was away from her phone. He'd give her a few more minutes and then try again.

Yet, once he was dressed, hair combed, and a cup of cheap hotel coffee brewed, she still hadn't answered the phone. A knot started to twist in his stomach. He reached into his wallet for the business card Lainie had given him at the crime scene a few days ago and punched in the sheriff department's number. The knot in his stomach twisted tighter when the lady at the desk informed him Lainie wasn't there. *Would she have left again without calling me first?* Trying a different tactic, he asked for Deputy Johnson. A moment later, the deep voice of the deputy answered.

"This is Rance Culpepper. Deputy Everest was supposed to call me about the video you retrieved off Roger O'Brien's phone. Do you know how long ago she left?"

"Left?" He could tell the deputy sounded confused. "I'm still waiting for her to arrive. I thought she was heading straight here."

Rance's knot twisted into nausea. "She did head straight there. I was with her when you called. Are you sure she's not there?"

He heard the squeak of a desk chair as Deputy Johnson moved. Didn't anyone take care of their furniture? "I haven't seen... Wait. Her car's here. Now that's weird. I would have sworn she would have come straight to me. Maybe Chet sidetracked her or something."

Rance closed his eyes and took a deep breath. As much as

he wanted that to be the case, he knew it wasn't. The Serpents finally made good on their threat. "Do me a favor. I'm on my way in, but can you look around for her. There were threats made against her."

"And you think they'd be stupid enough to try it in the parking lot of the sheriff's department?"

"Yeah, I do. And they have the guts for it. These people don't play around. Remember Roger."

"I'm on it."

The phone line went dead. Rance's wolf howled within him, fur sliding out of his flesh at the urge to shift. *We'll find her, but a car's faster.* Rance jumped off the bed, snatching up his keys. *Tell me you're all right, Lainie. I can't lose you after just finding you.* He shoved his way out the door and into the humid Florida air. It was time to cut the head off a snake.

Fourteen

ainie tried moving her head, but the pain that screamed throughout her skull forced her to hold still. She bit the inside of her cheek to keep from groaning out loud, needing a moment to think things through from what she remembered last. Johnson had called, saying he had the video for Rance, and she was on her way to check it out. No, she had arrived at the sheriff's department. She made it there, at least, and then…

She took slow, shallow breaths, trying her best to slow her breathing as well as settle her nerves. Voices could be heard nearby, and Lainie felt wind caressing her cheeks and tugging her hair. She was outside. That was a plus at least. She made it to the sheriff's department earlier but barely made it out of her car before someone had knocked her out from behind. Who did it wasn't hard to figure out. Having never left town, the Serpents must have grown tired of waiting and made their move. That they had the balls to attack her outside of the sheriff's department amazed her. They must have thought they were safe in such a backwoods town. She took another, deeper breath. *They really are idiots.*

Something scratched against her wrists when she tried to move. Rope, she assumed, since she couldn't move her arms apart. A futile attempt to bind her, she knew, but she would allow them to think her secure for now. The deception would allow time for her head to stop thumping an Army march behind her eyes and give her time to think about her next move.

"What if it doesn't work?" she heard one of the gang members say. If she remembered the scene at the rundown Lincoln in the woods the other day, the voice belonged to the skittish kid, younger, greener, than the other one. Definitely a follower.

"Then we kill her and find someone else," the other guy, tougher, more hardened against life, snarled. "You know as well as me that we ain't going back until we have that fucking phone, so stop acting like some chicken-shit schoolboy. God, how did you ever get into the Serpents? Snake must've been stoned that day."

"Dude, killing some scared old man is one thing. Hell, even killing a single cop isn't that big of a deal, but a whole damn department? The odds don't feel right, you know."

"Bullshit. The odds are what we make them, and that bitch is going to make our odds real good. Now, get some rest because tonight we're going in to get Snake his video."

Lainie heard the nervous kid pacing, his footfalls breaking and snapping twigs and small branches. She was worried that the kid would snap and make things even more difficult for her when she decided to escape. With her panther's strength, she could easily shift, snapping the ropes that held her and get the hell out of there. The two thugs would be scared shit-less once they faced a panther. Hell, she remembered how they responded to Rance's wolf.

She took a deep breath at the thought of Rance. She had no idea how long she had been out. Did he worry about her? Would he wait for her to reach out or get tired of her silence and try to find out where she was? He was a detective, so he'd investigate, she was sure, impatience a trait of the job. She didn't doubt his abilities. Hell, he was smart enough to follow her to Roger's cabin after all.

Forcing herself not to smile, giving herself away, she risked opening her eyes just a tad, the daylight stinging them, making her vision blurry. She took slow breaths, giving herself time to adjust before opening her eyes further. The man in charge said that whatever they had planned would happen later tonight, so Lainie assumed she had time to figure out how she wanted to play this.

The nervous kid could still be heard rustling around, his nerves making him too anxious to settle down. Lainie knew he would be the one to slip up if either of the gang members did. Why the Serpents sent someone out too green to do what needed to be done, she could only guess. The other one seemed to possess more years on the streets in the way he handled himself. That made him the dangerous one. *He'll be the one I take out first.*

Footsteps crunched their way toward her, and Lainie slowed her breathing. "Hey, TC, she hasn't moved since we dumped her here," the younger of the two said. "What if you hit her too hard?"

More footsteps headed toward her. "Chris, you're a paranoid idiot. I didn't hit her too hard. What? You think this is the first time I've done something like this? How the hell did you get into the Serpents?"

Lainie wondered the same thing. *At least I have names now.* Footsteps drew closer to her, the snapping of twigs sounding real close to her ears. She heard the tightening of material as the footsteps stopped and felt the presence of one of them near her face, his breathing heavy with the stench of cigarette smoke.

"Oh, she's fine all right," the one called TC said. "I would wager she's wide awake and listening to every word we've said, which is why I say you talk too much. Thanks to you, she knows our names."

"Hey, you said my name as well."

Lainie opened her eyes and would have shook her head, except it was against the ground. "That's because TC here doesn't want to be the only one to go down if I get loose." She turned her gaze until she could see Chris, his hands stuffed into his pockets, his shoulders slumped in that look of defeat that came with someone who was afraid. "I agree with your friend here. What the hell are you doing in a gang if you don't have the balls for it?"

TC laughed as he slapped his knee and stood up. "Lady, I

like you." He bobbed his head up and down, still laughing. "Yup, I really like you. So, don't make me kill you and just do what we need." His laughter died as he narrowed his eyes at her. Turning to Chris, he motioned to her. "Help her sit up and dust her off. We don't need her looking like shit when we send her back into the sheriff's department."

Lainie tried to ignore the rough way Chris handled her as he dragged her into a sitting position. Luckily, she was close enough to a giant pine that she could lean back on something for support, the rough bark digging into her back through her shirt. "You really don't think I'm going to help you, do you? I mean, why would I want to do that? As far as I'm concerned, you can rot in jail with the man who yanks your collar."

TC shrugged. "It's simple. You don't help us, then you die, and I find someone else. Either way, lady, I'm getting that video. It's up to you as to whether you live or not."

"Pretty sure of yourself, aren't you?" Lainie felt the bonds around her wrists. They were snugger than she would have given the gang members credit for, seeing as how she doubted either one of them were ever in the Boy Scouts.

He smirked as he gave a sarcastic shrug. "I've yet to fail or not be able to predict what people will do. You strike me as someone who prefers living rather than dying."

"How much longer, TC?" Chris asked. "I want this over with so we can get out of here."

"Who gives a flying fuck what you want, you moron?" TC moved away, turning back around toward the car. "We'll go when I say we go. It's still too early. I've been watching the place. They have less people there at night. We'll go then. Now, you watch her while I get some sleep and try not to screw it up."

"Screw it..? Gee, thanks, TC. You sure gotta lot of confidence in me." Chris yanked his hands out of his pockets and stretched his arms out. "I'm not a total idiot, you know?"

TC slid up on the back of the Lincoln, his hands clasped over his belly. "Oh, sure, I know. I know you're a buffoon, that's what I know. Now keep an eye on her and don't let her use any of that detective bullshit and try to get in your hollow mind."

Lainie watched as the skinny man closed his eyes, laying his head back on the glass. She doubted he would sleep for a while, choosing instead to listen to see if she said anything to Chris to give her hand away. She would not count on him being as stupid as his partner.

Laying her head back along the pine tree, she closed her eyes and thought of Rance and the way his arms felt around her naked form. He planned on moving to Bull Creek just to be with her, changing his entire life around and starting over. That was a far cry from what her parents wanted to stick her with back in Draven Falls. Lainie had to admit; she liked the way Rance made her feel. She wondered if he noticed how long she had been gone and started to wonder again. Would he keep waiting or would he reach out to someone to find out where she was? She smiled. He was too impatient to wait. He would definitely go looking for her, especially if she didn't answer her cell phone.

"Holy shit!" Chris's voice snapped her out of her reverie. He stood with his back to her, but his head swiveled all around. "TC! TC, we got problems."

"What the hell are you babbling about?" TC sounded about as put out as Lainie would expect. Maybe he had fallen asleep after all.

Turning her head in all directions, she tried to figure out what had Chris's underwear in a knot. Her smile only grew with everything she saw. Standing among the trees were a couple of panthers, two wolves, a bear, and two tigers, each focused on the two men, their mouths twisted in angry snarls. The place was surrounded. *I knew he'd be too impatient to wait.*

Fifteen

Rance pulled up into the parking lot of the sheriff's department, his hands gripping the steering wheel as if it were the necks of the Serpents. They would not succeed with whatever they had planned; he would make sure of that.

Johnson and Chet were already standing out in the parking lot near Lainie's car. As Rance pulled into a parking spot, two more cars followed him. He recognized Lainie's brother from when he followed her to Roger's cabin, but the others were all new to him. And there were a lot of them. Three women and three other men poured out of the cars, everyone moving to where Chet stood with his arms folded across his chest. The calvary had definitely been called.

Rance walked straight to Chet. "Any word yet?"

Chet shook his head. "Johnson says you think it's the

Serpents for some reason?"

Rance glanced over at Dimitri, recalling the man's name from what Lainie said at the crime scene that first day. "Lainie and I overheard their plans three days ago. They intended to force her to get inside the evidence locker to retrieve Roger O'Brien's phone." He turned his focus back to the sheriff. "Seems they made their move."

"Do you know where they are?" Dimitri asked as he stepped up to them, the others surrounding them. The expression on his face was a mixture of worry for his sister and anger at Rance for allowing her to be taken.

Rance wished he could give them a better answer. Shaking his head, he said, "No. The last time we saw them, they were hiding out in the woods. Looked like they were sleeping in their car." Then he took a deep breath, the memory of what happened when the one gang member threatened Lainie. "There was a little, um, scuffle, so I'm sure they've moved spots by now. Lainie saw them leaving town but obviously they circled back."

"A scuffle?" Johnson asked.

Everyone stared at Rance with quizzical expressions. "Don't ask." Rance then turned to Lainie's car, an idea popping into his head. He jerked his attention to Dimitri, not sure how much the sheriff or anyone else for that matter knew about Lainie's true self. "When your sister and I tracked the gang bangers…" Rance allowed the rest of what he wanted to say trail off, hoping Dimitri understood what he wasn't saying.

Dimitri stared at Rance a moment, waiting for him to

finish his sentence. Then, when it dawned on Lainie's brother that Rance wasn't going to say anything else, he stared at him harder, just before his eyes widened in understanding. "Your animals tracked them down."

Rance nodded as Chet said, "That explains why she couldn't arrest them." Rance turned to the man, thinking it odd how casual he was about having a shifter deputy. Apparently, there was more openness in Bull Creek than in other parts of the world.

"But it doesn't explain why she didn't tell the rest of us why someone had threatened her," Dimitri said, glaring at Rance. "A better question would be, why didn't you tell someone? Why did it take you so long to notice Lainie was missing?"

"Are you kidding me?" Rance shoved his hands onto his hips, not wanting to get into it with Lainie's brother, but also choosing not to bear the brunt of his anger either. "You know your sister better than I do. Would you tell her how to do her job?"

A thick man with a hairy chest and burly arms, just chuckled. "I wouldn't tell Lainie to do a damn thing." He turned to Dimitri, adding, "And neither would you, and you know it."

"Shut up, Ezra," another man said, obviously trying to avoid any fighting amongst the friends. He then turned to Chet. "So, how do we find them now?"

"Well, if they could be tracked that way once, we can do it again," a short blond said, hands on her hips as she stared off into the woods surrounding the sheriff's department.

A taller man, dark hair and muscles that tightened his shirt, wrapped an arm around her. "Eve, babe, we don't have any idea how far they went or even if they're still around."

"All the more reason to get started now," Eve said. She turned to Dimitri, ignoring Chet and Rance. "Don't you agree?"

Dimitri, ran a hand through his blond hair, staring at his sister's car and then out into the woods. "Agreed." He then turned to the dark-haired woman beside him. "Adira, can you track me if I shift and go after Lainie?"

She must be the witch Lainie mentioned, Rance thought as he watched the exchange.

"I can," the woman said. "I'll follow with Chet, and we'll be right behind you."

"Then let's do this." He reached for his shirt buttons, but Chet stopped him.

"How about you wait until you get into the woods for that. I'll send Johnson to fetch your clothes, so you have them when this is over. We don't need a rash of calls about nudists at the sheriff's department."

Dimitri nodded in agreement, and soon everyone except Adira and the two sheriffs marched into the surrounding woods, each unbuttoning their shirts and pants and yanking off shoes. Rance followed along. There was no way he would be left out of this. As they reached the woods, Dimitri turned to him, pulling his own shirt off his arms. "I assume you were working with my sister on Roger's death. You know who we're going up against?"

"Idiots. Gang members on a mission they can't turn back

from, which is why your sister is in this mess." He could feel the knots in his stomach tightening, his wolf anxious to get underway and for the talking to stop.

Dimitri's animal must have felt the same, for the alpha of Bull Creek said, "Well, those city boys are going to be in for a rude awakening. Let's go see what's left of them."

The talking ceased at that point as everyone around Rance finished stripping and began the shift. When Rance finished, the wind tousling his gray coat, he was surrounded by two panthers, a bear, another wolf, and two tigers. He didn't wait for Dimitri or anyone else to take the lead. As the sheriff's deputy collected the discarded clothing, Rance's wolf walked over to Lainie's car and started sniffing around, until he caught her scent. He could also detect the scents of the two gang members. He followed their trail until he could tell where they put Lainie in a car, and then the tire tracks of where they took off with her, with his Lainie. He turned to the others, snapping a yelp, and then taking off in the direction of the Lincoln. He didn't turn to see if the others followed; he could hear them behind him.

The path took several turns, but it didn't take long before they were weaving their way along a road cut into the woods, the sunlight peeking through the overhead branches as the afternoon breeze pulled at their fur coats. Rance couldn't help but think how odd it was for such a misfit batch of shifters to be gathered in one group and working together. Bears, panthers, wolves, and even tigers padded their way through the woods in search of another panther who was in trouble. Animals that would normally be at odds now worked in tandem to accomplish a common goal. There was more to Bull Creek than Rance knew, but he was determined to figure it out. He didn't have a choice. Once he marked Lainie as his, this would be his home.

Rance knew the gang members couldn't go far, wanting to stay near a road with their vehicle, seeing as how that would be their only form of shelter. Smart move on their part. Hotel rooms were easily discovered and traced. Hopefully, that was the extent of their intelligence.

He slowed his pace, the scent getting stronger. With his muzzle against the ground, he followed the road, the others in the woods and out of sight, trusting his instincts. That surprised him with as much as Dimitri seemed to blame him for Lainie's predicament. Of course, the idiots who took her didn't know the lady and what she was capable of. He was worried but also confident that Lainie could get out of the mess she was in when she truly wanted to do so. If those men knew they had taken a panther, they'd be halfway back to Pensacola by now. As it was, when they came face to face with the various animals coming at them, Rance could only imagine their panic.

"Pretty sure of yourself, aren't you?" Lainie's voice reached Rance's ears, bringing him to a halt as he shifted his focus ahead of him, lifting his head. *She's up ahead and to the left, it seems,* he sent to the others.

Everyone fan out, Dimitri said. *We need to surround them. No one moves until I say so.*

No, Rance said. He wasn't leaving Lainie's safety in the hands of people who didn't know what they were facing. *On my word, not yours. No offense. I know these thugs.*

"I've yet to fail or not be able to predict what people will do," the one Rance remembered on top of the Lincoln said. So far, it seemed the animals were unnoticed. "You strike me as someone who prefers living rather than dying."

"How much longer, TC?" the other gang member asked, and Rance could hear the nervousness in his voice. "I want this over with so we can get out of here."

Fine, Dimitri said. *But I want these idiots taken care of quickly.*

"Who gives a flying fuck what you want, you moron?" the one called TC asked as Rance watched him move away from Lainie, turning back around toward the car. "We'll go when I say we go. It's still too early. I've been watching the place. They have less people there at night. We'll go then. Now, you watch her while I get some sleep and try not to screw it up."

Oh, trust me, Rance said. *They'll be taken care of. Now, everyone spread out so we can come at them from all angles, not giving them a chance to escape.*

"Screw it..?" the younger of the Serpents said, his expression obviously not understanding what TC meant. Rance then saw when understanding hit him. "Gee, thanks, TC. You sure do gotta lot of confidence in me." The kid yanked his hands out of his pockets and stretched his arms out. "I'm not a total idiot, you know?"

TC slid up on the back of the Lincoln, his hands clasped over his belly as he settled in for his nap. "Oh, sure, I know. I know you're a buffoon, that's what I know. Now keep an eye on her and don't let her use any of that detective bullshit and try to get in your hollow mind."

Rance turned and watched as the kid who was left to stand guard over Lainie stood there staring at his partner for a moment, annoyance shifting across his face, but Rance knew the kid was too scared of the other to say anything that would get his ass kicked. Lainie was propped against a pine, her hands bound behind her back with rope. Glancing around, he noticed the others in place, all waiting for his word to attack.

"Holy shit!" The young kid's voice jerked Rance's attention back to where the kid stood near Lainie. He must have noticed the others as well, as his head swiveled in all directions, eyes wide as he noticed the wild assortment of animals staring back at him. "TC! TC, we got problems."

"What the hell are you babbling about?" TC sounded put out as he lifted his gaze to the kid.

Rance turned his focus to Lainie, and she stared right at him, a smirk turning up the corner of her lips. *You really don't want my help with this case, do you?* He sent to her, the animal's mindspeech working in either form.

It's not like I could keep you away, regardless. He watched as she turned her attention all around her, smiling as she took in the others.

Adira is bringing the sheriff and deputy, Rance said. *All we have to do is keep them from leaving until they get here.*

He watched as Lainie nodded. *Smart. So, what is the plan, if I might ask.*

Rance gave a mental laugh. *Well, you know how I like to have fun. Okay, everyone, let's scare the shit out of these guys.* And the woods erupted with howls, hisses, and roars.

Sixteen

The afternoon exploded with the sounds of animals on the attack. The panthers went after TC on the car, the man screaming and jumping to the hard-shell top of the Lincoln. The wolf and Bear charged Chris, who stumbled backward, falling to his ass on the hard ground, and crab-walking backward until he hit the trunk of an oak. The tigers prowled the perimeter, just in case the men slipped past the others, which Lainie highly doubted. TC was jumping into the air, trying to reach a branch to climb up on, forgetting, she supposed, that panthers could climb trees. Chris had tears streaking down his face and a giant wet spot on the front of his pants. If he could shove himself through the tree he was backed against, he would simply to avoid the bear that roared at him, but one of the wolves—Alanna, Lainie knew—was behind the tree, snapping at the man, keeping him in place.

Rance's wolf went straight to her, going immediately to the ropes at her wrists. She could break them, she knew, but didn't want to deprive Rance of his gallant effort. She thought of shifting and joining in the fun, but if this ever went to court, she didn't need it coming out that she was a shifter, not that the courts would probably believe the Serpents. Their claims would be assumed to be the wild accusations of men searching for an insanity plea. Besides, the others seemed to have it all well in hand.

Once the ropes were undone, Rance sat on his back haunches, his tongue lolling to the side. Lainie reached out and scratched his ears. "You just love to be in the middle of things."

No one messes with my mate, he sent.

Lainie jerked her attention to the others, hoping no one heard what he had said. If they did, it would be lost in the fight with the gang members.

Off in the distance, sirens were heard heading her way. Lainie scratched Rance's ear one more time and then stood, turning to where the men trembled. "So, I'm taking it, you're ready to surrender?" she asked, her hand still on the top of Rance's head. "Or should I just leave you to the local wildlife?"

"Tigers and bears are local?" Chris screamed, his eyes still on Ezra in front of him.

"They are, and much deadlier than snakes." She turned her attention to the sheriff's car that pulled up, smiling at Chet who sat behind the wheel. Adira waved before opening her car door. The animals all sat on their back haunches, eyes glaring at the Serpents who cried out to the sheriff to be rescued. Chet, of course, was in no hurry to help them out, his pace slow, casual.

Adira went straight to Lainie, her face revealing her concern. "Are you okay?" the witch asked as she drew nearer.

Lainie turned as Johnson pulled up behind Chet's car, sirens flashing but silent. The colors hitting the trees and leaves seemed way out of place deep in the woods, as if the city was intruding on something sacred. Lainie turned to the two Serpents, intruders themselves into a world they were clueless about and would never truly understand. Lainie placed a hand on Adira's arm when the other lady reached her, but her gaze was on the rest of her friends who had raced to her rescue. "Yeah, I'm fine. Thanks." She then turned to Chet. "Besides kidnapping a deputy, they planned on breaking into the sheriff's department and stealing evidence. They're also the ones who killed Roger O'Brien."

Johnson had walked up beside them as she spoke, his mouth open at the scene in front of him. He had seen the shifters in action before, and recently, but Lainie knew to humans it was always a sight to behold and threw many off.

Chet nodded. "Well, seems like you pretty well solved your case." Lainie couldn't tell if he was purposefully ignoring the animals in the small clearing or truly didn't consider them out of place. He pulled his sheriff's hat from his head and wiped his brow with the back of his hand. "Johnson, let's get them in handcuffs and back to the department." He then turned back to Lainie and then glanced down at the wolf at her side. "I guess this can put to rest two cases, actually. The detective is now free to return to Pensacola, I suppose. I see no reason not to give him the video and phone and let him put more of these gang members behind bars." He glanced back up at Lainie, and when he asked the next question, she wasn't sure exactly what he meant. "Are you sure you're okay?"

She glanced down at Rance, her heart twisting just a little before she remembered his words back at her cabin earlier that day. She felt the smile creep across her face. "Yeah, I'm fine." She scratched the top of the wolf's head. "Although I need to ask you if there's an empty spot at the department." She looked at Chet. "I know a detective looking for a job."

Chet looked at her for a moment, his eyes intense, searching. Adira just giggled and shook her head as she left them to join Dimitri's panther. Chet shook his head and gave a soft chuckle. "I'm sure we can find something for him." Then his grin turned mischievous. "I think there may be a spot on the K9 unit."

Rance yelped, hopping up on all fours as Lainie laughed. "That might be fitting."

Chet returned his gaze to Johnson who was busy slapping handcuffs on the Serpents. "Clothes are stacked in my trunk," he said. "But, I'd wait until we get these men out of sight before anyone does any shifting."

"Agreed," Lainie said. "No need freaking out the tourists."

Chet chuckled as he turned toward his car. "Now, that's

funny. See you back at the department. Take your time. Johnson and I will handle these morons until you get back."

Lainie thanked him, turning her attention back to the wolf at her feet, the smile curling her lips upward. Now that her case was over, she couldn't get to the department fast enough so that Rance could get his case behind him. A week ago, she was content with life as it was, but now that Rance was a part of her life, she was ready to get the next chapter started. Of course, she also worried that it had all been words, things he said just in the process of getting what he wanted. It wouldn't be the first time a man did that to her. She reached down and scratched behind his ears again, the confusion in her head creating a knot in her stomach.

Once Chet and Johnson were gone, the others started to shift, animal paws shrinking or stretching into feet and hands, fur slipping back into bodies as flesh stretched, and animals lifted off four legs to stand on two as their human counterparts took over. Rance did the same transformation in front of her, taking her in his arms and squeezing her to him, just as soon as his shift was over. "Are you all right?" he asked, kissing the top of her head. "Did they hurt you in any way?"

She kissed his bare chest, his flesh warm from the afternoon sun. "Are you kidding? I was just biding my time to see what they would do next." She turned her gaze back up into his eyes. "Besides, I knew you would be here." She shrugged. "So I had plenty of time." She then glanced around the clearing as her brother and friends started getting dressed, Adira having retrieved their clothes before the others left. "Of course, I didn't expect you to bring an army."

Rance kissed her forehead again, his lips bouncing along her head as he chuckled. "Chet called them. I don't think he trusts me yet."

"He will. I mean, after all, you're going to be working for him. Right?" He smiled at her but didn't answer right away. His silence twisted the knot in her stomach.

"Bull Creek getting a new resident?" Dimitri asked as he stepped closer, tugging his shirt into place as he did. Adira stood beside him, her hand slipped into his back pocket.

"Aren't we running out of cabins?" Josh asked with a laugh as he walked up to join the others.

Alanna ran her hand through her hair as she joined them, working the chaos of knots and stray strands back into some semblance of order. "I don't think he's going to be needing his own cabin by the look on Lainie's face."

Lainie just wanted them all to shut up so Rance could answer her question. Why wasn't he answering her question?

Seventeen

He never answered her question.

Luckily, Chet sent a couple of other cars out to gather everyone up and bring them back to the department. Rance wasn't looking forward to walking all the way back, although he could have thought of several things to do with Lainie in the woods. If they weren't surrounded by all of Lainie's friends, that is.

Once they were dressed, everyone made the round of introductions, all glad to see Rance and the "glow" on Lainie's cheeks. The one thing about a mating call, everyone around knew when someone was feeling that pull. The scent the animals emitted was unmistakable and to those exuding it, impossible to ignore. Everyone seemed to be great people to Rance, and he thought moving there would be perfect. A great change to his hectic city life.

By the time they arrived back at the department, Rance was inside gathering up his evidence, forcing his mind to turn back to the case waiting for him in Pensacola. He wanted it finished, so he could officially put in his notice and make his move to Bull Creek.

And Lainie.

He noticed she was quiet, probably worrying about the topic he wasn't discussing, but he didn't want to have that conversation in front of all her friends as well as her brother. No, that conversation needed to be had alone, because he didn't intend to just talk. He intended to make their mating official. He just needed to tie up all his loose ends. Nothing would keep him from achieving his goals. Or his future with Lainie.

Once back at the department, Dimitri helped him talk Lainie into going home and cleaning up, getting some rest. Her friends, Alanna, Adira, and Eve, vowed to stay with her in Lainie's cabin, making sure she didn't do anything that came close to resembling work. He promised to join her as soon as he was finished at the department. The Serpents would go to jail. and he could move on with his life, a life which suddenly seemed a whole lot brighter now that Lainie was in it.

Rance sat at Johnson's desk, patiently waiting for the paperwork to be finished, when Sheriff Einstein walked over and took a spot on the corner of Johnson's desk. "So, Lainie mentioned out in that clearing that you might be looking for a spot here in this department. Is that true?"

"It is," Rance answered as he shifted in his seat to face the older man. "Once I get this case back home finished, I intend on moving here."

Chet nodded, his hands clasped in his lap. "I'm pretty sure I could get you a spot, although it might not be as high up as you are in the big city. We're just a small township, you know."

"I'm not looking for a career bump. Just a new start. With Lainie."

"Well, she could use someone like you. She's a sweet woman and deserves someone who'll dote on her. Don't try to take charge of her, though. She'll have your nuts in a sling." He rapped his knuckles on the desk as he slid off. "Just give me a call when you're heading back this way, and we'll set something up."

"Oh, and Lainie needs the next few days off," Rance said before the sheriff could walk away. "I intend to take her with me to Pensacola. She helped me finish this, and I think she needs to be there to see the case to its conclusion."

Chet shook his head. "I'm sure that's why you want her along." Then he waved off the topic. "You two have fun. I'll take care of her shifts."

"Thanks," Rance said to the man's retreating back. By then, Johnson had arrived with the paperwork, just needing signatures, the phone and flash drive tucked and sealed in an evidence bag. "And thank you for this," Rance said to the deputy, lifting the evidence bag up into the air as if Johnson wouldn't know what he meant. "It'll be nice to cut the head off that snake back in Pensacola." He then pushed himself out of his chair and headed for the door. It was time to turn a page.

~ ~ ~ ~ ~

Lainie paced her quiet living room. She had forced the others to go home once they saw she was safe in the door. She didn't need mindless chatter outside of her head with as much as was happening inside of it. She knew her friends meant well, but she was just too on edge to be sociable. Rance should have his evidence by now and would probably be on his way to Pensacola, Bull Creek a memory in his rearview mirror. He hadn't even called or texted since they parted ways at the sheriff's department. Maybe she had rushed things asking Chet if there was a place for Rance in the department.

She was about to give up and take a nap when she heard a car pulling into her drive. Sliding off the couch, she went to the front window and peeked outside. Her heart pounded as she watched Rance get out of his car, and she could feel the wetness between her legs, her passion stirring. Even her panther was ready to pounce, and Rance wasn't even all the way out of the car yet.

Racing to the front door, she jerked it open, stepping out onto the porch just as his foot hit the first step. "You're back," she said, forcing herself to come to a stop before she appeared like a total idiot. She gave a feeble shrug. "I assumed you'd be heading back to Pensacola since you have your evidence now."

He reached out, wrapping his arms around her waist, and kissed her deeply. Her breath caught in her throat, his movement shocking her for a moment. However, the shock ended quickly, and she slipped her arms around Rance's neck, fully surrendering to the moment. When Rance broke the kiss and pulled away, she could see the passion in his eyes. "Sweetie, I'm not going anywhere without you. As a matter of fact, I've already cleared it with Chet. You're going with me to Pensacola."

She pushed back at him, her hands on his chest. "What? You didn't even ask me first? Just went around me to my boss? I have responsibilities here, you know?"

She almost laughed at how baffled he appeared right then. "What? I thought you'd want to go with me," he said. "Are you saying you don't?"

"I'm saying, next time, you need to talk to me and not my boss. I don't need a man making plans for me or deciding my life." She started to turn and walk back inside, her joy at seeing him quickly turning to anger at being coddled.

Yet, Rance gripped her arm and spun her back around. "You always have to do everything with a touch of sass, don't you?" His smile only made her temper smolder more. "Lainie, I'm not planning your life." He kissed her forehead and then gazed into her eyes, his golden eyes penetrating her soul. "I'm joining it." He gripped her hand, walking past her and into the cabin.

Lainie didn't have time to get away or to even think about stopping. Rance led her into the cabin, through the living room and kitchen toward the back. Her eyes went wide as realization dawned on her as to where he headed and what he intended. The passion between her legs stirred, and she could feel the wetness begin to pool as he shoved her bedroom door open and dragged her inside. He spun her around to face him, his smile devilish, his eyes full of passionate mischief as his words echoed in her mind. *I'm joining it.*

He jerked his shirt off. and the sight of his firm chest caught her breath in her chest as she soaked in his presence. He didn't stop there but unbuttoned his pants and jerked them down his legs, boxers as well, and kicked them off, his gaze never leaving hers. That is until she allowed her gaze to travel down his body, resting on his hard cock as it pointed at her as if claiming her for his own. Her panther purred within as Lainie forced herself to swallow the lump in her throat. It didn't make sense. She had already had sex with Rance before, so why was she as timid as a virgin at the end of prom?

He gripped her arms, turning her so that her back was to the bed. Reaching down, he pulled her shirt over her head and flippantly tossed it to the floor. Then he moved to her pants, his eyes fixed on hers, as he unbuttoned them. However, as he started to slide them down her legs, he lowered himself with them until her pants were at her ankles and Rance was on his knees. She felt his hands slide around her hips to cup her ass as he pulled her to him, his lips kissing her abdomen and then slowly making a trail downward to the wet valley between her legs that burned with desire. Her breath caught in her throat again and this time, she felt the tightness in her chest just before his tongue flicked over her swollen clit, sending electrical charges throughout her body.

With deft movements, he lifted her legs so that he could slip her pants from her body, and then he rose, his hands still on her ass as he lifted her in the air and moved her back toward the bed. She waited to be dumped down unceremoniously, but Rance had other plans. With gentle movements, he lowered her down to the bed, spreading her legs as he did until he knelt on the side of the bed, her legs on his shoulders, his face buried between her thighs. Again, she felt his tongue on her pussy, twirling around her clit as his fingers dug into the flesh of her ass. She moaned, one hand sliding down to the top of his head, holding him in place. *Oh, god, don't stop. Don't stop.* Her breathing came in ragged pants now as her head tilted back into the mattress, her mouth open and eyes closed. She clamped her legs around his head, hoping to hold him exactly as he was until...

Her eyes popped open as the first wave of an orgasm rippled through her, electrical charges bursting at all of her nerve-endings as she gripped the bedspread with her fists. She cried out, her back arching as she clamped down on Rance's head tighter. As the orgasm subsided, she glanced down and panicked, jerking her legs open. "Oh god, I'm sorry. Are you..?"

Rance just grinned as he crawled up her body, crossing his right arm over her waist and grabbing her hip. With one quick pull, he flipped her over onto her stomach, grabbed her hips and jerked her ass up into the air. "Oh, I'm fine. I've been waiting for this." With his fingers digging into her hips, he thrust his cock deep into her pussy, his grunts filling her ears. Her forehead was pressed to the sheet, her back arched, as she shoved back onto him, wanting him as deep inside of her as he could go. He pumped into her several times, hard, fast, pounding until she couldn't catch her breath. Then she heard his voice in her ear and felt his breath on the side of her face as he bent over her. "Tell me now, are you mine?"

"Yes! Oh god, yes."

Then she felt the stabbing pain as his teeth sank into her shoulder, just as he thrust all the way inside of her. His passion exploded inside of her pussy as pain flashed in her eyes. Once more, her body shuddered with her orgasm as he pinned her to his hips, spearing her with both his cock and his teeth. She was his, just as much as he was hers. Mated.

She felt his lips pull away from her shoulder, felt his hands ease up on her hips as he rolled her to her side, his arm around her waist, one finger stroking her nipple. He kissed the side of her head as he squeezed her to him, his cock still hard, her pussy drenched. Snuggling back into him, she pulled his arm across her tighter, wanting to wear him like another skin. Then she felt his lips on the mate mark, his tongue gliding over the impressions his teeth made, and she blushed at the thought of it.

I'm joining it. And he did. Completely. Wholeheartedly. And with a passion that she doubted would ever be quenched.

"Are you doing okay?" His voice was soft and still held the husky tone of a man sated.

She grinned, squeezing his arm again. "Mhm. I was just thinking how fun it will be when you move here and work for me."

She felt the bed shift around her and his body pull away from her slightly. "Work for you? Why wouldn't you work for me?"

"Work for you? Please. You needed me to solve your case. Don't worry, though. I think I can train you. I see great potential in you."

His chuckle warmed her heart and flamed the embers between her legs into another roaring fire. "Always have to add that touch of sass, don't you?"

"Oh, honey, you have no idea."

She felt his lips on the side of her face. "But I intend to find out." He settled in behind her again, his arms tightening around her waist.

Lainie closed her eyes. Pensacola would have to wait a few more hours. She wasn't done training this detective yet.

About the Author

Author of the popular series, *Destined Mates*, Robbie Cox started writing to escape—escape his teachers, escape his fears, even to escape his insecurities and doubts. However, his stories of seduction and adventure, not only allowed him to hide in the lives of his characters, but also captivated those who wanted to escape with him. Now, he enjoys a full-time career as a storyteller and novelist, creating rich worlds of fantasy adventure, paranormal action, and steamy romance. He invites readers to run away with him - to escape, getting lost in the seduction of adventure.

When not writing, Robbie is often found on his back porch enjoying a cigar, a scotch, and a good story. He derives pleasure from his large family and his crazy group of friends who provide the inspiration for his blog, *The Mess that Is Me*.

His series include, *Destined Mates*, *The Warrior of the Way*, *The Cauldron Coven*, *The Witches of Savannah*, and *The Bull Creek Chronicles*.

Connect with Robbie online:

Website ~ www.robbiecox.com
Facebook ~ https://www.facebook.com/robbiecoxauthor
Twitter ~ http://twitter.com/CoxRobbie
Pinterest ~ http://pinterest.com/robbiecoxauthor
Goodreads ~ http://www.goodreads.com/RobbieCox
Instagram ~ http://instagram.com/robbiecoxauthor
Bookbub ~ https://www.bookbub.com/authors/robbie-cox

For up-to-date news on Robbie's latest releases, book signing events in your area, and giveaways, follow Robbie's newsletter - https://landing.mailerlite.com/webforms/landing/z2c3u2

You can also join Robbie's reading group, Robbie's Rascals, for more updates, extra giveaways, and even more fan involvement - https://www.facebook.com/groups/RobbiesRascals/

Other Books by Robbie Cox

Warrior of the Way
Reaping the Harvest
Lore Master
The Warrior's Blade
Summerlands

The Cauldron Coven
Death's Shroud
Daughters of Darkness
Chaos Magicians

Halloween Seduction
Come Halloween
Behind the Mask
Halloween Seduction

The Witches of Savannah
Enter the Witch

The Bull Creek Chronicles
Alpha Rising
Panther Hunted
Bear Necessities

Destined Mates
Magic's Mate
Mate's Appeal
Mate's Touch
My Lover's Mate
My Mate's Wife

Visit www.robbiecox.com to find out more about these great books by Robbie Cox!

Also writing as R.C. Wynne

The Rutherford Series
Losing Faith
Roll the Dice
To Be Cherished
His to Command

The Harper Twins
Sibling Rivalry
Taming Karla
Always Aimee
The Harper Twins Box Set

Fangirls
Nikki
Lily
Cassie
Olivia
Willow
The Collection

Best of Both Worlds
Ribbons & Bows
Under the Wrapping
The Best of Both Worlds

Visit www.rcwynnebooks.com to find out more about these
great books by R.C. Wynne!

www.ingramcontent.com/pod-product-compliance
Lightning Source LLC
Chambersburg PA
CBHW030914050726
47498CB00003BA/736